FLIGHTS OF FANTASY

AN URBAN FANTASY ROMANCE ANTHOLOGY

Edited by
Sheellah Kennedy & Joy Wandrey

Wyld Stallions Press
Virginia Beach, VA

Chris Kennedy/Wyld Stallions Press
2052 Bierce Dr., Virginia Beach, VA 23454
http://chriskennedypublishing.com/

Publisher's Note: This is a work of fiction. Names, characters, places, and incidents are a product of the author's imagination. Locales and public names are sometimes used for atmospheric purposes. Any resemblance to actual people, living or dead, or to businesses, companies, events, institutions, or locales is completely coincidental.

Flights of Fantasy/Sheellah Kennedy & Joy Wandrey -- 1st ed.
ISBN 978-1648550225

To Ryan, Adrienne, and Erika for continuing to love me despite my unconventional ways. To Rodney and Gloria Jewell for always pushing me to believe in myself. And, finally, to Chris for giving me the courage and strength to try new things, even when I doubt myself.

— Sheellah Kennedy

My thanks, as always, to Mark, and to my family, blood and chosen, you know who you are. Thanks are also due to Sheellah Kennedy, my fabulous partner in crime, without whom this book would not exist, and of course to our awesome publisher, Chris Kennedy. My thanks!

— Joy Wandrey

Preface by Sheellah Kennedy

Where do authors and publishers come up with the greatest ideas? If you guessed in the bar of a hotel during a literary convention, you guessed correctly. "Flights of Fantasy" is a result of Chris Kennedy Publishing's newest imprint, Wyld Stallions Press. In November of 2019, Joy Wandrey and I were sitting in a hotel bar in Las Vegas, NV, during a writer's conference with our husbands. It was jokingly mentioned that the only imprint left to add to Chris Kennedy Publishing was romance.

Before Joy and I knew it, we were put in charge of running the imprint. Our good friend and author, Terry Maggert, just happened to be in the bar the same night, and he graciously agreed to write a short story for our very first anthology. Based on one of the genres that Terry writes successfully in, "Flights of Fantasy" was created. Like a flight of food or beverages, you are the lucky recipient of samplings of a variety of great stories by talented authors. Think of "Flights of Fantasy" as food for your mind.

Sheellah Kennedy
Virginia Beach, VA 23454

Contents

Welcome To Sherman County by Kylie Cross 9

Thus, With A Kiss by Kacey Ezell.................................... 47

Tiger, Tiger, Burning Bite by Julia May Vee............... 95

In Her World by Casey Moores 121

Sweet Simmer by Kat Beaty 157

Lions, And Tigers, And A Vampire...Oh My!
by Sheellah Kennedy 191

Shatter Me by Melissa Olthoff....................................... 223

Dark Side Of The Sun by Monalisa Foster............... 251

Ever The Dreamer by Donea Lee Weaver............... 305

At The Still Point by Marisa Wolf 339

Promised by Dawn Witzke.. 377

Pictures For Pleasure by Terry Maggert 407

* * * * *

Welcome to Sherman County by Kylie Cross

The two motorcycles raced along the empty backroads crisscrossing the Blue Ridge foothills. Surrounded by early morning fog, only their brake lights were visible as they hurtled through switchbacks that would give any rational man pause.

Justin Barbaro had stopped being a rational man yesterday. After returning from his tour overseas, he'd thought hiring on as a bodyguard would be an easy gig. He'd been so wrong.

Lil Dynamite might be the hottest thing to come out of Atlanta in the last year, but Justin didn't see the appeal. He much preferred classic anything to the noisy synth rap Lil Dynamite sang.

But a job was a job.

The first few weeks had been standard security and crowd control. But when Justin saw Lil Dynamite's manager passing out the new designer drug, he'd spotted the tip of the iceberg. After a few weeks of careful observation, Justin figured out Lil Dynamite was a front for a criminal enterprise much worse than just making bad music.

They'd been manufacturing drugs, and they'd been doing it by farming pixie dust. To get pixie dust that potent, they had to be harvesting from live subjects. Tailing the manager's assistant had led to a warehouse, lab equipment, and cages.

So many cages.

He should have told someone. He should have gone straight to the authorities. He should have waited to save all the pixies. He shouldn't have taken justice into his own hands. He shouldn't have engaged in a running gunfight and set off homemade bombs, blowing their warehouse sky high.

But that's exactly what Justin Barbaro had done.

After racing through the night, he was beginning to tire. He wasn't sure who was chasing him, although he had his suspicions. It was unlikely their connection with their motorcycle was as visceral as his was. They were riding a machine of combustion-fueled chrome, whereas his bike drew energy directly from him. While usually an advantage over human riders, his stamina wasn't limitless. His heart was beginning to feel the strain. His legs ached in a way no amount of resting them on highway pegs could help.

The pixies tried to help, but most were drained of magic and powerless. A few wind gusts were the best they could manage, not enough to speed him up or slow their pursuer down. Their troop leader, Zeph, rode in Justin's helmet, a tiny form vibrating near his cheek. The rest of the pixies were a negligible weight in his backpack.

This stretch of road snaked down the backside of the mountain like a classy medusa stripper's tattoo. As it leveled out along the valley floor, a road sign welcomed them to Sherman County. Justin had never heard of it, but as a Midwest colt born and bred, that was hardly surprising.

"There's an intersection up ahead," Justin said. "This is our best chance to get our persistent friend off our tail."

"They're no friend of mine, but I agree. We need to do something," Zeph said in his high-pitched voice. "My troop needs to rest and feed. Neither of those things we can do while strapped to your back."

"What if I toss the backpack into the woods before we get to the intersection? I'll lead them off, lose them, and circle back by tomorrow to pick you back up. Will that give your troop enough time to recover?"

Zeph hummed before replying. "With my wind magic, I can try to manage a safe landing. Oberon knows we don't need more broken wings than we already have. A day won't be enough for the worst off to fully recover, but it should give them enough strength to continue onward."

Justin cracked the visor on his helmet. "It's a plan then. There's a slight rise and dip in the road ahead. We should be out of sight long enough for me to toss the bag without anyone seeing."

"Do you have the whistle?"

Justin tapped the breast pocket of his leather jacket, feeling the small cylinder. "Still here." The whistle was enchanted with a compulsion spell. That was how the drug dealers had been controlling the pixies.

"Sunrise tomorrow," Zeph said. "Blow it, and I will come."

"You're sure?"

"Let's make that piece of fairy foulness work for us for a change. No matter how far away you are, I'll hear the damn thing."

"I'll find you tomorrow, I promise." Justin's right hand was cramped from putting sustained tension on the throttle. It was an effort to unshoulder the backpack and hold it so Zeph could drop from his helmet into it. The bike crested the rise, then dipped down into a pine-shrouded gully. Seizing the chance, he flung the bag low, its trajectory landing deep in the underbrush. He hoped the bushes and morning fog would conceal it as he rode out of the ravine like nothing had changed.

He didn't dare look back as he raced on toward the crossroads.

* * *

Rhodeghast the Crossroads Demon was bored. There were only so many faces screaming in the mist one could make over the decades before everything felt like it had been done before. Except for the occasional stupid mortal to liven its day, watching the sun rise on Earth was just as tedious as it had been in Hell.

The zooming of two motorcycles caught its attention. It waved a hand to disperse the anguish-filled faces it had been conjuring. They'd been uninspired, anyway.

The motorcycles were coming down off the mountain, winding their way down the road that always reminded Rhodeghast of a fallen angel's tramp stamp. As fast as they were going, it didn't seem like they were planning to stop in Sherman Township at all.

That was a shame.

Wasn't a road trip the perfect time to take in the sights, broaden one's perspectives? People were so narrow-minded. It was the same thing down in Hell, all the damned time. People should really stop to visit the historic sites. Rhodeghast's job was to keep new humans from entering Sherman. No one said anything about paranormals, and both of these riders fully qualified.

The first one had hooves big enough to make a succubus blush. And you know what they say about stallions with big hooves?

The second rider was even more delicious. It would have rolled out the red carpet for the witch hunter if it had known she was coming to Sherman. Maybe they could catch up when the witch hunter passed through the crossroads on the way out of town. Hopefully she'd leave a bloody trail in her wake. They could chat about it over mason jars of moonshine and some brimstone tarts.

With a wave of a taloned hand, Rhodeghast set both riders on what it affectionately thought of as the scenic route. The fog ebbed, and the rising sun momentarily blinded both riders. The road warped and reformed in an instant, then the grey mist returned thicker than ever. Unaware, the motorcycles raced on.

Welcome to Sherman County.

* * *

Sylvie Ellijay put her hands on her jean-short-clad hips and surveyed her handiwork. The lounge chair was placed at just the right angle to catch the morning rays once the sun cleared the mountain. Magazines were piled up on an antique tray table she'd dragged out of the back of the shop. The radio was tuned to her favorite country music station.

She was close enough to the shop to hear if a customer entered the store, but not so close as to pick up the incessant chattering of magical antiques. While many of the gifts and knickknacks inside were standard gift-giving fare, a few had much more magical histories. Sylvie's family went to estate sales and thrift shops to find enchanted items and save clueless humans from their influence.

Insomnia due to the owl cuckoo clock in the kitchen? Yep, seen that one. Haunted tackle box scaring away all the fish? Found one of those last week. Magic broom getting pushy about cleaning? Not great for a perfectionist, but Sylvie had sold one to some hygiene-challenged roommates yesterday.

All the magical items were gathered up and sold at the Silver Trinket. Along with their checkered pasts, the magical items her family recovered had opinions. Ugh, did they *ever* shut up?

Kicking off her sandals, Sylvie flopped on the lounge chair and braced herself for another long day of work. She grinned as she reached for a magazine. Her smile turned to a frown moments later when a motor revved as it pulled up the driveway. She wished she'd forgotten to turn on the "We're Open" sign.

The front door slammed open. Alarmed, Sylvie ran inside without putting on her sandals, her hand wrapped around her pentacle necklace.

A giant of a man stood inside the Silver Trinket. Easily six-and-a-half-feet tall, he towered over Sylvie, which didn't happen often. She hadn't been the star of the volleyball team four years ago for nothing. The way his jeans clung to his thighs was nearly sinful. With his black leather jacket and stubbled jaw, he looked like a perfect Saturday night to her.

"Do you have a map or something?" he asked in a deep baritone, sending shivers down her spine. "I got turned around this morning, and I really need to figure out how to get out of here."

His hands were empty at his sides. The bobcat statue by the door hadn't hissed at him. Sylvie released her necklace, letting it drop beneath the collar of her plaid shirt.

"We aren't a tourist bureau, but I might have something. Let me take a look back here." She chewed on her lip as she flipped through a bin of gift cards and other paper items near the register. If this motorcycle guy had gotten turned around at the crossroads, it meant the demon was causing trouble again. Sylvie would need to report it to the Poe sisters.

The framed treasure map on the wall shouted, "I'm a map, I'm a map," in a sing-song wail. Sylvie gritted her teeth and ignored it.

The man glared at his phone, his swipes growing more annoyed. "The GPS on my phone isn't working, either. I've restarted it twice now, and no change. And the map app keeps restarting itself."

"That happens a lot in the mountains," Sylvie said. "Everyone takes it for granted they'll have cell phone reception, but wide coverage isn't a thing up here." And she couldn't exactly admit there were any number of confusion and obfuscation spells woven about the town probably setting his phone on the fritz, too. She wasn't sure how a human like him had ended up in Sherman in the first place.

"Any luck yet?" he asked, shooting a glance toward the open front door.

She shook her head, her strawberry-blonde ponytail catching on her dangling earrings. She untangled them as she headed to the file cabinet in the corner. "Nothing yet, unless you want a get-well card. Might have better luck in here. Heavens know my family is allergic to getting rid of anything."

"Isn't there a gas station in this town? They'll probably have maps."

"Maybe where you're from, but not in Sherman. Scooter Jenkins runs the Flying D, and he barely believes in literacy. Best you'll find there is a beef jerky display and magazines with swimsuit models on the cover. Probably still believes the world is flat, too."

"I'm a map, I'm a map," the old treasure map sang. Sylvie wanted to wrap a hand around her pentacle, snap her fingers, and set the noisy thing on fire.

"Could you hurry it up? I'm sorry to push, but I really can't afford a delay like this."

Sylvie didn't think he was sorry at all. It was a shame, since he was the best looking guy to ever come into the shop. She was tempted to slow down her search out of spite, but that would just delay her return to her lounge chair. "Where're you wanting to get to? I could help."

"Don't worry about it."

She shrugged. Fine, if he didn't want to tell her so she could give him directions, that was his deal. She was halfway through the second drawer when she spied the old road atlas. "Eureka," she shouted, waving it about like a trophy. The man reached out to grab it, and she clutched it to her chest. "Hey, you gotta pay for it first."

"How much?" he asked, pulling a five dollar bill out his wallet.

Sylvie glanced down at the price printed on the back of the book. "You'll need to dig deeper in your wallet than that if you want to take this lucky book home with you. This rare find retails for $39.99."

"That's highway robbery. That book was probably printed before you were born. I'll give you ten bucks for it because I'm in a hurry."

She narrowed her eyes at him. How young did he think she was? It wasn't like he had any grey in his sideburns. "Well, I'm not in any rush, and it's my store. Forty bucks and it's yours. You know, collectors' items usually appreciate with time. This prized beauty has been racking up a lot of time. Maybe I should get it appraised first so I'm not losing out."

"I've only got twenty-eight in cash. That's my final offer."

"We do take credit cards," she said, spying the plastic cards in his wallet. "If you'd like to—"

"No, cash only." He slammed the money on the register, making the teapots rattle on their nearby shelf. The cracked pot on the end cried that it had fallen and couldn't get up. "Take the money, or I'm finding someone else in this town more agreeable to help me."

Sylvie snatched the money off the counter, dropping the dog-eared atlas in front of him. It was a shame he was so good looking, because his attitude sucked. "Fine, I'll consider this my community service for the day."

His hand reached for the book, then changed trajectory, reaching instead for his neck. Two small darts were embedded in his skin. He yanked them out, but his eyes were already rolling back in his head. He slumped over, falling to the wooden floor like a bull in a china shop.

A slim woman wearing green camo pants and a tank top stepped inside the Silver Trinket. A small pistol gleamed in her hand. The bobcat statue by the door hissed, and the hunting hounds painting began to howl.

Sylvie reached for her necklace, but a faint pinch in her neck and a wave of confusion slowed her down. Her mind grew foggy as she watched the woman close the door and turn off the "We're Open" sign before Sylvie crumpled behind the register.

* * *

The girl looked like a Southern fantasy Justin didn't know he possessed when she sauntered from the back of the shop with bare feet. He'd had to grip the doorknob for support. Her shirt was knotted under her breasts, exposing a delicious amount of tanned skin. He wanted to trace her curves with his tongue all the way down to where her cutoffs hung low on her hips. Then he wanted to pull them off and keep going.

Asking for a map had been a challenge. He'd had to resort to thinking about roadkill to rein in his cock. It was interested in getting lost in her valleys, not finding a way out of these mountains.

She was an aggressive negotiator. Damn if that wasn't hot, too. Justin wondered if he should find his way back to this town after this clusterfuck had subsided. He should leave his phone number along with the money. He was getting worked up again imagining her tanned legs wrapped around his waist. Or imagining her bent over his Harley. Or imagining her long torso arched backward, his hand wrapped around her ponytail, her pussy impaled on his cock.

He felt two pinches in his neck. He barely had time to rip the darts out and think, *oh shit*, before falling over like a chain-sawed log.

* * *

We are so screwed.

Those were Justin's first thoughts when he swam back to consciousness. The country music had stopped playing. Two women were talking.

"You've got to untie us right now. This rope isn't safe."

A harsh laugh mocked the first woman. "Right now you've bigger things to worry about than a rope, unless I decide to wrap it around your pretty little neck."

"Please, you don't understand. This thing is cursed. Tie us up with whatever else you want, but get this rope off now."

More laughter. "No, I don't think I will."

Justin's awareness came back to his body. He was bound to a chair at wrists and ankles. The cute but annoying shopkeeper was tied up behind him. He could feel her straining against the restraints with no success.

Eyes still closed, he tried to shift forms, but the drugs in his system inhibited his ability. His connection to his motorcycle was faint, but present. Normally he could feel it the same as this body's arm or foot, but it was ghostly and distant. *What had been in those darts?*

"Stop playing possum, Barbaro. I heard it the moment your breathing changed. Wake up so we can talk like civilized people."

He opened his eyes, and a woman's sharp face came into focus— sharp nose, sharper cheekbones, and when she smiled, canines filed to razor-sharp points. Nina Nijinsky, former squadmate and witch hunter extraordinaire.

"What are you doing here, Nijinsky?" he asked, attempting bravado. The woman was very good at her job. He didn't want to square off with her if he could avoid it. He scanned the small kitchen in the back of the shop. Faded yellow wallpaper, tiny coffeemaker, small wood table, and the two chairs they were occupying. Not much to work with here.

"Just as rude as ever. No greeting, no asking how I've been lately, no asking how the guys are doing, nothing."

Justin tried to laugh, but it came out as a hoarse cough. "I didn't realize you were in the habit of making social calls."

She flashed him a toothy grin. "Only on special occasions like this, where a horse has broken off from the herd and needs to be rounded up."

"I don't know what you're talking about."

"Don't play dumb with me; it's insulting. I'm here to recover some stolen property and bring you in on charges of suspected arson."

"What property?"

Nijinsky arched a thin eyebrow. "The pixies, of course. Tell me where they are, and I won't make this any worse than it needs to be."

"Dammit, Nina, you'll just be taking them back to their slave pens. Those people were torturing them just to manufacture drugs."

"Since when did you grow a conscience? You were never like this overseas."

"Well, maybe I got tired of everyone blowing smoke, telling me we were the good guys doing the right thing, when what we were actually doing didn't feel a damn thing like that. Blowing up the warehouse was just a bonus."

She sighed. "Are you going to tell me where you stashed the pixies?"

"No," he said, knowing what would happen next. It would hurt, but she wouldn't kill him yet. Not until she had what she needed. At least the shop girl was smart enough not to draw attention to herself. "Not a chance."

Nijinsky shrugged. "If you'll excuse me, seems I'm stepping outside for a bit. Feel free to shout when you're ready to talk." She wiggled her pointed elf ears at him. "I'll be listening."

The front door slammed shut, then the girl asked, "What's she doing?"

"Right now she's looking for something to hit with, then she'll smash my motorcycle. If that doesn't get the results she wants, she'll probably come inside and break my arms and legs in multiple places."

"And if she still doesn't get what she wants?"

Justin exhaled slowly through his nose. "Then she might start working you over, too."

"But I don't know anything."

He heard the tremor of fear in her voice. "What's your name?"

"I'm Sylvie. I really wish you hadn't come into my store this morning."

"I'd have kept driving if I'd known this would happen. My name's Justin." He tried the restraints, but he was too weak and drugged to break them.

"Don't bother," she said. "The rope is cursed. It can't be undone by cutting or breaking it."

Justin sensed some hesitance in her voice. "But there *is* a way to get out of it?"

"It's a binding rope, used in courtship and matrimonial rituals by a warlock cult that lived up on the hills years ago. They were some really sick folk. They used the rope to marry teenaged witch girls to their old warlocks, binding their fates together so they couldn't—"

Pain shot through Justin's knee, and he screamed. That was followed by white-hot pain in his other knee, dragging out another involuntary shout. Outside were the sounds of smashing metal and laughter.

"Keep talking," he said. "How do we get out?"

"The story goes that, um, the man and the woman had their wrists bound with the rope and they—are you sure you're okay?" she asked

Justin grunted as several blows smashed his feet and shins. He couldn't stop twitching and knew she could feel it too, tied back-to-back as they were. "Just keep talking."

"Okay, so the man and woman were, uh, bound together with the rope, then they had to speak some ritual words. I don't know the words, but I don't think it was very different from a normal wedding. We could try something similar and see if it works."

"Feeling more talkative yet?" Nijinsky yelled from the driveway.

"Go to hell, Nina!" he shouted back, groaning as more spikes of pain blossomed. It was growing hard to focus through the red haze. "What now, Sylvie?"

"Now I think we try to get married. But what do we do about afterward?"

"Let's just focus on getting out of this alive first." He paused. "Please tell me you're at least eighteen."

"I'm twenty-three years old, you jackass."

Nina was ripping off lug nuts and spokes now. It hurt worse than pulling off his toenails. Justin hissed through his teeth, trying to focus on the words and block out the pain. "I, Justin Bucephalus Barbaro, take you, Sylvie, to be my lawfully wedded wife, as long as we both shall live."

"I, Sylvie Mythril Ellijay, take you, Justin, to be my lawfully wedded husband, as long as we both shall live."

They were simple words, but binding all the same. The rope slackened, then dropped to the floor. Bereft of its support, Justin toppled forward, too, curling in a ball as pain lanced through his spine. He moaned and blacked out.

* * *

Sylvie felt Justin tumble to the floor behind her. She would check on him in a moment, but first she had to get this crazy woman to leave. Now that her hands were free, she seized her pentacle in her hands and began to chant. *"Trinarii quodam dimittere, et canes dimittere, primos belli canibus."*

All around the shop, the magic animated the dogs, from tiny figurines and stony statues, to shadowy photographs and oil paintings. They leapt and grew until they were a howling pack thick across the floor, each hound with a sharp set of fangs. Sylvie waded through them and opened the front door.

The witch hunter had heard the noise and had already backed up to her parked motorcycle. At the sight of so many dogs howling for her blood, she wisely scrambled for her seat. Sylvie watched as the dogs chased her down Main Street and out of Sherman.

The spell wouldn't last forever. The spirits would return to their bodies by sundown, but they should keep Nina occupied long enough for Sylvie to figure out what was going on.

Justin was still unconscious. Sylvie's heart broke as she saw the bruises on his hands and face. It looked like he'd been in a brawl, but Nina hadn't touched him physically.

She smoothed the hair off his forehead, unable to resist touching him. Her bones tingled with the pull of the bond between them. That was another problem she'd need to solve. She wished she could go back to first thing this morning when tan lines had been her biggest concern.

His wounds were beyond her ability to heal. She wasn't a full witch; she'd never claimed her heritage, never wanted to. This was the first time she'd ever regretted that choice.

She needed to call someone to help, someone who had the magic to do what she couldn't. Sylvie grabbed the landline from the wall, the phone cord long enough for her to sit and hold Justin's hand. She asked the operator to put her through to the veterinarian's office.

* * *

Gramercy Poe pulled up in her van less than an hour later. She knocked and let herself into the shop, a quiet, soothing presence with braided blonde hair and a large medical satchel. Sylvie was relieved to see her. Being a veterinarian for Sherman as well as a witch meant Mercy was called in for things that weren't exactly animal related.

"Hey, Sylvie, what happened here?" she asked softly as she knelt down in the kitchen.

She was one of Sylvie's favorite cousins. All the Poe sisters had strong magical talents and took their responsibilities as white witches seriously. Most of them couldn't understand why she didn't want to embrace her heritage, but Mercy had never pushed. She was a sweetheart like that.

Sylvie smoothed the blanket she'd draped over Justin. It barely covered half of him, but she hadn't known what else to do while she waited. Mercy listened while she explained. She hoped her cousin would be able to fix him.

"Help me get his clothes off," Mercy said. "I need to see what we're dealing with."

As they pulled his jeans off to inspect the bruising, Sylvie couldn't help but notice the way Justin was stuffed into his black boxer briefs. If he lived up to his potential when aroused, a girl would need a step stool to mount him. But it would be a hell of a ride.

Her thoughts climbed down off the stripper pole as she saw the patches of black and purple covering his legs. Whatever that crazy woman had done outside had really hurt him. His legs were covered in bruises from hip to heel.

She wished she could cook up a batch of chicken noodle soup and make it all go away.

Mercy continued her inspection, checking his eyes, feeling his pulse, listening to his lungs. "Why did this witch hunter leave? Did she know what you were?"

"She assumed I was human. I didn't let her see my necklace. Since I don't actively use my magic, she couldn't smell it on me." Each witch's magic had a particular fragrance unique to them. The Poe sisters were lovely, and all smelled like different kinds of flowers. Sylvie's magic smelled like flowers too, as long as you like the scent of verbena mixed with silver polish.

Mercy sniffed. "But you used it today." She placed her hands on Justin's chest. The fragrance of honeysuckle and hay filled the kitchen as she used her healing magic. Unlike Sylvie, she didn't need to touch her pentacle with her hands to use her powers.

"She was outside, so she didn't sense anything," Sylvie said. "I animated all the dogs and set them on her. They chased her off."

"Hmm, if she was a witch hunter, what makes you think he isn't one, too?"

"Torturing one of your own seems a bit extreme, doesn't it?" Sylvie hadn't even told her yet about the bonding ritual they'd done to escape. What would her cousin think of that?

Mercy squeezed her shoulder. "Hunting witches and other paranormals is extreme. That's why our family set the wards around Sherman County in the first place, so we'd have a sanctuary in the hills to be safe from such xenophobes."

"But this witch hunter was an elf."

Her cousin made a face like she was going to vomit. "That's just sick, but it explains why she made it through the crossroads."

Justin coughed and rolled on his side, starting to come around. Mercy took the opportunity to examine his back and listen to his lungs again.

"Hey there, you're safe now," Sylvie said. "You need to wake up. We need to talk to you so we can heal you." But even more, she needed to hear his voice and know he was alright.

"Body won't heal while the bike's messed up." His voice was raspy, and Sylvie got him some water. "She ripped me apart headlamp to spoiler."

Mercy put her stethoscope back in her bag. "I don't think you're going to die, but my healing magic didn't seem to help. All I can do is give you something for the pain."

"Nothing strong," Justin said. "Have to keep my head clear. Got to fix my bike. No offense, but you'd be a lot more useful to me if you were a mechanic."

The cousins exchanged glances. "We know a mechanic." Sylvie hopped up to make another phone call.

* * *

Meridian Poe pulled up with a trailer hitched to her truck just as the sun was setting. Justin had never been happier to see a complete stranger before. After a quick round of introductions to Sylvie's latest cousin, they went to work hauling all the pieces of the motorcycle around to the backyard. Justin dragged himself to the back porch to supervise.

After the big pieces were moved, Mercy excused herself, mentioning something about a coven meeting. Justin's legs were twin pillars of pain. While Mercy had done her best to relieve the aches, not much else could be done until the motorcycle, the other half of him, was repaired. Justin leaned his head back against the side of the house and closed his eyes.

This was all his fault, trying to save the pixies, blowing everything up, and setting the drug lords on him, not just driving through town and leaving himself to fate. Stopping to talk to a cute girl when he should have known to keep moving. He knocked his head back against the house, savoring the headache it caused, believing he deserved every bit of pain for being such a complete idiot.

This wasn't the first time he wished he could time travel and fix his mistakes, but it was the messiest.

Meridian stepped into the trailer, gathering her tools together so they could start bending back the bigger pieces of metal. While it didn't take long to put a normal motorcycle together, fixing up the tangled hash of metal would be an overnight job at best.

Sylvie had confirmed that all the dogs had returned to their spots in the antique shop. Now that Nijinsky was left free to her own devices, Justin knew she'd be aiming for another shot at him. The only solace he could take in that was knowing the pixies were still safe.

Sylvie rounded the corner of the house. Justin felt immediately drawn to her, like a lodestone. It had to be the bond from the rope tying them together. She was carrying a box with the last pieces of metal from the front yard. She must have been searching the grass with the flashlight to find everything. She looked up at him sitting on the back porch and tried to smile. It quickly dissolved into tears as she cradled the box.

Justin wished he could go to her, but there was no way he could move in his current state. "Sylvie, can you put the box down and come up here for a minute? I want to talk to you."

Sylvie gingerly set the box on the steps before slumping down next to him. She pulled her knees to her chest and wiped her eyes. The sight of it broke his heart.

"Come here," he said, wrapping an arm around her shoulders. Her knees jostled his thigh, but he stifled his grunt of discomfort. No need to make her feel worse than she already did. She had to be freaked out about today. Normal people don't get tied up with strangers in their own kitchens and threatened at gunpoint. "I'm sorry I got you all mixed up in this. I wish I could tell you it was all a bad dream."

"I'm not a child," she snuffled.

"Good, you can hold me instead. I'm terrified of what Nina could do if she returns."

"What do you think will happen?" she asked.

"Nothing's going to happen," he said, kissing her temple. She smelled sweet, like strawberries. Noticing how good she smelled should have been the last thing on his mind. But other parts of him never listened to common sense. "Your cousin's going to get me patched up, and I'll be on my way. Once I'm gone, there's no reason for Nina to hang around. Fix whatever problem you've got at the crossroads, and no one will ever find Sherman again."

"But what if she doesn't leave?"

"Then I'll drag her down the highway with me. I promise I won't leave her here to torment you and your cousins."

Sylvie snuggled closer. Justin loved the way her head tucked right under his chin. He would miss it when he left. She toyed with his dog tags.

"Bucephalus? What kind of a middle name is that?"

"My father is fond of history, especially ancient Greece."

"I can relate. My mother adores anything sparkly. Being named after silver isn't so bad, but who gets saddled with the middle name Mythril? It isn't even a real metal."

Justin watched the last rays of sunshine fade behind the mountains. The stars sparkled overhead. He decided to tell her everything. He owed it to her after bringing this mess to her front door. He tucked the blanket tighter around her.

"You and your cousins are all witches, right?"

Sylvie shook her head. "They're real witches. I never claimed my heritage or went through the initiation, so I'm not an official part of the coven."

"Why not?" he asked. "Wouldn't that expand your powers?"

"And give me more responsibility. Not something I'm looking for heaps of. White witches are obligated to help people in trouble. I'm obligated to run this shop and pay my taxes, nothing more. I like it just fine this way."

"I can understand that," he said, squeezing her tighter to his side. He tried to ignore her fingers brushing across his chest and biceps. He wanted those slim fingers all over him. *Remember, it's only the bind-*

ing rope's magic. "I haven't been completely honest with you, and I think you need to know what exactly you bound yourself to."

Sylvie stilled. "Are you dangerous?"

"To you? Never." Justin pressed another kiss to her temple before continuing. "I'm not human. You've figured that out by now. But my species is different from werewolves or vampires. We aren't humans who were changed by drinking blood, like vampires. And transformation magic is not a power we originally possessed, like werewolves. In order to hide from humans, we've needed to conceal parts of ourselves in plain sight. It isn't easy to hide when you're normally ten feet tall. Transformation was a power we had to learn, but there are some concessions."

"Your motorcycle is a part of you, right? That's why Nina went after it first instead of you."

"Exactly. My middle name is Bucephalus because history remembers it as the name of Alexander the Great's horse. But he wasn't Alexander's horse, he was one of his advisors and mentors, back when centaurs were respected for their wisdom. Before we had to become creatures of myth like the harpies and minotaurs. I'm named Bucephalus because he was my ancestor, and because I'm a centaur, too."

Justin watched her reactions as she processed this new information. He had no idea how she felt about other paranormal species. She could be looking for a nice witch or druid to settle down with and have beautiful strawberry-blond babies for all he really knew. Damned if that didn't cut deep. *It's only the stupid rope*, he reminded himself.

He wasn't really in love with her.

"So what did you use before motorcycles? There's a lot of history between Ancient Greece and the invention of the combustion engine."

He was surprised by the question, but glad she hadn't immediately pushed him away. "Horses mostly. Transforming half of ourselves into wagons and carriages was unwieldy at best. No matter what form we take, we still have to obey the laws of physics. The rest of our mass has to go somewhere."

"Makes sense, I suppose. Are there a lot of you, then? There's a lot of motorcycles on the highways these days."

"Not every biker gang you're imagining is a herd in disguise, but yes, there are more of us than you might suspect."

"I'm happy I met you in the present. Motorcycles are much sexier than wooden wagons."

Justin couldn't help but laugh at that. "Glad you feel that way." Forgetting their attraction wasn't real, he pulled her up to his mouth for a kiss.

* * *

Sylvie leaned into him, offering her lips up to him like a flower seeking the sun. His mouth seared hers as he deepened the kiss, masterfully sliding his tongue along hers.

It felt right, so very right.

She returned his kiss, trying to say what she was feeling with her lips and tongue. She hoped he heard her, hoped his heart responded the way her heart responded to him. It beat like a frantic hummingbird as he trailed kisses down her neck. Her heart wanted more.

Not just more, she wanted everything. Whatever Justin would give her, Sylvie would willingly take so long as he didn't stop.

He traced her collarbone with his lips as his fingers worked at the buttons of her shirt. His stubble tickled her skin. She arched toward him, offering herself to him as a feast. He could indulge until they were both sated.

Meridian slammed the trailer door shut. Startled, they broke apart. "Hey, lover boy!" she shouted. "You ready to put this heap of scrap back together or not?"

Sylvie searched Justin's face, wondering if he was as affected by the kiss as she was. Her pulse was racing, and her cheeks were hot. She could feel his heart like a galloping horse under her palm.

"I'm sorry," he said. "The stupid rope, the bond, I didn't mean to—"

"Sandwiches, I should go make everyone sandwiches," Sylvie said, releasing his dog tags and pushing away. "No one's had anything to eat all day. I should make myself useful, too." She darted into the kitchen without a backward glance.

Sylvie heard Meridian and Justin talking as she pulled the fixings for turkey and pimento cheese sandwiches out of the fridge. How stupid could she be? He wasn't really attracted to her. It was just the binding spell messing with their heads. It didn't help that she'd thought him attractive when she first saw him.

She would look for a counterspell. She would keep her hands and lips to herself. That was the plan. It was simple.

Why did it seem so impossible for her to do?

She brought plates of food outside. Meridian had propped the main body of the motorcycle up, and Justin was working on the engine. She left their plates on the porch steps and retreated inside, heading to the stuffed bookshelves. With a sigh, she pulled the first book from the top of the shelf. Finding a spell to undo the binding between her and Justin would take a while.

Her presence agitated the large steamer trunk chained up in the corner. It growled and gnashed its compartments at her. A troublesome piece of baggage, it had a habit of eating stray cats if it slipped its leash. Sylvie frowned at it, took another book from the shelf, and left the room.

Dawn found everyone asleep. Sylvie was stretched out on the porch swing, a quilt around her shoulders and a book under her cheek. Justin was stretched out on his back in the grass, a hand resting on a tire. Meridian's boots dangled out the open window of her truck.

Sylvie groaned and stretched. Coffee; she needed coffee.

Meridian and Justin had worked as fast as they could to rebuild the motorcycle. Sylvie was amazed at the progress they'd made. At this rate, they'd have it fixed by the end of the day. Justin said he'd be able to shift once the repairs were complete, and his body would be healed.

And then he would leave.

Sylvie closed her eyes against the feelings of loss that washed over her. *Remember, it's not real.* But as she watched him sleep, dark bags under his eyes and motor oil under his nails, she knew she didn't want him to leave.

But he had no reason to stay in Sherman. He'd never planned to come to her small mountain town. His life was outside.

She shook off the cobwebs of her thoughts and stepped into the kitchen. Everything would seem better after coffee.

After breakfast, Meridian went back to her truck. Justin hung back at the table, toying with a crust of toast. He'd limped inside to eat, and Sylvie had barely restrained herself from hugging him. She closed her eyes. *It's just the magic of the bond.*

"Hey, are you okay?" Justin asked. "You aren't hurt anywhere, are you?

Sylvie's eyes flew open, and she stepped back just before he would have touched her cheek. The two of them alone in the kitchen, who knows where that caress would have led?

With toast and jam on the floor, and me spread across the kitchen table, her helpful imagination suggested.

"Fine, I'm totally fine." She forced a smile then put the jam safely in the cupboard. "Just tired. How are you feeling? You're walking around better this morning."

Justin stretched a leg out, then winced. "Better, but we've still got work to do today. Since I'm tied up here and not fit for roaming around anyway, I have a favor to ask."

Anything for you. "What kind of favor?"

He pulled a thin silver whistle the size of half a pencil from his jacket pocket. "The pixies are still out in the woods. I dumped them yesterday in case Nijinsky caught up with me. Probably the only smart thing I did. I promised them I'd find them today. I'm in no shape to retrieve them myself. It's a lot to ask, but I was hoping you could go get them for me."

"Why the whistle?" she asked.

"I threw the backpack they were riding inside into the woods before the crossroads. We weren't sure if they would have to hide further in the trees, or if I could even find the exact spot. Blow this whistle, and the troop leader will find you. Tell Zeph I sent you."

"What about Nina? Won't she be watching?"

"You're right, it's too dangerous to send you out there." He ran a hand over his face. "We'll just have to hope the pixies are okay, hope they can hold out until I'm all patched up."

Sylvie didn't want to leave the pixies alone. If they needed help, making them wait seemed cruel. She chewed on her lip, considering the options. "There might be a way I can get to them. I can take a path through the Witchwoods."

"Where are the Witchwoods? I've never heard of it."

"It's a shadow realm alongside this one, a place where witches can step and be closer to the old paths that lead to the deep places. We don't talk about the Witchwoods with outsiders."

"It still doesn't sound safe. Why would you do this for me?" Justin asked.

Because my heart aches when you're close, and it'll break apart when you leave. "Because someone has to find those pixies. I might not be a white witch, but someone needs to save them."

"Promise me you'll be careful. I've gotten you mixed up in so much, and I keep asking you to do more. It isn't fair to you that—"

"It's fine. I'm going to change into some jeans, then I'll head out. Maybe Nina will decide to sleep in this morning."

Later, as the Witchwoods wrapped their dark shadows around her, Sylvie wished she'd brought a map, even the obnoxious treasure map, with her. Like had happened to her mom, she was afraid she'd never find her way home.

She should be safe if she stayed on the path to the crossroads, but it could go wandering off if you lost your focus. If you worried about what lurked in the shadows. If you searched for sharp-beaked shapes in the branches. If you glanced over your shoulder for ghost-pawed stalkers.

Sylvie kept her eyes on the ground in front of her and prayed. She wanted to make it back home. She tied the knot on her bandana tighter and hurried.

* * *

It had taken most of the morning, but they were just about done. Justin now felt only battered, which was a huge improvement over feeling like the remains of a childhood toy strapped to some cherry bombs. He could finally walk and had stumbled to the bathroom with some dignity.

Sylvie was cradling the backpack and crying when she came out of the woods. Her bandana was missing. He opened his arms, and she set the bag on the porch step before letting him embrace her. Something had upset her. Justin wanted to ask, but he stayed patient, rubbing her back until the tears stopped flowing.

"They were having a funeral when I found them," Sylvie said.

"How many?" he asked, sick to his stomach.

"Too many," Zeph said as he emerged from the bag, "but fewer than it would have been if we'd kept going yesterday."

"I'm still sorry," Justin said. In that moment, imagining those small, cold bodies, he didn't regret his rash escape from the warehouse. He only wished he'd found the pixies sooner.

"There is no debt you owe us," Zeph said. "The harm done to us was not by your hand. Without you, the whole troop would have perished eventually. But you gave us a chance to carry on their songs. It's enough."

"I'm glad you're safe."

"You have our appreciation for sending this young witch to find us."

"Yes, I appreciate it as well," a sharp-tongued voice said as Nina sauntered out of the woods. "I would never have found my way back through the barrier without this lovely guide. And I appreciate you gathering everyone together for me in one place. It really *couldn't* be more perfect." She brandished the pistol—Justin's pistol—which she'd taken yesterday.

"Nijinsky, you don't have to do this," Justin said. "Let everyone else go, and I'll come back with you."

The elf laughed at him, a sharp sound like breaking glass. "The only ones I'm bringing back are the pixies. That's what they're paying me to retrieve. Shooting the rest of you is just a bonus."

Meridian stepped out of the trailer, chanting loudly. Her pentacle burned like star fire on its chain. Embers swirled around her raised fist. "*Dirigentes stella, procidens stella, meteororum pluam vo—*"

Nina shot Meridian in the chest. She crumpled heavily to the trailer floor, a puppet with its strings suddenly severed. Sylvie screamed.

"Witches are a plague, every one of them. Pretending to be human, when they're no better than magical cockroaches. You should thank me for removing them from the face of the earth."

"Dammit, Nina, you're shooting innocent people!" Justin exclaimed. Sylvie moved to check on Meridian, but Justin grabbed her arm and pulled her behind his back. "Don't," he said, "she'll shoot you, too."

Nina pointed the muzzle at Justin. "You were always so concerned with right and wrong. Don't shoot these people. Don't blow this up. Don't do anything where someone could accidentally get hurt. Why couldn't you understand that killing people was our *job?*"

He put his hands out in front of himself, wide and nonthreatening. "Killing might have been your job. My job was to protect lives. Yes, sometimes that meant people died, but it was so other people could stay safe. What you're doing here is nothing like what happened over there." How could he stop Nina before she shot everyone dead and took the pixies back to their lives of slavery?

"Shut up! You don't know what you're talking about. You're just another holier than thou prick no one will miss."

Behind him, Sylvie started chanting. Despite her claims of not being a full witch, he hoped she was casting something good.

"Shut that bitch up," Nina said. Twice she squeezed the trigger. Twice her shots hit Justin squarely in the chest. Her marksmanship skills were as sharp as ever.

Justin struggled to keep his footing. If he fell, she'd shoot Sylvie next. He couldn't let that happen. Digging deep into his core, he reached the foundation, where his body and the motorcycle were the same, where his legs were all the same, where his spirit ran free. He willed the pieces of his body to merge and transform. His senses swam and refocused, as he was now twice as tall, and ten times heavier than before. Dark mane and tail, silvery sharp hooves. Power surged through his body as he tapped into his full strength.

Behind him, Sylvie continued to chant. "*Venit pectore repono, at contra   gazophylacium,   et saturabitur festum.*" There were horrible thumping and gnashing sounds, but nothing happened. She chanted louder.

Justin was still wounded by the bullets, but they were placed much lower in his torso, not next to his first heart. And now that he had two hearts, he was much, much harder to kill.

He charged.

Nina unloaded the remaining rounds into the charging centaur, but he didn't falter. He trampled her and wheeled around for a second pass. The witch hunter rolled her broken body into a crouch. "You won't stop me so easily." Her teeth were stained with her blood. Reloading her gun, she took aim at Sylvie.

Hand around her pentacle, Sylvie stared her down unwaveringly and kept chanting.

Justin raced to stop Nina, but he knew he wouldn't reach her in time to stop her shot.

The gnashing sound was thunderous. The ground rumbled all round Nina and fell away. Out of the freshly turned earth surged the trunk from the library. Its enormous maw was filled with rows and rows of shark-like teeth. And like any orca lunging from beneath the waves to snatch a sleeping seal, the trunk gulped the elf down in a single move. There hadn't even been a chance to scream.

Safe from her attacker, Sylvie stumbled away, running to help Meridian, who lay unmoving.

Justin came to a halt, stunned. As quickly as she'd appeared, Nina was gone. Only the disturbed ground hinted at her demise.

Sylvie ripped off her shirt, pressing it to her cousin's stomach. She was crying and begging her to hold on.

The adrenaline was fading from Justin's body, giving way to shakes and pain. He wondered when he would finally stop hurting. He slumped down next to Sylvie, resting his head on her shoulder. Blood was running freely down his chest. "I love you," he whispered, but his voice was drowned out by the sound of a van rumbling up the driveway.

Mercy wasn't alone. Her witch sisters were with her, and they swiftly took over the house and yard. They tried to separate him from Sylvie, which he refused, holding tightly to her hand after transforming back to his more human form. Mercy made a comment to the cousins that he couldn't hear, and they relented, for which he was grateful. He wanted to spend every moment he had left with Sylvie. He committed her to memory, the freckles on her nose, the curve of her ear, the shine of her hair as she tucked him into bed, after Mercy had healed him with her sisters' help.

And when everything had settled down, Justin decided he would leave, taking the threat of violence to Sylvie away from her. And when she found a counterspell, she would have her future back, too.

* * *

Sylvie quietly closed the door to her bedroom behind her and crept down the stairs. Justin had kept such a tight grip on her hand, she'd worried she'd need to gnaw it off to escape. He'd let her go long enough to change into a sundress, the first clean outfit she'd found.

Her cousins had set the house and yard to rights and were leaving. They were loading Meridian into Mercy's van, despite the mechanic's loud protests.

"I'm not some livestock you can just load up and cart around."

"Then stop braying so loudly I confuse you with a jackass," Mercy said. "Let's get you home so you can rest. The healing seal I put on the wound should hold, but I don't want to take any chances. Who'll fix my van if you're not around?"

"Damn skippy," Meridian said, relenting with a sigh.

"Thank you," Sylvie said, squeezing her cousin's hand.

Meridian gave her a lopsided smile. "Anytime, sugar. So what are you going to do with that boy of yours when he wakes up?"

Sylvie frowned. "He isn't mine, not really. When we were tied up, it was with that cursed rope from the shop. We think we're attracted to each other, but it isn't real. That's why you saw us kissing on the porch."

"What rope?" Mercy asked. "You didn't mention this yesterday."

"It didn't seem as important at the time as helping Justin and stopping Nina."

"It wouldn't happen to be a blue rope cursed by mountain-dwelling warlocks, would it?" Meridian asked.

"Yes, that's the one. You wouldn't happen to know what the counterspell is, would you?"

Mercy and Meridian exchanged glances, then both burst out laughing. The mechanic's laughs turned to guffaws of pain as she covered her healing wound with her hand, which made the vet laugh even more.

"I don't understand what's funny about this," Sylvie said.

Mercy wiped tears from her eyes. "We made up that story years ago, told it to your mother, and tried to make money selling stupid things like that in the shop. That rope was nothing special. She must have missed it when she was cleaning out the random stuff we brought into the Silver Trinket to sell."

"But that doesn't explain how the rope untied itself. It didn't happen until we said the vows."

"It wasn't the vows, it was your magic. You believed it would happen when you said the words, so that's what happened. You aren't any more bound to him than any other witch who falls in love." Mercy gave Sylvie a hug. "Now go back upstairs and give that guy of yours the good news. I need to get my sister home before she finds some more trouble."

Sylvie was stunned as she watched them drive off. She didn't understand how it was possible, but her cousins wouldn't lie to her about something like this. The knowledge that her feelings were real had her grinning from ear to ear.

* * *

Justin threw a leg over his bike. The cars were leaving, and he planned to follow after them. They'd said the crossroads demon wouldn't bother him again. It was best that he left now.

The pixies had decided to stay. The Poe sisters had promised to take good care of them.

Justin didn't dare kiss Sylvie goodbye. He felt like his heart was being torn in half. He kept reminding himself that it wasn't real. He didn't truly love her. It was just a magic spell caused by a twisted artifact tricking his head and his heart.

"Where do you think you're going?" Sylvie asked. The late afternoon sun turned her hair into burnished gold, and the light in her eyes was all fire. "Were you going to sneak away without saying goodbye?"

"It's better this way. The way we feel, it isn't real. This way I could save us doing something we might both regret."

"Oh, what kind of things might that be?" Sylvie asked as she strode toward him. Her sundress clung to her hips, outlining curves he wanted to worship with his hands and mouth. "Something like this?" she asked as she wrapped her hand around his neck and pulled his mouth down to hers.

And god help him, he let her do it. He was powerless to resist, drawn to her like a moth to a flame. Her tongue danced along his lips, sending sparks of fire to his cock, igniting a passion that threatened to consume him.

"It's real," she whispered. Her breath was warm on his cheek. "The rope was just a rope. The magic to unbind us was mine. That's why I couldn't find a counterspell."

"Truly? You're certain?"

"As certain as I am about how much I want you." Sylvie drew his hand off the throttle and to her breast, moaning as he squeezed with tender pressure. He mirrored his touch with his other hand. Her nipples tightened, and she arched her back, pressing her hips into his thigh, asking for more.

Asking for everything he wanted to give her.

Justin pushed the straps of her sundress down, baring her breasts. Her rosy nipples puckered in the air, too enticing to resist. He took one of her nipples into his mouth, licking and sucking until she clutched at his shoulders. Then he swapped his torment to her other breast, listening to her moans. It sounded like she'd orgasm from just that.

He pressed the full handfuls of her breasts together, sucking both nipples into his mouth at once. Sylvie gasped as her orgasm slammed into her, and Justin was nearly undone by the feel of her coming apart in his hands.

She blinked at him as he pulled off her sundress, followed by his shirt. She swayed unsteadily, dazed by her unexpected orgasm. Her panties were blue with little yellow pineapples on them. It was so unexpected, he laughed. "What's with the pineapples?"

"Don't you know, it's a sign of Southern hospitality?" She pressed her mound into his hand. Her panties were soaking wet.

"Very hospitable," he agreed, capturing her lips with his as she wiggled out of her last item of clothing.

Justin was still straddling the black leather seat. When he pulled her up, Sylvie wrapped her legs around him without hesitation. He skimmed his hands down her body, feeling the same curves that had so captivated him the first time he saw her. She was fiery and sweet and smelled so deliciously of strawberries.

Sylvie's legs were open for him, and she was dripping. She pressed herself into the ridge of his jeans, where his cock clamored for release. She rode his erection, trying to get the friction she needed to relieve the tension that was building. She trembled in his arms like a tightly strung bow. He slipped a hand down, rubbing her clit, matching it to the tempo of his tongue on her nipple. She was writhing on top of him, begging him for more. He slid a finger inside her, reveling when she reached her climax riding his hand.

Coming back to awareness, she reached for the button on his jeans. "I need you inside me."

He'd never had sex on his bike, had never even taken a woman for a ride on it. It was too much a part of himself, but this felt so right. Mesmerized, he watched as she undid his jeans, shoving them down and releasing his cock.

"Oh my god, you're like—"

"A horse, I know. I'm sorry, it's too—"

"It's perfect," she said, pumping him slowly. Her slim hands were magic as they gripped him, using her wetness to get him ready for her. He was so fucking ready.

She guided him inside her, slowly at first as she adjusted to his length. There was a lot of him to take, but she bore down on him inch by inch until she took him fully. They locked eyes as he rocked into her, moving faster, rolling deep into her.

Fully impaled on his cock, she arched back over the handlebars, the perfect fantasy he'd had of her embodied in his arms. He could feel his climax building with every thrust. He was at the mercy of her hot sheath, slamming down as she rode him faster. Being on the motorcycle, fully connected with himself, made this so much more.

He sucked a nipple into his mouth, tugging on it with every give and take of their bodies. "Oh, yes, please," she moaned, tugging on his hair as he tormented her breast. "Please make me come," she begged.

He grabbed her hips, rubbing her clit as she ground against him. Her orgasm rocked through her, and her pussy squeezed him tightly, bringing him to the most profound completion of his life.

As they rode out their aftershocks of pleasure together, she whispered in his ear, "Welcome to Sherman County."

* * * * *

Kylie Cross Bio

An old romantic soul in a young body. Romance writer born and raised in the South. Enjoys traveling the world through books and food. Involved in a scandalous relationship with cupcakes. Don't tell gelato!

www.kyliecrosswrites.com

# # # # #

Thus, With a Kiss by Kacey Ezell

The teenaged girl shuffled forward, her steps slowed by the fog of hormone-induced fatigue. She fumbled for the light switch and flinched as blinding white light flooded the bathroom. With a squint and a scowl, she knuckled her eyes and forced herself to focus blearily on the image in the mirror. Death stared back, the witness of eons deep in her icy-pale eyes.

"Oh," Death said softly. "Oh, I see. We're sixteen this time."

"Eliane!" her mother's voice echoed up the stairs, her tone strident with urgency. "Are you up? You're going to be late!"

"Yes, Mom!" Death called back. Her voice sounded shriller, sharper than she'd intended.

"Watch your tone, young lady! Get your butt up and dressed! You can't miss the bus today; I don't have time to take you to school this morning!"

"I got it, Mom!" Eliane, who was now also somehow Death, shouted back. Try as she might, she couldn't entirely keep her frustration out of her words, and she felt her mother's rising anger at her apparent attitude. It reverberated through the house like the *crack* of a bullet in flight. Since she was both Death and Eliane, the teenager felt equal parts detached interest and echoing dread. She hadn't meant to sound nasty. She hated fighting with her mom.

Downstairs, the back door slammed as Eliane's mom stormed out to the garage. *Probably better that way*, Eliane thought as she walked back down the hallway to her bedroom. Mom couldn't be late for her shift as an ER nurse, and their "discussions" about Eliane's attitude were never productive anyway. They just ended in everyone shouting and feeling miserable.

"Ain't nobody got time for that," Eliane said softly as she turned to her closet. She slid the door open, and her eyes fell upon the single, bright spot in the forest of black within. Blue and gold polyester. Stripes and geometric patterns. A sparkly, glitter-encrusted ribbon bow looped over the hook of the hangar. A cheerleading uniform.

Correction. *Her* cheerleading uniform. She, Death incarnate, was a varsity cheerleader at her high school. And if Eliane's memory was to be believed, today was the day of the school's pep rally. So rather than any of the eminently suitable black outfits in the closet, she would be wearing the cheerleading uniform during her first day of this existence.

Perfect.

Eliane let out a sigh and pulled the brightly colored uniform off its hangar. She dressed with neat, economical motions, making sure to center the embroidered chenille of the rearing horse on her chest. The skirt was almost unforgivably short, but the body-hugging short pants that hung beneath it made wearing it less intimidating.

"Gotta love Nike Pros," Eliane said as she smoothed her hands down over the outfit and looked at herself in the mirror that hung on the closet door. "At least my ass won't be hanging out when I find my siblings. I would *never* be allowed to forget that. Not in a million lifetimes. They're going to give me enough grief about the bow."

She pulled her tight blonde curls up into a ponytail atop her head and wrapped the bow's rubber band about the base with neat motions. Then she headed back to the bathroom to finish getting ready. Death may not have had any idea how to put foundation and eyeshadow on Eliane's sun-kissed golden skin, but Eliane did, so it didn't take long to get to the point where the teenager, at least, was satisfied with her appearance.

She was brushing her teeth when her phone buzzed.

Death hadn't even realized she *had* a phone, but it seemed to be a natural extension of her hand as soon as she picked it up. Words flashed across the screen, apparently a message from someone named "Ivy." Eliane recognized the name of her best friend.

Did you catch the bus?

Eliane clamped her toothbrush between her teeth to hold it while she used two hands to tap out a quick reply.

No.

Need a ride?

Yes.

I'm out front.

KK. Be right down.

Eliane leaned forward and spat the last of the toothpaste into the sink. She swiped her toothbrush under the running water, turned it off with her wrist, and grabbed the hand towel to dry her fingers. She slicked on a coat of a pinky-mauve lipstick, which she then dropped into the front pocket of the sparkly backpack she'd found at the foot of her bed. It was blue and entirely covered with the same light-catching glitter as the bow, with a small exception. There was a satin infinity symbol stitched on to the front of the backpack, which Death found incredibly amusing. Eliane knew it was the logo for the bag's manufacturer, but Death and her siblings had used that symbol to identify themselves to one another for millennia, so it was really quite apropos.

Her phone buzzed again. *Where RU???*

She tapped out a quick reply, zipped up the backpack, slung it over her shoulder, and ran down the stairs. It was nice, Death reflected, to have such a young, strong body this time around. Last time she'd joined a woman who'd just given birth to her seventh child. The only thing she remembered feeling from that incarnation was fatigue.

Eliane grabbed her letterman jacket and let the front door slam behind her as she headed out into the world.

* * *

Ivy drove a green Mustang.

Eliane knew that, but Death found it amusing, especially since the rearing horse logo on the car resembled the one stretched across the chest of her cheerleading uniform. She found herself staring at it as she ran down the walkway to where the car idled at the curb. So much so she didn't notice at first that the driver had rolled the window down.

"Oh, thank God!" Ivy said. "It's you! That's perfect!"

Eliane blinked and opened the door, slinging her backpack between the two seats and onto the floorboard behind Ivy.

"What are you talking about?" she asked as she slid into the seat. "Of course it's me. You came to my house, remember?"

"Not you, Eliane, you..." Ivy trailed off, frustration threading through her voice. She let out a muttered curse, dug in the purse slouching in the footwell of Eliane's seat, and came up with a black permanent marker.

"Perfect!" Ivy said again and uncapped the marker. She then drew the infinity symbol on the inside of her left wrist. "See?"

"Ohhhh…" Death inhaled deeply and then looked narrowly at Ivy. She appeared perfectly ordinary, if rather on the pretty side. Long dark hair parted over her left eye and hung ruler straight and smooth past her shoulders. She wore a blue sweatshirt bearing the logo of a local university's sports team, and jeans shredded up the front of both legs. She smiled thinly, her red lipstick bright against the pale ivory of her skin.

But her eyes…

Bright and virulently green, they shone like the underside of new leaves. Death looked into them, and ages of simmering rot looked back.

"Pestilence," Death breathed.

"Death," Ivy said and reached over and wrapped her arms hard around her sister. "I didn't think I'd find you this quickly!"

"Nor I, you," Eliane said, hugging back. "This is lucky. Our incarnations know each other."

"We're best friends," Pestilence said matter-of-factly as she let go. "At least, Ivy thinks so."

"So does Eliane," Death said. She reached over her shoulder to grab the seatbelt and buckled it into place. "So do I, I mean."

"Oh, right. I forget how you like to integrate so closely with your host." Ivy put the car in gear and eased away from the curb.

"That's the point, isn't it?" Eliane asked. "We incarnate within these humans so we can taste the lives of those who will experience the next Eschaton. We can't really do that if we don't integrate with them."

"So *you* say," Ivy shot back, a thread of petulance in her tone, "but you don't know why we have to incarnate before every Eschaton any more than the rest of us do. I hate it when you pull that 'all-knowing eldest sibling' crap."

"I never said I knew all—"

"You didn't have to."

"Pest—"

"Call me Ivy," Pestilence interrupted her as she turned the wheel sharply, making Eliane bump against the inside of the door.

"Ivy," Death said, inhaling slowly. Within her mind, Eliane's knowledge simmered. Apparently teenaged Ivy disliked any situation where she didn't feel perfectly in control. "I never said anything of the sort. And you're a fine one to talk to me about over-integrating. *You* appear to be letting your host's insecurities cause you to act irrationally and drive dangerously. In other words, stop being a drama queen."

Ivy stomped on the brakes, causing them both to lurch forward in their seats. She turned, her green eyes alight with rage, to stare at Eliane. Death stared back, her voice and face calm, her eyes empty of judgment or censure. She even permitted herself a tiny smile.

After a long moment, Ivy's lips curled upward at the corner, too, and she let out a little laugh.

"Damn," she said. "I've missed you. I'd forgotten how much fun incarnation can be when we're all together."

"Well, we're not all together yet," Death told her sister. "But I've missed you, too."

"This host is something else," Ivy said. "My emotions are all over the place. One minute, I feel like I could take over the world. The next, I despair that no one cares for me at all."

"I care for you," Eliane said. "Both as Death and as Eliane. And, as you're well aware, you *can* take over the world. But we should find our other two siblings first."

"Do you think we'll all be teenage girls?"

"It's a possibility."

* * *

The school wasn't far from Eliane's house. Which was a good thing, because Ivy didn't go directly to the school. Instead, once she reached the main thoroughfare outside Eliane's neighborhood, she turned right and wheeled the green Mustang into a busy parking lot in front of a Starbucks.

"Apparently we like this place," Ivy said as she killed the engine.

"We shouldn't be late for school. We might find the others there." Eliane glanced over her shoulder toward the school, and then down at her watch. They had about fifteen minutes until classes started.

"Then I guess you'd better hurry, sis, because we might find them here, too." Ivy winked one of those impossibly green eyes at her and opened the car door to step out into the crisp fall morning. Eliane sighed and followed her out and into the spice-scented warmth of the coffee shop.

A few minutes later, they emerged, tall, warm cups in hand, and returned to the car. Ivy unlocked it with a click of her key-fob and folded herself down into the seat with the ease of long practice.

"Don't spill," she called out, "but hurry up, you're the one who didn't want to be late."

"Hang on," Eliane said, her voice distant, her attention on a small figure walking toward the intersection that led to the school. She knew the girl, she realized. Her name was Dora, and she was a freshman whose mother worked for the same company as Eliane's mom. They weren't close friends, but Eliane always said hello to her in the hallway at school, and Dora usually smiled back.

She wasn't smiling now.

She walked quickly, her shoulders hunched and her head down. At first, Eliane thought she was just cold, but the sunlight streamed down like a benediction, and despite the tiny bite to the autumn breeze, it really was warming up to be a nice day. Eliane's bare legs weren't chilled at all, even in the cheerleading uniform's short skirt. So why—?

"Hey, look! It's Whore-a the Explorer!" The shout came from a young man exiting the convenience store next to the coffee shop. He wore a letterman's jacket similar to Eliane's own, but instead of a cheer megaphone, it held the round patch of a baseball player on the sleeve. The name "Kevin" was embroidered on the chest. Two more boys similarly attired followed him out, laughing at his crude joke.

"Come on!" Ivy urged from inside the car.

"Just a minute," Eliane said as Death stirred within her. She closed the Mustang's door and walked up to the trio of boys as Dora picked up the pace and fled toward the dubious safety of the high school. She could hear Ivy's gusty sigh behind her but then the Mustang's door opened and closed again. Ivy and Pestilence might both have been capricious, but once given, their loyalty was absolute.

"Hey," Eliane called out to the boys. Kevin, the leader, turned from his laughing mockery of Dora and smiled at her. This was a genuine smile, devoid of the mean edge his earlier laughter had held.

"Hey. Eliane, right? You're Ivy's friend," he said. Then he blinked as Ivy came up to stand just behind her and to the side. "Oh. Hey, Ivy."

"Yeah. Do you know that girl?" Eliane asked as Ivy jerked her head in acknowledgment.

"Which girl?"

"The one you were just yelling at. The one running down the street to get away from you."

"Oh, her. Yeah, she's just some freshman that likes my little brother. Why, is she a friend of yours?"

"Something like that," Eliane said.

"Look, I didn't know she was anyone cool, all right? I'm sorry. I'll apologize to her at lunch if you want."

"Does it matter?" Death asked.

"What, if I apologize?"

"No, if she's 'anyone cool' or not? What you said was rude regardless."

"I guess. Is this some feminist thing that's happening right now? Hashtag me too or whatever?" Kevin rolled his eyes and shrugged his shoulders, then pulled his phone out of his pocket and began to scroll through it, ostentatiously projecting an air of insouciance.

Death reached out and wrapped her hand around his wrist. "Look at me," she said, in a voice that held the weight of eons. The boy blinked his brown eyes twice, and stopped, staring dead into the icy abyss of Death's gaze.

"All people are equal in the eyes of Death," she said, her voice low and throbbing with intensity. "And none can escape her grasp. Stop being an asshole, Kevin, lest you waste your infinitesimally short mortal life in misery. Because I promise you, that's how it will be. Do you understand me?"

"Yes, ma'am," he whispered, eyes wide with fear.

"Good boy," she said and let him go. Then she turned her back and looked at Ivy, who stood blowing the steam off her coffee.

"Ready to go now, sis?" Ivy asked, her tone dry.

"Yes, thank you." Eliane said and took a sip of her own latte. The spiced warmth of it ran through her, feeling almost as good as what she'd just done. She followed Ivy back to the car and got in, taking care to buckle her seatbelt. They really did work, after all. She had more reason to know than most.

"Well," Ivy said as she backed out of the parking spot and turned back onto the main street, "that was entertaining."

"You know I can't stand bullies," Eliane said.

"I know Death can't. I also know Eliane isn't usually the type to stand up to anyone. People are going to notice if you have a sudden personality change."

"Do we care if people notice?" she asked.

"I'm not sure," Ivy replied. "My gut says it's probably for the best if we don't go out trumpeting our new identities to the entire world. They might try and do something dumb like kill us in the hope of staving off the next Eschaton."

"That's not how it works." Eliane took another sip of her latte. It was surprisingly good. As Death, she'd tasted coffee before, but this was sweet, almost like a dessert.

"I know that, and you know that," Ivy said, flipping on her turn signal and pulling into the parking lot at the school. "But other than our two missing siblings, no one else knows our whole purpose is to see that humanity makes it *through* the Eschatons. That damn passage in Revelations really screwed the story up."

"Not entirely," Eliane said. "We *are* Harbingers."

"Yes, but that's only half of our job. Speaking of which—" Ivy put the car in park and killed the engine, then grabbed her marker and Eliane's left wrist. She flipped Eliane's hand over and inked in the same infinity symbol that graced her own wrist. "In case you don't have your backpack with you. Try to stay focused today, all right? No more crusades. Just find War and Famine."

"I'll do my best," Eliane said as she stepped out of the car and slung her backpack over her shoulder.

"Cool," Ivy said. "See you at lunch."

* * *

The bell rang, reverberating through the halls of the high school. The long, shrill sound was punctuated by several slamming doors, and the cacophony of last-minute rushes into classrooms for the beginning of the day. Eliane sat quietly at her desk in the back corner of Ms. Smith's world history class and looked around the room. At first glance, none of the students in the classroom resonated in her awareness. Not that the presence of War or Famine would automatically activate some mystical "Spidey sense" or anything. Her task would be a lot easier if it did. But that was the reason for the infinity symbol.

She nudged her backpack with her toe so the sign faced out toward the rest of the class and turned her left arm upward on the desk.

"New tattoo, Ms. Jenkins?"

Ms. Smith stood over her, frowning down with an expression that made her look forty years older than she truly was.

"Uh, it's temporary," Eliane said, rubbing at the edge of the marking to show how it smeared.

"Hmm. Not terribly classy, writing on oneself. But tattoos have a long and storied past in humanity's history…" Like the pedant she was, Ms. Smith turned and continued droning on as she approached the front of the class. Eliane ducked her head and breathed deeply, forcing herself to remain calm in the face of such casual disrespect.

"She's so fucking rude," the boy next to Eliane whispered, and it felt like someone had kicked her in the gut. She turned her head to see Braeden Jumper's green eyes smiling at her.

It was suddenly very hard to breathe. Confusion swirled in Death's mind, but Eliane knew exactly what was happening. She'd spent many a night dreaming of those green eyes.

"Now," Ms. Smith said as she turned back to face the classroom. "I've decided to try something a little bit different as we move into the Middle Ages. When you're in college, you'll have to do research papers and presentations. I thought it would be fun if I broke you up into pairs and had each pair take a topic and present it to the class next week. You can present it however you like, though I'd encourage you to use multiple media forms. Get creative, get edgy! If you'll look up here, you'll see your group and topic assignments." She tapped the remote control she held in her hand, and the large computer monitor mounted over the whiteboard flashed up with a table of names.

"Hey," Braeden said, "we're partners; that's cool! And what's our topic?" He squinted at the screen, leaning forward over his desk and making it creak under his weight.

"The Black Death," Eliane said softly. "The Bubonic Plague of the 1300s in Europe."

"I don't know much about it, do you?" He turned and hit her with those green eyes again, and she nearly lost her lunch. What was it about the way his mouth twisted as he smiled at her? It made it hard to look at anything else.

"A little bit," she managed to say. She'd been there, after all. Just as she'd been there for every Eschaton that ended life as humanity had known it. The Black Death, the Fall of Rome, the Plague of Justinian, the Mongol Conquest of China, The European Invasion of the Americas, the Great War; she and her siblings had been present at all of them, and countless others. And they would be there for countless more—

"That's great!" Braeden said, scooting his desk around to face hers. All throughout the classroom, noise reigned as others did the same, rearranging desks and starting conversations about how, exactly, they were going to present the pertinent facts to the classroom in a creative, edgy manner. "What do you know? I heard it was really wicked."

"It was," Eliane said, gaining confidence with every word. "Literally. They thought it was the Judgment of God. Nearly a third of the population died, all told. In some places, entire villages were wiped out, with corpses rotting in the streets because there was no one left alive to bury them. After a while, once the smell died down, usually someone came by and burned everything clean."

"That's really cool that you know that," he said, smiling at her. "Most girls would be too squeamish to talk about stuff like that."

Eliane laughed.

"Why is that funny?"

"Just, girls being squeamish. During the plague, a lot of times it was the women in the family who would end up nursing the dying. It wasn't a pretty death, either. Do you know where the name comes from?"

"What, the 'Black Death?'"

"Yeah."

"Not really." He cocked his head to the side and ran his fingers through the fringe of sandy hair atop his forehead. He wore it shorter than most boys, Eliane noticed. More like a military cut, which she supposed made sense. His dad was in the Marines or something like that.

"Do you?"

"What?"

Braeden chuckled at her inattention. "Earth to Eliane. The Black Death. Where does the name come from?"

"Oh! The buboes. So the disease would cause the victim's lymph nodes to get infected and swell up to create these puss-filled lumps they called buboes. They would turn black and start to rot before the person was even dead."

"Gross," he said, wrinkling his nose.

"Yeah. And painful. But that's why it's the 'Black' Death. Because of the colors of the buboes."

"It's the 'bubonic plague,' right? Is that where they got 'bubonic' too? From the buboes?"

"Exactly." She felt her smile growing, felt herself leaning forward over her desk in order to be closer to him.

"You're a cool chick, Eliane Jenkins."

"Thank you," she said, hating the way her cheeks heated up at his compliment. What was wrong with her? She was an eternal harbinger of chaos, a steward of humanity, why on earth was one adolescent boy tying her insides in knots with every blink of his long-lashed eyes?

"You know what would be awesome?" Braeden said then, breaking her circling train of frustrated thought.

"What's that?"

"You know the long-beaked masks they wore? To try and protect from the Black Death?"

"The plague doctor masks. Sure."

"What if we got some and brought them in for our presentation? Then you can tell everyone about the disgusting effects of the plague, and how whole towns died, and we can make a point of all the crazy shit they tried to pull to protect themselves." He flashed that brilliant smile again and leaned back, obviously satisfied with his suggestion.

"Oh! That's smart. I wonder if we could find some of those online."

"Probably. You can find everything online. Hell, it's probably on Amazon." He leaned further back in his seat, extended his right leg, and fished his phone out of the pocket of his jeans. The movement accentuated his long, lean musculature, and Eliane felt her mouth go dry.

"Yeah," Braeden said, surging back forward to show her his phone screen. "Here it is, look! Shit, they've got all kinds of 'em, even these cool, steampunky ones. And they're not too expensive. This is gonna be badass."

Eliane leaned in, saw the familiar shape of the long beaked masks, then turned to look up into his face.

"Yeah," she said softly. Her gaze fell to his mouth, and without realizing it, she wetted her bottom lip in response. "Badass."

Braeden's smile faded, drifted away, and a peculiar intensity lit in his green eyes. He inhaled, just a little bit, and Eliane felt as if he were pulling her forward with his breath. The sounds of the classroom faded, drowned out by the thundering of the blood in her ears. She felt her lips part, felt him lean closer—

"How's it going over here?"

Ms. Smith's forcibly cheery voice sliced through Eliane's intoxication like a scythe through wheat. She sat back so suddenly that her chair creaked against the linoleum floor with a grating sound.

"Really good, Ms. Smith," Braeden said, leaning back as well and smiling up at the teacher in the half-false way of a teenage kid charming an authority figure. "Turns out Eliane knows all about the Black Death."

"Really?" Ms. Smith's eyebrows shot up, and she turned skeptical eyes to Eliane. "Is that true, Ms. Jenkins? You've never shown much interest in medieval history before."

The older woman's barely-disguised contempt seeped through her words as she looked down her nose at Eliane. The part of her that was sixteen was used to it. Sometimes, teachers seemed to not like their students at all, particularly not the ones like Eliane who were just a little too brown, a little too pretty, a little too young, and a little too much of a cheerleader/basketball player/whatever. She'd learned to let it go; it usually wasn't worth the pain a confrontation would bring on the back end.

But she wasn't just a sixteen-year-old biracial cheerleader anymore. And the eternal harbinger part of her wasn't accustomed to letting small-minded pedants think they were in a position to be condescending.

"Perhaps you haven't seen my interest, Ms. Smith," Death said, "but I assure you, it's there. It's hard not to be interested when you've walked the ruined streets of extinct villages in the Italian highlands and seen the effects of a community eradicated."

"You've been to Italy?" Ms. Smith asked, her skepticism clear.

"*Ovviamente! Io amo l'Italia. Ci sono stato molte volte,*" Eliane said, her accent perfect, if a bit antiquated.

"Well," Ms. Smith said, straightening up and pursing her lips. Her expression resembled nothing so much as the puckered rear orifice of a cat, and the comparison caused Eliane to have to press her own lips together in order to avoid laughing out loud. "Just make sure you document your sources thoroughly, young lady," the teacher said before turning away to check on another group.

"That," Braeden said slowly, "was awesome! I didn't know you spoke Italian!"

"Yeah," Eliane said. "A little bit. You pick it up."

He shook his beautiful head and hit her with that megawatt smile one more time.

"Like I said, you're a cool chick, Eliane Jenkins."

She wanted to say something cool and edgy back, something like how he wasn't so bad himself, but both the teenager and the ageless harbinger foundered in the face of his obvious admiration, so she settled for giving him an awkward smile and a shrug.

You win some, you lose some.

* * *

By the time lunch rolled around, Eliane's mood had soured. The morning's coffee had long since worn off, and both her head and her stomach throbbed with hunger. Death didn't appreciate the reminder of the more inconvenient aspects of incarnation, not one bit. Eating for pleasure was all well and good, but the dull, gnawing ache was something she'd have gleefully forgone for the rest of eternity.

"There you are!" Ivy's voice cut through the dull roar of conversation as soon as Eliane stepped out of the hallway into the commons. The central hub of the school served multiple purposes, including functioning as a cafeteria during lunch time. While people swerved around them from all directions, Ivy linked her arm through Eliane's and drew her out into the swirling mix. "I've got a table over here. How was your morning? Any luck?"

"Pretty good," Eliane said. "He said I was a cool chick."

Ivy froze. "Who said? Did you find our brother?"

"Oh! N-no. I was talking about something else."

Ivy looked closely at her, her green eyes narrowing to speculative slits. "Mmhm," she said. "Okay. Well, sit down, and you can tell me all about it."

"Ivy, I'm starving. I gotta get something to eat."

Ivy looked over her shoulder at the window where ladies wearing hairnets passed out trays of dubious-smelling food.

"You're *not* considering eating that," Ivy said, her voice flat and laced with command. "Besides, I've got you covered. Just sit down."

"Got me covered how?" Eliane asked, but Ivy just shook her head and pointed imperiously at a circular table with six plastic chairs arrayed around it. Eliane breathed out a sigh and let her backpack drop off her shoulder into one of the seats, then fell into the one next to it.

"Ivy! Ivy!" A girl with red hair in two French braids and freckles across her nose pushed through the crowd of people, holding up a red and white paper bag in triumph. "I got it!"

"It's not as if it's the Holy Grail, Samantha," Ivy muttered under her breath, but she turned to face the girl with a smile. "Niiice," she said. "And you remembered no pickles on my chicken sandwich?"

"I did," Samantha said. She plunked the bag down in the center of the table, beaming. A drink carrier with three large drinks followed, then Samantha helped herself to one of the other chairs. "Hi, Eliane," she said belatedly.

"Hi, Sam," Eliane said. "You got us lunch?"

"Yeah, Ivy said I could sit with you guys if I brought Hate Chicken," Sam said, nearly breathless with excitement.

"Nobody calls it that anymore, Samantha," Ivy said, rolling her eyes, but she sat down and began digging in the bag.

"Well," Eliane said, glancing sideways at Ivy. "Thanks. Do you want some money?"

"Oh, no! It's my treat," Sam said. She grabbed the drink carrier and pulled one of the cups out. She stabbed the top with a straw and sipped as enthusiastically as she'd done everything else up to that point. Eliane knew Sam as one of Ivy's annoyingly sycophantic hangers-on, but she was hungry, and Death actually took pity on the girl. She so obviously wanted to be accepted and welcomed.

"Well, thanks again," Eliane found herself saying as she followed suit and helped herself to one of the drinks—it was delicious lemonade—and a box of nuggets. "This was really nice of you, Sam."

"So," Ivy said as she unwrapped her sandwich and found that, indeed, there were no pickles present. "Tell me about the guy. Who is it?"

"There's a guy?" Sam asked, her voice climbing the register toward what could only be called a squeal. "Oooh!"

"Samantha, if you can't control yourself and let us have a conversation without butting in, I'm going to send you away," Ivy said, her green eyes dark as she turned a glare on the third girl.

"Oh! Sorry, Ivy," Sam said, shrinking back into herself.

"Ivy," Eliane said, warning in her tone. Ivy turned her glare to Eliane, and then rolled her eyes.

"Fiiine…" she said, letting out a gusty sigh, "I'll be nice. But tell me who he is and why he's got you so distracted."

"Hey, Eliane."

Braeden's voice rolled through her like thunder, reigniting the fire that burned deep in her belly. She turned around so quickly she nearly knocked her lemonade off the table. Braeden reached out at the same time as Eliane, and their fingers brushed over each other as, together, they prevented the full beverage from tumbling to the ground.

"Uh…hey. Braeden."

"Dude, you guys got Hate Chicken for lunch, that's awesome! I'm jealous." He lifted her drink up, holding the straw close to his lips. "Wanna share?"

"Sure," she said, her voice breathless.

His smile grew, and a buzzing sensation started under her skin and spread across her body as he held eye contact and took a long sip of her lemonade. Then he lowered it, winked at her, and set the cup back down on the table.

"Anyway," he said, "I wanted to tell you how badass I thought it was the way you shut Ms. Smith down in History today. I thought she was going to stroke out when you started speaking Italian."

"You speak Italian?" Sam squeaked, disbelief soaking through her voice. "Since when?"

Eliane immediately regretted forcing Ivy to be nice to her.

"Since we did all those language learning apps over the summer," Ivy broke in, her eyes shooting poisoned daggers at Sam. "Not that it's any of your business, Samantha."

"Plus Eliane's been to Italy, right?"

"Yeah," Eliane said, glancing over at Ivy, who turned back to her, eyebrows arched.

"Yes, I know," Ivy said. "Several times."

"You should have seen it. Smith was being her typically fake bitchy self, doesn't believe Eliane knows anything at all about the Black Death, and Eliane tells her about visiting an Italian ghost town and then starts spouting off in Italian to prove it. It was the most awesome thing I've seen on a Monday in a long time."

"Thanks," Eliane said, unsure what else to do.

"No sweat. I can't wait to work more on our project. Thanks for the lemonade. I'll see you around!" Braeden gave her another wink and a smile, then raised his hand to wave at someone calling out to him.

"Bye," Eliane said to his retreating back, then closed her eyes in mortification and turned to face her friends.

"Wellll," Ivy said. "I guess that answers that."

"Ohmigosh! I can't believe you like Braeden Jumper!" Sam bounced in her seat, clapping her hands together like a delighted toddler. "He's a *senior*. He's way too cool to be into you…"

Ivy rounded on her.

"Samantha!" she snapped. "I *told* you. Quit butting in to other people's conversations!"

"Sorry, Ivy," Sam whispered, wilting.

"You're going to have to go," Ivy said, her voice hard. "Take the trash with you."

Sam's eyes filled with tears, and her hand trembled as she reached out for the fast-food bag. "I'm really sorry," she said again. "Can't I stay?"

"No. You were rude, and you were mean about Eliane speaking Italian, like you didn't think she was smart enough to learn a language. *And* in front of the boy she likes!"

"I didn't mean it, I promise," Sam said, her eyes overflowing. "I would never—"

"But you did, didn't you? Just go, Samantha."

Sam stared at Ivy's unforgivingly stern face, and then turned to Eliane in a silent plea for help. Eliane said nothing, as the insult still stung. And as much as Death pitied the poor girl, Ivy *had* warned her.

"You're both a pair of stuck up bitches!" Sam hissed as she shoved her chair back with a scrape. "I don't know why I ever tried to be friends with you!"

"Believe me, Samantha," Ivy said, "we ask ourselves that all the time. Run along now and let the adults speak."

"Fuck you!" Sam said. She flung the empty fast-food bag at Ivy, who caught it in midair. Ivy's green eyes narrowed, and Sam opened her mouth to say something else, but suddenly found herself obliged to cough. Several times. The sound was deep and chesty, and the redhead girl's blue eyes widened as she found herself unable to do anything but cough harder and harder.

"Poor thing," Ivy said, her voice like poisoned honey. "You don't look like you feel very well. Maybe you should have the nurse call your mom. We wouldn't want anything bad to happen to you!"

"Ivy," Eliane said quietly, her voice a warning as the crying, coughing Sam turned and fled toward the front office and the school nurse.

"Oh, spare me. It's just a little viral infection. She'll be fine in a day or two. She's a nasty piece of work, anyway. She spent all of second period trying to tell me what a bad friend you were. She's working the social angles to get close to me for some reason."

"Because everybody wants to get close to you, Ivy. You're the top of our class, class president, and you know everyone. You've got all the social power of a Russian Tsarina."

"Yes, but that doesn't mean I'm obliged to suffer social climbing fools. Besides, we need to talk seriously about a few things. I found our brother!"

"Who?"

"Famine. He's here, in our school. Which means War probably is, too. I don't know what's so special about this little town, but apparently it's going to be the center of the next Eschaton, if we're all incarnating here at once."

* * *

Eliane stared out the passenger side window of Ivy's Mustang and watched as the city lights slid away behind them. They were winding their way up into the hills, headed to a party thrown by Hiro Ikeda. Hiro was the son of

Mashiro Ikeda, a local biotechnology magnate. The Ikedas lived in Magnolia Hills, a development sprawled across the foothills of the local mountain range, filled with breathtaking, grandiose mansions.

"How far up is it?" Eliane asked, turning to see Ivy's beautiful face lit only by the reflection of the headlights as she followed the twisting mountain path.

"All the way to the top, baby," Ivy said, a wry note in her voice. "Only the best for the Ikeda clan."

"You're sure Hiro is Famine? I've never been to any of his parties before. I don't know what he's like at all."

"He's…a rich kid," Ivy said with a shrug. "He lives in a world without consequences. He gets whatever he wants, whenever he wants. He goes through girls like underwear, but he throws a good party."

"That's why Mom would never let me go before. She said she's seen too many kids come out of his parties all fucked up."

"Oh, yeah," Ivy said, nodding emphatically. "Hiro can always get shit. Whatever you're into—or not. I usually watch my drink pretty closely." She glanced over at Eliane before turning her gaze back to the road. "How'd you get her to let you come out tonight, then?"

"I didn't tell her," Eliane said, shrugging. "I just said I'm spending the night with you."

"Smart," Ivy said. "My parents aren't home to confirm or deny. Look at you, little rebel, sneaking out without telling your mom!" She grinned as she delivered the tease.

"Well, you said Hiro's our brother Famine. We have to talk to him."

"I *think* he's Famine," Ivy corrected. "I wasn't able to actually confirm it at school. But he's carrying the symbol, and too many things fit."

"What fits?" Eliane asked. "What are you talking about?"

"Well, besides the infinity symbol, look at it. You're Death, but you incarnate as a cheerleader. Except that unlike the stereotype, you're actually kinda reticent and dark. And super egalitarian. I'm Pestilence, and I'm the pre-pre-med frontrunner for valedictorian next year—"

"Also the queen bee mean girl," Eliane added.

"Also that," Ivy agreed. "But that fits too, right? What is gossip but another type of infection?"

Eliane nodded, conceding the point.

"So yeah, with both of us, it's totally obvious—and also not. Who else should be Death but a shy, emo cheerleader?"

"Okay, so Hiro is Famine because he lacks for nothing?"

"Yeah. He's never gone hungry, but he also builds people's hunger—as in addiction. 'First one's free,' right?"

"Shit, you're right. Ivy, you're brilliant."

"Yeah, I'm really smart this time." She turned the wheel sharply, gliding around a switchback. A building loomed up ahead at the top of the hill. As they drew closer, Eliane could see that it was really just a gatehouse. Ivy eased to a stop and rolled down her window.

"Here for the party?" a male voice asked.

"Yes, sir," Ivy said, fluttering her eyelashes. Eliane snorted to keep from laughing.

"Name?"

"Ivy Anders."

"And?"

"Eliane Jenkins," Eliane said, leaning forward to look up at the stone-faced man standing with a clipboard in his hands and a Bluetooth earpiece in his ear. He consulted the clipboard, and then nodded before stepping back to wave them through.

"Main house is off limits. Follow the lights to the parking area for the pool house. Have a good time."

"Thank you!" they chorused, and then Ivy put the car in gear and rolled forward, the well-manicured gravel crunching beneath her tires. She turned to follow the strings of twinkle lights that led around the huge, darkened edifice of the main house. On the back side, they found rows of cars parked on a wide gravel lot, with more lights leading to a fragrant, flowering hedge ahead.

Ivy pulled her car into the first available spot at the end of the row and put it in park.

"Ready?" she asked.

"I suppose," Eliane said.

"Here," Ivy said, holding out a tube of lipstick. Eliane took it, a question in her eyes. "Just in case," Ivy said with a wink, and opened the car door to step out. Eliane shrugged and slicked on a coat of the wine-dark color, and then followed her friend out into the night.

Ivy was dressed to the nines, her long, mahogany hair loose and flowing over a simple metallic green strapless minidress that made the most of her figure and her mile-long legs. Eliane had opted for skinny jeans and a cream-colored beaded crop tank that showed off her toned belly and muscular arms. She might be the incarnation of Death, but Eliane had to admit it was gratifying to see heads turn as the two of them walked through the hedge gate and out onto the beautifully sculpted swimming pool deck.

"Keep your eyes out for Hiro," Ivy said quickly, turning her wrist over to show the infinity design she'd reapplied to herself and Eliane back at her house. "See if you can find a way to talk to him, see if he recognizes you, or vice versa."

"Got it," Eliane said.

"Ivy!" someone called out to the left, and before she realized it, Eliane was on her own. Anxiety reared up inside her mind, threatening to drown her, but she took a deep breath and shoved it back. She wasn't just a scared, shy teenager anymore, was she? She was a harbinger of chaos! The Pale Rider of the Eschaton! Surely she could handle a simple teenage pool party. Right?

Ivy had gone left, so Eliane decided to move to the right, wandering through the crowds that ringed the softly glowing swimming pool. It sat perched on the side of the cliff, and had an infinity edge, so it looked as if it just fell off into the twinkling lights of the small city below. Eliane found herself stopping to stare at the breathtaking view.

"Pretty, isn't it?" Braeden's voice came out of the night to brush against the skin below her ear, making her jump. She turned and found him standing near enough to make her shiver.

"Yeah," she said. "No wonder they built their house up here."

"Oh, yeah, the view is pretty, too," Braeden said, winking at her.

"Cute," she said, pushing down the sudden swarm of overexcited butterflies that exploded into her stomach and going for a tart, sassy tone. "You need some wine to go with that cheese."

"Hiro's got some wine inside," Braeden said. "You want some?"

Eliane wrinkled her nose. "It's not my favorite."

"Something else then. Come on, let's get you a drink." He reached out and grabbed her elbow lightly, then let his hand slide down to find her hand. His touch left trails of fire burning under her skin. She tried to breathe, tried to say anything, but then his fingers were threading between hers, and they were walking toward the brightly lit windows of the pool house not far away. She could feel the rhythmic thumping of music reverberating through the night in counterpoint to her racing pulse. They stepped through the open doorway into a wide room packed with bodies swaying and grinding in response. Braeden began to thread his way through, keeping a firm hold on her hand as he made a path for them through the main room back to the pool house kitchen.

"Pick your poison," he said. "Beer? Vodka? Something else?"

"Um," Eliane said, biting her lip. She wasn't much of a drinker. Plus, Death knew alcohol would no longer have any intoxicating effects for her, so why bother? It had never really tasted that good to her anyway. "I'm probably gonna drive Ivy home. Can I just have a Coke or something?"

"Of course," Braeden said easily, and Eliane smiled in relief. He squeezed her fingers briefly before letting go and reaching for the stainless-steel professional-grade refrigerator handle. He pulled out a glass bottle and popped the top open with a nearby bottle opener before handing it to her. "Hiro gets this from Mexico; it's got real sugar in it."

Eliane took a pull and smiled as the sweet acid poured over her tongue. "It's good," she said, watching Braeden help himself to a longneck beer.

"Yeah," he said. "It is. Only the best for my boy Hiro."

"Do you know him well?" Eliane asked. She didn't want to stop talking to Braeden, but she knew Ivy was right. They couldn't afford to be distracted for long. They had to find their missing siblings sooner rather than later.

"Hiro? Yeah. Since we were kids. We played tee ball together and stuff. He's a good guy, despite his rep." Braeden leaned his elbows on the counter and dropped his voice to a conspiratorial murmur. "He'd kick my ass if this got out, but he's more than just a spoiled rich kid. He spends every Sunday afternoon downtown at the Mission soup kitchen, feeding the homeless. It's crazy, he wears a disguise and everything."

"Did he get community service for something?"

"What, Hiro? There's not a judge in this county that'd dare to convict Mashiro Ikeda's son. Nah, he does it on his own. Has for years. Sometimes I join him, but he's always afraid I'm going to give him away."

"That's wild," she said, only half talking about the prospect of Hiro working at a soup kitchen. Her eyes fell to Braeden's lips, and she became abruptly aware of his nearness. Maybe alcohol couldn't intoxicate her anymore, but the slightly spicy scent of Braeden Jumper's skin had no trouble spinning her head around. His smile grew, his eyes darkening with intent as he leaned closer, close enough she could feel the heat of his breath on her lips.

"If you don't want me to kiss you," he whispered, "you need to say so now."

"I want you to," she whispered back.

"Good," he murmured and brushed his lips against hers. Fire and need exploded inside her, tangling up in a wet inferno centered somewhere deep in her body. She felt her lips part under his, felt his hand brush up along her jaw, under her hair, to cup the back of her head. Her own free hand somehow found the tight, lean muscles of his back under his t-shirt. His tongue darted into her mouth. He tasted like beer and desire, and it was enough to make her rethink her dislike of the beverage.

He pulled her up hard against his eager, straining body, and she tensed slightly. He instantly let go and backed up a step, breathing heavily.

"Oh, damn," he said, his eyes wide and a bit frantic. "Did I hurt you? I'm so sorry—"

"No!" Eliane said, reaching out a hand to reassure him. He caught her fingers and closed his eyes as he brought them to his lips. "You didn't hurt me. I was just…surprised."

"I'm sorry," he said again, opening his eyes. She could see real regret in his gaze. "I know I'm moving too fast. It's just…you're maybe the coolest chick I've ever met, you know that? I always thought you were pretty, but then earlier today you were just so different. So…confident? I guess. And when I look into those damn gorgeous eyes of yours, it's like I can see…"

"Centuries?" Death asked, her heart sinking.

"What?"

"Oh, no—nothing. Never mind. It's a movie quote. A bad joke," she said, trying to cover. Sudden hurt flashed in his eyes, and he looked away.

"Ah," he said. "A joke. Cool."

"Um, not a joke…that's not what I meant."

"What did you mean?"

"Um…" her mind failed her, went absolutely blank with sudden panic.

"Look, Eliane. I like you, all right? I like you a lot. And I think you like me. Am I right?"

"I—" Did she like him? Like *like* him, like him?

Yes. Obviously she did. But she wasn't just Eliane, was she? She was Death now, too. An Eschaton was coming. Centuries of heartache spiraled through her as she remembered other lifetimes, other loves. Loving a harbinger was a terrible fate for any human. Could she expose this boy—not even a fully-grown man—to that doom?

"Oh." Braeden's expression closed down like a vault door slamming shut. "Okay. Cool."

"Braeden…"

"Hey, look, I gotta go."

"Braeden, wait!" Eliane called, but he just turned and walked out of the kitchen, chugging his beer as he went.

"Don't bother, B," a new voice said from behind Eliane. "My boy Brae wants what he wants. Ain't no use in chasin'. I'm sure I can better give you what you need, anyway."

Eliane turned and found herself staring into the depthless black gaze of crushing, hopeless, aching hunger.

"Famine," she breathed. Hiro Ikeda, resplendent in his designer jacket and jeans, with an infinity symbol embroidered in metallic thread on his breast, stopped dead and gaped at her.

"The fuck did you say to me?" he whispered. Death smiled and turned her arm over, letting him see the inked-in infinity symbol.

"I said hello, little brother." Eliane smiled and let her own eyes show her true nature.

"Death!" he said then and surged forward to wrap his arms around her in a hard, crushing hug. "Oh, God, it's not a dream!"

"It's not," she said. "Pestilence is here too. She's Ivy Anders."

Hiro laughed. "Of course she is. That's perfect. It's been forever since I incarnated as one so young! I was worried it would be damn near impossible to find you guys. Any sign of War?"

"Not yet, but Ivy thinks it's probably one of the students at our school. Since three of the four of us incarnated that way, it would make sense that we all did."

"Yeah, but that means—" he broke off, horror flowing over his features. Eliane nodded and squeezed him a little tighter in reassurance.

"Yeah. I don't know why yet, but this sleepy little town is going to be important in the next Eschaton. But that's for the future, you know that. For now, we need to find Ivy, and then figure out who our other brother or sister is—"

"Eliane—" Braeden's voice was thick with emotion and apology as he pushed back through the doorway into the kitchen. Eliane dropped her arms from around Hiro and stepped back as if she'd been burned. Braeden's eyes went wide again, then pure fury and hate filled them, and his expression twisted into something between a snarl and a smile.

"Braeden—"

"Never mind," he said, holding out a hand. He lifted his now-empty beer bottle in Hiro's direction. "Have fun, bro," he said, then turned and threw the bottle into the metal farmhouse sink with enough force to shatter the glass. He lifted two fingers toward the pair of them, and then stormed back out again.

Eliane's eyes filled with tears.

"Oh, shit," Hiro said. "You *like* him."

"More than that, I think," Eliane said, with the benefit of Death's experience and context. She sniffed mightily and swiped at her eyes with the back of her hand. "I think I might actually love him."

"Fuck."

"Exactly."

* * *

The party continued through the night, but Eliane, Hiro, and Ivy stole back to Hiro's wing of the main house in order to talk in privacy.

"Parents are gone for the weekend," Hiro said, his grin flashing white in the darkness as he ushered them down the hallway toward his game room. "So it's just me and the crew. I'll have Zara send up some snacks."

"What about the party?" Eliane asked. "Don't you need to be there?"

"Nah," Hiro said. "Security's there. They'll take care of anything that happens and shut it down at one. I just go for fun, but I'd rather talk to you, sis."

"Sisses," Ivy corrected.

"Yeah, exactly. Speaking of which, we probably should figure out who our fourth is, and quickly." Hiro stopped in front of a set of beautiful mahogany double doors. He opened one and gestured for the ladies to precede him inside. Ivy led, with Eliane following close on her heels.

Motion sensor-activated black lights kicked on as soon as they crossed the threshold, bathing the entire room in an eerie, purplish glow. Ivy turned and put her hands on her hips, her teeth glowing as she bared them in a ferocious smile.

"Cute," she said. "This doesn't make you seem at all like a psycho serial killer."

Hiro laughed and snapped his fingers twice. The black lights faded away, replaced by a kinder, softer golden glow issuing from a hidden slot that ran around the edge of the ceiling. The rest of the room was minimally, if comfortably, furnished with plush recliners and various game tables here and there. In the far corner, a pair of antique video game consoles stood next to an old pinball machine.

"I'm pretty sure we all qualify for that title, sis," Hiro said. "You as much as me. And Eliane is Death herself, so…"

"Yeah, yeah, smartass," Ivy said, dropping elegantly into a recliner. "You know what I meant. You don't always have to be so creepy."

"I am who I am," he said with a grin, but he pulled up a smaller chair and sat as well. Eliane chose another recliner next to Ivy's and tried to focus on her siblings' interplay and not the rending pain she felt every time she thought about that hurt, accusing look in Braeden's eyes.

"So," Ivy said, after a pause, "what's the next step?"

"Find War," Hiro said promptly. "Don't you think, Eliane?"

"Wh-What?" Eliane shook herself and forced her eyes to focus on her brother's face. "I'm sorry. What were we talking about?"

"Shit." Hiro leaned in, his eyes filling with concern. "He really got to you, didn't he?"

"What?" Ivy sat forward. "What's wrong? What happened?"

"Braeden kissed me," Eliane said. "And then I said something wrong, and he got confused and hurt. And he left for a minute, but then he came back, only I'd just found Hiro, and we were hugging…"

Ivy's eyebrows went up. "And he got jealous?" she asked, her voice carefully neutral. "And that bothered you?" Ivy's eyes flicked to Hiro. Eliane saw him nod slowly.

"Yeah," Eliane admitted. "A lot. I told Hiro…I think I love him."

"Oh, *damn*," Ivy breathed, her fingers coming up to her lips. "Oh, Eliane, I'm so sorry."

Eliane's eyes filled with tears. Her siblings' sympathy made the tearing sensation in her chest so much worse. They, too, had loved and lost countless times before. All of the harbingers had. It was part of the process.

"I want to push him away," Eliane confessed in a tear-soaked whisper. She brought her hands up to cover her face. "I want to make him hate me, so he'll be safe and have a good life and marry and have kids— but he hates me right now, and I don't think I can bear it for another second."

"No," Hiro said, his voice low. He reached out, grabbed Eliane's right hand, and pulled it away from her face. She looked up at him to see the aching hunger of millions in his gaze. "No, you can't. And you can't push him away, you know that. We're here to experience humanity. If you fall in love, you *have* to experience that love."

"I know," Eliane whispered as the tears began to trickle out from under her eyelashes. "I just…it's so new, you know? I thought maybe—"

"Hiro is right," Ivy said, her voice gentle. "If you love him, you have to *love* him. He might even be a catalyst for the coming Eschaton."

Eliane pulled in a deep breath and nodded, lowering her other hand to her lap.

"You're right," she said. "You're both right. This is why we're here."

Ivy took hold of Eliane's free hand and squeezed it. "This is why we're here," she repeated. "You, me, Famine…and War."

"Right! War. How do we find our brother or sister?" Eliane said, latching on to the new topic like a drowning woman clinging to a life raft.

"We're all in high school," Ivy said. "War has to be there, too. Unless either of you has another idea, I think at this point, we just go back on Monday and keep our eyes open."

Then she looked over at Eliane.

"And we figure out how to get you and Braeden together."

* * *

Monday was a crap day.

Since the high school ran on an alternating schedule, Eliane didn't have to worry about sitting through class with Braeden. Relief and regret tangled up inside her. She wanted more than anything to talk to him, to explain that what he'd seen wasn't what he'd thought he'd seen. But she had no idea how to do that. How was she supposed to make him believe Hiro was her brother when a few moments earlier she'd just said she didn't know him at all?

She could tell the truth, but Death quailed at the thought. Things tended to go wrong when ordinary humans found out a harbinger's true nature. At least they didn't do witch burnings anymore, but being locked up in a psych ward was just as counterproductive to their mission. Besides, it wasn't like Braeden was going to believe her, anyway.

So she was just as happy to start her morning with Algebra II instead of World History. At the very least, it gave her a day to figure out a game plan. However, by the time school ended and she headed to the locker room to change for cheer practice, she was still trying to find a good avenue of approach.

Which was why, when she rounded the corner of the locker-lined hallway and found him talking to Ivy's frenemy Samantha, Eliane froze. She must have made some kind of sound, because both Braeden and Sam looked over at her. Something hot and needy flickered in Braeden's eyes before he blinked and deliberately looked away. Sam, on the other hand, smiled nastily and stepped closer to Braeden, putting her hand on his chest and pressing her body up against his.

Ice flashed through Eliane, followed by hot, boiling rage. The insane desire to fly down the hallway and rip every one of Sam's fingers from its socket roiled in Eliane's brain. She felt her skin blanching, her sun-kissed coloring fading to the archetypical pale. Somewhere in the distance, she could hear the rustle of a thousand wings…

No. Eliane closed her eyes briefly and held herself very still, willing her anger to slow, to calm, and to fade away. When she opened her eyes, she could see Sam stretched up on her tiptoes, her lips firmly pressed against the underside of Braeden's jaw. Eliane forced her expression to stay blank, her lips to curve in a noncommittal, nonjudgmental smile, and she inclined her head briefly when Braeden's eyes once again met hers.

Something dark and dangerous flowed in his expression.

She ignored it, hitched her cheer bag higher up on her shoulder, and walked by them toward the girls' locker room. Her hands shook, but she kept her spine straight, her chin high. "Bless your heart," she murmured as she passed them.

She was Death, a harbinger of chaos, and no attention-grubbing, slutty-ass thot was going to make her feel inferior. No fucking way. She swept forward and through the doors of the girls' locker room.

* * *

Eliane's hands still shook while she changed clothes, but she felt a tiny flicker of triumph in the midst of her miserable mind. She'd done the right thing. It was difficult, and her stomach still roiled at the mental picture of Sam kissing Braeden, but she'd retained control. She hadn't broken her incarnation and revealed her true nature in order to hurt the girl. She was still on the right side of things.

Within a few minutes, she'd changed into practice wear and was outside on the track with the rest of her team. They spent a few minutes stretching and warming up before the coach announced that they would practice their new basket-toss. Eliane's flyer, Dana, was a tiny, slender sophomore, but she'd been cheering on all-star teams since she was four, and she had serious skills. At Friday's game, they'd unveil a heart-stopping kick double basket for the first time. This meant that Eliane and the two girls designated "bases" would throw Dana over ten feet into the air, where she would kick one leg out, then spin twice as she fell back down into their interlaced arms. It was a crowd-pleaser and guaranteed to wow an audience. It was hard work, but fun, and Eliane generally enjoyed practicing the skill.

"That was better!" Coach called out after they'd done the toss for the third time. "Dana, I need just a bit faster rotation! Get that hand down to your hip, all right?"

Dana nodded, her face set in determined lines as she got back into her ready position.

"C'mon, Dana," Julie, one of the bases, said softly. Kyara, the other base, nodded in agreement. "You got this!"

"Five! Six! Seven! Eight!" Coach called out, and as the counts continued, the four cheerleaders snapped in sequence to the body positions that loaded Dana into the basket. "Clean, One! Set, Three! Dip, Five—"

"Eliane!" Braeden's voice echoed across the track as he burst through the double doors from the school gymnasium and came running toward them. Eliane and her teammates were focused on the basket, but the sound of her name bellowed in such agony caused Eliane to flinch. That tiny movement communicated itself through their interlaced arms to Julie, who instinctively tossed out and away instead of straight up.

Dana let out a scream as she felt her body arching up over Kyara's head. Eliane swore and dove, mindful of the one and only unbreakable commandment in cheerleading: No matter what happens, the flyer never hits the ground. Kyara lunged, too, and the two of them got tangled up enough that Eliane stumbled, reaching her arms out in a desperate attempt to grab onto the body of her falling friend.

She got a hand around Dana's waist. She hauled in tight with all her strength.

Dana pivoted, her head striking the cinder track with a sickening *thud*.

The rest of the team screamed as well. Coach yelled for everyone to get back, and for someone to get the trainer. Eliane crumpled to the ground, reached out, and put her hand on Dana's twisted neck.

Death reached out through that touch, feeling the currents of the myriad life forces swirling around. Dana's was there, thready and thin, a breath away from dissipating.

This doesn't have to happen, Death thought as she read the patterns of the currents. In the grand, eternal scheme of things, even most "accidental" deaths were actually a part of the plan. They caused ripple effects that had meaning down the line. Most of the time. But sometimes…

Sometimes, there was wiggle room. And Death could work with wiggle room.

She turned her mind inward to the knowledge of her true nature. There was a connection there, an energetic thread that bound her to her siblings in a way no being could ever trace. That thread was the reason they always incarnated at the same time. That thread bound them to each other, to their mission, and to eternity. Death touched that connection and *pulled*.

I need you! she sent in a message without words or form. *Come to me!*

Ivy, who was a student athletic trainer, had been sitting in the bleachers doing homework while she waited for Eliane to finish practice. She tossed her books to the side with a clatter and began clambering down the metal seats. Hiro, who'd been engaging in an illicit pharmaceutical transaction behind the closed-up snack bar shed, came around the corner of the building at a dead run.

And on the football field, starting defensive back and varsity football captain Marshall Stevens straightened up, removed his helmet, and stared, his eyes a red roil filled with oceans of blood.

She'd found War. He ignored his coach's yelling and took off running toward the cluster of cheerleaders on the sidelines.

"What do you need?" Ivy asked as she skidded down to her knees next to Eliane on the track

"Power," Eliane said. "I'm going to manifest. Dana doesn't have to die today."

"Sister, are you sure?" Hiro asked. "The Plan."

"I said what I said." Death turned to look at him, her expression iron hard.

"I—I'm here," Marshall said as he joined them, looking half-dazed. He fished a thin gold chain out from inside his uniform. On it, a slender gold infinity symbol twinkled.

"War," Death said. "You can slow time. Like you do on a battle-field. Do it."

"I need a human anchor," he said, and Marshall's uncertainty faded under the clipped confidence of War's pronouncements. "Someone for whom it won't slow."

Eliane looked up and saw Braeden standing, staring at her, his face wreathed in horror.

"Use him," she said, pointing.

"Done," Marshall said, and Eliane felt the life forces around her start to slow, like swimmers caught against a current.

"Famine, when I'm done, I need you to eat the memory of what they'll have seen here today," Death said then, turning to her other brother. "Everyone but Braeden."

"Of course."

"And Pestilence—"

"I'm here," Ivy said, reaching out to take her free hand. "I'll fix her body, if you can keep her soul from leaving."

Death nodded, and then looked once more at the bewildered and terrified face of the boy she loved.

"Watch now," she said, knowing that he'd hear her, even though he was several yards away. "See what I really am."

As she'd started to do in the hallway, Eliane let her humanity fade away. Her skin once again paled, going bone-white against the pale gold riot of her hair. She felt her pupils open up, dilating into yawning voids from which not even light itself could escape. She heard the sound of rustling wings and knew them for her own dark-feathered majesty arching up above her human form as she called upon her true nature: the power of life and death itself.

Dana's life force had become the barest whisper of energy. Death reached out her skeletal hands and cupped it with her essence.

"Stay," she whispered. "Stay, young one. It's not required that you go just now. Be healed, and stay."

With every word, she pumped her own power into Dana's life force, feeling it slowly still and strengthen. Next to her, Death could feel her sister Pestilence manipulating the biological material of Dana's body, pushing the cells back into place, pulling the fluids into their proper courses. War stood over them all like a sentinel, holding back the enemy onslaught of time. Their final brother Famine moved from life to life in this milieu, excising and devouring every memory of this event as soon as it happened.

Every memory but one.

Throughout it all, Braeden watched, a human witness to the mysteries of eternity as the four harbingers pooled their power to save the life of a girl who shouldn't have died.

Dana let out a moan and turned her head slowly to the side. Her foot twitched, and slowly, so slowly, she rolled to her hands and knees.

Eliane felt the life forces around her begin to move normally again.

Marshall stepped back, holding his football helmet by its face-mask. "She's, ah," he said, "gonna be okay?"

"Yes," Ivy said, her voice thready with exhaustion. "She'll be bruised, but she's miraculously okay."

"Damn, so much drama for nothing," Hiro groused, slipping back into his asshole rich kid persona. "Glad you're alive, though, B," he said, winking at Dana. She grimaced and pushed herself up to stand.

"Thanks for catching me," she said to Eliane. "That one's gonna hurt in the morning."

"It's my job," Eliane said softly. "The flyer doesn't hit the ground."

"Oh, I hit it," Dana replied, her lips twisting up in a smile. "But thanks to you, I bounced. I'll be okay."

"All right, enough baskets for today," Coach said, pushing her way into the cluster of students. "Ivy, take Dana to the head trainer's office and have them run concussion protocols, please. The rest of you, we're done for today. Let's come back and hit it hard tomorrow. Stevens, I appreciate your concern for my athletes, but don't you have your own practice to go to?"

"Yes, ma'am," Marshall said, pulling his helmet on over his head. "I'll, uh, see you guys later?"

"Count on it, bro," Hiro said. Then he, too, smiled and started walking away as Coach turned her gimlet glare on him.

"Eliane," Coach said, beckoning her over. Eliane took a deep breath and followed as Coach drew her off to the side.

"Look, this isn't your fault, I know that. But if that boy is your boyfriend or whatever, I expect you to explain to him exactly what happened today, and just why he absolutely *cannot* be interrupting our practice like that. Dana could have died. We were lucky you caught her the way you did! Do you understand?"

"Yes, Coach," Eliane said. "I'll take care of it."

"I know you will," Coach said with a smile. She clapped Eliane on the shoulder then turned to begin gathering up her boombox and other equipment.

Eliane took another deep breath and turned to collect her backpack and cheer bag. She guessed she'd just wait for Ivy outside the head trainer's office.

"What was that?"

Braeden's voice cut through the resumed babble of football practice, and Eliane turned from gathering up Ivy's scattered homework. Even now, with his eyes haunted and his face pale, looking at him sent a shock of desire arrowing right through her body.

"That was what I said it was. That was my true nature."

"So, what?" he asked, frustration in his tone. "You're some kind of angel?"

"Not exactly," she said with a sigh. She looked around, but they were all alone on the bleachers, with no one else in earshot. "Look, I'm two things, all right? I'm Eliane Jenkins, the 'coolest chick you know.' But I'm also Death, the Pale Rider, Harbinger of the Eschaton."

"Don't you mean Apocalypse?"

"No. 'Apocalypse' is just the Greek word for revelation. The word for the end of life as we know it is Eschaton."

"So you're going to cause the end of the world?"

"We don't cause it," she said, "my siblings and me—the Riders, or Harbingers, whatever you want to call us. Humanity always causes it. We just bring causal factors together, and then see to it that humanity makes it through to the other side."

"You mean this has happened before?"

"Innumerable times."

Braeden snapped his fingers, his eyes lighting up as he made a connection.

"*That's* why you knew so much about the Black Death! You spread it!"

"No, my sister, Pestilence—she's Ivy in this incarnation—spread it. But I helped. I was there, like I told you."

"You really did walk the streets of empty villages."

"Yes."

"Ivy is Pestilence..." he trailed off, thoughtful. "And Marshall and Hiro?"

"War and Famine," Eliane said. In the back of her mind, a voice reminded her that in general, it was a terrible idea to tell humans too much, but the nearness of him still sang under her skin, and she didn't want to stop talking to him just yet.

"Huh. You...you all had wings."

"They're mostly metaphorical," she said with a smile. "They only manifest when we're acting in our...official capacity."

"Why are you called Riders if you can fly?"

"Well, we can ride, too. You pick these things up over the eons."

That got her a laugh. She smiled, reveling in the way the haunted look was fading from Braeden's eyes. He reached out a hand and took her fingers in his own. Heat and light curled within her at his touch, and she felt her body tighten down low.

"Why are you telling me this?" he asked, still smiling. "You know this sounds crazy."

"It does," she said, "but it's the truth. I—I really do like you a lot, Braeden. When you saw me at the party…I'd just found Famine for the first time in this incarnation. That's why you saw us hugging. Eliane doesn't even know Hiro Ikeda. But Famine is my brother, and we're a very close family."

"I'm sorry about that," Braeden said. "I really like you, too. More than that, if I'm honest. I can't stop thinking about you. Even with all this—" he waved a hand at the now-empty track. "Even with everything you're telling me, I just want to get closer to you. I want to spend all my time with you. I'm sorry I got so jealous. I'm really sorry I asked Sam to help me get even with you. *That* girl is a psycho!"

"Did she hurt you?' Death asked, eternity roaring back to the forefront of her gaze.

"Fuck! That's terrifying!" Braeden said, starting back, and then leaning close to look into her eyes. "No! No, she didn't. But…"

"I will destroy her," Death said, meaning every word, "if that's what it takes to keep you safe. I protect what I love."

Braeden froze, his eyes searching hers. Then a slow smile spread across his lips.

"You love me," he whispered.

Eliane swallowed, blinking her eyes back to normal. Then she nodded. His smile grew, and just as he'd done so many times in her dreams, Braeden leaned forward and ran his hand up under the back of her hair, gently cupping her skull.

"I love you, too, Pale Rider," he whispered just before his lips touched hers in a delicious explosion of sensation.

* * * * *

Kacey Ezell Bio

Kacey Ezell is an active duty USAF instructor pilot with 2500+ hours in the UH-1N Huey and Mi-171 helicopters. When not teaching young pilots to beat the air into submission, she writes sci-fi/fantasy/horror/noir/alternate history fiction. Her first novel, MINDS OF MEN, was a Dragon Award Finalist for Best Alternate History. She's contributed to multiple Baen anthologies and has twice been selected for inclusion in the Year's Best Military and Adventure Science Fiction compilation. In 2018, her story "Family Over Blood" won the Year's Best Military and Adventure Science Fiction Readers' Choice Award. In addition to writing for Baen, she has published several novels and short stories with independent publisher Chris Kennedy Publishing. She is married with two daughters. You can find out more and join her mailing list at www.kaceyezell.net.

# # # # #

Tiger, Tiger, Burning Bite
by Julia May Vee

BANGKOK

I was dressed to slay, but it didn't matter since none of the men who frequented Club Whispers would even look at me. Magic eaters like me were shunned here. Whispers is where all the magical elite like to party, which is why I usually avoid it when I have to come to Bangkok for work. But Misty had really wanted to come, and she was my best friend from Academy, so I'd given in to her desire to have our girl's night out here.

That meant we'd gone extra with our club wear. Heels, tall; skirts, small. The bouncers had waved us past the roaring foo guardian statues, and the magic of Whispers surrounded us. The illusionists on staff wove a dreamy vista of waterfalls and lights against the ceiling of endless sky. Pretty dancers gyrated in cages of dazzling sparks, looking like they were suspended in the stars themselves. Wisps of red flame lit up the dais where the DJ mixed the latest Korean pop notes with thumping bass beats.

Misty was poured into a hot pink latex dress, and her hair was tinted a pastel pink. Under the shimmering club lights, she looked like an extra in a sci-fi alien flick. To humor her, I'd gone full makeup, teased up my chin-length dark hair, and sprayed it to ridiculous heights. When you're five feet two, you'll do a lot to look taller. So my go-to was big hair and platform-heeled boots. Today, I went for the full white leather effect. Laced bustier, leather skirt, and shiny boots. I loved this skirt. It had pockets. Small pockets, but handy nonetheless when you need to carry around vials of powdered magical flaked gold.

We stayed at the bar, but I was looking forward to dancing. If I was going to have to spend time at Whispers, at least I could do something I actually liked. While Misty got her drink on, the men lined up at the bar conspicuously avoided me. Their gazes passed right over me like I wasn't even there. This is why I dated Norms. At least they actually looked at me—they didn't know to be afraid of my magic.

The bartender came back with Misty's vodka martini, dirty style. I'd been watching this bartender work, and she dazzled the patrons. Between her extraordinary height and the long blue wig, she was already eye-catching. Then her showmanship took it to the next level. Her sleek muscles rippled in her ribbed white tank top as she moved. The tank read "Firebird" in loopy red script. When Firebird poured the liquor, it arced high in the air, defying gravity. She topped all her drinks with a little extra spark. Patrons tipped her generously.

Unlike Misty, I wasn't inclined to get tipsy, so I had a Shirley Temple. Yes, boring, but then I was an accountant. And I liked maraschino cherries. My hot outfit notwithstanding, my boring drink was totally on brand for me.

The bartender snapped her fingers, and the sugarcane straw smoked with a tiny flame. My eyes widened with pleasure, and I blew out the flame and sucked on the straw. The taste of Firebird's magic lingered, a cinnamon heat on my tongue. Delicious.

Misty tapped on my shoulder and yelled into my ear, "I heard the Tiger Clan is coming tonight!"

No wonder she'd lobbied so hard to come to Whispers tonight. We both followed members of the enormous, and enormously wealthy, Apichai family of Thailand on social media. The Thai Tigers were socially elusive, which made them all the more alluring to the magical world.

Misty knew I crushed hard on Aran Apichai and teased me mercilessly about it.

Aran's social media feed largely consisted of him playing soccer with his shirt off, or him on a boat with his shirt off, or him running in a forest with his shirt off. Well, you can understand why he was the highlight of my Insta feed.

I wondered what they were doing in Bangkok. The Tiger Clan preferred to live on the Malaysian peninsula, just outside the border with Thailand. I sipped my drink and scrolled through my phone to check Aran's feed. Nothing since yesterday's video of him walking by the ocean. I'd watched it three times already. No new pictures of Bangkok; Misty was shining me on. I laughed at myself for falling for her teasing and tipped my glass to toast her. Misty had never shunned me, and she'd stuck with me through the Tourney. For that, I would always give in when she wanted to go to Whispers. We were having a girl's night out, with or without Tiger shifters. That was more than enough for me.

A hush came over the club. I looked up from my drink to see what had caused the people at the bar to stop talking. I set my glass down with a heavy thunk. The loud music faded into the background, and all I heard was my heart thumping. Three guys in crisp navy linen blazers sauntered in. They wore their tight white t-shirts and dark blazers with panache, and the soft silk of their tan trousers molded to the taut muscles of their legs with just the slightest amount of drape. The front man finished the look with bright white limited-edition Supreme sneakers. Their graceful strides ate up the marble foyer as they approached the bar. I felt the sudden urge to fan myself.

The Thai Tigers had arrived.

Aran headed up the trio and was aimed right at me. To his right was a beefier man with broad shoulders and not much neck. Everything about him screamed bodyguard, from his slow stride to the way his eyes quickly scanned the occupants of the club. To Aran's left was a taller bald man, probably twice my height. Aran wasn't short in my eyes, maybe 5'10" or so, but then again, to me, most people were tall. They were both handsome, but I only had eyes for one particular Tiger.

I looked up at Aran and an electric sizzle passed between us. I'd dressed to overcome my invisibility. I had certainly caught his eye. *Did he remember me?*

I was looking at Aran in the flesh again, and it was almost too much. He wore his hair in a high fade, and the top had a slight curl over his forehead. It was shorter than when I'd seen him last. A year ago he'd come to Hong Kong, and I'd run into the Tiger at the goldsmith. He'd smiled his almost bashful smile as we passed in the gilt-covered foyer. I'd been too startled to do more than stare after him.

After that, I'd followed Aran's meteoric rise online. He was the youngest of the reclusive Apichai clan but refused to follow his clan's secretive lifestyle. He worked with lenders to build schools and train farmers throughout southeast Asia. I traveled extensively in the region, too, to deal with my family's holdings, but rarely crossed paths with the Apichai clan. But we were both here now. This was my chance.

I plucked the cherry from my drink, gently catching it between my teeth before biting into the bright red flesh. My fangs were small compared to those of a shifter, but long enough to signal I was something different. I kept my eyes on his as I sucked the rest of the sweet fruit into my mouth. I had just enough of Firebird's magic in my system to take a page from her book. I held the cherry stem on my bottom lip, and then puffed softly. The stem sparked and flamed from my breath. I looked at Aran, and his dark eyes stared at my lips. Gotcha.

I flicked my tongue quickly to absorb the fire. Fire elementals had the best party tricks. If only I could borrow Firebird's magic more often. But the cherry trick had literally burnt up the tiny magic spark I'd eaten earlier.

Aran was standing directly in front of me. I washed down the ashes of the stem with my sweet, bubbly drink and drank in his handsome features. That jawline of his could cut glass. He finally spoke, "*Sah wah dee khrap.*"

I smiled at the very polite greeting and held out my hand. "I'm Evelyn. I don't speak much Thai."

He grasped my hand, his grip firm, but he didn't shake it. Instead he bowed without letting go of my arm. I saw his lips part, and I knew he was scenting me with his Tiger senses. *That's right, drink me in.*

Then I felt a pang of guilt. He probably smelled fire magic. I wouldn't smell like that in a few minutes as Firebird's magic wore off. And if I ate anything else that was magical, I'd smell different soon.

He switched to English, and like mine, it held the British accent of boarding schools and London-bred tutors. "I'm Aran."

I almost said, "I know." Instead, I just smiled.

I leaned in so close we were almost touching. Still seated on the bar stool, I shifted to the edge of my seat, and could feel the heat rising off his body. Shifter metabolism. Being so close to him after months of just seeing him online was overloading me. I felt giddy from both the proximity and his clear interest.

But I'd forgotten entirely about his entourage. A heavy hand came down on Aran's shoulder, and we both stared at the bald Apichai. Aran shook off the hand and turned back to me. "This is my cousin, Chakan."

Chakan wouldn't be put off. He wrapped an arm around Aran and almost lifted him away as he said to me, "Please excuse us. We have an appointment."

Disappointment rushed through me. I merely waggled my fingers at Aran. "Nice meeting you, Chakan. Come back and buy me a drink, Aran."

Now the beefy one flanked Aran, and together he and Chakan practically dragged Aran toward the back of the club. Aran gave me one last apologetic look before succumbing to his entourage's heavy-handed direction.

Misty bounced over. "Woo! Is it hot in here or what, girl?" I grinned at her and tilted my head in the direction of the stairs where the Apichais had been hustled off by Chakan. "Maybe it'll be cooler there."

Misty fluttered her eyelashes at me, "Yeah, we'd totally cool off while hanging with those smoking hot Thai Tigers."

I laughed. Misty knew I wasn't going to let this chance go. "I'm sorry; you don't have to watch me obsess over Aran Apichai. You could go dance and we can catch up after."

She shrugged then patted her pink hair. "I'm single, too. Maybe that tall one could use some company." Misty had always liked bald guys.

I hopped off the stool, and we sauntered off to the back of the club. The DJ had switched from K-pop to Cantopop. My hips popped to the beat, and my body warmed and loosened as we moved through the bodies gyrating to the catchy music.

Aran Apichai wasn't getting away from me tonight.

* * *

I hadn't counted on not being able to find him in the up-stairs lounge. Misty, of course, managed to find friends of hers there. She settled in with them and ordered another drink. I wandered back downstairs to search for my elusive quarry. Whispers had continued to fill up, and it was slow progress navi-gating the bumping and grinding crowd.

Disappointment coursed through my veins. How had I missed him? I ran a hand through my hair in frustration. We'd had a moment. I didn't want to be a stalker, but I knew I'd regret it for the rest of my life if I didn't give this a fighting chance. I wove my way to the ladies' room. I powdered my face and refreshed my lip gloss. My gloss was a custom blend from a magical herbalist in San Francisco. Grandma Chen made sure what I put on my lips was pretty—and potent. Then I checked the vials in my pocket, where I kept the source of my power. Gold flake was the best way for me to ingest magic, as it didn't put me in the hospital afterward.

I took a deep breath and let it out. I adjusted the girls in my bustier for optimum positioning. I would try one more pass around the club to see if I could find Aran. If not, maybe it wasn't meant to be.

People kept streaming into the club. I could barely turn sideways in the hallway where the restrooms were. To my right I saw the "Staff Only" swinging doors, steel with square windowpanes. Was that a blue blazer? My pulse sped up. Of course! That's why we hadn't seen them anywhere else in the club—they were behind closed doors.

Well, not exactly closed. I elbowed my way past the people vaping in the hallways, their sickly sweet vanilla clouds of smoke getting in my way. I stepped over a couple of people passed out on the floor. I hadn't thought through what I would do if it turned out the Apichai Clan members were having a private meeting so I pushed the door slightly open and peeked in. It was basically a supply room with stacked crates of liquor bottles and other linens. A gentleman in a charcoal blazer had his back to me. Damn. Wrong guy.

Before I could back away, Charcoal Blazer bent down and started dragging something from behind a dolly stacked high with boxes. I squinted in confusion. Wait, was that a leg? Two legs…silky tan slacks? My eyes narrowed as I recognized those sneakers. My breath caught in my throat as I realized what was happening.

Charcoal was dragging Aran out toward the back entrance from the supply room. My pulse raced, and I struggled to figure out what I should do next. I took a step back from the door and continued to watch from behind the window. I tapped out a message on my watch to Misty. <<Code Red—Aran needs help.>>

Who knew when Misty would check her phone to even see my message, but she'd know what to do. I looked around. The drunk people in the hallway were oblivious to what I was doing. I reached into the tight pocket of my skirt and pulled out a small vial with a red lid. This one.

I measured out five flakes. They glowed with the red undertone of Hoard magic. I tossed them in my mouth and swallowed. There, that should give me ten minutes of luck. Hopefully I wouldn't need any more than that. I popped the vial with the gray lid. Five flakes would give me ten minutes of steel limbs. If I couldn't take the guy down with that, things would get hairy.

Aran was no lightweight, and I saw Charcoal struggle to get him across the floor. Finally he turned and faced toward me to reach under Aran's arms and lift him by his armpits. I bobbed down, ducking below the window.

I counted to three, and then risked a peek at the window. Charcoal was all the way out the back door, which was closing behind him, and only poor Aran's sneaker remained, left behind on the gray concrete floor.

I held my breath for two beats and decided Charcoal was unlikely to come back in to retrieve the shoe, even if it *was* a Supreme Limited Edition.

With trepidation, I dashed across the storage room, stopping by the shoe. I knelt down, and something caught my eye behind the supply shelves. Collapsed in the corner was Chakan, the bald cousin. Slumped just beneath him was the robust other cousin. *Oh, no!*

The need to go after Aran tugged at me, but I checked on the cousins. Strong pulses, but slow. They also felt cool to the touch, as if all their shifter metabolism had left them. Drugged.

I texted Misty from my watch. <<Aran's cousins were drugged, come get them from supply room downstairs by restrooms.>>

I crept back to the back door and opened it slightly. A large white van was running in the alley behind the club, the rear doors wide open. Charcoal was making slow progress carrying Aran to the van. I hardened my arms, readying for combat.

Without stopping to think, I darted out and launched myself at Charcoal. I aimed for his head, clapping with my stone-hard fists. He dropped Aran and staggered. Blood flowed from his ears. *That's right, buddy.* I drove two more hits, one after another, into his solar plexus. He grunted and went down. With an iron foot, I smashed his knee. He howled in pain and scrabbled backward like a crab to get away from me. No way this guy was getting his mitts on Aran again.

My chest heaved from the exertion and the adrenaline spike. I mean, I worked out, but let's face it, my life as an accountant hadn't really prepared me for this type of exertion. I knelt down to where Aran lay on the ground. I touched his neck and felt his pulse, deep and slow. He was so drugged he hadn't come to, despite the excitement in the alley.

The driver's side door to the van opened. *Uh, oh.*

I stood quickly, and charged low, hoping to surprise him. Luck was with me, as the driver grunted from the impact. I stomped hard on his instep, then followed with a fist to the groin. The driver went down, and exhilaration and relief flooded me as I went to finish him off. The van's side door slid open, but as I turned to face this new threat, I was too slow. My luck had run out. Pain blasted through me as I took an uppercut to the jaw. The back of my head smashed against the alley floor.

* * *

I came to with a massive headache and a dry mouth. Worse, I was locked in a cage. A small cage. I assessed my surroundings and my options. We were in a huge, empty warehouse, our crates against a rusty corrugated steel wall. How long had we been in that van? The two guys I'd fought in the alley were nowhere in sight. Were there more of them? My magic vials were gone. They'd stripped me of my watch, phone, and magic stores. Even my boots. *Bastards!* Those were Fendis from two seasons ago, and I loved them with a mad, mad passion.

There was only one source of magic left in the warehouse, and he was in the crate next to me. Tiger shifter strength, the fear-inducing roar, rapid healing, and the ability to crunch the skulls of our captors between massive jaws. Perfect. Except for one thing. A wide red jade collar was wrapped around his neck. *Blood Jade*. Deadly to shifters. Aran was barely conscious.

"Aran, wake up." I tried to pitch my voice above a whisper, but not loud enough to get the kidnappers running in. Sound traveled easily in this cavernous warehouse. I didn't know how much longer he had with that collar. Surely they didn't intend to kill him with it? They'd gone through an awful lot of trouble to take him alive from Whispers. I'd bet all my gold flakes they were planning to transport him. I scanned the area around us more closely. This wasn't a warehouse, it was an airplane hangar. They were going to fly Aran out of here! I was lucky they hadn't just killed me in the alley. I had to get us out of here.

He shook his head slightly, then winced. When he turned to face me, his eyes widened. "Evelyn?"

I nodded. "I saw them take you out the back. Tried to stop them, but there were three of them." I shrugged.

He licked his lips, and his words were slow. "I'm sorry you got dragged into this."

He was too adorable. "Do you know what they want with you?"

He frowned. "I was supposed to meet with the club owner, talk about funding a clean water project…" His words trailed off, and I could see fatigue in the droop of his shoulders.

He lifted his head and gave me a half smile. "I was hoping to finish and come buy you a drink."

I got a pang in my chest hearing those words. I'd be lucky if he didn't spit on me after this, because he was fading fast, and I knew I couldn't count on anyone but me to get us out of here.

I reached through the bars of my crate into his and tugged his arm until it extended into my crate. I touched the brown flesh of his forearm, stroking it softly. It was cold, the Blood Jade collar inhibiting his shifter magic. He looked at me in confusion.

"I'm sorry; I can't figure out any other way to get us out of here." He blinked, and I could see what a struggle it was for him to keep his eyes open, let alone to stay conscious. This strong, vital man collared and imprisoned in a cage. My heart broke looking at him and thinking about what I had to do next. It would be so much worse after this, but at least we'd be free, and that would be worth him shunning me forever. So I made myself do something I hadn't done since the Tourney.

I bent over his wrist, my fangs extending. I bit down, and the coppery tang of his blood filled my mouth. I drank steadily, even as he struggled. The blood coursing through me warmed as I swallowed, and I could feel Tiger magic pooling in my gut. My skin began to tingle as the heat suffused it. Even my scalp tingled as the Tiger magic filled me. *Enough*. From the discipline borne of years of training, I told myself to stop. I'd taken enough.

Reluctantly, I stopped drinking, and my fangs retracted from his wrist.

Aran's dark eyes held dull accusation. I'd seen worse before in my friends' eyes. Horror usually followed.

Now all we had to do was wait. I didn't have the metabolism of a shifter, but taking magic directly from blood meant my body would process it quickly. It had been five years since I'd drunk from any living thing, but I'd never forgotten how it felt. The self-disgust, the pleasure, and the guilt. All of that rushed through me now as I waited for the tiger magic to circulate throughout my system.

Unlike Aran, I wasn't bound by a Blood Jade manacle around my neck. That meant I'd be able to shift and punch out through this crate. My eyelids drooped in pleasure as I felt the shifter magic spreading throughout my limbs. It felt so good, like the time I'd eaten a bushel of magical snow peaches in Japan. I closed my eyes and sank into my newly acquired magic.

Shifter magic was so potent. I had a feeling it might last for days. I needed to use it or lose it, and I had too many clothes on. I unhooked my bustier and shimmied out of my skirt. The thong was a little trickier. This was NOT how I wanted to get naked with Aran. I squeezed my right hand a few times, clenching it into a fist and opening it. I concentrated on my fingertips. Unlike a natural born shifter who had the training to transform in one fluid burst, I had to do it piecemeal.

Claws punched out of my nailbeds, and my fingers widened and grew. The air around my hand shimmering a soft blue from the use of Tiger magic. I concentrated now on my other hand. Soon I sported two enormous Tiger paws from my still human arms. I looked around the warehouse, and suddenly every detail of the dark warehouse came into focus. *Tiger night vision was amazing.*

Aaron looked at me, eyes wide in what I'm sure was abject horror. I was still me, but Aran was looking at the petite woman from the nightclub who'd drunk his blood and was now naked, but with two Tiger paws and Tiger eyes. I'm pretty sure he wouldn't be asking me out for dinner after this.

I turned my attention to the top of the crate. The wire was continuous. I didn't want to shift entirely inside this tight space, though, so I studied the corners and finally realized the bottom of the crate was the weakest link. Only small loops wrapped around the bottom to secure it to the rest of the crate. I looked at my bare feet and sighed.

There was no hope for it. I got on my hands and knees and called forth a full shift. First my feet, and then all the way up my legs toward my torso. Soft orange fur encased my limbs, and I shrugged and rolled my shoulders, arching my back. Sure enough, my body grew rapidly, and as my back hit the top of the cage, my body kept going, and I pushed downward. I opened my mouth wide and extended my tongue. I had whiskers, too, which were giving me all sorts of sensory input. It was all I could do to keep from yowling at the sensations coursing through my body. *Shifters must feel so good all the time.*

I flexed and strained against the confines of the crate, bending the weak, plastic-coated metal wires. These cheap crates were never meant to hold a shifter. Clearly the kidnappers had relied on the Blood Jade collar to restrain Aran. They hadn't counted on little ole me.

Well, not so little anymore. My head felt enormous. I'm sure I was still smaller than a normal shifter, but for me it was a novelty to feel so massive. The wires on the crate were cutting into my flesh, not painfully, but annoyingly, like when you sit on plastic patio furniture too long and it leaves marks on the backs of your thighs.

My paws pushed at the bottom corners of the crate, and I saw the small hooks that looped around to secure one corner pop off.

Bingo. I kept shoving at that edge, and then eventually that end of the crate bottom dropped off from the rest of the crate. A few more pushes, then I stood on all fours, and the top of the crate hung uselessly over me. I shrugged it off and padded over to Aran's crate.

Aran's eyes fluttered open, and he whispered, "What are you?"

Fair question. I opened my jaw wide, testing this new mouth. My tongue curled as I formed the words. Challenging, but doable. "Magic eater."

Some from Academy had called me a vampire. That wasn't a compliment in our world. Then I felt compelled to add, "Your rescuer." The *rrr*'s rolled in a pleasing manner from my tongue.

His eyes closed again, and his head bobbed. I had to get that damned collar off of him. This next part would be trickier. I studied the padlock on Aran's crate. No key, so that was a no go.

Tiger paws were strong for running, but not particularly dexterous. I'd have to do some maneuvering. "Aran, I have to tilt you."

I'm not sure he even heard me. I stood on my hind legs and pushed two giant paws against the top of Aran's crate, turning it sideways with a giant thud. Aran didn't make a sound. I paused to listen. No shouts or footsteps. I turned my attention to the bottom of the crate, then opened my mouth and bit down on the corner nubs, crunching through them. I spat them out, then did the next corner, and the next. Eventually I'd weakened the entire bottom of the crate. If Aran had the strength to push out, that would have been ideal. But instead, I found myself yanking the bottom with my teeth while pulling the top away with my paws. With one last tug, I got the bottom off. *There!*

I reached into the rest of the crate and gently bit down on Aran's pant leg to tug him out of the crate. He had one sneaker on, and the other foot was encased in a low white sock. The tugging motion roused him, and he cooperated with me, crawling out of the crate. He pulled heavily on the ruff around my neck as he tried to stand. He fell backward onto his ass next to me and leaned his face against my fur in fatigue.

This wouldn't do at all. I worried if I'd have to take blood from him again after this to regain the form, but if we were lucky, he'd have enough energy to climb on my back once I got the collar off. I lifted one big paw and wiggled. I withdrew the shifter magic from my paw, and it felt awful. But after a few seconds, I had my right hand back, and I worked on the clasp of the Blood Jade collar. Twenty-four carat gold was very soft, and very bendy. I twisted off the clasp and yanked the collar from Aran's neck. He moaned in relief.

Normally I would have taken the collar with me, as it was clearly a precious Hoard piece. Hell, under ordinary circumstances, I would have ground it down to ingest its magic. But in this tiger form, it was detrimental to me. I concentrated on using my borrowed magic stores to shift my arm back to tiger form.

To my relief, it worked. I licked Aran's face. He nodded. "I'm ok." He got up, wobbly, but already more alert than before. Together we walked to the door. Aran turned the knob and opened the door just enough for him to look around. It was as dark outside as in the hangar. That meant it was still evening. I wondered how long it would be before Misty got my message and realized I was gone.

* * *

We stepped quietly out onto the airfield. Two small planes were parked over at the other hangar. The hangars were dark, and I couldn't hear anything other than Aran's breathing. I thought about shifting back and searching the hangar we'd just left. Maybe we could find our phones? I wondered how far out of Bangkok we were. I didn't know what kind of staying power I had in this form, but I felt great. Maybe Aran could hang onto me while I ran us back to safety. That was also a terrible idea, since I had a lousy sense of direction and absolutely no idea where we were.

Aran held onto the ruff of fur on my neck. It felt good, possessive almost. Or maybe that was just me, feeling possessive about him.

He knelt down next to me and murmured. "I still can't shift. It'll take a while for the effects of the Blood Jade to wear off."

I was the one who'd drunk his blood without his consent, but here he was, apologizing to me. I gave a small shake of my head. Before I could respond, my heightened senses picked up something. Faint pinpricks of light shone in the distance, growing larger as they approached. The kidnappers had to be coming back. I bit Aran's sleeve and tugged, wanting to head back to the hangar we'd come from.

We dashed back inside to wait to ambush them. I listened for their footsteps. Aran wasn't in any position to deal with them, so he wisely stayed behind me. I heard the crunch of gravel as they approached, chatting in Thai. It sounded like two guys, which comforted me, because I had been worried about a clown car full. Who knew what kind of magic they had? I'd have to dispatch them quickly.

My body tensed as they approached the door. My whiskers quivered, and I could smell them. Meaty and garlicky. Probably Norms.

The door swung open, and I lunged, taking the front man down. His scream was cut short as I bit through his neck. The sensation of crunching through human bone and chewing the flesh was a new one. He wasn't a threat any longer, but I found it hard to let go of my downed prey. I didn't have time to experience more as the second man yelled and started shooting. Damn Norms and their guns.

I roared in pain as the bullet burned into my flank. I leaped over the dead man and opened my jaws wide to bite down on the shooter's arm. He let out a bloodcurdling scream I found quite satisfying. The gun fell to the floor, and blood spurted from his arm. I growled and moved in, ready to kill this one, too.

"Stop!" Aran waved his arms. "I need him alive."

I whined, but my logical self knew Aran was right. So I bit the shooter in the leg to prevent him from running. He collapsed into a heap and cried. I sat back on my haunches and tried to lick my wound.

Aran checked the shooter's pockets, found a phone and a wallet, and tucked them into his pockets. I watched Aran's movements. He seemed to be recovering well from the Blood Jade collar. That was a relief. Aran took off the shooter's belt and wound it around his arms, immobilizing him. Then he searched the dead guy and held up a ring of keys in triumph. I licked my bloody paw, cleaning it.

The guy blubbering on the floor rolled around in pain. Aran reached down and grabbed his chin, speaking Thai in a low menacing voice. I wondered if they knew each other. Sadly, I realized I wouldn't know what happened after this. It's not like I'd be able to text Aran to chat with him later.

We made our way to the car. It was a tiny, beat up sedan. I tilted my head. There was a small logistical problem getting my large tiger form into that little beater. Aran shoved the shooter into the trunk, face down, then turned to face me.

He shrugged off his blazer and unbuttoned his shirt. I watched with not a little interest. Aran pointed at the passenger seat. "You need to shift back. I'm ok to drive now."

Oh.

I gave one last body stretch. I would miss this form. It had been glorious to be a ferocious Tiger, even under the circumstances. I closed my eyes and let the magic go. It hurt to burn up the last of Aran's shifter magic so soon. Then I was cold and naked, standing barefoot on the tarmac. Aran wrapped his shirt around me, then his blazer. I got into the car and buttoned up the shirt.

My bare legs stuck to the seat. My right thigh was still bleeding, but it didn't look bad. The weight of this evening's activities hit me all at once, and I realized I was dizzy. I hadn't burned this much magic in such a short time since the Tourney. My stomach churned. Probably all the blood I'd consumed. I tried not to think about the human flesh I'd eaten.

Aran drove in silence. I had trouble thinking of anything to say, so I just said, "I'm sorry."

He looked away from the road and stared at me, silent. I had trouble meeting his eyes and looked away. My stomach was really hurting now. I leaned my head back against the headrest, and tears burned in the back of my eyes. Shudders wracked my body, and I blinked as my brain froze. Just as suddenly as the seizure had come, it stopped. *Oh, no.* I knew what came next. More seizures. I thrashed against the seat now, arching my back.

Aran braked and then pulled over. "Evelyn! Evelyn!"

He reached for me, but it was too late. The seizures were coming fast and frequent, and I hit my head against the window. My vision hazed, and I passed out.

* * *

I clutched the lapel of my fluffy pink robe close together. Maybe today, I'd finally leave my flat. Since my brief hospital stay in Bangkok in a private care facility used to us magical folks, getting my stomach pumped, and returning home to Kowloon Tong, I hadn't seen another human being other than my older sister, Marilee. Mari had been solicitous, and she'd done a good job dodging my parents. It helped that she lived in the flat above me.

But now Mari was turning into a nag. "Evie, you should really shower today."

I rolled my eyes. *So* demanding. Just because I hadn't showered all week. *Jeez.*

So I let her bully me into taking a shower. Of course she was right, and I felt so much more human after. She was so bossy. Yesterday she'd insisted on cleaning my place. Not that I was messy, but she'd aired out the place, vacuumed, and changed my sheets.

Next she was threatening to get me out of the house for a Boba tea. But she'd left me alone, satisfied I'd showered and brushed my teeth. I sat on my bed in my pink robe, my hair still wet. I'd exhausted myself just washing my hair. It wasn't physical exhaustion that was the real culprit, though. I knew I was wallowing, but I couldn't help it.

Misty kept texting me. I hadn't called her. She'd finally sent me a giant bouquet of pink roses and an overnight parcel. When I opened the parcel, a single white sneaker lay inside. Aran's Supreme Limited Edition that had gotten left behind at Club Whispers. How embarrassing. I'd put it on my coffee table like a centerpiece.

I'd read through all Misty's texts and watched all her video messages. She apologized a million times for not looking for me sooner, but I wasn't mad. She'd found Aran's cousins and had gotten medical help for them. My watch and phone had gotten pitched out on the street in Bangkok, so she'd had no way to track me. But Aran was safe. He'd gotten me to the hospital. I don't know what happened to him after that, but Misty said Whispers had shut down. I assume the Apichai clan had circled the wagons.

My doorbell buzzed. Marilee had a key to my place, so she never even bothered to knock, let alone ring the bell. I walked over to the door and looked at the security screen. My breath caught.

Aran stood on my doorstep, holding a giant bouquet of brilliant orange orchids.

Thank God I'd showered. I opened the door.

He looked scrumptious. I drank him in.

"Hello, Evelyn." His voice was low. He handed me the bouquet of fiery blooms. I took them, feeling self-conscious.

"Thank you, please come in." Now I was super grateful Mari had cleaned my place, though I was starting to sense a conspiracy. I stepped back and let him in. Aran Apichai in my flat. All my senses were screaming. It hardly seemed real.

I gestured to my white leather sofa. "Would you like to sit down?"

As he sat down, I realized his shoe was on my coffee table. Wow, this was awkward. I put the beautiful flowers on the console and sat in the armchair next to the sofa. "Mmm, here's your shoe back."

His eyes lit up with surprise, and he grinned. "Hey! I thought I'd never see that again."

Yeah, that was how I felt about my Fendi boots.

"I don't know why, but my friend Misty sent it to me." I was mortified. I wished the armchair would swallow me whole.

Aran nodded like that was totally normal. "Is your leg ok?"

Relieved to have something safe to talk about like injuries, I lifted up my robe to show him that the gunshot wound had healed up with only a small scar from the stitches. Then I realized I was practically showing him my ass. I dropped my robe and yanked it down. Of course he'd already seen me buck naked. This was confusing. "It's fine now."

He looked up from my thighs, and his eyes twinkled with amusement. "You're a hard woman to find, Evelyn."

I hadn't realized he'd ever try to find me. I flushed. "I'm sorry?"

He shook his head. "No, please let me apologize. It's entirely my fault you were injured." He reached out and grabbed my hands in his. "I want to thank you. You saved my life."

I struggled to process what he was saying. I had no script for this. He hadn't even mentioned that I'd violated him by drinking from him and stealing his magic. Bygones?

I settled on, "You're welcome."

He was still holding my hands. Delicious heat from the contact spread up my arms. Shifter heat. I studied his handsome face, so earnest as he spoke to me. He hadn't rejected me. He'd clearly conspired with Misty and my sister to find me. He'd brought me flowers. He'd flown to Hong Kong to see me in person. What the hell was wrong with me? Aran Apichai was holding my hands.

"It doesn't bother you that I'm a magic eater?" I just wanted to be clear.

He gave a lazy shrug. "Evelyn, I'm a tiger. We eat *people.*"

He had a point. I'd gotten a second chance, and I wasn't going to wimp out. I leaned until we were nose to nose. "You owe me a drink."

"Yes. Please take me up on that."

I gave in to the instinct that had driven me to flirt with him at the club and brushed my lips against his, a soft invitation. He responded, letting go of my hands to cup my face as he deepened our kiss.

I moved off the chair and slid into his lap, winding my arms around his neck. Aran swooped in, and our kisses grew more heated, a battle of lips and tongues. Excitement bubbled up in my chest, and I felt giddy, like I'd drunk champagne. I pulled away and put my hand on his chest, feeling the thump of his heart. Strong and steady. His eyes burned into mine, and in their depths I could see the tiger prowling, patient and watchful.

I reached over and unbuttoned the top of his shirt, placing kisses along his neck and all over the beautiful chest I'd fantasized over so many times. I leaned my cheek against his bare skin and closed my eyes. He rested his cheek against the top of my head, continuing to hold me close. I let my breath slow, and the heat came down and pooled low in my belly. I wanted to savor this moment forever.

"So about that drink…"

I turned and looked at him. He gave me a slow smile, the kind a man gives his lover in private. Wow. I was going to have my hands full with this one.

"How do you feel about Boba?"

He laughed and nodded. I wanted to gobble him up, but forced myself to stand up, and waited for him to do the same. He placed his hands just below my elbows, his grip gentle, but firm. "Whatever you want, Evelyn."

Perfect.

* * * * *

Julia May Vee Bio

Julia loves stories about heroes, monsters, and heroic monsters. Fans can find her at http://juliavee.com where she has more great stuff for voracious readers.

# # # # #

In Her World by Casey Moores

Text Message Transcript:

Me: Are you sure this is okay?

Her: You ask this every time, I've said yes

Me: But that doesn't mean you're okay with it.

Me: How can you actually be okay with this?

Her: Because I imagine how I would feel if it was me.

Her: She has no one else. Please, trust me, you should do this.

Her: I've always known this about you

Her: I've always accepted it's something you have to do.

Her: Go to her

Me: Okay, though I think it's starting to tear me apart

Her: Welcome to my world

Me: <typing, deleting, typing again... deleting again>

Her: I'm sorry, that wasn't fair

Her: Just go to her

Her: I'll be fine

Me: Okay

Me: I love you

Her: I love you too

* * *

The city of Beluanox always projected a somber, sinister mood, from which it rarely deviated. I couldn't fathom the passage of time since my last visit, not that it mattered. As I glanced around and got my bearings, I found some businesses replaced and a few buildings altered according to their owner's moods, but the overall character of the city lay eternal.

Somewhere back in history, the creators of the city had manufactured a strange blend of Gotham and Venice. Narrow alleyways interspersed with the occasional waterway made vehicular traffic impossible and pedestrian traffic difficult. Worse, they followed labyrinthine paths detestable to the unfamiliar. It seemed intentionally set to ensnare the unprepared. The Minotaur of Crete would approve.

The architecture, on the other hand, blended modern highrises and ancient gothic monstrosities. Above, gargoyles glared disapprovingly at me amongst lichen-covered stone crenellations. Elsewhere, glass and steel expanded upward and disappeared into not-so-low flying clouds.

I inhaled the misty air to complete my nostalgia. Fog and mist acted as constant companions to the melancholy façade. Seldom did it actually rain, but the threat of such was consistent. Conversely, the overcast clouds weren't perpetual, but they were frequent. Clear skies don't exist there.

Focus, there's only so much time. Every second not spent with *her* was a moment wasted. On the other hand, every moment *with* her was a betrayal, wasn't it? Guilt tore at me.

Go to her, I heard in the voice of a woman from another world. I pushed my thoughts aside.

Fortunately, the old leads maintained their usefulness. Her habits, it would seem, changed little over time. I would've thought she'd become bored, but apparently not. My heart pounded stronger and faster the more I thought of her.

Soon.

The mere word ignited both my imagination and my inner conflict.

Can I actually save her? Do I actually want to? Stop that; of course I do.

Like a hound, I set off on the scent. The usual contacts placed her in Croftvale a short time prior. The busier alleys gave way to quieter alleys, until I found myself in a dark, silent part of the quarter. With the ambient noise gone, the sound of my footsteps on the stone became audible. I stepped softer, quiet as a mouse. Though the rush of my excited blood threatened to overcome my senses, I felt confident no one else could hear my passage. I didn't fear anything that might have resided in those alleyways, I didn't fear any traps that might have laid in wait. I feared only the delay such encounters might cost me.

As if conjured by my mere thoughts, I spotted the telltale shuffle of a thug casually stalking prey. His clothes were well-worn and his demeanor rugged as if to feign homelessness, but he was bulky for a vagrant. My interest piqued at the thought of just who that prey might be.

A nearby apartment building sported stone windowsills lined vertically, with perfect spacing, all the way to the roof. I leapt to grab the second story, used the momentum to launch myself upward and past it so I could place my feet on it, briefly balanced on the window, and jumped to the next ledge. In this manner, I climbed the remaining twelve stories like a ladder.

Werewolf body, how I missed you so.

When I caught the lip of the roof itself, I pulled myself up and rolled over onto the top. I nodded to a gargoyle who stood watch. Thankfully, it understood I meant no harm.

I sprung back to my feet and slowed at the edge. My eyes refocused on the darkness below, and I regained sight of the stumbler.

His pace quickened, yet remained soft and silent. I headed him off at the far edge of the rooftop. My blood pressure rose drastically as I caught the slightest glimpse of *her*. I only spied a small flash, but it was all I needed. My instincts were correct, his intended victim was, indeed, my shadow witch.

The shiny, wavy, beautiful brunette hairstyle *could* have belonged to just about anyone in the city. The fringed black poncho and the black leather miniskirt *might* have belonged to anyone. It wasn't even the black Louboutins she wore which confirmed her identity. No, my confirmation came from her masterful gait over uneven cobblestone in *those* shoes.

That, and her clever "lost and confused" act. I knew it well. Ever dramatic, she'd always played the part of helpless, soon-to-be victim exceedingly well. I knew she reveled in portraying the mouse when she was, in actuality, the cat. Her poor, unsuspecting mark blundered happily into the trap.

Another scent pierced my awareness. More than one predator approached. While the pathetic thief stumbled toward his doom, a quieter, better trained assailant waited up the next alley. He stood deathly still in the shadow of an inset door. Thinner, calmer, and dressed in tight-fitting black sportswear, he had a pistol at the ready. The stumbler was, perhaps, a bit too obvious, likely by design. His purpose, I imagine, hinged on garnering her attention so she would focus on him. Meanwhile, the professional clearly intended to wait for her to be distracted.

These convolutions of predator and prey, the ebb and flow between hunter and hunted, were my shadow witch's forte. Above everything, this was her raison d'être, the attraction that drew her to the city. From my perspective, however, it seemed her ego would soon fail her. To my delight, she required a protector. It would infuriate her to receive help, but she'd get over it. She always did.

She "mis-stepped" in her high heels and "twisted an ankle" with an embellished whimper. The stumbler closed the distance as she crouched to fumble with the "injured" side. When she twisted to deal with the stumbler, the professional stepped out.

I leapt from the rooftop. Wind whistled through my ears, and adrenaline surged through my body. The sinking feeling, which usually sent me into panic, invigorated me.

I dropped, as if magnetized to my target. My timing was perfect.

She sprung up on the ball of one foot to kick the stumbler in the face. My boots landed on the professional's collarbone. Despite the loud crack I heard, he retained his footing and threw me off.

I dropped behind him and drew a knife.

Deftly I slashed the blade across the wrist that carried the pistol before he could bring it to bear.

He released it in pain but produced a knife of his own with the other hand. I'd hoped for a quick, clean kill, but instead we fell into a struggle that involved a lot of stabbing. Lucky for me, the blade wasn't silver, and my wounds healed faster than he could make them.

Eventually I wound up on top, fighting to drive the knife down.

My muscles tensed, my power surged, and the knife started to give way in my favor.

"You two can stop now," she announced in that haughty, authoritative tone she used when she held all the cards. Behind her, the stumbler lay crumpled in the shadows.

I relaxed, but the professional flipped the knife.

Black tendrils shot out from the shadows, wrapped around the professional's neck, and wrenched him away from me. They held him up in the air like a freshly hung criminal.

The shadow witch sighed in disgust.

Crap! Now I've made her mad.

"What exactly do you think you're doing?" she asked. Her eyes, wild and dangerous, burned through to my soul. I basked in the sensation.

Play dumb, act cute, she always likes that.

"I, uh, thought I was saving you," I said, making big, innocent eyes. Her intense stare held onto me while the shadows lifted the stumbler.

"You mean from this one?" The shadows flung the stumbler across the alleyway and slammed him into the opposing wall. The remains dropped limply to the street. The tentacles of shadow swung the professional to hang immediately in front of me. He kicked, squirmed, and pulled uselessly at the black constraints. "Or this one?"

I shrugged and glanced side to side like a child with a hand in a cookie jar.

"You understand it'll be harder now," she lectured, "and I'll have to kill them both. I mean, I was going to kill them both, but...well, now it's going to be much less fun."

"Sorry?" I muttered with an embarrassed half frown. The professional spun around to face her, legs still dangling like a marionette.

"Not as sorry as this one," she muttered. Simultaneously, a mound of darkness grew beneath her feet and lifted her to meet him eye to eye. The tendrils drew up and pressed on both sides of his head. "Where is it?"

He screamed for half a moment, until another shadow poured into his mouth and silenced him. He spasmed, and more shadows held him still.

"Where iiiis it?" she sang. The corner of her mouth curled into a smirk, and her eyes wandered to the side as if she was listening to something.

"Thank you!" she announced.

His head twisted, and another crack sounded. The shadows withdrew, and he dropped like a broken doll. She lowered the remaining shadows, and they dispersed.

"See? Easy, just…boring," she said. "I prefer to play with my food. Tell me again what you're doing here?"

"I, uh, *thought* I was saving you from that guy," I pointed to the crumpled corpse. She chuckled in condescension.

Her gaze moved from me, went up the adjacent wall, and traced to the top of the building I'd leapt from.

"You're cute and kind of delicious looking," she remarked. Her eyes dropped back to me and made a not-so-subtle evaluation. "But perhaps not incapable. That was quite the jump, and though I *obviously* didn't need your help, you might be useful. Even if not *during* this endeavor, you can definitely be useful *after* it."

The seductive look and the coy edge to her voice made the implication crystal clear. *If* I survived whatever quest she was in the midst of completing, I would be her "after party." I knew it to be her modus operandi…to celebrate successful missions that way. Jealousy welled inside me as I envisioned how many times, and with how many other people, she'd "celebrated."

Don't let it get to you. It's simply the state of things now and none of your business.

"Are you there?" she asked. She huffed in feigned indifference and walked away.

"Yes, miss, sorry, and I would love to accompany you," I said and stood to follow her. I caught her eye, smiled, and winked. "I'm here for you."

There it was, my first key phrase. The seed had been planted. Now it simply required reinforcement. She paused half a breath in thought and manifested a suspicious look. Just as quickly, it passed, and she regained her playful, cavalier persona. She stalked off, the tap of her heels echoing down the alleyway.

* * *

"Can I ask where we're going?" I asked, as I caught up.

"You may," she replied, in a flat tone.

I let a small chuckle escape. "Okay, so where are we going?"

"This way," she answered.

"I see. Well, then, may I ask, er, I mean, would you please tell me what we're doing?"

"You know, you haven't even asked who I am yet," she said with a hint of frustration.

Oops, she's right. I'm not supposed to know her, and people who don't know each other introduce themselves.

"Well, you haven't asked me, either," I said, hoping to salvage the mistake with playfulness. "But I will graciously relent. I'm David."

She stopped, turned, and looked me over once more.

"David, hmm?" She said. "Do you have a last name?"

"I do," I replied, with a sly grin. "Now, might I have your name?"

Amusement flashed across her face, and she smiled. A genuine smile, one that warmed my soul.

"Theresa," she said, and held out her hand as a lady would.

I took the fingers and kissed the back of her hand.

"Enchanté," I said. "Now, would you please tell me where we're going and what we are doing?"

"Fine," she responded, and held the smile. "*Where* is irrelevant; just follow me. *What* is the important bit, but my problem, not yours. So would you prefer to walk in front, and be my big, manly protector, or would you rather walk beside me where you can keep sight of me?"

"Well, I'd prefer to walk ten feet behind you to watch you walk. But I assumed I didn't have a choice. Where would *you* prefer me?"

"Take your pick," Theresa answered. "Now, tell me why you're really here. You *were* following me."

Blunt as always, but a beautiful opportunity for me.

"Well, truth be told, I'm looking for someone," I explained, while I took stride immediately next to her. "I believe your boss might be able to help me. Scratch each other's backs and all."

"Not sure you'd survive if I scratched your back." She snickered. "But that's fine. Survive, and you can tag along when I report in. Who is this person you're looking for?"

"Well, it's actually quite a story, uh, how far do we have to go?" I asked.

"It's a couple dozen blocks actually, so talk away," she answered. "Just keep your eyes, and *nose* open."

I tilted my head respectfully.

"So, there's this girl," I explained, "whom I'll describe as a stunning, beautifully proportioned, athletic brunette. On one particular night, she wore a red satin dress that accentuated all the curves, hair done up to show off her neck, classy jewelry, and dazzling hazel eyes."

"Sounds like my kind of girl," Theresa said. "Is there any chance you could set us up?"

"Let me tell my story," I scolded. "Anyway…she works for this billionaire, pretty-boy twenty-something—"

"Ugh, the rich, good-looking princess story trope," she groaned. "Really?"

"No, not really," I teased. "She's not really into him, but we'll get there. But this limo driver, our hero, picked her up one night, but realized she's way out of his league."

"Don't be mean. I've met some very nice and very *capable* limo drivers in my time," she said. I bit my tongue. "By the way, did you just head hop?"

"Did I what?" I asked.

"*Head hop*," she responded. "It's when you're telling a story from one perspective, but then swap to another perspective inside a single scene."

"I, uh, I don't know, just…"

A scent caught my nose. Perspiration, cologne-scented deodorant, and sushi breath trailed behind us. Other noises and smells came and went, but this had followed us for four blocks.

Head locked forward, she grabbed my arm casually and whispered, "He's not being too inconspicuous, is he?"

"Not so much," I answered. I half glanced at her, careful not to show any concern. "Think he's after what you're after?"

"Honestly, he probably just recognizes we're after something," she mused, "and wants to join in the fun. Then again, he might have been sent to stop me. Or, for all I know, he's here to kill you. You never can tell around here."

"Well, I'm glad we've narrowed it down," I replied. "Let's avoid letting him know *we* know. Do I have time to continue?"

She nodded and smiled, artificial, yet pleasant.

"Well, I'll try to stick with one perspective. The limo driver, whom it appears you might be sympathetic to, having *known* several…" I gave her a teasing side glance. "It was his first day with a particular client as an emergency replacement, and he hadn't gotten any real information yet, just a set of destinations. He drove to the directed spot in a somewhat middle-class neighborhood and picked up this gorgeous brunette, as I said. Naturally, he fell deeply in lust on sight."

"But, as you said, totally out of his league, right?"

"You'd think. But based on where he picked her up, he wondered if, just maybe, she's more on his level, like maybe the limo is a gift from a friend. She left the divider down, and he takes a chance, strikes up a conversation. Somewhat superficial, he steers clear of job and life stuff, just makes some good, flirty-bantery small talk.

"She played along, and he started to think, maybe, just maybe, there's a chance. At some point, he asked if it was a special occasion, and she explained it was a birthday party. At that moment, they arrived at the next destination. Limo driver waited while gorgeous girl retrieved a rich, good looking, famous guy."

"Billionaire pretty boy," Theresa said.

"Yes," I replied. "But he doesn't know that. He's crushed when the two get in the limo, and rich boy gets handsy, lovey dovey, and puts up the divider. He can only imagine what happened en route to the next stop, where the party took place. While he hung out in the servant's area, he searched the internet for rich boy, found out he was married, but the buzz claimed the marriage was rocky, and people were wondering who gorgeous girl was."

"I love how you call her gorgeous girl," Theresa interrupted. She tugged at my arm. With a flash of her gaze, she indicated our destination. We stood a couple dozen yards from a generic small grocery store, part of a chain that littered the city. In disbelief, I asked, "It's in a Mercury's Mart?"

"You go around back," she said. "See if you can drag our tail there and work out his purpose. Then take whatever action you feel necessary."

"You don't need me inside?" I asked. She scowled with eyes that asked, *Are you kidding?*

I gave a sarcastic salute and wandered to the alleyway. Before I disappeared into it, I gave an overly dramatic look around, verified she entered, and actively ignored our follower.

It came as no surprise the objective lay in a Beluanox corner store. The city only had so many abandoned churches, subterranean hideouts, hidden libraries, night clubs, haunted mansions, etc. Considering you couldn't walk five steps in the city without running into another sinister plot by this evil sect or that, it actually made sense. The only relatively safe places were the pawn shops and the hospitals. Except, of course, the abandoned hospitals…

* * *

As soon as I turned the corner, I leapt fast and far into the darkness. The alley ended in a tall wall a few yards past the back entrance to the store, and I hopped over it. On the other side, I waited for the scent of our interloper.

The possibilities ran quickly through my head. By the smell, he was merely human. Shifters carried the lingering scents of whatever they changed into. Mages, warlocks, witches, and the like always carried a scent commensurate with whatever medium they worked with—herbs, concoctions, sulfur, or even just plain ink and parchment. Outside perspiration, cologne, and mild (non-shifter) halitosis, he only smelt of gunpowder. A hunter.

A hunter, however, wouldn't be so obvious, even if he was a noob. This indicated a hapless adventurer who recognized some sort of quest and hoped to join in the fun. The denizens of the city were strange in that way. Ultimately, regardless of his reasons, my conclusion remained firm. As quietly as I could, I undressed and waited.

The scent strengthened, and a soft crunch of gravel announced his presence at the door. His feet shuffled about as he searched.

When the shuffling stopped, I figured he'd stopped looking and planned to enter.

Another great leap into the air took me in a high, tight arc, over the wall and down onto him. In the few seconds while airborne, my claws pushed painfully out through my fingers, my muscles swelled into bundled masses, and my jaw jutted out from my face to make room for my great fangs. Dark gray fur blossomed all over my body.

Airborne, I took stock of my prey. He was fairly tall, wiry, and had long, dirty blonde fashion model hair. Sunglasses straight out of *The Matrix* adorned his face, atop a mustache and six-inch goatee. Camouflage cargo pants, a black leather vest with lots of pockets, and semi-scuffed black boots made up the ensemble. Ambiguously militant or survivalist clothing, but still naturally fashionable. Over his back he carried a holstered shotgun and a machete. Though totally impractical in most places, somehow the setup worked in this city. Definitely a hunter, and clearly a ladies' man as well. Theresa would eat him up.

Excellent reflexes served him well. Though he nimbly blocked my attempt to rake him with my claws, my sheer weight knocked him onto his back. Undeterred, a blade appeared in his right hand and pressed gently toward me. It burned against my skin, and I flinched. A silver blade. I'll give him his due, the guy was fast. I suppose one has to be when you're a human who fights the supernatural.

"Easy, pal, don't hurt yourself," he said with a strained chuckle. "Not looking for trouble, not with you at least."

The blade gave me pause, which gave him room to scramble backward and onto his feet. He flicked out a second blade in his left hand and defensively shifted them about.

"No quarrel with you, just wondering if I can help out," he stated calmly. The weave of his knives was relaxed, skilled. He wouldn't be easy to take down. "Three's company, right? Can I ask what it is you're after?"

I forced myself to relax, and I grinned as best I could with my werewolf jaws.

"Honestly, I'm not too sure myself," I growled. I've always found it somewhat annoying how difficult speech is in that state. "But she wanted me to sneak up on whoever's inside. If you're game to join us not knowing the payout, be my guest."

With a wave of my big, gangly claws, I motioned to the door. I imagine it was comical, like the Beast trying to be polite to Belle at dinner. Doubt flashed in his eyes. In addition to my voice, my acting sucks in that form as well.

"No, please, you first," he said, eyes narrowed. My ruse had failed.

Screw it.

I charged into those shiny, sinister silver blades.

He danced backward and took a swing with one knife, and then the other. One slashed my left arm, which sizzled. The other missed.

As I closed in, I allowed him to stab me in my gut with the left blade so I could focus on grabbing the right arm, which I did. After he buried the blade in me, I grabbed the left arm as well.

Though fire exploded in my side and welled up inside me, I jerked him closer with both arms.

With a snarl, I snapped my jaws on top of his head.

He struggled about, left hand still firmly gripping the hilt of the knife he'd shoved into me. As it wiggled about, I began to see stars. By translating all that pain into anger, which I had in abundance, I tightened my bite until his skull cracked in my mouth. The hunter went limp, and I released the corpse to the ground.

With an angry roar, I fought to tear the cursed blade from my side. The tremendous agony sent my muscles into enough shock that my clawed fingers became numb. The fine motor skills necessary to tear the knife out simply weren't there, so I pressed both palms against it and slid it out, shaking the whole time. As soon as it left my body, I reverted to my human form and fell to my knees.

Then I spit everything out. Using my jaws to kill humans was another aspect of being a werewolf I'd never adapted to. Pieces of human flesh that stuck in my teeth made me retch, and for a moment I forgot the horrendous pain in my side.

"Sorry, *pal*, but three's a crowd," I sputtered weakly. I must have sat there for a good long time, unsuccessfully attempting to regain my strength.

When she opened the door, she found me on all fours, gasping for air, gagging, and spitting.

"Wow, attractive," she said. "But I guess that settles his intentions. Do you know if he was here for *you* or for *me?*"

I shook my head to convey I didn't know and spit one last time. Feebly, I attempted to stand. My legs failed me, and I immediately fell backward. The pain made me somewhat apathetic to the fact that I remained completely nude. I also knew she was the last person on Earth to be bothered by it.

Shadows stretched out from the walls and cradled me. She glanced around and took in the scene, focusing for a moment on the bloody knife that lay in front of me. Then she turned her attention to me.

"Ooh, that looks pretty bad," she said as she examined my side. "I can patch that up, but I'm guessing that won't heal too quickly."

I shook my head in agreement.

"Did you find what you were looking for?" I asked in a daze. A tendril of shadow worked its way up to my side and placed a small patch of black, nebulous material over the wound. Then it placed another on top of the cut on my right arm. *Huh, that's a new one*, I thought.

"No, in fact, I did not," she said. "They all confirmed it was there, but they all broke before giving me any meaningful info. Seeing as there were several of them—I really coulda used your help, by the way—I had to use what you might call excessive force once again. Anyway, think you're up to searching the place with me?"

* * *

"So, what happened with limo boy?" She asked as we meandered about the Mercury Mart. We'd locked the front door and switched the sign to "Closed." I downed my third "Demonic" energy drink and smiled on the inside. I had her hooked.

"Well, he waits around in the servant area." My gaze tracked around the store. "Where, somewhat oddly, gorgeous girl passes through a few times and even sits down once to talk. It kind of strikes him as odd that she would be back there, with the servants, in the middle of the party, but he doesn't want to ruin the chance to talk to her by asking about it." I stopped and sighed in frustration. "Hey, did the manager or workers here say anything at all? Any clues whatsoever?"

"The only thing I got was 'lowest level of hell,'" she answered. "Dramatic much, am I right?"

"Well, the lowest level of hell was frozen, right?" I said.

She smiled, we locked eyes, and she rushed to search the freezer section.

"So, late, late, after the party, gorgeous girl and rich boy hop back into the limo," I continued while I opened a freezer door, dug through the vegetables, and closed the door. "Rich boy was inebriated, handsier than before, and, as the divider went up, limo driver realized she was very disinterested in his advances."

"Ooh, the plot thickens," Theresa responded in a slight mocking tone, while she dug around in the pizzas.

"It ate at him for a good part of the drive," I explained. I slammed another door shut and huffed. "There's another freezer, right? Like a separate one they use in the back?"

Theresa closed the door to the ice cream section and stuffed a spoonful of mint chocolate chip into her mouth.

"Mmm, fink so," she mumbled. We trekked toward the doors to the back area and hunted for said freezer.

"A short while in, he heard actual arguing in the back and feared rich boy was fighting to take more than she wanted to give," I said. "He stopped the limo, raced to the back, and found rich boy completely unconscious."

"Well, that's a fun twist," Theresa said. "He rushes in to be the hero but finds out she most definitely doesn't need a hero."

"Yeah, so good on her, right?" I paused the tale again as I approached the industrial freezer. She got there first, as I was still moving pretty slowly. She jerked the handle and pulled. With a clunk and rush of air, the large metal door swung open. She stepped inside and resumed the search.

"Any buttons, handles, anything?" As I asked, I noticed the freezer door itself actually had two handles. One on the door, which she'd used to open it. The other, totally identical, was on the wall *next* to the door, which made it seemingly useless. Impulsively, I reached out and yanked on that handle. The insides of the freezer gave a loud hiss, and then a grinding noise.

Theresa gasped and jumped out.

"I don't know what I did, but I did something!" She chuckled. I pointed casually to the handle I'd just pulled. Her amusement turned to feigned anger, and she punched me on my good arm.

"You could have waited until I got out first!" she exclaimed. "You could have killed me just now."

"I didn't know what it could do," I retorted indignantly. "Plus, I assumed you could handle yourself."

She put a hand up, indicating I should wait a moment, and went into a sort of trance. The shadows wove their way down the stairs that had appeared like a pack of bloodhounds, sniffing their way around. Her gaze flickered around blankly. Then I heard a muffled cry, followed by a loud thudding noise. The shadows broke apart spontaneously, and I saw her snap back into her own mind.

"It's clear," she said with a sinister grin. She dramatically waved her hand forward. "You first."

"As you wish," I teased. With a sniff of the air, I picked up the scents of dust, mold, unfinished wood, candles, and fresh blood. Cautiously I stalked down the steps, doing my best to make little noise. The further down I went without any sign, sound, or smell of danger, the more brazen I got. As I turned the corner at the bottom of the stairs, I found a generic thug-type guard on the floor. Blood pooled around his head. He wouldn't be getting up anytime soon.

I continued down the narrow hallway, which wound around like a spiral toward the center.

"So?" she asked.

"Oh, so gorgeous girl explained she'd drugged him, as he usually got a little too frisky when drunk. Limo driver realized she'd used the term 'boss' when describing him, so he inquired on the nature of the relationship. Turns out she's the rich boy's bodyguard, whenever he leaves his swanky high-rise apartment, where he actually still lived with his wife."

"Ooh, game on, limo boy, get some!" Theresa said with excitement.

"Yeah, exactly. Ecstatic, limo driver helped her drop off the 'drunk' rich boy at his swanky apartment. As both were then off duty, she invited limo driver out for a drink."

"*She* invited *him?*" she asked. The conversation paused when we turned the last corner. The spiral opened into a large room with a stone pedestal in the middle.

A tall, jade statue of a dragon sat atop the pedestal. Its thin body, adorned with intricate gold inlay, wound its way up to a large, grinning head with emerald eyes. I'm going to be honest; I've become somewhat apathetic toward whatever "thing" we're always meant to find. Sometimes it's a talisman, some special book, a gaudy but wholly useless weapon, or sometimes even a media drive of some type. I've seen all types and kinds; at this point, my mind simply labels it the thing, and I remain unimpressed.

"Isn't it beautiful?" Theresa exclaimed. "Imagine, something so intricate, so valuable, and so powerful."

So gaudy, so dramatic…

"What's it do?" I asked. She shrugged.

"Whatever it does, my boss assures me it's the key to everything," she said with confidence. "Let's get it to him as quickly as we can."

We worked our way quickly back out of the spiral, too excited by our success to continue my story.

Remarkably easy to obtain. Before I could berate myself for such a careless rumination, I caught the sound of a small, hard object as it bounced down the stairs.

"Grenade!" I shouted.

I grabbed her and spun in order to shield her from the blast. The explosion sounded, but I felt no shrapnel rake into my back. I turned and found a wall of shrapnel falling to the ground as a shield of shadow dissipated.

"You keep trying to save me," she sneered, but then her smile warmed. "Don't think I don't appreciate it."

"Good to know," I said with a grin. "Anyway, we might have loitered too long down here."

Boots stomped down the stairs. I released her and flexed with all my might to initiate the change. My vision went red, my muscles bulged outward, and fur grew out all over. Claws pushed out from my fingernails, and my teeth lengthened to fangs once again. When my vision cleared, I found those familiar tendrils of shadow sneaking down the hallway toward the stairwell. My nose and ears foretold a pair of machine gun-wielding henchmen creeping cautiously down.

A crack of glass and a hiss resonated from somewhere above. Then, another...and another. Slowly, the sound of roaring flames and the scent of burning plastic overpowered my senses. The two henchmen on the stairs shouted and stomped back up. A cacophony of gunfire erupted from both inside and outside.

"Sounds like backup's arrived," Theresa said cheerfully. "Let's go!"

"Who's backup?" I asked skeptically.

"Does it matter?" she replied and crept to the stairs. Light danced unevenly from above, but the henchmen had disappeared. As I joined her, I found the freezer door through which we'd entered lay open, and flames crackled away beyond it. Theresa became noticeably concerned. She asked, "How are you with fire?"

"Fine for a little bit," I responded. "Why? Is it a problem for you?"

"Well, I don't like to admit it, but my shadows are weak in a blaze like that," she answered. Wide, uncharacteristically frightened doe eyes peered up at me. Long years prior, it had been exactly this type of vulnerability in a woman normally so self-assured and confident that had stolen my heart in the first place. "I'm embarrassed to admit that something as elemental as fire is a weakness. A mage's flame, or even a flamethrower, sure, but that assumes I have shadows to draw from. Up there, however, I just don't have...I mean there's—"

"It's fine," I said with a reassuring grin. I always found it endearing when insecurity caused her to babble. "Grab the idol, wrap yourself around it, and I'll carry you out. Cover yourself in whatever shadows you can, and I'll get you out."

As she huddled around the idol, I scooped her up off her feet with an arm behind her knees.

I gently folded her into the fetal position and molded my arms around her like a cocoon. She filled in the narrow gaps around my massive, fur covered arms with amorphous darkness.

After a quick, calming breath, I stared up into the great blaze, steeled my nerves, ducked my head, and charged up the steps. Eyes narrowed, I blocked out the immense pain of the flames, and stomped through the rapidly disintegrating Mercury Mart.

Several burning, unidentifiable corpses littered the floor, and the rows of prepackaged goods had been shredded by gunfire. All the windows were destroyed, save a low metal bar from the frame, so I leapt over that and into the street beyond.

The sting of bullets immediately replaced the burn of the flames as my charge continued through a line of pseudo-military looking a-holes lined up outside. More than a few of the bullets were silver, and they sizzled deep into my muscles.

One snapped my ankle, and I stumbled forward. I nearly dropped my precious cargo when I reached an arm out to catch myself.

I slowed, and the lead and silver that poured into me increased.

"He's out, pour it on, people!" I heard someone shout. "But try not to kill him, just weaken him and hold him here until Jeremy catches up!"

Who's Jeremy? The answer presented itself, and I mentally grimaced. I confirmed my conclusion by taking in the general clothing and grooming styles of the gunmen.

Frantically I attempted to muscle through the agony to drag us forward but felt myself weakening. I thought, perhaps, it was time for me to pop "the pill," but I reconsidered. Although we had cleared the Mercury Mart bonfire, things always got worse before they got better.

Theresa opened her eyes and looked into mine. Over the course of a brief eternity, her eyes went from fear, to concern, to realization, and then to anger and fury. She drew up a ball of blackness to engulf us.

The incoming fire stopped, and the cacophony of gunfire softened as if it drifted into the distance.

The ball wrenched around awkwardly in short jerks. The firing ceased entirely.

As much as I tried to block out the suffering, it overwhelmed me. Dazed, I barely perceived the darkness dissipate.

"David!" she cried, as she ran to cradle me. I discovered I'd reverted to human form, though a dozen silver slugs were still buried inside me. Each one burned like a tiny fireball. "David? Are you still with me?"

Through cloudy vision, I scanned about and found pieces of the gunmen strewn about. Each appeared ripped up by some great beast, torn apart by immensely powerful arms.

"You did this?" I croaked out.

"Yeah…once you got me clear, I could gather the darkness again," she said. She'd become far more powerful than the last time

I'd visited. It almost unsettled me. Faintly, I heard a single set of footsteps approach. Theresa and I turned our heads as one to regard our new arrival.

"Come for seconds?" Theresa snarled, her rage clear. The hunter, the one I'd killed earlier, stopped abruptly and looked around. He raised his hands to the air timidly and gave an awkward, uncomfortable grin.

"Nothing personal, I just, I mean, it *was* personal, but I can—" his words were cut short as a tendril of shadow shot out from an alleyway, wrapped around his neck, and snapped it, all in the blink of an eye.

"Why don't these assholes ever stay dead?" she mused. For a moment I feared she might attempt to sort out the answer to her question. Thankfully, as far as I could tell, she didn't. "Let's get you to my boss. When I explain you helped me retrieve this for him, he'll straighten you right out."

I assumed, since she didn't offer, that her shadow couldn't dig out the silver bullets. We limped along down the street. As is the norm in Beluanox, none of the people we passed seemed in any way perturbed by our appearance.

* * *

"So, what happened at drinks?" Theresa asked, as we hobbled along. She tried hard to support me, but even as a human, I weighed quite a lot. She mostly just braced me slightly as I hopped a little at a time on my good leg. "Good" meaning the leg that *only* had a bullet in the thigh, and not the calf and ankle as well.

"What?"

"The adventures of gorgeous girl and limo boy...what happened?" she asked.

Clearly she meant to take my mind off the excruciating trip through the streets. In my wretched state, I nearly lacked the motivation to finish the story. I began to doubt whether I cared to tell it.

"Oh, well...I mean sparks flew...crazy mad love ensued," I explained weakly.

"You mean, like, that night?" she said with big, interested eyes.

"Yeah. They didn't even finish their first drink. They played pool, she noticed him staring at her, um, 'curves' in the tight black pants she'd changed into..."

"You mean she caught him ogling her ass?" Theresa clarified.

I nodded.

"She practically dragged m—, *him* out of the place and back to hers," I said.

She turned us and led me through the automatic glass doors of a great high rise. A pair of security guards looked at me, then her, and let us pass without a word. We limped along the white marble floor toward a set of elevators reminiscent of ancient luxury hotels.

"So was this just a quick, passionate fling, or...?" she inquired. I assumed it was to keep me talking.

"Oh no, it was such an intense night, and he was such a gentleman the next morning, she decided to see where it would go," I explained. Indeed, I did find it easier to ignore the pain as I wracked my mind for details to supply. "Turns out they had quite a bit in common, hobbies, interests, dreams, et cetera... The whole thing blossomed into a several months' long relationship."

"So, happily ever after?" she asked. A ding sounded from the elevator, and the doors slid open to the sides.

"Not quite," I answered as we shuffled in. The doors closed slower than they'd opened. The darkest, most sinister elevator music I'd ever heard played quietly in the background. Parts of this whole city were seriously overdone.

"Rich guy?"

"No," I replied softly. "There was another woman."

Focus! Don't say things like that! Quick, fix it…

"Limo boy had another woman? I should've guessed he was a player. Or was he still reeling from an ex or something?"

"No, uh, rich guy's jealous wife, who assumed, just as everyone in the media did, that rich guy was screwing his gorgeous bodyguard."

Nice.

"Ooh, another decent plot twist," she joked. "And I'm guessing, just to make this a better story, it impacted limo boy instead of gorgeous girl. So, what…car bomb, cut brake line?"

"Well, you're right in principle, but not detail," I replied, though I had to pause to catch my breath. "The wife tried to poison…girl via the water bottles…knew husband never drank them… gor-g-girl did."

"Hey, stay with me now!" Theresa shouted, getting animated. I looked up to see the never-ending, slow-moving floor needle pass fifty-seven and continue. I assumed our destination to be the eighty-second floor, the top.

"Sorry," I gasped. I inhaled a long, deep breath. "Guy was in back of limo, waiting with girl for rich guy, took a sip, got sick…girl rushed him to hospital."

"Well, obviously he lived," Theresa said. "Because he's looking for this girl. So while recovering, did gorgeous girl lay the smackdown on rich bitch wife?"

"No," I said. "Just got him to a hospital, got him better, and the two ran off to another city."

"That's it?" she said, disappointed. "Just like that? I thought you were building up to some exciting conclusion or something. I mean, you just made this whole story up, right?"

I laughed. "Yeah, well, parts of it. It's mostly real, and in real life, there's seldom any kind of climax." I grinned cleverly. "No pun intended, but I mean, life just goes on in real life. It's not like most stories."

"So, what happened that he's looking for her here and now?" Theresa asked, lost in thought. With another solid *ding*, the door slid open again. The needle was pegged; we had arrived at the top. I wondered whether any of the intervening floors even had anything in them.

"She came here, to this city, and got herself lost," I said. "So here he is, searching for his beloved. Because he promised her he'd love her always and forever."

"Always and forever..." she said, and the words sat upon her lips. Her eyes wandered as if in a dream. I sensed the answer to the great question forming in her head.

"Sounds like I'm getting the tail end of a very touching story," a new, crisp, well-enunciated voice intruded.

We exited the elevator directly into a giant, luxuriously furnished penthouse. To our left stood a great intricate marble fireplace in which a large wood fire blazed. Along the far wall, beyond several different arrays of furniture, I found a fairly expansive mirror-backed wet bar. Further to our left, I discovered the "boss," a bespectacled businessman, immaculately dressed in an expensive silk suit. He sat at a large polished oak desk. The individual was relatively diminutive, at least compared to the rest of the city, but particularly noble looking. He displayed a very sour look on his face, a projection that he carried the weight of the world on his tragic shoulders.

In short, another damn brooding vampire.

"You have the idol, I take it," he inquired. As if in a trance, Theresa nodded and held it out. It floated from her arms and flew to the man. Theresa half-heartedly pointed to me.

"My Prince," she said hollowly, "he's injured, I told him you would heal him." She looked at me as she pointed, and her gaze locked onto me. Her eyes narrowed, and confusion seemed to clear.

"All in good time," the "Prince" responded with a sneer. "But before that—"

"I'm sorry, dude," I cut in. "But, let's be real, you're going to betray her because you're trying to start a gang war, or cover up some wrong doing, or whatever, to gain more power and whatnot, and you know she'll stand in your way, but, let me be real." I causally pointed to Theresa. "I think I just made a breakthrough here. You're kind of inconvenient right now. Can we just cut to the fight so I can get back to the girl?"

I fumbled in my pocket for a tiny capsule.

"How do you know of my machinations!" the prince shouted. Then he laughed the standard maniacal cackle. I retrieved my pill and tossed it into my mouth. "Never mind! It makes no difference. You're correct, and the answer is everything you've just said. I can't have this Girl Scout interrupting my plans with her lofty ideals!"'

He slammed his hand against a button, and the entire ceiling lit up with a blinding, harsh light. Theresa and I winced at our sudden blindness. The prince's laughter increased.

"Her magic is now useless, and you can barely walk!" He jumped nimbly on top of his desk and bared the fangs which sprang into his mouth. Theresa cowered against the wall and ignored the "boss." She continued to stare at me with squinted eyes.

"Dave?" she said. "Is it really you?"

"Yeah, Terry," I replied with a tender smile and tears building in my eyes. "It's me, I found you. Everything's gonna be okay. Now, you stay there a second, I gotta handle something."

I rolled my shoulders and writhed at the sting while the pill took effect. The bullets inside me pressed back out through their entry wounds. The tiny lumps of silver fell harmlessly to the floor. I roared and went full werewolf once again as the vampire charged at me.

Master vampires, as powerful as they are, are obnoxiously predictable in this city, the prince in particular. They'll invariably flash by and appear behind you, just off center, and slash at your throat or rake your back. However, timing is key. If you turn too early, they'll readjust and still appear behind you. I've had a good deal of practice getting the timing correct. That, and a few tricks to make it all easier.

I dispatched him quickly and tossed him into the fire so he'd burn up and intrude upon us no more. As I settled back into my human form, I walked to the desk and turned off the brilliant ceiling lights.

"Dave, what's going on?" she asked. These moments were always the trickiest. I had to maintain the façade of the world she lived in, and somehow remind her of who I was and who we were to each other.

"I've been looking for you for a long time," I said. It was mostly a lie, but there was a kernel of truth.

"How did you take my Prince down so easily?" she asked with wonder in her voice. The great, predatory, invincible shadow witch was gone. Only my vulnerable, bright-eyed love remained.

"They're really more intimidating than tough," I said. "But the important thing is, you remember me. I was so worried you might not remember me."

In a rush, she ran to me and made to wrap her arms around me. I dropped slightly and put my arms out to wrap around her underneath her arms, so when I stood, I lifted her off the ground. With a hand she pressed my face to hers, and we held a long, deep, kiss. Eventually, we broke free from each other.

"But why didn't I?" she asked softly. "How could I have forgotten the great love of my life?"

"Think of it as a curse," I said. "But I'm here now; that's all that matters. Come, let's sit by the fire."

She glanced around as I set her down gently. With a smirk and a tilt of the head, she moved toward the couch as I'd suggested.

"I suppose the late prince won't object, now will he?" she joked. "What about guards, will anyone come—"

"No, they won't," I said truthfully, and with confidence. None had ever shown up before. I gestured to the bar. "Wine? Pinot Noir?"

"I suppose that's awfully cliché in a place like this, but yes, please." She smiled. Her posture relaxed.

The situation became more familiar, more comfortable to her. I grabbed a crystal wine glass, poured the red liquid into it. Then I poured myself an amber glass of scotch. We sank into the green velvet couch and snuggled against each other. She grabbed the glass from me, took a sip, and melted into me. I wrapped my arm around her tenderly and leaned my head against hers. A tear of joy, sadness, or both slid down her cheek.

"So then is the curse broken now?" she asked with a hint of worry. Her muscles tensed back up a little. "Can you stay with me now?"

"Yes, it's broken," I replied. As usual, I huddled around that tiny little verisimilitude. At that moment, the "curse," a perfectly reasonable thing to call it in Beluanox, was in fact inactive. Any elaboration could have been disastrous. "And I'll stay as long as you want. Let's talk about all the good times, refresh your memory."

"What was that story you told?" she asked, a little confused. "That wasn't us, it—"

"Our real story doesn't really make sense here, does it?" I asked, and she shrugged. "It's part of a process someone thought up. The important thing is to tell you *a* love story, but one that makes sense for this city. The story itself opens up the part of your mind that the,

<cough> *curse* normally blocks. The mere fact of your imagining a love story can help bring our story back to the surface."

"That sounds a little complicated," she asked, and doubt crept back into her voice. "You brought me back on the first try?"

"Persistence saw me through," I replied. A lie of omission, I admit that freely. My first couple dozen tries were epic failures. It had taken a long time for me to find the right process, the right formula, to bring her back. Even so, it seldom succeeded. "But let's not speak of it. I'm here now. Say, does this fire remind you of that hot springs resort in that sleepy desert town, up in the mountains?"

"Ojo Caliente, yes." She smiled and snuggled deeper. Her fingers danced across my chest dreamily. "The one with the private open-air hot tubs. God, how could I ever forget that place? You lit that fire in the kiva fireplace and almost smoked us out. Mmmm...but that bed sure was comfortable, wasn't it?"

* * *

Hours later, light poured into the suite, and we awoke. We'd spent hours talking, remembering, dreaming of places we'd been and things we'd done. Some we'd never actually done, but only talked about, or "planned to do someday." It was all the same to her. She'd made some advances, but I'd gently redirected her with a new discussion. Thankfully, she drifted to sleep before she pressed the issue. I held her as she slept, stroked her hair, and whispered confessions to her.

"Where are we?" she asked sleepily.

"In the prince's suite," I responded. "Relaxing on his couch."

"Is he here?" she asked, befuddled. Her tone sharpened, as it had when I'd first found her.

"No, he's out just now, he said we could enjoy the suite," I answered.

"And you…you're that werewolf who helped me get the Green Dragon, right?" she asked, eyes narrowed. "Did we…?"

"No, I was a perfect gentleman," I said, doing my best to choke back tears. The worst part of my visits always occurred when her emotions reset. "And I'm sorry to say, but it's time I got going."

"Well, you're pretty boring, aren't you?" she asked indifferently and waved her hand. "See ya. I'm sure I'll have a new mission when the prince returns anyway."

"Certainly," I said. Instinctively, I leaned forward as if to kiss her, but caught myself just as she jerked away with an angry look of surprise. My heart sank. "Sorry, I, uh, take care."

I sullenly left the suite without another word from either of us. She likely forgot me the moment I left the room. I rode the elevator down, walked a few blocks to an apartment building, trudged morosely up the stairs, and let myself into an empty apartment room. I went to the terminal and logged out.

* * *

"Hey there, blue eyes," a hazel-eyed, athletic brunette said affectionately, but also cautiously. I can only imagine what she's thinking whenever I come back. She didn't always wait for me to come back, but over time she did so more and more. Now, she's always there when I return.

Snapping out is nothing like what's depicted in the commercials. You don't calmly awaken back in the real world, fresh and content. I believe it *was* like that in the early days, when they administered drugs to ease the return. Those drugs, however, proved to be *exactly* what caused the complications that left the alpha-testers trapped. Thus, without the drugs, the return is called "snapping out" for a reason. It literally feels like your brain pops loose from something, and you get quite a jolt to your heart. For some, the rush becomes addictive. I just get a minor headache and a good deal of nausea.

"I love you," I replied, as my heart calmed down. Forcing strength into my sleepy muscles, I reached out for her hand. She hesitated for a moment, but then she nervously reached out to grab it. We interlaced our fingers. Her eyes dropped to the floor and shifted around uncomfortably.

"Did she remember?" she asked.

I nodded.

"You know, I told her our story, yours and mine, with some embellishments, to get her to remember me?" I explained. "How sick is that?"

"She took *our* story?" she asked, bewildered. "How does that even work?"

"I don't know; maybe it's the emotion I put into it when I tell it. The point is to get her thinking romantically, and I have to be careful to avoid anything that might make her realize she's trapped in the alpha test of a fully immersive virtual reality world."

Her eyes wandered into space. The "Alphas of Beluanox" were famous in the gaming world. The first-round testers of a revolutionary fully-immersive gaming system never came out. Their minds became so inexplicably tied to the world that the first few they'd attempted to remove died instantly. Years later, court cases consistently ruled against removing them without liability. In the end, it was cheaper for the gaming company to leave them in than risk the damage of removing them.

"What embellishments?" she asked.

"I was a limo driver, not a bus driver, you were a bodyguard, not a security guard, your creepy old hostile workplace boss was a pretty boy billionaire," I said. She laughed. "I had to tie her in at the end, though. It doesn't work otherwise."

"I understand," she said. The smile evaporated from her face.

"I need to stop doing this," I said. "It's killing you, and it's not fair."

"No, it's not fair," she replied, her eyes welling up with tears. Her gaze shifted to look at Theresa, who lay comatose in the bed next to me. "Pretty much everyone who knows about this doesn't understand it, and I'm not even sure if I do. They all think I'm crazy loving someone like you, who has this." She motioned to the table where my first true love lay, immobile and unmoving. "But it's not fair to her, either. None of this is fair to anyone. If that were me lying in that bed, trapped in some si—, some…simulation, I can't imagine I'd want you to abandon me. I mean, part of me says I'd want you to move on, but…it's…I find it incredible how committed you are to her."

"It's not just her, I'm committed to you, too. More so, really…I spend most of my life…all of my *real* life, with you," I pleaded. Now tears welled in my eyes, too. "You're my island. You saved me when I was…lost and adrift. You're the reason I still live in the real world, that I don't just stay in there with her…"

She put a hand out to silence me.

"I know, and it's your love for her that made me fall in love with you, if that makes any sense," she said, though her face betrayed that the concept still confused her.

"It doesn't," I answered, "but it doesn't have to. I really don't know how much longer I can do this, as much as I love her. It's barely even her anymore. When we met, if you'd made me choose between you and her—"

"I'd never have made you make that choice," she protested.

"But *if* you had, I'm sorry, but it would have been no contest," I continued. "But *now*…if you made that ultimatum today—"

"I wouldn't."

"—I'd choose you," I said. "I mean, *I choose you. You* are the one I want to grow old with, here, in the real world. I love you, forever and for always."

"I know," she said softly and kissed my forehead. "So come on. Let's go home."

* * * * *

Casey Moores Bio

Casey Moores was a USAF officer, as well as a rescue and special ops C-130 pilot for over 17 years- airdropping, air refueling, and flying in and out of tiny little blacked-out dirt airstrips in bad places using night vision goggles. He's been to "those" places and done "those" things with "those" people. Now he is looking forward to a somewhat quieter life where he can translate those experiences to fiction. He is a Colorado native and Air Force Academy graduate, but has also become a naturalized Burqueño, planning to live in New Mexico forever.

# # # # #

Sweet Simmer by
Kat Beaty

I t was supposed to be a boring night, but Kenneth ensured that was not to be the case.

"Kára!" He flopped into the booth next to me, slightly sweaty and smelling like he was on fire. I double-checked to make sure he wasn't *literally* smoking or on fire. It happened from time to time. He'd been dancing with several of the young ladies in the club, and I hated it. Not that I could tell *him* that, as he was my boss, and criticizing one's boss generally wasn't a good idea. And if I told him, then he'd *know*. He couldn't *know* under any circumstances. So I kept my mouth shut, tried to ignore him, and did my job. I kept my eye on a few people in the area for their potential to do violence. I only intervened if they got too close to Kenneth. Then all bets were off.

"You should have a drink! Dance with me!" He wasn't drunk, though he had been drinking, which wasn't that unusual. He liked to be in control, and being drunk was decidedly *not* in control.

"Is that an order, sir?" I asked, keeping my gaze on a man at the bar. He was getting very frustrated that the bartender wasn't paying him enough attention. He was also getting snubbed by a young lady out with her boyfriend. The boyfriend was trying to keep things civil, but the other man was preparing for a physical altercation. Too much testosterone and alcohol. My sisters would've loved him.

157

"Can't you take some time off working just for a *minute*?" Kenneth complained, lounging across my lap. He deliberately tried to aggravate me. He knew I was very territorial about my personal space, but he took every opportunity to invade it.

"I'm on the clock," I reminded him patiently, "that means I *can't* stop working, sir."

"Ugh." Kenneth stretched out, securing his position across me. Three of the women he'd danced with glared daggers at me from across the club. "When are you going to loosen up, woman?"

"I relax on my days off, sir."

It was a long-standing discussion. I'd been Kenneth's bodyguard for nearly thirteen years, and we'd been friends for over twenty. Kenneth had always hated my work ethic, even when we were kids, and I didn't go out and play before finishing my homework.

"You don't *take* days off, Kára!" He finally sat up, getting off me. I could have moved him easily, but once again, I tried not to offend my boss. He settled into the booth next to me and flung his arm around my shoulders. "Do you even *have* a life?"

"My job is my life, sir."

"You're impossible, do you know that?"

"You've told me so many times, sir."

"Are you *ever* going to drop that 'sir' nonsense?" Kenneth snapped at me, exasperated.

"Not while I'm on the clock, sir."

"You're *always* on the clock," he mumbled grouchily. He didn't like that I was a workaholic, and I didn't like that he flirted with everything on two legs, but there was nothing to be done about either one. The man at the bar had decided enough was enough. He swung at the boyfriend and got a face-full of bar for his trouble. I wrapped an arm around Kenneth's waist and lifted him to my other side. The new position put him behind me if the fight got too rowdy. I didn't really expect it to, considering George was the bouncer that night, but it didn't hurt to be cautious.

Kenneth, for his part, didn't seem to have a reaction to me bodily moving him, and continued complaining about my lack of work-life balance. Considering how often I had to move him to keep him out of trouble, he'd gotten used to me maneuvering him around. He gave the fight a cursory glance and then ignored it, focusing on me. The trio of women across the club were gossiping about me and trying to see what made me so special to someone like Kenneth. Of course they saw a woman sitting next to him and assumed she was a fling, rather than his bodyguard.

I got that a lot.

Kenneth was *beautiful*. That was the best word to describe him, and honestly, it was unfair how pretty he was. He had ginger hair that was a deep rust color rather than orange. The messy locks were almost always styled in a "bro flow" cut (his words, not mine), because Kenneth thought it made him look dashing. Unfortunately for my sanity, he was correct. It gave him that windswept, knight-in-shining-armor look that made women swoon when he passed. He kept a short beard and mustache combo, because if he ever went clean-shaven, he'd look like a teenager. (He had a rough case of baby face.) There was a smattering of copper freckles across his nose and high cheekbones. The real slap in the face for his beauty was his bright blue eyes. I'd witnessed many an individual getting lost in said eyes. I had myself on several occasions, but I was professional enough to keep it to myself.

Kenneth was taller than me, but I was barely average height, so that wasn't particularly surprising. He was broad and lean, built like a swimmer, though I'd never seen him willingly jump into a pool. He was my best friend, my employer, and the most infuriating person I'd ever met. In short, I was utterly in love with the man.

Not that I could say anything, because he couldn't *know*. That would be the end of my career. And since my career was my life, I'd have to give that up, too. I'd die of embarrassment. Him *knowing* would just ruin absolutely everything. So I made a concerted effort that he never, ever find out. It would only be worse if my sisters found out. I'd probably be excommunicated if they did.

"Why don't we ever go out as *friends* anymore?" Kenneth was still whining.

"Because I'm a workaholic and going out with you means coming to crowded places like these, which is just asking to get attacked," I replied blandly, "sir."

"We don't have to go *clubbing*," Kenneth muttered with a pout. I might've just upset him. Damn it.

"I'm paranoid, and that means going out is *not* in my future, sir," I continued, trying to lessen the blow of my dismissal.

"If you can't leave the house, you should see a shrink for that," Kenneth replied, stifling a grin. Well, at least I hadn't offended him.

"I can quite obviously leave the house, sir," I pointed out, "seeing as I'm *here*."

"Yeah, but this is *work*, Kára."

George got his hands on the drunken upstart at the bar and hauled him from the club. I let out a sigh of relief. Guarding a man who liked being surrounded by loud music and warm bodies writhing against each other with the heavy stink of alcohol in the air was not the easiest job in the world. But I didn't have much of a choice. Wherever Kenneth wanted to go, that's where I had to be. The three women still glowered at me from across the club. They didn't intend to do any physical harm to me, but they wished it upon me. They'd likely confront me before I left for "stealing their man." As if Kenneth would even be interested. I'd seen him flirt with every person under the sun, and yet he *never* went on dates.

"Shall we go, sir?" I didn't want to be out anymore and, considering Kenneth hadn't had anything new to drink *or* gone out to dance again, he seemed to be winding down for the evening.

"Sure." He sighed a bit but followed me out of the booth obligingly. I collected his wallet, phone, and keys from the booth where he'd left them and grabbed our coats.

"Bitch!" Cold liquid drenched me as I turned around, and I blinked in shock. The women from across the club had *thrown* their drinks at me. It was so unexpected and utterly pathetic that I almost burst out laughing. People didn't throw drinks at me, they threw knives, or better yet, spears. I considered my options and decided to just ignore them. They were all human and not worth the effort of a confrontation. Besides, I guarded *Kenneth's* body, not my own. Any altercation would just put him in danger. In no way were these women enough of a threat to be taken seriously. It was a little comical how much they thought they mattered.

"Shall we, sir?" I shrugged on my coat and offered Kenneth his. Fortunately, I stood between him and the women, because his eyes burned with fire. Literally. I cleared my throat to get his attention. His gaze focused on me and he took a deep breath, shutting his eyes carefully. When he looked back at me, the baby blues were back, though he didn't look any happier about the scenario.

"George," Kenneth said, voice calm, "escort these ladies out." The bouncer had approached us as soon as the drinks had been thrown. Without hesitation, he herded the trio away from us, ignoring their drunken protests. When the owner of the club kicked you out, there was nothing you could do. Kenneth followed me through the throng of people, staying close to my back, as I'd instructed him.

When we stepped out into the cold winter air, I was sticky from the sugary drinks and a little irritable. I was a patient individual, but even *I* had my limits. Kenneth shivered against the cold and rubbed his hands together, bouncing in place.

"Let's get you out of the cold, sir," I said, gesturing toward his car. Resolutely, Kenneth didn't move toward the vehicle.

"Why'd you let them do that?" He glowered at me.

"I didn't let anyone do anything, sir."

"That's bullshit, Kára. You can sense violent intentions. Why'd you let them throw their drinks at you?" Kenneth shivered in earnest as a gust of wind nearly knocked him over.

"They didn't *have* violent intentions, sir. They just wanted to embarrass me," I explained. Magic worked in strange ways. My magic allowed me insight, a gut feeling really, into the violent natures of people around me. I didn't have to see them to feel their intentions, but I could only really sense aggression. Anything else existed beyond my magic, so I was totally guessing on the embarrassment angle. I experienced enough of humanity to be pretty good at assessing other intentions without the use of my magic.

"Throwing drinks is pretty violent."

"Yes, sir." There was no point in arguing. Even though I was *his* bodyguard, Kenneth was notoriously protective of me. It had taken a long time for us to come to a compromise over his protectiveness and my job. He knew to obey me when I was focused on protecting him, and I let him mother-hen me when we weren't in danger anymore.

"Trying to humor me won't work, Kára." Kenneth tried to glare at me, but he was shuddering too hard for it to be effective. I stepped forward, angling my body so the wind crashed into my back, trying to offer him some sanctuary from the cold. It didn't work particularly well, but it was the thought that counted.

"Let's get you out of the cold, sir," I said, "then we can continue this discussion."

While Kenneth *wanted* to be the one calling the shots, he was highly sensitive to cold. He gave in without much fight, and I got him settled in the back seat of the car with a heavy wool blanket on top of him. I kept the blanket in his car during the winter for these particular circumstances. At first Kenneth had made fun of me, but after the third time using it, he realized it was a genius idea.

"I hate it when you do that," Kenneth grumbled as I slid behind the wheel.

"Do what, sir?"

"Patronize me."

"I only patronize you when you act like a child, sir."

"You know," Kenneth said, "you add the 'sir' bit to be respectful or something, but then you say crap like that, and it's obvious you're just trying to hide your sass."

"Yes, sir." I bit back a smile and drove him back to his house. Technically I lived there, too, but Kenneth owned it. I shuffled him into the warmth of the house and made him wait in the front hall while I checked the place out. It took a few minutes, because Kenneth's house wasn't small, but he stayed by the front door the whole time it took me to make sure we didn't have any unexpected visitors. I'd never found someone before, but the danger to Kenneth's life was too much to let myself get lazy.

"Clear," I told him. Kenneth shrugged out of his coat and went to flop on the couch in the living room. I went to the front door to lock it, because he hadn't.

"Go relax, Kára," Kenneth ordered, "we're safe in the house. Get cleaned up."

"Yes, sir." I made my way to my side of the house.

"Stop calling me 'sir!'" Kenneth yelled after me, making me grin.

The staircase split the house down the middle. The kitchen and dining room were on one side, while the living room and office were on the other. The upstairs had a master suite over the living room side, and two guest rooms and a bathroom over the kitchen side. The basement was finished, and Kenneth had turned it into his own private gym. Kenneth had given me the two guest rooms for my own space. The landing on the top of the stairs separated the bedrooms. While he might not have any respect for my personal space, Kenneth never intruded onto my side of the upper floor.

I showered, washing the sugar and alcohol from my body, and blatantly ignored my clothes. I'd take care of them later. I felt too lazy to do anything about it tonight. My hair was a tangled mess after washing it, so I spent a full five minutes combing it out. The platinum blonde locks were the envy of my sisters. (I was the only one of us to have such a pale color.) I methodically scrubbed my streaked makeup off. It didn't take long before it was just me and my tattoos.

Part of the reason people judged me harshly when they saw me were because of my deep green tattoos. They were gifts, and I'd worked hard to earn them, so I wasn't ashamed of them, but it did influence how others perceived me. I had a thick line that ran from the top of one ear to the other, across my cheekbones, and curving over my nose to show the completion of my training. My second tattoo was another thick line from the center of my lower lip, down over my chin, indicating my mastery of all weapons. I had a small valknut on the right corner of my jaw, with an equally small runic "k" on the left corner, representing my allegiance to Odin and the first letter of my name respectively. I had a Web of Wyrd along the right column of my neck to symbolize the interconnectedness of fate and time. My shoulders were capped with the Helm of Awe on my left to grant me physical, mental, and spiritual protection, and a Vegvísir on my right as a compass to keep me from getting lost.

Each one had taken all my strength and will to earn, and I wouldn't trade them for anything.

I threw on my favorite pajamas (bright pink, fluffy, and covered in kittens), which were at least two sizes too big, and tromped back down the stairs to get some water before going to sleep. Kenneth was still on the couch, but he'd fallen asleep sometime while I was getting ready for bed. It honestly wasn't fair how attractive he was, even asleep. Most people would get bedhead or drool or something, but not Kenneth. He stayed perpetually perfect.

I filled up my water bottle and looked at him with a heavy sigh. He hated sleeping on the couch. He said it hurt his back. He must've been too lazy to walk up the stairs. I sighed again and hoisted him into my arms, bridal style. He was lucky I had superhuman strength, because otherwise he'd be whining about a sore back in the morning. I hauled him up to his bedroom and deposited him on his bed, covering him up with a thick, downy blanket. I allowed myself the luxury of watching him for a few moments before brushing some stray hairs from his face.

Then I realized how absurdly creepy that was and snuck out back into my room. Why did I have to be in love with my boss? I was being punished for *something*, I just knew it.

* * *

As a light sleeper, when the window downstairs crashed, I awoke instantly. I got out of bed and grabbed my sword and shield, cursing that I'd forgotten to turn on the alarm before passing out. Most intruders would be scared off by the loud noise without any violence whatsoever. I crept silently across the landing to check that Kenneth was still asleep. Which he completely was. The man could sleep through an earthquake.

Downstairs, I felt four different people moving through the broken glass. Each of them felt aggressive and violent, all directed at Kenneth. Not much of a surprise there. Why they'd decided a broken window was the best idea, I had no clue. Perhaps they couldn't pick locks. But they weren't expecting me, or they'd have used a quieter entrance. I studied their intentions for another moment. They wanted to do violence against Kenneth, but they didn't want to kill him. Maybe they wanted to kidnap him. Well, that wasn't going to happen. Not while I had breath in my body.

I slipped down the stairs, taking care to step on the sides of the treads so they didn't creak. The four people stood in the dining room, trying to arrange themselves in such a way that they weren't making noise anymore. Too little too late. I stepped into the foyer and eyed them while they were frantically hand-waving at each other. Two werewolves, a vampire, and a human, all male. Weird. Vampires and werewolves didn't usually get along, and humans were just food to vampires.

When they finally looked up, they froze. They weren't expecting a tattooed woman in too-big, pink, fluffy, kitten pajamas wielding a sword and shield standing in the foyer.

"You've entered the wrong house," I told them calmly. One of the werewolves swore under his breath.

"We just want the phoenix, and we'll be on our way," the human said.

"The phoenix is under my protection," I answered, "You will not touch him."

"You idiot, that's a Valkyrie!" the vampire hissed.

"How did we not know he had a Valkyrie?" one of the were-wolves snarled. I *tsk*ed loudly, interrupting their little spat.

"Someone didn't do their research." I shook my head. "Too bad. This is your last chance to leave now, or I'll kill you."

"She can't take on all four of us," the human muttered.

"Yes, she can." The vampire backed away from me.

"Kára?" Kenneth's sleepy voice distracted all of us. I didn't look away from the intruders because I wasn't an idiot. The vampire wouldn't do anything, as he was showing proper deference to my station, but the human wasn't well-versed on Valkyries, so he'd try something stupid.

"Stay back," I ordered. Of the two of us, it was a toss-up who was more deadly, but Kenneth's fire would destroy the house. I would, at most, destroy the furniture.

"I'm not fighting a Valkyrie," the vampire insisted, trying to get back out the window without letting his gaze leave me.

"You have ten seconds to leave," I said, keeping my focus on the intruders.

"Or what?" The human had bravado, but his werewolf buddies weren't liking their chances, especially with the vampire half out the window.

"The number one rule of dealing with a Valkyrie," I told him with a small smile, "is we don't make threats; we *are* threats."

The werewolf who hadn't yet spoken was getting agitated by Kenneth's presence. The sight of their goal was proving to be too tempting. He was going to get violent sooner rather than later. The human was on the edge, trying to decide if Valkyries really *were* that scary. The other werewolf hesitated, his urge to fight quelled by his knowledge of Valkyries. The vampire finally got out the window and fled.

"It's three-on-one, we've got the advantage," the human insisted. That excited the werewolf who was itching for a fight. His eyes started to glow yellow, the tell-tale sign a werewolf was going to change. I needed to take care of him before he shifted. Claw marks were impossible to get out of hardwood floors.

"Time's up." I heard the grin in Kenneth's voice. He'd fully woken up, apparently. He always enjoyed watching me fight, though he'd never told me why. I moved forward a couple steps, to get out of the way of the stairs, and readied myself for their attack. The antsy werewolf took the bait immediately, throwing himself at Kenneth with a snarl. A werewolf would normally be able to make that jump with ease, but not if there was an obstacle in the way. That obstacle being me.

I spun around, slamming my shield into the werewolf's shoulder with a sickening crunch. The wolf howled in pain and crumpled to the floor. Ugh. What a weakling. Most werewolves could handle broken bones, no problem. They were more irritating than painful, especially since werewolves healed so fast. But this one just fell apart. Either he'd never had a dominance fight in his pack, or he was a new wolf. The pain triggered fury, and his intentions went from "attack and maim" to "tear apart" in a blink. I brought my sword down, separating his head from his body before he could so much as growl.

The other two stepped forward to attack me, hoping I'd be distracted by the first attacker and wouldn't notice them. I sensed their intent a moment before they moved. I turned into them with my arms outstretched, knocking them both flat on their backs. I reversed my grip on my sword and brought it down on the werewolf's neck, while I brought the shield down on the solar plexus of the human. The human wheezed out, eyes tearing up as I knelt down next to him.

"Three-on-one against a Valkyrie will *always* be an advantage in her favor," I told the human before stabbing him through the heart.

"Anywhere to go?" Kenneth asked. I turned to look at him. He sat on the steps, his chin in the palm of his hand, watching me with literal fire in his eyes.

"No," I replied, getting to my feet. I was obligated to bring the souls of warriors to Valhalla, but frankly, there weren't many *real* warriors in the world anymore. None of the intruders were worthy of anything more than a quick death. "I'll clean this up. Go back to sleep."

"No."

I looked at him, brows furrowed.

"This is my house, and when you call the police, they'll want to question me, too. So you'll have to wake me up anyway. How about *you* go rest while *I* call the cops and clean up?" Kenneth suggested. I gave him a dark look, and he laughed. "Here, you call the cops, and I'll make hot chocolate." He always bribed me with chocolate. And it always worked.

"Now you're speaking my language." I smiled at him. Kenneth grinned back, showcasing a pair of dimples, and got off the stairs, meandering to the kitchen.

"Oh, and *try* to sound freaked out this time; the cops already think we're weird," he called over his shoulder. I rolled my eyes and went to the house phone, dialing the police.

"There are *intruders* in my house!" I said frantically, once the line connected, "I thought they were going to *kill* me!"

* * *

It took seven hours for the scene to be completely processed, for us to be interrogated, and for everyone to leave. By that point it was morning already, Kenneth had bribed me with several mugs of hot chocolate, and I was exhausted. For his part, Kenneth didn't look much better. But the human authorities assured us it was an open-and-shut case of self-defense, so they shouldn't need any more information from us. We'd met the detectives before, thanks to all the previous intruders, but there was a selkie on the force who helped us stay under the radar. For the most part. He was a selkie, not a miracle worker.

"Long night." Kenneth draped himself over me on the couch.

"Yep." I didn't fight him, mostly because I liked it too much.

"One of these days, you'd think it'd get out that the phoenix in the area has a Valkyrie bodyguard." Kenneth sighed and stretched himself more comfortably over me.

"One can only hope," I agreed, "maybe then people will stop trying to kill or kidnap you in the middle of the night."

"They wanted to kidnap me?"

"Sure did."

"Can we let them try? Just once?" Kenneth asked, excitedly.

"No."

"Kára!" He whined.

"Kenny!" I mocked him. That had been my nickname for him when we were children. He got to a point in our teenaged years where he refused to let *anyone* call him such a "juvenile" name. Well, anyone except me. He said since I had come up with it, only I was allowed to use it.

"You should call me that more often." Kenneth grinned.

"When I'm not on the clock," I agreed.

"You're the best, Kára."

I let his words warm the little cockles in my heart and pretended like my sisters wouldn't make fun of me for the rest of my life if they ever found out about this. Odin help me, they would absolutely ruin my life if they knew. But it would still be better than if Kenneth knew, because then I'd never be able to talk to him again without dying of constant embarrassment.

"There's something bothering me about this," I said slowly. Kenneth *humm*ed a question mark. "Kenny, why would two werewolves, a vampire, and a human team up to kidnap you? It just doesn't make sense."

"Maybe they don't like my nightclubs?"

"They specifically called you 'the phoenix,' as if that were your only interest to them. I don't think it's the nightclub thing." I looked at Kenneth, chewing my bottom lip. "There's something else going on here. I don't like it."

"You're too paranoid, Kára." Kenneth shook his head. "*Everybody* wants a phoenix. We're pretty rare, you know. That's why I need the best bodyguard in the business." His charming grin did nothing to assuage my fears.

"I don't like this at all," I informed him.

"You don't like *anything.*"

"That's not true," I argued. "I love chocolate."

"Do I have to worry about losing you to Willy Wonka?" Kenneth teased.

"Of course not, sir."

"Don't call me that!"

I laughed. Kenneth's stomach rumbled horribly before I could respond any other way. That made me chuckle again. He sighed heavily and sat up, getting off me.

"Ugh. I don't wanna cook," he whined, scratching at his scalp and mussing his hair up.

"I'll go fetch breakfast," I offered. Kenneth brightened up immediately.

"Doughnuts?"

"Fine." I rolled my eyes. "But you have to promise to stay inside, away from windows, and—"

"*Don't* answer the door for *anybody.*" Kenneth rolled his eyes. "Yes, Kára, I've done this before. It's less effective when there's a window missing."

"I boarded it up." We both looked at the plywood I'd put up after the police had left. It was pretty shoddy work. I could fight just about anything, but actually *building* something was beyond my capabilities. And I wasn't a very good cook. Hence why I'd offered to go purchase breakfast instead of making it. It was safer for everyone that way.

"I'll go work out in the gym," Kenneth offered, "will that satisfy your paranoia?"

"It's only paranoia if I'm wrong," I reminded him, "and considering how often I'm right, you should be thanking my preservation instincts."

"Go fetch me doughnuts, woman!" Kenneth shoved at me, barely moving me. He might have been a phoenix, but he didn't have super strength. I did.

"Yes, sir." I forced myself to get off the couch. Kenneth protested the title vehemently as I got myself ready to leave. It took longer than was really necessary, but I had an image to maintain. No self-respecting Valkyrie would be caught dead without her hair and makeup done. Thankfully, the makeup part was easy, as it was just thick kohl around my eyes. My hair was more of a chore, as I had to put my hair back in a thick faux-hawk plait with a few tiny braids pulling the rest of my hair back from my face. Each Valkyrie had a specific braid that was hers and hers alone. Mine was a little more elaborate than most of my sisters, so it took longer to do.

By the time I was presentable, Kenneth had made himself coffee and was loudly complaining about the lack of doughnuts in his life. I made sure he went down into the basement and then departed. The local doughnut shop had the best pastries in the city, and Kenneth and I had been buying doughnuts from them since we were children. That was how we'd met. Because of that, we got a pretty nice discount for anything we wanted from them. We never took advantage of it, on principle really. Kenneth said he had enough money to buy whatever he wanted, so it didn't make sense for him to get a *discount*. He argued he should pay *more*, but Mrs. Chopra wouldn't hear of it.

Because the shop was fairly close, I decided to just walk over. I warned Kenneth I'd be back in a half hour and he yelled at me to "feed me already!" I laughed almost all the way to the bakery. Mrs. Chopra, as always, manned the register with a pleasant smile and quick eyes. I doubted the shop ever had issues with petty theft or anything like that. She was scary enough *nobody* argued with her. Odin's beard, I was a *Valkyrie*, and she scared me.

"Kára, where is your young man?" I always thought I was prepared to see Mrs. Chopra and, without fail, she caught me off-guard and feeling self-conscious. It must've been a Mom Thing.

"He's not my young man, Mrs. Chopra. He's at home."

She sucked her teeth, pursing her lips and eyeing me up and down. I felt like a piece of meat under that stare.

"You are getting old. Why do you wait for him?"

Yup. There it was.

"I have plenty of time, Mrs. Chopra."

"He will never figure it out. You must make him see." Mrs. Chopra ignored me. "I can help."

"No, thank you, Mrs. Chopra." The *last* thing I needed was a meddling Indian mother in my life. She sucked her teeth at me again and rang up my usual dozen doughnuts.

"Do not wait too much longer," she ordered me.

"Yes, ma'am." I averted my gaze, knowing better than to aggravate a higher predator, and slipped out the front door.

I blame it on the fact that I was trying to escape the third degree from the closest person to a mother I had, combined with the significant lack of sleep. That was the only reason I wasn't paying attention

when the van skidded to a stop next to me, right in front of the bakery. Of course, once the doors opened, and three trolls jumped out
at me, I perked up pretty fast.

I dropped the box of doughnuts, but a troll had already gotten
his arms around my torso, pinning my arms to my sides. I jumped
and kicked the second troll in the chest, knocking him backward and
shoving against the troll holding my arms tight. I threw my head
back, hearing his nose crunch under the force. He let go of me due
to his watering eyes. With my arms free, I was able to dodge the
punch from the third troll and kick him in the knee. He howled and
dropped down onto said knee. The second troll grabbed my wrist. I
pulled back against his hold and slammed my fist onto his forearm.
The first troll tried to get a new grip on my torso, but I kicked him in
the face, blinding him with blood. The second troll still had a tight
grip on my wrist. I turned into his chest and flipped him over my
shoulders, forcing him to let go. The third troll had gotten back to
his feet. He tackled me into the van. I smashed my fist into his temple, causing his eyes to roll back in his skull as he lost consciousness.

"Go!" one of the trolls yelled. I rolled the unconscious one off
me, but the other two had already gotten in and shut the door. I
threw myself bodily at one of the trolls, knocking him over. He
threw his fist out, catching me in the jaw. It hurt. Trolls hit like
freight trains. The other troll clamped his arms around my torso,
pulling me off his buddy. I tried to lash out with my feet, but the
troll who'd hit me grabbed my legs.

"We got her!"

I stopped fighting. I needed to preserve my strength for escaping
from them. It wouldn't happen in transit, as I had two trolls literally
holding me still. The third one was still unconscious, but he wouldn't

be for very long. They'd probably chain me up. Ropes couldn't hold me. Why did they want me? It had to be something to do with Kenneth. They'd figured out they needed to get me out of the picture to get to him. And he had no idea I'd been taken.

Shit.

"Let me go, and none of you will die," I told them. My calm demeanor freaked them all out, but the trolls didn't let go of me. That was fine. As soon as I had more space, I'd make my move.

"How were you planning on killing us?" the man in the front seat, a human, asked. Humans always thought they were the top of the food chain. I rolled my eyes.

"I figured that was obvious," I replied.

"You have no weapons," he added, "and I have three fully-grown trolls."

I couldn't help it; I started laughing.

"You told him you were fully grown?" I looked at the trolls, who seemed a bit abashed at getting caught. "These trolls are adolescents *at most.* You could barely fit *one* fully-grown troll in this van. The fact that you have three means they're not adults."

The human glanced over his shoulder to scowl at the trolls.

"Besides, if you think I have no weapons, you truly have no idea what a Valkyrie *is.*"

The trolls shifted uncomfortably, tightening their grip on me in their nervousness. That was actually a good thing for me. As long as they had a tight grip, they were exerting themselves. Then, whenever we got to where we were going, they'd be weaker and easier to get away from.

"Shut up," the human growled at me. I looked at the trolls and shrugged. I'd been kidnapped before. And the fact that the human didn't even know what a fully-grown troll looked like told me the entire operation was amateur. They'd learned about my existence from the vampire the night before and had thrown together a slap-dash attempt to get me out of the way to get to Kenneth. I was irritated that it had worked at all. I had to get out of their captivity so I could get home and protect Kenneth. Assuming they weren't going after him right now, which would be the smart thing.

The trolls didn't like my blasé attitude. They kept eyeing each other, not liking anything about the scenario. The troll I'd knocked out groaned as he came to. If I had to guess, they'd just been hired recently, so their employer would send them off as soon as they delivered me. Or maybe kill them. I didn't know. I knew they wanted me alive for some reason. No one, to date, had been able to capture and hold a Valkyrie. That the person in charge thought he *could* was incredibly arrogant.

"Put that bag over her head!" the human snapped. Neither troll holding me wanted to release me to grab the bag in question. The troll who'd just regained consciousness sluggishly grabbed it and threw it over my head. The black bag wasn't anything special. It wasn't even particularly thick, as I could still see light through it. Amateurs. It pricked my pride that I'd been kidnapped by *amateurs*. My sisters would *kill* me for this. And who knew what Odin would do.

"You know, I still know where we're going," I informed the human obligingly. I could *feel* the surprised looks being tossed around. "You haven't done anything to ensure that I couldn't keep track of where we were going. A left turn, down a mile, another left turn, four miles, a right turn... You're taking me down to the warehouse district. Which, frankly, is a mistake."

Nobody liked my words.

"Shut her up!" the human snarled.

"There are few people in that area, which means any sort of screaming for help is useless. But that also includes *your* screams," I continued. Amateurs were easy to frighten.

"*Shut her up!*"

One of the trolls punched me, trying to knock me out. Unfortunately, he missed the spot, so it hurt, but it didn't make me lose consciousness. Still, I let my body go limp. It would be easier for me to get away if they didn't think I was awake. The trolls were wary of releasing me, even though I'd gone limp. Smart trolls. It took only another few minutes to reach our destination. Regrettably that was way longer than a normal knockout lasted. Luckily no one around me was smart enough to know that. The van pulled to a stop, and I heard the door open. I waited for them to pull me from the van. If I jumped too soon, they'd just shut me in the van again.

"Is this the Valkyrie?" The voice that spoke halted my plans immediately. It was most definitely Jason Harter. He was a wendigo, a powerful, cannibalistic creature who loved to torment and torture his victims before eating them. Most wendigos were feral, but Jason Harter had somehow retained his sanity, and that made him all the more dangerous. I'd kept Kenneth away from him for a long time, but Jason probably wanted to eat him. Apparently all supernatural creatures tasted different, and Jason was a connoisseur. He'd made it his life's mission to taste every different being out there. He'd accomplished quite a lot. But phoenixes were rare enough that he hadn't had the opportunity. Yet.

His intention wasn't to kill me. Not yet. He *was* going to kill the three trolls and the human who'd brought me to him. I was pretty certain he wouldn't eat the trolls, at least. They were notoriously bad at maintaining any form of hygiene. He might want to eat me, since I knew he'd never eaten a Valkyrie before, but he wasn't thinking about that at the moment.

"Yes. And she was a lot of trouble," the human piped up. He didn't have much in the way of self-preservation. I was dragged bodily from the van, and it took all my self-control *not* to react when my body hit the pavement. I couldn't get away from Jason Harter. He had a cadre of various creatures on his payroll that could scent me and track me easily, to say nothing of his personal ability to track his prey. But Jason himself was also a problem. Wendigos were fast—not faster than a Valkyrie, but it was close. I would have to somehow slow Jason down so I could get away, even temporarily. But I couldn't go back to Kenneth, because then he'd be in even *more* danger.

Getting away was no longer an option.

I had to stall Jason long enough to find an opening to kill him. That was the only way Kenneth would be safe. Killing a wendigo was notoriously difficult. Luckily, I knew exactly how to do it.

"We want double," the human continued.

Jason laughed, a dark, sadistic sound that made chills run up my spine. I didn't like wendigos normally, but killing one was like putting down a feral animal. Jason Harter was evil, pure and simple. Strangely enough, he wasn't fit for the halls of Valhalla because he took too much delight in the pain and suffering of others. He wouldn't be a good fit for Ragnarök.

"You'll get what you deserve." I felt Jason kneel down next to me. The three trolls and the human all screamed in terror. I heard them die, one by one, the human being last. He had never been more terrified in his entire life. The bag was pulled off my head. "You don't need to pretend anymore, Valkyrie."

"Good." I opened my eyes and faced the blood red gaze of the wendigo. "Do you *really* think this plan of yours will work?"

"Plan of mine?" Jason smiled as I sat up. We were playing nice for the moment, but it wouldn't last long.

"You want to eat my phoenix," I said, unaffected. The man wanted to play games, but I wasn't going to buy into it. He had a group of seven people behind him. There was a werewolf in wolf form, covered in blood; a fully-grown troll with bloody knuckles; a lamia, who was also licking blood off her hands; two elves; and two fae. Weird. I didn't know what Jason Harter was touting to make himself so appealing to various supernatural creatures, considering his reputation was eating *everyone*. Now the lamia and vampire I understood, because eating humans was their shtick as well. But werewolves hated wendigos, as wendigos ruined their reputations.

"I'll eat you first, if that makes you feel better," Jason replied calmly.

"Tell me, what do you know about Valkyries?" I asked.

"Well, you work for Odin, you bring worthy warriors to Valhalla, and you're surprisingly easy to capture." Jason got to his feet and looked down at me with an unforgiving smirk. He was trying to upset me. Or maybe manipulate me. Too bad I'd been trained out of acting on impulse.

"What can I say?" I shrugged. "You caught me on a bad day."

If that was everything he knew about Valkyries, he was in for a world of hurt.

"You don't seem convinced this is the end for you and your phoenix." Jason eyed me carefully.

"That's because I'm not."

"I have you captured, Ms. Valkyrie. You have no weapons. You're stuck. And because you're stuck, your phoenix will be taken shortly."

"Sure." I got to my feet, brushing the dirt off my jeans. "I'm captured. What next?"

Jason and his posse stared at me. They were trying to figure me out. People didn't usually respond like that to their intimidation tactics, apparently.

"Shall we go in and sit down?" I continued blandly. "It'll probably be more comfortable for everyone." Nobody really liked that response, either. "Fine, I'll lead the way."

I walked into the building, followed by the group, in what was probably the most bizarre kidnapping of all time. Inside the warehouse was a long hallway that split off into separate rooms. The first room seemed to be a generic office. The second room was a security room, with screens showing a myriad of other rooms, presumably on the premises. The third room was what appeared to be a meat-carving station, as there were knives all over the walls, and blood all over the floor. There was a series of freezers on the far side of the room. The fourth room seemed to be a torture chamber, with one chair in the middle of the room, and ropes and chains all around. It didn't look particularly sanitary. The fifth room was a lounge-type area with a couple couches and a coffee table.

There was plenty more to the building, but this room would do. I walked in and settled down in one of the chairs. I needed time to examine the intentions of the rest of the group so I could determine the best way to get out. Jason, of course, had to die, but the others could live if they played their cards right.

"Are *all* Valkyries this creepy?" I heard someone whisper. I smiled.

"If you'd met any of my sisters, you'd find we're all about the same in hostage situations," I replied. The posse all sat, keeping their bodies angled away from me in their discomfort. Jason scowled and glowered at me, crossing his arms and refusing to sit.

"This isn't a negotiation," he snarled.

"It is now." My calm demeanor pissed him off more. His hand snapped forward and closed around my neck. I didn't react.

"I'm going to harvest the meat from your bones while you're still screaming before I take your phoenix and eat him alive," he said with vitriol.

"There're a few problems with that scenario," I told him.

"What would those be?" He'd lost his patience and was losing grip on his human form. His forearms got hairy, his ears became pointed, and his teeth sharpened.

"Firstly, you'd have to keep me captive longer than the next couple minutes. Secondly, even if you *did* manage to hold me, you're assuming cutting me would make me scream. Thirdly, you'd have to fully kill me before you could take my phoenix alive. And fourthly, what makes you think my phoenix would just *allow* you to eat him alive?" I took the opportunity to read the room, finding little interest in violence against me. Interesting. Jason *definitely* wanted to kill me, but his posse didn't want anything to do with me anymore. Probably because I weirded them out. Good enough. It would make escaping easier if I didn't have to kill them all.

The claws that grew from his fingernails pricked into the skin of my neck as he snarled wordlessly at me. Before the situation could escalate further, a loud, buzzing alarm rang throughout the warehouse. Everyone jumped, me included. Irritation flooded me at the sound. If that was what I thought it was, I was going to *murder* Kenneth.

"What's that?" Jason growled at one of the fae.

"That would be a fire alarm." I sighed in defeat. Right when I was about to make my move, too.

Everyone looked at each other. It took them a moment to put two and two together.

"Capture him alive!" Jason roared, sending his people into a frenzy. He turned back to me, eyes fierce.

"None of them will survive this," I informed him. "My phoenix is vengeful."

"So possessive over him." Jason lifted me from the chair by my neck. Normally such a maneuver would put undue strain on the throat, preventing me from being able to breathe. Unfortunately for Jason, I was taller than he was, so my feet were firmly planted on the floor. "If I didn't know better, I'd say you were in love with the bird."

"I am." Honesty was the best policy, my eldest sister always said. Blunt candor shocked and startled people. Jason simply stared at me, completely aghast that I willingly admitted a weakness like that. I slammed my fist into his throat, making him choke and release me, trying to protect himself from more pain. He stumbled backward, giving me all the space I needed.

"He's *my* phoenix," I said coldly. "You will *never* touch him. I will kill you, and then he will burn every inch of your empire to the ground. And unlike him, you *won't* rise from the ashes. Make your peace with death before I deliver you there myself."

Terrified screams pierced through the fire alarm. Smoke trickled into the room. Well, *someone* was mad. Jason seemed to recognize that his plan had gone awry. He glanced at the doorway.

"Go on," I suggested. "Run for it. It won't change your fate. I've declared your death. It will be so."

Jason considered me for a long moment, and I saw fear flash in his eyes. Not so stupid after all. He'd taken two steps toward the door when the frame erupted in flames. The figure of a man stood in the doorway, enormous wings of fire sprouting from his back. His body was sheathed in a heat shimmer, and his eyes literally burned. The inferno forced Jason back a few steps, trying to escape from the very angry phoenix.

"You've been hurt, Kára." Despite how livid Kenneth was, his voice was gentle when he spoke to me. His eyes focused on the bruises on my face and the tiny dots of blood on my neck.

"I was handling it," I told him, a bit exasperated. We had rules and safeguards in case of this *exact scenario*, and guess who'd ignored all of them?

"Not fast enough," Kenneth replied, "Mrs. Chopra saw the whole thing. She called me when you were taken."

"I was handling it," I repeated. "If you come running after your bodyguard, you're not particularly safe, are you?"

"I won't stand by while you're kidnapped, Kára."

"It's my *job* to be kidnapped in your stead."

Kenneth sighed in frustration.

"I was about to kill him and be on my way. If you'd waited five minutes, we'd be talking at home instead of here."

"Kára…"

"Did you have to set the *whole* building on fire?" I gestured to the smoke pouring into the room. It was already making my eyes water. Kenneth abruptly looked a bit embarrassed. Weird.

"Let's handle this wendigo first and talk about this later." He turned to look at Jason, who'd shrunk into one of the corners. He couldn't leave through the door, as Kenneth was blocking that path, and I was positioned such that he couldn't hide behind any of the furniture. He was closer to me, probably because he thought I was the lesser threat. Silly man. Jason looked panicked and kept glancing between me and Kenneth. The big, strong alpha machismo had died pretty quickly in the face of certain death.

"I get to kill him," I said.

"What?" Kenneth frowned at me. "No, *I* get to kill him."

"You killed everyone else," I pointed out.

"Yeah, but *he* was going to eat you."

"But he didn't."

Jason kept inching towards me, bit by bit. Just a few more steps...

"Kára, I demand satisfaction. He kidnapped you and was going to eat you before coming after me," Kenneth was also distracted. Good.

"*I'm* the one who was kidnapped. Where's *my* satisfaction?"

"I'll make you hot chocolate when we get home."

"That's not even the same, and you know it."

Jason stepped into range. Perfect. I took a breath and brought my magic forward. Jason turned to look at me, to figure out where the surge of magic had come from, and my sword and shield materialized in my hands. His red eyes widened in terror right before I cut his head off. His body dropped unceremoniously to the floor. I took a few precious moments to dismember his body, to slow down his regeneration. Simple decapitation wasn't enough to kill wendigos, but dismemberment followed by cremating the pieces did the trick pretty well. I did the first part, and my phoenix would do the second. I looked at Kenneth, who was *pouting*.

"What's with the vengeance act?" I asked, kneeling down to wipe the blood from my sword on Jason's shirt. "I was perfectly fine."

"I just...saw red." Kenneth shrugged, putting his wings away. The building was still very much on fire, but waves of heat and magic stopped emanating from him. He stepped into the room, fidgeting awkwardly. I'd never seen him so uncomfortable in my life. He was hiding something from me. He *never* hid things from me.

"Kenny, you can tell me anything," I reminded him. "What's going on?"

"You've never been kidnapped before." Kenneth shrugged, shoving his hands into his pockets as he stepped closer. I got to my feet and frowned at him.

"It's an occupational hazard. I'm bound to get kidnapped or hurt on the job at some point."

The fire that had been extinguished in his gaze returned with a vengeance in an instant. Jason's remains burst into white flames so hot he almost immediately turned to dust.

"Kenny..." I didn't know what to say. What was making him so upset?

"Kára, when I got the call from Mrs. Chopra, I've never been more scared in my entire life. And *that* includes the first time I was reborn," Kenneth said, staring hard at the floor.

"You know I can take care of myself," I reminded him patiently. I was going to choke on the smoke any minute.

"It's not that." Kenneth shook his head.

"Then what is it?"

"I'm in love with you!"

My heart stopped in my chest.

Kenneth flushed bright red.

"I've been in love with you since grade school," he said. "You're strong and funny and brilliant, and gorgeous beyond reason. I thought, when I heard what had happened, that I'd lost you. And if I'd lost you, you'd never know that I adore every little thing about you. Like how you snore a bit in your sleep, but you'll never admit it. And how you have the *biggest* chocolate addiction, and you're proud of it. And how you can't carry a tune in a bucket, but you still sing in the shower anyway. And that you hate having people in your personal space, but you've never pushed me away. And that's why I keep doing it. Because I'm the only person you trust enough to let that close."

It was a good thing the room was filled with smoke, because I had plausible deniability as to why my eyes were tearing up, and why I was choking. Immediately Kenneth grabbed my arm and pulled me through the smoke-filled hallways. The bodies of the other members of Jason's posse were strewn around, burnt to little crisps. I followed Kenneth out and away from the building. We didn't have much time before the authorities arrived. The cool and clean air somehow made the tears worse. And the lump in my throat would *not* go away.

"I'm in love with you, Kára, and I can't stand going one more day without you knowing that I would give up my ability to be re-born so long as I got to keep you in my life." Kenneth looked at me like I was the last person on the planet.

"You're an idiot, Kenny," I replied. It obviously wasn't the answer he was expecting, because he just blinked at me, blankly. "I've always loved you."

"I'm not joking around, Kára." Kenneth didn't allow himself to believe me. The idiot. I dropped my sword and shield and dragged him down to my level to kiss him. He hesitated for a fraction of a second before sliding his arms around me. Pleasure burst in my gut in a way I'd never felt before. Kissing him felt like coming home. It took every ounce of my willpower to pull back from him.

"Does it sound like I'm joking, Kenny?" I asked, breathless and giddy. I'd never been breathless before. It was making my head swim.

"I love you," Kenneth chuckled, "and I'm going to die if I don't get to kiss you again."

I started to laugh, but the sound was swallowed up by his lips as he kissed me again and again and again. My sisters were going to have a field day with this. I found myself not caring so long as I got to keep kissing my phoenix. He'd come to rescue me, the adorable idiot. We'd have words later, but for now, I had to get him away from the scene of the crime. Arson was much harder to explain than self-defense.

Kenneth always *did* make sure my days were never boring.

* * * * *

Kat Beaty Bio

Kat Beaty lives in North Carolina with her husband and son, a short distance away from her siblings and parents. She has been reading and writing as long as she can remember, usually instead of paying attention in school. (Don't do that, kids.) She is thrilled to have her first publication in "Flights of Fantasy" and hopes that this will help her put out more of her scribblings in the future. She would like to thank her husband, Richard, for always supporting her and pushing her to write, write, write. She would also like to thank her beta readers and best friends, Tori, Sara, and Mary Byrd, for never being afraid to give her constructive criticism. Finally, she'd like to thank her son, Wesley, for giving her the courage and strength to continue despite impossible odds.

# # # # #

Lions, and Tigers, and a Vampire...Oh My!
by Sheellah Kennedy

"**I** can't believe I let you talk me into going," Liza said as she bent over, pulling on her worn cowboy boots. "The fairgrounds are going to be full of kids and teenagers running wild, and you know how I feel about them. I'm sure it's one of the many reasons Pete left me for somebody almost half my age!"

"Pete is an ass, and he knew when you married him you didn't want kids. That's not on you," Heidi said, dragging her best friend since childhood toward the door. "And besides, I don't recall you having better plans this evening? And please don't tell me you need to catch up on your TV shows. They'll be here next weekend, but the circus certainly won't."

Heidi paused. "I also heard through the grapevine that Jack is back in town for the weekend, visiting his mom, and is planning on taking his niece. There's talk that his relationship with Tess is over. I'm not missing out on an opportunity to bump into him this weekend, and I can't go to the circus alone. Just the thought of running into him makes me wet."

191

"Seriously! Here I was thinking my best friend wanted to get me out of the house because she felt sorry for me," Liza said, tossing her long blond hair over her shoulder. She added a derisive snort to emphasize her displeasure at being dragged along as the wingwoman. "Whatever! I'll go, but you're going to owe me big time."

* * *

Stepping out of the truck into the grassy parking area, Liza was impressed with the sight before her as the sun set over the Rocky Mountains. There was a reason her state was called Big Sky Country. The view never got old. What *was* getting old was watching Heidi apply yet another layer of red lipstick and fix her hair for what felt like the hundredth time. "Oh my God, Heidi! It's a circus, not the freaking inaugural ball!" Liza exclaimed. "I can't believe I let you drag me out to this."

"Oh, lighten up, Francis!" Heidi teased, getting out of the truck. "This is going to be fun! And remember to be on the lookout for Jack. I need to bump into him tonight, and hopefully do some other 'bumping' with him later this evening…if you know what I mean." Winking at Liza, she grabbed her hand and pulled her toward the fairgrounds.

As they approached, Liza had to admit the view was spectacular. Growing up on a nearby ranch, she'd spent plenty of time at the grounds showing off livestock as a 4-H member. There was nothing glamorous about her childhood, though, and she sometimes wished she could've traded places with Heidi growing up. Heidi's parents were free spirits to this day, and they still owned a local artisan shop on Main Street. Where Liza'd had plenty of responsibilities as a teenager, Heidi'd had none.

The fairgrounds had been transformed into a magical playground, and lights twinkling from canopied tents provided a soft glow around the biggest circus tent Liza and Heidi had ever seen. Even with the garish red and yellow stripes, it was a sight to behold.

"I can't believe how many people are here tonight! It's like the entire town descended on the fairgrounds," Heidi said as she scanned the crowd looking for Jack.

"Are you kidding me?" Liza asked. "This is the most excitement they've had in months! Our little town has a handful of bars, a movie theater, and a bowling alley. It gets old after a while. The same places and the same people. Honestly, I get depressed just thinking about it. Why do you think I spend my weekends catching up on my favorite shows? Because there's nothing better to do! Come on; let's see if we can find a beer tent."

"Now you're talking! I think that's the most positive thing to come out of your mouth all evening. Plus, I could use a little extra liquid courage for when I see Jack."

Liza could feel the locals' eyes on her as they walked through the freshly cut grass in search of the beer tent. "Why don't they just put me on the cover of the weekly newspaper?" Liza muttered to Heidi. "They can headline it, 'Lonely Liza's Lover Leaves Her For 26-Year-Old Lolita.'"

Heidi shook her head. "A slutty girl is like the first piece of bread in a loaf—everybody touches it, but nobody wants it! He'll get tired of her eventually. And are you seriously going to let Darci and her gossipy crew get to you? They've pretty much slept with the whole town, and the ones they haven't slept with are related to them. I wouldn't be surprised if your asshole husband has banged at least three out of the five bimbos in that group," Heidi said.

"Soon-to-be *ex*-husband," Liza reminded her. "And it can't come soon enough."

"Speaking of coming…look who's walking this way!" Heidi lightly elbowed Liza in the side. Jack was walking toward them holding hands with his young niece, who was carrying a big swirl of cotton candy. Heidi's face flushed pink in the glow of the tent lighting.

"How do I look?" she whispered, tugging down her tank top ever-so-slightly to show off a little more cleavage.

"Like you're ready to ride the Jack train! Be cool and don't forget he's got a kid with him. Remember to use your filter."

Jack was certainly easy on the eyes, and Liza could appreciate why Heidi was so into him. It wasn't just his looks, but the way he carried himself. "Jack, I didn't know you were home for a visit," Heidi said as he approached. Liza smirked, knowing full well that Heidi had been obsessing about what to wear all day.

"Yeah. My mom is tying up a few loose ends before she heads off to sunny Florida. Now that my dad is gone, she doesn't want to brave the winters alone. Liza, aren't your parents living in Florida?"

Liza replied, "They moved a few years back. Keeping up with the ranch was becoming too much to handle, so they sold everything, bought an RV, and traveled around for a while. They recently settled in the Ft. Myers area. I'm sure your mom will love it there." She could see Heidi chomping at the bit out of the corner of her eye, so being the perfect wingwoman, she said, "I'm going in search of the beer tent. Can I bring either of you back anything?"

"Sure!" Heidi said. "I'd love a hard cider if they have it, and if not, surprise me."

Jack's niece began tugging on his shirt and whined, "Uncle Jack, you promised you'd take me to the bathroom," as she shifted her weight from one foot to the other.

"I don't mind walking with you to the bathrooms and escorting her," Heidi volunteered. "You never know who's going to be hanging around the bathrooms late at night."

"Sure," Jack said. "That would be great." Turning to Liza, he said, "I'm going to pass on the drink offer. Why don't we meet up under the big top? It's bleacher-style seating, and we can save you a spot."

Liza smiled and said, "I'll catch up with you in a few."

Heidi gave Liza a subtle wink and said, "See you soon."

* * *

As Liza continued in search of the beer tent, a gentle, warm breeze caressed her neck. It was the perfect night to be out under the big Montana sky, enjoying the starry night and the transformation of the fairgrounds. She smiled and reminded herself to thank Heidi for dragging her out of the house. She needed to do it more often, rather than wallowing in self-pity. She knew Heidi only wanted what was best for her, but sometimes it was a little much. She swore to herself that she'd start putting herself back out there. Maybe they could plan a girls' getaway sometime soon. Somewhere tropical, with lots of hot, bare-chested guys. Getting Heidi to go along with the plan wouldn't be hard—that is, unless she hooked up with Jack. She'd been crushing on him since high school.

Walking past some smaller tents, she noticed several of them had their flaps down. She was curious to see what was behind the flaps, but not curious enough to get kicked out of the fairgrounds. Rounding the corner, she ran into a line of at least 20 people. Assuming it was the beer tent, she quickly jumped in line with them.

Two women in their early 20s caught her attention as they walked past the line, giggling like schoolgirls. She heard one say to the other, "Oh my god, he was mind-blowingly hot," and the other responded, "I'd blow him any day of the week," which resulted in another fit of giggles. Liza was pretty sure it was the Pederson girls, but she wasn't going to be obvious by turning around and looking.

As the line slowly approached the front of the beer tent, she heard several more inappropriate conversations between women as they walked past. *That's weird*, she thought, *none of these women are carrying drinks*. Puzzled, Liza tapped the shoulder of the woman in front of her. She was surprised to see her old high school teacher turn around. Mrs. O'Grady had to be pushing at least seventy. She hadn't seen the woman in years and kicked herself for getting the woman's attention. Mrs. O'Grady had also become the town gossip after retiring from her teaching position several years ago.

"Oh, hello dear," she said. "I'm so sorry to hear about your marriage, but I must say I'm not surprised to see you in this line now that you're a free woman. Please don't tell George you saw me. I was supposed to be headed to the ladies' room and getting popcorn for our granddaughter, but I decided to take a little detour." She winked at Liza.

Confused, Liza asked, "Isn't this the beer tent?" Mrs. O'Grady chuckled and said, "Oh, honey, this is far better than any old beer tent. This is where the fortune teller is, and you're in for a treat. Rumor has it you get a reading and a lot *more*, if you know what I mean." She gave Liza another knowing wink. "The news is spreading like wildfire among the women. Word has it he has movie star good looks. Just look at this line. Do you see any guys?" Mrs. O'Grady asked. Liza leaned out of the line to look, and sure enough, they were all women. A sign ahead read, "Tarot Card Reading—$20."

Liza felt anger beginning to bubble inside of her. Yet another man taking advantage of women! Deciding to stay in line, she looked forward to coming face-to-face with him. *It'll be the best therapy EV-ER,* she thought to herself.

Texting Heidi, she said, "Met up with Sarah, and we're discussing a shopping trip to Fernie. Are you in?"

A few moments passed, and Heidi responded with, "Definitely! And take your time coming back. It looks like the Jack train might be heading south—and I'm not talking about Florida."

Liza rolled her eyes.

* * *

L iza watched as Mrs. O'Grady parted the curtains and exited the tent. Beads of sweat glistened on her forehead, repulsing Liza. What the Hell was this man doing to these women? A little shaky on her legs, Mrs. O'Grady leaned over to Liza and whispered, "He doesn't disappoint." Liza's nose wrinkled at the thought of Mrs. O'Grady and this hot mystery man together.

"Next in line," an exotic-looking woman in a rhinestone bodysuit announced in a sultry voice. Collecting Liza's $20, she parted the velvet curtains, ushering Liza in. "Damian is ready for you."

A salt lamp provided a soft glow inside the tent, and incense burned in a pot, giving off a dark, earthy aroma that smelled just like the patchouli oil Heidi's mother wore. She'd once told Liza that patchouli was used for both the attraction of sex and money. It wasn't shocking at all that she smelled it in this tent.

The only furniture in the tent was a table, behind which sat an incredibly handsome man. Placing her hands on the table, Liza leaned over the tarot cards and into his face. She hesitated for a moment, staring into his amber eyes—it wasn't any surprise to her that women were making up excuses to visit the "ladies' room" or "beer tent." He had a rogue look about him, wearing a partially unbuttoned white dress shirt and a burgundy velvet blazer. "What do you think you're doing?" she angrily asked.

* * *

Damian looked up from the cards on the table and came face-to-face with a gorgeous blonde who was clearly not there for a tarot reading.

This one is trouble, the wisp hiding under the table said to Damian. *There's something different about her. Get rid of her as quickly as possible.*

Damian's mouth lifted in an amused smile. He'd never been challenged by a human. *This is going to be fun!* he thought to himself.

Get rid of her! the wisp repeated, giving Damian's leg a pinch. *She's only going to draw more attention, and we can't afford to be caught.*

A little mind control never hurt anyone, Damien replied. *Let these women believe they're fulfilling a sexual fantasy with me. We need the extra money to help pay down our debt.*

"I'm preparing the cards for your tarot reading, of course!" Damian answered. "Please, have a seat."

"Don't patronize me. I know you're giving more than just readings," Liza said heatedly, "and I intend to report you to management as soon as I exit this tent. What you're doing is completely unacceptable and downright disgusting!"

* * *

Damian picked up the tarot cards and began shuffling them as Liza continued to rant. She was certainly a firecracker, and he was enjoying every second of it. *This is the most fun I've had all night!* he thought to himself. He loved the way her breasts rose and fell, and delighted in the sound of the throbbing pulse coming from her neck. The angrier she became, the more he smiled, and he found himself becoming aroused.

Surprised at his reaction and feeling like he was beginning to lose control of the situation, Damian entered Liza's mind. Instantly, he was sucked into a tornadic, molten lava pit. Fighting to regain control, he heard laughter from above. Looking up, he spotted Liza standing on the edge of the pit—a stunning beauty, smiling and enjoying his torture. He gave out a loud, piercing howl as she disappeared from his sight, and the hot lava consumed him.

"Ahhhhh!" he yelled, exiting Liza's mind. The wisp had sunk her teeth into Damian's leg and wasn't letting go. Shaking his leg as hard as he could without drawing any more attention to himself, he made every attempt to get the wisp off his leg. *Damn it! Let go!* he commanded.

Once she's gone! We're not going to get any extra out of this one. There are other customers waiting, and she's bad for business.

Selene parted the curtains and walked in. "Is everything okay in here?" she asked, placing her hand on Liza's shoulder. "Our customers are growing impatient and a little worried after they heard you yell," she said, directing her attention toward Damian.

"Yes. Everything is fine, Selene," Damian curtly responded. "Her ten minutes aren't up, and we're preparing the cards for her reading." Dismissing the woman, he said, "Please excuse us."

Giving Damian a smoldering look, Selene gave Liza's shoulder a squeeze and exited the tent.

* * *

Liza found herself fighting to string words together in a complete sentence. *Calm down, Liza. This man is obviously humoring himself with your antics. Just take your complaint to management and be done with it.* Getting control of her emotions, she asked, "Have you heard a single word I've said?"

"Of course I've been listening to you," Damian said, "and I take great insult at what you're implying. You're welcome to take your complaint to management, though, as I have nothing to hide." Pushing back from the table, he continued, "It saddens me greatly to see such a beautiful face marred by anger. Please take a seat and allow me to give you a reading before you run off to report me. You *have* already paid."

I don't have any proof he's done anything wrong, Liza thought, *and I'll only draw more negative attention to myself—giving the busybodies more to talk about if I report him.* He certainly wasn't wrong about her anger, either—it had been pent up for months since Pete had left her. And she had to admit, she was intrigued by the mystery of the tarot cards. Deciding to stay, she said, "Read my cards."

* * *

"Have you ever done this before?" Damian asked, handing her the stack of tarot cards. His hand accidentally brushed against hers, causing him to suck in his breath. There was no denying his attraction to her. Such a simple touch awakened every fiber of his being, and feelings of guilt washed over him. It had been a long time since a woman had affected him this way. A wave of sadness washed over him.

Not now, the wisp said, releasing herself from Damian's leg. It gave him an affectionate squeeze.

* * *

"I haven't," Liza replied, shuffling the cards. The simple touch of Damian's hand had caused a thrilling flutter in her chest. Struggling with this unexpected feeling, she did her best to remain composed and said, "My best friend's parents have a deck of cards at their place, but I've never been interested." Noticing Damian's mood change, she asked, "What's next?" and placed the cards on the table.

Clearing his throat, Damian said, "I am going to read three cards you select from the deck. The first card will be the past—what you need to let go of. The second will be the present—what you need to know now. And the third will be the future—an upcoming opportunity." Damian instructed Liza to cut the cards in half. Pulling the top three from the bottom half, Damian placed them face down on the table.

Watching Damian flip the cards over, Liza hesitated as each one was presented face up. *Don't freak out. It's just crazy hocus-pocus bullshit,* she reminded herself. Looking at the first card made her giggle.

"It's a picture of a man hanging upside down from a tree titled *The Hanged Man*. This is my past, correct?" Liza asked. "And if that's the case, does this picture represent my lying, cheating, soon-to-be ex-husband? Because if so, he can stay hanging on the tree permanently." Damian responded with a deep chuckle, and Liza felt warmth spread through her lower half. She found herself enjoying the sound of his laugh.

"Well, you certainly have an interesting spread of cards," Damian said, "and judging from the comment you made, your first card is right on the money. *The Hanged Man* represents sacrifice and letting go. If you're divorcing your husband, I'd say it's very accurate. It appears you've already begun the process of letting go and need to focus on the second card, which leads us to the present."

* * *

Liza eagerly leaned forward to study the second card, making it hard for Damian to focus as he breathed in her heady scent. He fought the urge to lean forward and devour her lips. It wouldn't be hard. She was only a few inches away from him.

"Time's up," came an annoyed voice from behind Liza. It was Selene again, and she didn't look impressed. "You're actually a few minutes past," Selene said, "and we need to finish up before the show begins." She gave Damian a look of disapproval, and glared at Liza, before angrily tossing the curtain aside and storming out.

Listen to her, Damian. We haven't collected enough tonight and can't afford to be under, the wisp reminded him.

Damian wasn't ready to let Liza go, and he could see the disappointment in her face, knowing she wouldn't get to finish her reading. Gathering the second and third card, Damian put them to the side. He'd never done this before, but he needed to see her again.

"If you are willing to come back after the show, we can continue where we left off," Damian said, walking to the front of the table where Liza was seated.

Liza gasped at the nearness of him. *Pull yourself together, Liza. Don't show him any weakness. He's playing you, and you're falling for it,* her inner voice shouted. She was definitely having an out-of-body experience when she heard herself reply with, "I'd love that. I'll come as soon as the show ends."

* * *

Not wanting to show up empty-handed, Liza carefully balanced two full cups of beer and a bag of popcorn as she made her way over to Heidi, Jack, and his niece. Heidi was looking quite cozy sitting next to Jack in the make-shift bleachers.

"We were wondering if you were going to make it back in time for the start of the show," Heidi said, taking a beer. "You missed the excitement. Katie and I got to ride an elephant, didn't we?" Smiling, she reached over and squeezed the little girl's hand. Liza wasn't fooled by the gesture as Heidi's hand grazed Jack's lap in the process. "Liza, would you mind driving the truck over to your place tonight? Jack and I are going to drop Katie off after the circus and grab a drink or two. He can give me a ride over tomorrow," she said, winking.

"Of course," Liza said with a smile. Heidi certainly hadn't wasted any time while Liza had been gone. She'd never had a problem going after what she wanted. Liza was the complete opposite. She found herself wishing she possessed some of Heidi's boldness. This also solved the problem of explaining to Heidi why she needed to visit Damian's tent afterward.

Liza's thoughts were interrupted when the lights dimmed, and a voice announced, "Ladies and gentlemen, children of all ages, welcome to the greatest show known to mankind!" A spotlight followed a colorfully dressed ringmaster as he rode a huge black stallion into the center of the arena. Clowns of all sizes and shapes riding small motorcycles circled around him, while attractive men and women dressed head to toe in sequined, form-fitting bodysuits walked out in formation, waving to the excited crowd. The audience went crazy, clapping wildly.

Liza's eyes locked on one of the couples. Holding hands and waving to the crowd were the tarot card reader and his helper. An unexpected wave of jealousy washed over her watching them together.

* * *

Damian felt Liza's eyes watching him as he circled the arena with Selene. He knew Selene could feel it, too, because she possessively gripped his hand a little harder. Concentrating on the show, he pushed Liza from his mind. He didn't need to have an erection in a tight-fitting body suit. It was a family show, after all.

* * *

The wisp enjoyed her quiet time while Damien and Selene performed. Hiding under a table all day listening to readings was *not* her idea of fun. Tidying up the inside of the tent, she fantasized about spending some quality time with Damian in between shows. Sometimes she regretted her decision to become a wisp. Her heart ached, remembering the life she and Damian had enjoyed while she was human. As memories bubbled to the surface, luminescent tears rolled down her delicate cheeks, and her wings drooped. The choice to become a wisp had been hers to make, and she needed to own her decision—even if it wasn't easy. She could have succumbed to her illness, but the thought of leaving Damian had been too much. And, in all honesty, death had frightened her. She knew Damian still loved her, but his feelings for her had changed. She'd become a confidante to him, not a lover. It hadn't been easy, accepting the fact that Damian was mind-sexing the women who entered his tent for additional money, but it eased her mind that it was helping Damian to repay his debt. Occasionally she would join in on the fun, but it only left her feeling sad and empty afterwards. It had been a long time since the wisp had seen him react to a woman the way he had tonight. He'd made a point of reminding her before he left to save out the two cards that hadn't been read.

The wisp sensed trouble. Trying to convince Damian to stay away from this woman was futile. He was in control—or at least the wisp hoped he was.

* * *

"**L**adies and gentlemen, and children of all ages, thank you for supporting our circus," the ring-master addressed the crowd as the show ended. "Don't forget to stop by our merchandise stand on your way out and purchase a fun souvenir to commemorate tonight. Anybody who purchases a souvenir will get an autographed photo from one of our many talented performers located in the stand next to it." His stallion reared on its hind legs as he gave one last wave to the crowd, and the performers exited the tent with several clowns trailing behind them.

Jumping up from her seat, Katie excitedly asked, "Uncle Jack, can we pretty please get an autograph from the pretty lady that flew through the air?"

Liza knew exactly who Jack's niece was referring to. It was Selene from the tarot card tent. As impressive as she'd been as a trapeze artist, Liza wasn't a fan of the negative attention Selene had directed her way during the show. Selene had thrown at least three nasty glares her way. Knowing Selene wouldn't be going back to the tent immediately with Damian helped put Liza's mind at ease.

"We'll stop on the way out, but we should get going before the line gets too long," Jack responded to his niece, standing up. "Heidi, are you ready?" he asked, looking over at her.

"Oh, I'm *ready* alright," she whispered just loud enough for Liza to hear. Liza nearly choked on the last of the beer she was drinking. Giving Jack a light pat on his butt without his niece noticing, Heidi said, "Why don't you get a head start? I'll catch up with you in a few." Saying goodbye to Liza, Jack and Katie followed the crowd exiting the tent. Heidi's eyes followed him until he was out of sight and said, "That man certainly knows how to remote start a vagina!"

Liza looked around to make sure nobody had heard Heidi's comment. "You certainly don't mince words, do you?" she asked. "Really, though, I'm glad you two hit it off." Liza smiled, adding, "Did you see any of the show tonight?"

"Oh, believe me! The best show is yet to come...pun definitely intended!" Heidi exclaimed, laughing. She struck her best seductive pose. "Seriously though, thanks for driving Big Red home tonight." Heidi handed her the truck keys. "I'll have Jack drop me off at your place tomorrow...hopefully sometime in the afternoon." Hugging her goodbye, Heidi took off in the direction Jack had gone.

* * *

Checking to make sure Heidi was nowhere in sight, Liza made her way back to Damian's tent, doing her best not to be seen by any of the circus employees. She'd wanted to tell Heidi where she was going but wasn't sure she'd be able to explain her little side trip. Even admitting to herself that she was curious about the readings of the last two tarot cards, she knew her real reason for returning to the tent was the magnetic pull she felt when she was in Damian's presence. Her thoughts ran wild as she pictured his muscled body up against hers, skin to skin. She'd witnessed what his body was capable of, watching him perform on the trapeze with Selene.

Focus, Liza! You're here to finish your card reading, she thought to herself. Approaching the tent, Liza heard soft, peaceful music emanating from it and could see the outline of Damian's body through the fabric. Parting the velvet curtain, she quietly stepped inside.

Damian's back was to her as he pulled up the black pants he'd been wearing earlier. Liza let out a small gasp, causing Damian to turn around bare-chested. "Sorry," he said, with an amused smile. "I didn't realize you'd make it back to the tent so quickly. I saw you talking with your friends after the show and figured you might be a few minutes late," he said, zipping his pants.

Liza found herself staring at the bulge behind his zipper and forced her eyes upward. *Damn! It's been a long time since I've felt like this,* she thought to herself, envisioning her hands running through his raven hair and traveling down his smooth, muscled chest. Pulling herself out of her trance, she shakily said, "I was just getting my friend's key from her. She's spending the night at a friend's house and wanted to ride back with him."

* * *

D amian smiled, happy he'd replaced the salt lamp with votive candles. They cast a golden hue inside the tent that set the mood perfectly.

"Please, have a seat," Damian said, gesturing to the chair. He finished buttoning his shirt, purposely leaving the last four buttons open. Enjoying the effect he had on Liza, he mentally applauded himself for creating the right ambiance. Mind-reading had never been a problem for him, although she was proving to be a challenge. Catching bits and pieces of the conversation within her psyche, he was thrilled by what he was hearing. Her attraction to him was mutual, but he could also tell she was holding herself back. *The soon-to-be ex, perhaps? Regardless, I'm taking it slow this time,* he thought. *Going too quickly last time was painful, and I certainly don't want a repeat of that!*

* * *

The wisp hiding under the table felt a pang of jealousy, but pushed it back. Damian deserved to have someone in his life, and Selene wasn't the answer. She was tired of the witch and the financial hold her group had over the circus. Unfortunately her powers were never going to be great enough to get rid of Selene. Quietly counting the day's profit, the wisp eavesdropped on the conversation between Liza and Damian.

* * *

Damian took his seat across from Liza, sliding the three tarot cards back in front of him. Pointing to the second card, he said, "This is the *Five of Swords*. It symbolizes that you're currently engaged in a conflict of sorts, or you're in a disagreement with something or someone. It's also suggests there may be jealousy, malice, or spite surrounding you."

"Wow! Is there anything positive with this card?" Liza asked.

Damian had done his best to be gentle when delivering the reading on the second card. There wasn't a lot of positivity with the *Five of Swords*. He'd left out the parts about possible violence and a rivalry or competition over a relationship. Hiding his concern for her well-being, he did his best to lighten the mood. Reaching over and touching her hand, he said, "To put a positive spin on it, I believe the card is telling you to forgive yourself and get rid of any negative thinking you may have. Earlier this evening you mentioned you were in the process of getting a divorce. I don't know the details, but from what I've gathered, you appear to be a genuinely kind woman—and I must admit, very easy on the eyes."

* * *

He winked playfully at her, making Liza's stomach somersault and her heart thump in her chest. "Would you like to continue?" he asked.

Liza struggled with her feelings. He'd been the perfect gentleman toward her, and all she could think of was kissing him. And if she were truly being honest with herself, she wondered what it would be like to have him inside her. She hadn't been with anybody since Pete, and the thought of being with Damian both scared and excited her. Stepping outside her comfort zone, she channeled her inner-Heidi. "I'd like to add something to my *Five of Swords* card," she said, leaning over the card table just inches from Damian's face, hoping he'd accept her invitation.

* * *

Surprised by Liza's boldness, Damian hesitated for a split second. He was used to women chasing after him, but with her, it was different—she had an innocence he found endearing. Leaning into her, their lips lightly touched—a simple kiss that left Damian wanting more and wanting to pull back at the same time. It had been forever since he'd felt this way kissing a human. Corinne, his last relationship, had broken him, watching her struggle toward the end with a terminal illness. The thought of losing her had frightened him. The decision to become a wisp had been her choice, and he was thankful to still have her in his life, though their relationship had become no more than a friendship.

"I'm so sorry," Liza said to Damian, flushing. Grabbing her purse off the back of her chair, she apologized again as she stood to leave and added, "I'm not the type to kiss somebody I just met."

"Wait," Damian said, walking around the table to her, close enough that it caused her to suck in her breath. He wasn't going to lose Liza—not now that he'd found her. Caressing her cheek with his hand, he said, "We haven't discussed your future card, *The Knight of Cups.*"

Locking eyes with her, Damian could tell Liza wanted him as badly as he did her. Pulling her toward him with his free hand on her back, their lips came together in a soft, passionate kiss. *God! She tastes of all that's good in the world—sugar, sunshine, and music.*

* * *

Forcing all the negative thoughts from her mind, Liza felt her body relax. It was a very freeing experience—she'd always been an overthinker in the bedroom, and with Damian, he made her feel confident and sexy. The scent of Damian's cologne heightened her senses, and her hands began slowly unbuttoning his shirt, coming to rest on his waistband. Damian moaned and pressed up against her. Enjoying the control she had over him, Liza lightly cupped his hardness through the fabric of his pants with her hand. Releasing him, her fingertips traveled back up his now bare chest, teasing him as she lightly brushed upward through his chest hair. Reaching the top, she began to trail her fingertips downward again. Damian grabbed her wrist.

* * *

"Enough, woman!" Damian rasped in ecstasy, taking her hand and bringing it up to his mouth. Putting her index finger into his mouth, he sucked on it, lightly dragging her finger back and forth over his teeth. He greatly enjoyed watching her response—head tilted back, eyes closed, and her lips slightly parted. *God! She's beautiful!* Slowly pulling her finger out of his mouth, he said, "Turn around." Liza turned her back to him.

Removing her t-shirt and bra, Damian continued to explore her body. Lifting her long blond hair up and over her left shoulder, he trailed his hands down to her firm breasts, gently massaging them and pressing his mouth against her exposed neck. Practicing great self-control, Damian lightly bit her, causing her breathing to quicken. Feeling Liza's head turn toward him, he gently caught her earlobe between his teeth, blowing warm breaths into her ear at the same time. He felt her body shiver. "Do you like that?" he whispered in her ear. Liza's small moan was answer enough. Damian huskily said into her ear, "Let me see you." Damian wasn't sure how much longer he could wait—he wanted her now. Liza turned back toward him, raising her hands up to cover her breasts.

He felt a tug at his heart at the knowledge that she didn't realize how beautiful she was. It made Damian desire her even more—wanting to protect her, mind, body, and soul. "Come here," he said, overwrought with desire. Taking her hands in his, he pulled back just far enough to admire her, and said, "Liza, you're perfect!"

Releasing her hands, Damian pushed her hair back, bending his head down toward her bosom, and grazed her right breast gently with his teeth. He heard Liza moan as she grabbed his hair. Her breathing quickened as he swirled, sucked, and bit her taut nipple.

* * *

"**M**y turn," Liza said seductively, bringing him back up to her face. Lightly biting his neck, she inhaled his masculine scent, and began unzipping his pants at the same time. Guiding his pants and boxers down toward his feet, she made her way down the length of his body, nipping and biting. Damian grabbed handfuls of her hair as he groaned in pleasure. She bit a little harder than planned on the inside of his thigh when she saw his erect manhood. Having only felt him through his pants, excitement filled every inch of her body. The thought of him inside her was highly erotic.

* * *

Damian wasn't sure how much longer he'd be able to control himself. "I need you soon," he said, groaning. With Liza's assistance, Damian stepped out of the clothing bunched around his feet. His eyes locked on hers. She flushed with anticipation as she rose back up to meet him, while undoing her shorts, and let both her shorts and panties fall to the ground. Kicking all of it aside, she looked at Damian in eager anticipation.

Turning Liza around, he guided her forward, resting her hands on the table. Caressing her ass, he reached further down and inserted a finger into her, finding her more than ready for him. She pushed back against him, moaning, and he heard her say, "Now, Damian, please!" It was more than he could take, and he stepped forward and slowly entered her.

Liza gasped at the fullness of him as he slowly thrust in and out, picking up the tempo with each stroke. The combination of him pulling her hair and riding her from behind pushed her to heights she didn't know existed. *Oh God, yes! I'm so close!*

Damian felt Liza's body tense as he released himself inside her, and both cried out in pleasure. He reached forward to cup her breasts and hold her, but as his eyes came down on her shoulder, he saw something he'd missed before—Selene had put one of her marks on her. He didn't know what Selene planned to do; all he knew was Liza had raised Selene's wrath somehow, and Selene intended something unpleasant for her.

No matter what else happened to him or the circus, he knew he couldn't allow that to happen.

After a few seconds, she turned around, her face flushed. "I'm sorry," she said. "I've never done anything like that before. I don't know what came over me." She gathered up her clothes, putting them on as quickly as she could.

"It's okay," he said. "It's a first for me, too."

"I'm sure," she said, although Damian could tell she didn't believe him.

"Really, it is," he said. "Wait, don't go."

"I have to. I…I…" Without another word, Liza ran from the tent.

Damian sighed.

"Well, that went well," the wisp said. "Right up until she ran from the tent." She paused and then asked, "Aren't you going to get dressed?"

"No," Damian said, "I have to save her."

He concentrated, dropped to all fours, and turned himself into his wolf-form. "I'll try to be back by sunrise, but don't wait up." He raced out of the tent after her.

* * *

Fumbling for the keys in her purse, Liza cursed herself. *What was I thinking? Having sex with a stranger! Have I lost my mind?* She found the keys and opened the door to Heidi's truck. Quickly jumping in, she slammed the door. *Thank God nobody saw me! Wouldn't that have added fuel to the fire for all the town gossips!*

Starting the truck, Liza looked around, secretly hoping Damian had followed her. He was nowhere to be seen. *That's probably for the better,* she thought, although she couldn't shake him from her mind. She was already missing everything about him—his hands moving over her body, the way he looked at her, him biting her neck, and more. For a split second, she had the irrational thought of running back to him, but instead she put the truck in drive and drove away from the fairgrounds.

* * *

Thankful the roads were curvy, and Liza wasn't speeding, Damian loped after her, just beyond the tree-lined road, out of sight. The locals weren't happy with the wolf problem they were having in the area, and Damian certainly didn't need to draw attention to himself, especially with some of the trigger-happy locals who liked to shoot animals out of season.

Panting hard, he hoped Liza's place wasn't too much further—and more importantly, that he'd beat Selene to Liza's place. There were so many things that could go wrong, and he wished he'd had more time to come up with a better plan. Seeing the mark on Liza's shoulder, Damian knew not only was it a tracking device for Selene, but also a death sentence for Liza. Damian would do everything in his power to protect Liza, even if it meant losing his life. Selene's powers were mighty, but her temper could work in his favor—and that's what he was counting on.

* * *

Using her left turn signal, Liza turned onto the gravel road leading up to her place. When her parents had sold their ranch, they'd gifted her and Pete with enough money to move out of their apartment and into a house. Timing had been everything, and when old Mr. Jacobs had died during their house hunting, they'd quickly put in an offer to his son, who just wanted to get rid of the place. It was a beautiful one-story house overlooking Loon Lake. Liza's parents hadn't been happy about her separation from Pete, and she felt like her mother had blamed her for Pete running off with the tramp—that maybe she wasn't fulfilling her wifely duties. *Wouldn't she like to know what I did tonight,* Liza thought, which brought her back to thinking about Damian. How was it possible for her to miss somebody she'd just met? She longed to be back in his arms. There was still so much to discover about him. An overwhelming sadness came over her, realizing she'd never see him again. She kicked herself for leaving so hastily.

Her sadness wasn't helped when she pulled into her driveway and looked at the dark house. *Shit! I thought I left the outside light on. I guess Heidi turned it off,* she thought. Liza wasn't a fan of coming home to not only a dark house, but an empty house. She'd thought about getting a dog or cat to keep her company, but it would be too hard. Getting a pet-sitter this far away from town would be a challenge. Sighing, she turned off the truck and got out.

When is Heidi going to break down and buy a new vehicle? Liza wondered as she fumbled to lock the old Ford pickup in the dark.

"Shit!" she exclaimed as the keys slipped out of her hand to the ground. Feeling around and not finding them, she fished for her cell phone in her purse to use the flashlight. *There they are,* Liza thought as she stooped down to pick them up. Coming back up, she was startled by the figure standing a few feet in front of her.

"Oh my God!" she shouted. Fear enveloped her body. "What do you want?" Trying to decide whether it would be best to try to run into the house and lock it, or reason with him, Liza came to the conclusion that it wouldn't matter either way. If he was here to kill her, she wouldn't be able to fend him off. *Reason with him,* she decided. *But how the Hell did he get here so quickly, and how did he know where I live?"* she thought.

* * *

Damian took a few steps backward, seeing fear in her eyes. He'd known it was going to be a problem showing up unannounced. "Liza, it's okay. I'm not here to hurt you," he said, trying to remain calm. He scanned their surroundings for Selene. "We need to talk," he said, "and we don't have much time. It would be better if we could go inside. Trust me." He hoped she'd agree; protecting her inside would be a lot easier than out.

"Not much time for what?" she asked. "You're scaring me."

"Please, Liza! I'll explain once we're inside." Damian said, once again checking their surroundings.

Hearing the urgency in Damian's voice, Liza glanced down at her phone. *Shit, shit, shit!* As expected, she didn't have a signal. That was one of the few disadvantages of living lakeside. "You can come in, but you need to keep your distance," she said, hoping for a better signal from the WiFi inside. She really wanted to trust Damian—he'd been so loving toward her in the tent—but her red flag count was high.

* * *

Damian had insisted on entering the house first, with Liza following behind at a safe distance. "You really should lock your doors," he admonished Liza as he flipped on the lights and glanced around.

"It's not necessary, living this far out," Liza said, making a mental note to lock the doors in the future…if she survived. *A big, scary dog might not be a bad idea, either,* she thought. "So…like I said earlier, I'm not the type to have random sex with strangers. I don't know what came over me," she said, pacing back and forth in the kitchen, rambling on about how great it was as she stalled Damian and waited for a better signal to call emergency services.

"You bitch!" Selene yelled as she stormed out of the walk-in pantry Damian had failed to check. Selene angrily stuck her hand out toward Liza and put a holding spell on her.

"Selene, no!" Damian shouted as Selene squeezed Liza's lungs with her spell. The look of terror on Liza's face was enough to drive Damian crazy, and he leapt at Selene. He hit her, throwing her backward and into the edge of the granite countertop. Her head hit with such force that it rebounded forward with a sickening snap, and she collapsed. Selene's eyes stared lifelessly at him from where she lay.

The spell broken, Liza slumped to the floor, sobbing uncontrollably.

Damian rushed over and took her in his arms. "Shhh…it's okay now," he said, whispering into Liza's hair as her head fell onto his chest. She was shaking uncontrollably, and Damian angled her away from Selene's body lying on the floor.

Several minutes passed as Damian rubbed her back and whispered into her hair before Liza was able to speak. Looking into his eyes with confusion, she asked in a shaking voice, "How? Why? I don't understand!"

Damian knew without a doubt he loved this woman. Selene had killed in the past, but Liza was different. He was also now in great danger, having killed Selene to protect Liza. Selene's bosses would want answers, and he knew they wouldn't be happy with his response.

"We're in this together now," Damian said. "Please don't doubt my feelings for you." Damian reached into the pocket of his pants, pulling out the third tarot card—the *Knight of Cups*, Liza's future. "Before I tell you everything, I need to give you the reading for your third card—the *Knight of Cups*." Liza looked down at the card he was holding in his hand—a knight riding a magnificent white horse, holding a cup, as if he were a messenger of sorts. She looked back up at Damian with a hint of trust, and he continued, "The *Knight of Cups* wants you to prepare to be swept up in the whirlwind of new love. If you're in a relationship, an epic night of major charm and romance is headed your way!" His voice grew huskier. "I have many things to explain, and I promise I will."

* * *

Liza could see the love in his eyes as he looked at her. She had lots of questions—and she intended to get her answers—but for now she was going to take advantage of the *Knight of Cups*, and she leaned in for what she knew would be a passionate kiss. For the moment, everything was right in the world.

* * * * *

Sheellah Kennedy Bio

Sheellah Kennedy was born in Toronto, Ontario, Canada, and raised in a remote area of British Columbia. From the time she was a little girl, she loved to read. It's no surprise that she became a children's librarian for several years. She is pleased to have her first ever short story published in "Flights of Fantasy," and intends to turn it into a full-length book. Her family means everything to her. She would like to thank her three children, Ryan, Adrienne, and Erika for continuing to love her despite her unconventional ways. She would also like to thank her parents, Rodney and Gloria Jewell, for always pushing her to believe in herself, and of course her ever-patient husband, Chris Kennedy, who continues to believe in her, giving her the courage and strength to try new things even when she doubts herself.

# # # # #

Shatter Me by Melissa Olthoff

"Second Squad, check in."

I automatically reached for the radio attached to the front of my vest before I remembered it wasn't there anymore. The wireless upgrade we were field testing had some serious advantages, like no longer having a cord a perp could strangle us with, but there were downsides. Muscle memory needed to be retrained, costing precious seconds in an altercation. Relocating the transmitter to a secure pocket high on my vest also came to mind. Seriously, every time I transmitted, it looked like I was feeling up my left boob.

I bit back a growl as I replied, "Second Squad, checking in. We're on Cascadian Road, approaching Stage Parkway. No issues. How copy?"

"Five by five," Dispatch said. I could hear the smile in his voice. It must be Rogers on duty tonight. He always sounded like he was on the verge of laughing and persisted in using older radio terms for the fun of it. "The new radios are working out great. Anything interesting happening?"

"Oh, it's a regular party out here." I snorted as I wiped rainwater off my face for the millionth time.

Jena Cole, my best friend and partner, rolled her eyes. Her silvery blonde hair was in its usual high ponytail, water dripping nonstop off the end. Terrance Hendricks, who normally looked like he could be a linebacker, was hunched down in his jacket and more closely resembled a pissed off bear woken early from hibernation. His tall and gangly partner, Shawn Sanchez, was trudging along beside him. Neither bothered to respond. Unless you counted Terrance growling. Like a bear.

"You know, with the pouring rain," I continued. "Nice and balmy out here, too."

There was a pause. "You're being sarcastic again, aren't you?"

"Yes. Yes, I am."

"Copy all. Dispatch, out."

Jena gave me the side eye. "I think you pissed him off, Hannah."

"Wouldn't be the first time," I muttered, scanning the cross street as we trudged through the intersection.

"Boss, if you could avoid pissing off Dispatch just once, we'd really appreciate it," Sanchez called from behind me.

Hendricks growled in agreement.

I glanced back at the big man and raised a dripping eyebrow. "Nonverbal much?"

Hendricks just glowered back at me. With his large size, he could be intimidating as hell, but his rough exterior hid a soft and gooey center. Out of the four of us, he was hands down the best with kids. And God help anyone who hurt a child with him around. We'd been patrolling together for a few years, and it was easy to see the misery behind the grumpy face.

I took pity on him. "Coffee break when we reach Lakeside?"

That got me a smile and a nod. It was the best I could hope for at this point in our patrol. It was late fall, and the temperature had fallen to the upper forties over the past hour. He wasn't the only one who could use a hot drink to get through the rest of our shift.

"Join the City Guard," they said, "It'll be fun," they said. Yeah, right. Crappy pay, crappy hours, crappy weather, and worst of all—boredom. We walked the same route every day, patrolled the same section of the city, passed the same shops. Suggestions to the higher ups to switch up our routes every so often to keep us sharp were met with disdain and snide comments. I gave up after the first year.

We were nearing the end of our route when a flash of movement in an alleyway caught my eye. I raised a fist to halt my squad and used hand gestures to indicate Jena and I would check it out while Hendricks and Sanchez kept watch on the street. I panned my flashlight around the alley, searching the shadows. Jena placed a hand on her baton, only to relax and snort a laugh when the light revealed the happy face of a large dog. Make that a *very* large dog. His back looked like it would be even with my waist, and I wasn't a short woman.

"Holy shit, he's huge," Jena breathed, taking a cautious step backward.

I stayed still, watching the dog's body language.

"Friendly though," I finally decided. "Tail's up and wagging, and he's relaxed. Think I see a collar, too. Must be a pet, not a stray."

The dog's ears perked up at the sound of my voice. He took a few cautious steps my way, fully into the light from the street. He was gorgeous, with sandy brown fur and the most beautiful green and gold eyes. He sniffed the hand I held out to him. I got a lick for my trouble, but when I reached out to pet him, he backed away.

When I made no move to chase him, he turned around and disappeared into the shadows of the alley.

I shrugged and looked at my partner. "I'll call it in to Dispatch, and they can relay it to Animal Control. I'm sure there's someone looking for him."

I notified Dispatch once we were on the move again. We were all eager to get out of the rain, and moving faster now that the end of our patrol was in sight.

"Copy all, Second Squad. Lot of dog sightings tonight. Must be a full moon," Rogers joked.

"Yeah, sure," I muttered, rolling my eyes.

* * *

After our shift was over, Jena and I met up at the neighborhood bar a short walk from our apartment complex. It was nothing special, just a hole in the wall with decent food, better beer, and a nice selection of eye candy. It was crowded tonight, and we hadn't been able to snag a pool table. Hell, we were lucky to get our normal barstools.

I scowled at the packed room but changed it to a smile for the bartender when she passed me my usual drink. Jena chugged half her rum and coke in one go before setting it forcefully on the bar.

"God, today sucked," she moaned, wiping her mouth with the back of her hand.

"Yeah it did," I agreed, sipping at my beer. "You know, I've been thinking. Our squad is senior enough now. Maybe we should try applying to the border wall patrol again."

Jena looked at me like I was crazy. "Why would we want to do that?"

I shrugged. "Change of pace."

"It's nothing special," Jena argued, slinging back the rest of her drink and signaling for another. "Just the border between city districts. It'd just be the same ol' shit, different patrol route."

I tugged at the bottom of my long blonde braid and sighed in frustration. "But at least it'd be *different*."

"Whatevs." Jena snorted. "They'll just deny us again anyway."

I turned away from her and looked out at the crowded bar again. I recognized most of the people here. It was the same people I saw every time we came here, though there were definitely a few new faces tonight.

Jena was silent for a moment before she said, "What's up your ass, anyway?"

"I'm bored," I said honestly. I turned back to my best friend. "We do the same thing every day. We get up, go to work, patrol the same damn streets, and usually end up here after our shift. We're like goddamn clockwork figures."

Jena kept a straight face for all of five seconds before she snorted a laugh. "How long has it been since you got laid?" I rolled my eyes at her. "No, seriously. You need to get those endorphins going. You'll feel so much better!"

That got a reluctant laugh out of me. She bumped her shoulder against mine. "The hottie at the end of the bar keeps checking you out. You should go for it."

I glanced to my left. She wasn't wrong; the guy was hot. I pulled my eyes away and sipped at my beer again.

"Not my type," I muttered, my face turning red.

"Uh, yeah, I'm pretty sure tall, dark, and handsome over there is every girl's type."

I sighed and pushed away my nearly empty beer.

Jena groaned, shoving her silvery blonde hair out of her face. "I know that sigh. You're thinking about *him*, aren't you?"

"I was actually thinking about that dog," I said absently, spinning my ID band around my wrist.

Jena narrowed her blue eyes skeptically and tapped her fingers on the bar. "Really."

I blew out a breath, exasperated. "Okay fine, you caught me," I snapped. "I was thinking about him."

Matt had been my first boyfriend, my first love, my first…everything. Right up until he walked out of my life six years ago. My best friend, just gone.

"*Technically,* I was thinking about the dog. His eyes reminded me of him. They were that same mix of green and gold…"

My best friend's expression softened just a little bit. "Oh, honey, you have *got* to let that boy go."

"I know," I replied softly. "But not today."

I pushed away from the bar, my tab already settled, and shrugged my jacket on. "I'm out. You?"

Jena muttered under her breath but got up anyways. "Nobody worth going home with tonight. I'll walk with ya."

I snorted a laugh as we walked out the door. "I thought that guy was every girl's type?" I teased.

"Yeah, and he didn't look twice at me," she grumbled.

"Ouch," I laughed as we walked out into the night. "And of course it stops raining *now*."

"You couldn't have done that a few hours ago?" Jena shouted at the cloudy sky.

We shared an exasperated look and set off on the short walk home. Skittering claws drew our attention across the street to yet another oversized dog, this one a pure black. A slightly smaller gray and white one cautiously stepped out of the shadows and into the pool of streetlight where the first paused. It was a weird moment. We stared at the dogs, and they stared right back at us. Almost like they were studying us. The moment broke. The dogs wagged their tails and trotted off.

"Well," Jena said after a silent beat, "Dispatch wasn't wrong. They really are everywhere tonight."

I released a breath as the strange tension left me. "Okay, yeah, I've had enough for today."

My best friend raised an eyebrow at me but didn't argue as I picked up the pace for home. Five minutes later, we'd reached Silver Springs Villas. It sounded fancy, but it was nothing more than a random collection of old three-story vinyl-sided buildings scattered around a muddy pond. It wasn't the most secure place, either. All of the apartments were outside access, and mine was ground level. But at the time, it was the only one available, and now I was too lazy to move to a higher floor.

Jena and I waved goodnight and split off to our own apartments. I slowed abruptly as I neared my front door and saw the shadowy figure leaning against it. I slowly reached for my pepper spray, silently cursing the fact that even the City Guard weren't allowed firearms.

"Who's there?" I said sharply.

The man slowly stepped forward, the porch light highlighting his green and gold eyes. The bottom dropped out of my stomach.

"Matt?" I gasped.

"Hey, Hannah Banana."

I just gaped at him wordlessly for a long moment. I'd forgotten the sound of his voice. It was deep with a hint of rasp to it, making my toes curl. He was taller than I remembered, with a lean, muscular frame. His hair was the same sandy brown, but longer, down to his jawline and messy, like he'd been running his hand through it while he waited.

Matt took another step closer and gave me an uncertain smile. "It's been awhile."

I unfroze and stalked toward him. The moron opened his arms like he thought I was moving in for a hug. Instead I balled up my fist and socked him right in the gut, twisting at the waist to put my whole body into the hit.

"You son of a bitch!" I yelled as he doubled over, gasping and...wait, was he laughing? What. The. Fuck.

Matt slowly straightened up, amusement and guilt battling for supremacy on his face. "Okay, I deserved that."

"You think?" I demanded sarcastically, swiping angrily at the strands of blonde hair that had escaped my braid when I punched the bastard.

Remorse won. Matt licked his lips nervously. "Hannah Banana, can we talk—"

"Oh, no you don't," I interrupted. I stabbed a finger at his face and added, "You lost nickname privileges a long time ago. You know, when you *left*."

"Can I please come in? I'll explain everything," Matt replied, green and gold eyes pleading with me.

I crossed my arms stubbornly. "Whatever you want to say, you can say out here."

The clouds chose that very moment to open back up with the kind of downpour that soaked you to the skin in ten seconds flat.

"Seriously?" I shouted up at the sky. I closed my eyes for a moment and slowly let out a breath through my nose, fighting to control my anger.

"Fine, you can come in," I finally said through gritted teeth.

Matt was a smarter man than he looked. He didn't say a word as he stepped aside so I could get to the front door. I jammed my key into the lock like I was stabbing a certain someone. I paused for a moment. It belatedly occurred to me I hadn't seen him in six years, and I was trusting him at my back. Just like I always had.

But I trusted my gut, too, and while it was full of rage and other emotions I wasn't ready to examine, I didn't have any alarm bells going off. I mentally shrugged. *Fuck it.* I unlocked the door and stomped into my rather messy one-bedroom apartment. I kicked off my shoes, went straight to the hall closet, and grabbed two towels. I wrapped my nice fluffy purple one around my shoulders and flung a cheap brown one at Matt. He caught it without looking as he shut and locked the door.

I threw myself onto my small couch and crossed my arms again. "You want to talk, talk."

"Do you remember the last time we spoke?" Matt asked as he slowly sat at the other end of the couch. His face was relaxed, but the towel clenched tightly in his hands gave away his real feelings. That was the thing with Matt. You had to pay attention to his hands.

I glared at him. "Are you freaking kidding me? Yes, Matt, I think I remember the last time we talked before you *left* me."

Green and gold eyes winced. He took a deep breath. "I said I was going to go see what was on the other side of the wall."

I launched myself off the couch and paced as much as the small living area would allow. I needed to move.

"And what did you find? More city?" I demanded sarcastically in an echo of our last conversation.

I remembered everything about that day. I remembered what we were wearing, how the wind felt as it played with my hair, how the city looked from our perch on the top of a high rise. Gray, gloomy, endless. Matt wanted to see the other districts up close. I didn't. You weren't supposed to cross the border walls without permission. We fought. And he left me alone on that rooftop with only the wind for company.

The devastation I felt that day flooded over me. Like I was drowning all over again. Like I'd never take another full breath of air.

My ex must have seen the look on my face. "Hannah Banana, I'm sorry—"

I spun to face him, rage burning out the sorrow and leaving ashes in its wake. "No. You don't get to call me that ever again. We had one little argument, and you left me. You *left* me, Matt. You walked away without a word. You knew what that would do to me, and you did it anyway. And now you've got the balls to show up at my door after six years? I don't want your apology. I want to know *why*."

My voice wavered at the end, and I hated it. I couldn't even look at him without risking tears, so I went back to pacing. Waiting for his response.

"Did you know the border patrols carry guns?"

I stopped abruptly. Whatever I'd expected him to say, it definitely wasn't that. "What? No, they don't. None of us do."

"Yeah, Hannah, they do. They like to use them, too," Matt replied, voice hard as he pulled down the collar of his shirt to reveal a ragged scar on his shoulder. It looked an awful lot like a bullet wound. His voice softened as he added, "I didn't mean to leave you, Hannah. And I'm so, so sorry I did. I'm sorry it took so long for me to find a way back in—"

"What are you talking about?" I demanded, ignoring his apology for now. It hurt too much to think about.

Matt took a deep breath, his hands flexing until his knuckles were white. "The wall, it isn't what it looks like. It's not a border between districts. It's a border between the city and the outside world."

"The outside world," I repeated slowly.

"When you cross the wall, there's nothing but wilderness, miles of it, until you get to the next town," Matt said earnestly, leaning forward and looking directly into my eyes. "I almost didn't make it; I was bleeding out. And what I found out there…"

I fought back the surge of pure panic at the thought of him dying and tried to hold onto my anger as a shield. I cleared my throat and said, "What did you find?"

"Magic and monsters, Hannah."

He sounded so serious that for just a second, I believed him. I snorted a humorless laugh and shook my head. "Did you get shot in the head, too?"

Matt grinned at me. It was the same grin that dared me to climb the tallest tree in the park, to kiss him for the first time, to run around after curfew and sneak onto the roofs of high rises. He knew exactly what he was doing, that fucker.

"I can prove it to you if you want. Or I can walk out the door. Your choice." He shrugged like it didn't matter to him. But I saw his hands. This mattered to him.

I snorted and walked back over to the couch. I made a bit of a production of wrapping my towel back around me and getting comfortable.

Matt raised a sandy brown eyebrow and asked, "You done yet?"

I gave one last wiggle and smirked. "Yup. Go ahead, show me some magic. And when you're done playing, you can tell me why you really got...shot..."

I trailed off as Matt stood up and pulled his shirt off. Holy hell! That was a lot of muscles. Soooo many muscles. I literally had to brush my hand over my lips to make sure I wasn't actually drooling. Matt had always been fit, but sometime in the past six years he'd gone from lean to full-on *ripped*. There were some new scars, too. The biggest four were in parallel lines wrapped around the golden skin of his ribcage. They looked like claw marks of all things. My view was abruptly cut off when Matt threw his shirt in my face.

"Hey!"

I pulled the shirt away to glare at the shirtless asshat. He just winked at me. "I thought you could use something to wipe the drool off."

"Shut up," I muttered. I raised a questioning eyebrow when he unbuttoned his jeans. "I thought you said you were going to do some magic, not a strip show."

"Well, you always thought those were pretty magical," Matt teased with a wicked grin. His smile abruptly fell away as he added, "I never said I was going to do magic."

"But you said—"

"Magic and monsters," he interrupted grimly. "And I'm one of the monsters. Please, just...don't be afraid of me."

His hands were white knuckled again as he stripped off his jeans, jaw clenched tight. He was starting to scare me a little. Six years was a long time. How much had he changed? How much could I really trust him? Those thoughts didn't stop the slight pang of disappointment when he left his boxer briefs on, though. Damn it.

A grunt brought my eyes whipping back up to his face, which was contorted in pain. What followed was the most horrifying thing I'd ever seen. Not because of the sound of his bones breaking or muscles tearing, though that didn't help. It was the look of burning agony in his eyes. Those green and gold eyes stayed steady on mine as everything else about him changed, as if he was holding onto me like a lifeline. After a minute that stretched into eternity, there was a panting dog standing in his place. A ridiculously huge dog, with pointed ears, sharp teeth, shaggy brown fur...oh fuck.

"You're not a dog, are you," I whispered, voice hoarse and barely audible even to me.

The dog—no, the *wolf*, sat down as visible tremors shivered down his long legs. The move put his head higher than mine. If I was standing, his head would be even with my shoulder. The wolf tilted his head to the side and whined.

"Oh yeah, I'm fine," I reassured him, my voice stronger but somewhat high pitched. "I see ex-boyfriends turn into wolves all the time."

Those green and gold eyes narrowed at me. What? Oh. "You disappeared for six years," I pointed out. "I thought it was reasonable to assume the relationship was over."

The wolf snorted and stood back up. He shook his fur out and perked his ears forward. He raised one oversized paw into the air and tilted his head at me again. In response, I held my hand out to him like I would to a dog. He snorted again and slowly walked over to me. Our eyes were nearly level. He ignored my outstretched hand and licked my cheek. I jumped and bit back a shriek of surprise. He winced, ears turning back slightly, before pushing his head against my hand. In a daze, I scratched behind his ears.

"This is fine," I muttered. "I'm just sitting here, scratching my ex-boyfriend the wolf behind the ears. No big deal. Everything is fine."

The wolf—no, Matt—whined again. I blinked at him. "I hope you don't have fleas," I said seriously.

For whatever reason, that struck me as funny as hell, and I laughed hysterically. I couldn't stop. Between one breath and the next, it turned into sobbing. I covered my face with both hands and just let it all out. The shock of seeing Matt again, the bullet wound, him turning into a wolf. I just, I just couldn't…

"Hannah," he said softly.

I physically couldn't answer him, not while crying. I also couldn't *stop* crying. I felt the couch dip as he sat next to me, the man, not the wolf. He must have changed back. The thought triggered another wave of hyperventilating, and it was a good minute before I managed to calm my breathing. Then the idiot placed a comforting hand on my shoulder, and I completely lost it again. This time I turned into him, and his arms wrapped around me. I buried my face in his warm chest, and he rested his head on top of mine. He didn't say a word; he just held me until I was ready to let go.

I took a couple of deep breaths and pulled away.

Matt smiled at me. "There's those blue eyes I love. Storming when you're upset, clear skies when you're happy."

"And bright red when I cry," I added wryly.

I wordlessly took the tissue he held out to me and cleaned up my face. I sat back against the corner of the couch so I was facing him.

"Tell me everything," I said simply.

It took hours. He talked until he was hoarse. At one point, I got up and walked the five steps to the kitchen nook and grabbed us both waters. When I sat back down, I pretended I didn't notice my leg was pressed against his. Magic and monsters, he'd said, ripped their way back into the ordinary world about thirty years ago. Cascade City was created as a kind of Humans Only zone and existed as a separatist state from the rest of the country. He told me about the wall, which was layered with an illusion spell to give the appearance of an endless city, and what he called an avoidance spell, to make people want to stay away from it. He told me how the city government somehow suppressed any magical talent or monstrous tendencies in its citizens. And how the border patrols enforced their orders to keep anyone from getting in. Or out.

I sat quietly for a while after he finished. It was a hell of a lot to process.

I frowned slightly. "How come the avoidance thingy didn't work on you?"

"I'm a wolf shifter," he replied with a shrug. "We've got strong pack instincts. That drove me outside the walls to find more of my kind."

I took a deep breath and asked the big question. "Why are you back?"

Matt hesitated. "There are concerns the city has overstepped the bounds of their treaty. They say they just suppress magic, but we think they're actually siphoning it off anyone with talent, which is highly illegal. There's also been a recent increase in the disappearance of magic users, specifically children with high potential. There's no proof, but if the city is already stealing everything from its citizens, it may be looking for more power. We were sent here, unofficially, to investigate and look for any sign of the missing kids."

Missing kids. Oh god. I stomped hard on the memory that tried to rise and focused. "Any luck?"

He shook his head slowly. Damn it. I spun my ID band around my wrist for a moment. Even after six years, it turned out I could still read Matt. He wasn't telling me everything. And he kept saying 'we,' not 'I.' I looked down and braced myself.

"You said we?" I asked carefully.

"My team, me and five other members of my pack." He shifted closer and ducked down, his green and gold gaze capturing mine effortlessly. This time there was no hesitation. "I fought tooth and claw to get added to that team. I swear to you, I didn't abandon you. Yeah, I walked off when I was mad, but I figured I'd just hop over the wall and come right back to tell you what I saw. I never dreamed it would take me six years to do it. I never stopped fighting to get back to you. I *never* stopped loving you, Hannah. You want to know why I really came back? I came back for *you*."

I closed my eyes as fresh tears poured down my cheeks. Well. If that wasn't what every girl wanted to hear. His warm hand came up to cup my cheek, and I leaned into it without thinking. It was automatic with him. It always had been.

"I may have exaggerated about the ex-boyfriends earlier," I said, my voice a little hoarse.

Matt snickered. "You mean they didn't really turn into wolves?"

"I mean they didn't exist." I opened my eyes and looked up at him. "There was never anyone else. It's always been you."

His eyes flared, and he growled before pulling me into a searing kiss I felt down to my toes. I made a desperate sound in the back of my throat and kissed him back. My arms came up and gripped his muscular shoulders. After a moment, he pulled back. I protested wordlessly, but he just laughed and lifted me into his lap without any apparent effort.

Damn, that was hot.

Matt's hands came up and cupped my face. His green and gold eyes searched my stormy blue ones. He must have found what he was looking for, because he let out a relieved breath and gently kissed me again. I loved it, but right now I didn't want gentle. I opened my mouth and demanded more. He obliged with a kiss that scrambled my brains and made me forget my own name.

After a few minutes, he drew back. His hands flexed on my hips, and his eyes were more than a little wild. "Hannah…"

I bit my lip. Oh, I knew that look. That look promised late nights and lost sleep.

I gently moved his hands off my hips and got to my feet. The poor guy looked so disappointed I almost snorted a laugh and gave the game away.

Matt took a deep breath, closing his eyes and visibly forcing himself to relax. Well, most of him. "It's too soon, isn't it? Sorry, Hannah, it's just been a long six years."

I walked away without a word. I somehow managed to hold in my laughter until I reached my bedroom door. The sultry sound had his eyes snapping open. He focused on me with a predatory intent that made my pulse race.

I cast a smug grin over my shoulder. "How about we make up for lost time?"

* * *

The next morning I woke up slowly, more than half-convinced last night was nothing more than wishful thinking and a dream. The warm weight at my side put that fear to rest, and I sighed happily. Matt let out a quiet laugh, wrapped a well-muscled arm around my stomach, and tugged me closer, my back to his front. I took a few minutes to just enjoy it. He dropped a gentle kiss on my shoulder and trailed his fingers over my belly. His fingers ever so slowly dipped lower. I caught my breath and pushed back against him with a wicked grin, my thoughts immediately jumping straight into the gutter.

The shrill sound of my stupid alarm clock rudely interrupted. Damn it. I leaned over and turned it off, barely resisting the urge to throw it across the room.

"I've got to get ready for work." I sighed, shoulders slumping in dejection.

I turned back in time to see him sit up, the blankets falling down to his hips and revealing his defined torso. Oh, holy hell. His hair was sleep mussed and hanging in his face, partially obscuring his eyes. Blonde scruff lined his jaw, and his lips were quirked up in a smile.

"Are you sure I can't persuade you to be late?" he asked, that ever-present rasp in his voice deeper than usual.

"Yeah," I groaned, hating myself. "I'm sure."

Tearing my gaze away from all those muscles was damn near physically painful. I may have whimpered a little. I went to get out of bed, but he reached out and gently gripped my arm, pulling me around to face him again.

"Okay, I think this now qualifies as torture," I teased.

"I want you to come with me when I leave."

I froze. A part of me knew he wouldn't be staying—hell, it even knew he'd ask me to go with him. And after the wolf thing, I didn't doubt anything he'd said. But I had a life here. Even if it was a boring, clockwork life, it was *my* boring, clockwork life. And like a clockwork figure, I had a safe, comfortable path to follow. My days already blurred together, because they were all the same. Gray, gloomy, endless.

I could easily see it continuing that way forever.

Seeing Matt again was like taking my first real breath in years. Like I'd been living in the darkness and could only now see enough light to remember there was color in the world and not just shades of gray. But…I was scared. To break away from that path, to leave everything I'd ever known behind…it was too much, too fast.

I let out a slow breath and met his eyes. "I need to think. How long can you give me?"

"Only until tonight," he replied, face troubled. His hands clenched and unclenched several times before he added, "We're supposed to meet up outside the west wall after dark."

I started spinning my ID band around my wrist again. It was an old habit, and it had always helped settle my nerves. Matt reached out and stopped me. I glanced down at his warm hand on mine and raised an eyebrow in silent question.

"We think that's how they suppress our powers," he explained quietly. "Everyone wears them, nobody thinks to question it."

"And it's against the law to take them off," I added absently, thinking through the implications.

I flashed him a teasing grin as one implication in particular occurred to me. "Think I've got any magic powers?"

"I think you're a Pegasus," he immediately replied.

I blinked at him, taken aback by the serious look on his face. "You think I'm a winged horse?"

Just saying the words out loud had me cracking up. Matt grinned that wicked smile at me. My pulse picked up.

"It's a nickname for an air mage. The wind has always loved you, Hannah. Even suppressed, it's done everything it can to help you. Remember the tree?"

"You mean the tallest tree in the park? The tree you dared me to climb? The tree I fell out of? Nope," I said dryly, popping the 'p' at the end of the word. "I don't remember that at all. Or how you barely saved my ass from hitting the ground."

Matt rubbed the back of his neck, face reddening. "And at thirteen, I was more than happy to take the credit for saving you. That got me my first kiss, after all." I smirked at him. I remembered. "But I really didn't do much more than grab hold of you. The wind gusted so hard, I swear you were weightless."

I looked back at him skeptically. "You sure you're remembering that right? Maybe the kiss scrambled your brains."

"Only one way to find out. Give me your hand." My pulse leaped until I realized he wasn't talking about kissing. When I hesitated, his green and gold eyes met my stormy blue ones. "Hannah, do you trust me?"

I scowled at him and stuck my wrist with the ID band out. "You really have to ask me that after last night? I just…don't like breaking the rules."

"I know," Matt said quietly as he gently took my wrist. His fingers tightened slightly. "I'm grateful for it. If you'd been with me all those years ago, you could have died."

He bent his head, sandy brown hair falling across his face as he examined the band. There was no clasp, just a solid circle of metal embedded with all my information. It was more than identification, it was all my personal, health, and professional records. And I'd never once thought to question it. He gripped the band with both hands and looked up at me.

"Hold still."

His muscled shoulders and arms flexed, and he literally ripped the metal in half. Holy shit. I suddenly felt a lot less tired as he carefully pulled the jagged pieces away from my skin. But that could be attributed to reasons that had nothing to do with suppressed magic. Incredibly hot, muscly reasons.

"Okay, that was hot," I admitted, trying not to drool again.

Matt's green and gold eyes flashed to me, filled with heat. I could almost see him fighting for control. I smirked, beyond smug that I still had that effect on him. He dragged his eyes up and down my body, but unfortunately regained control quickly.

"Feel any different?"

I shrugged. "Not really."

"Try making a breeze," he suggested.

I thought for a second. Feeling awkward as hell, I waved my hand through the air. Nothing happened. Unless you counted my face turning beet red.

Matt coughed to hide his laugh. "I don't think that's how it works, Hannah Banana."

I raised an eyebrow. "Oh, so you think you've got nickname privileges back, do you?"

Matt raised a sandy brown eyebrow right back at me, a mischievous glint in his eyes. "You've really got to ask me that after last night?"

"Touché." I glanced at the time and licked my lips. "You know, I've got a little bit of time if you want to…persuade me some more."

I'd barely gotten the words out before Matt pinned me to the bed, his muscular body pressing down on me in the best way possible. Those green and gold eyes filled with heat again, and I felt an answering heat rise up inside me.

* * *

I was more than a little late to the mid-morning briefing before shift change.

"Where have you been," Jena hissed as I sidled in next to her as unobtrusively as possible. "And why are you glowing?"

Before I could answer, her eyes widened. "You got laid, didn't you? Details! Now!"

The patrol supervisor saved me from having to answer. "Nice of you to drop in, Sergeant Barrows. As I was saying, Animal Control can't keep up with all the strays roaming the streets lately. The City Council has requested our assistance in this matter. You'll be issued tranq guns before you head out on patrol. Tag any dogs you come across and coordinate with Animal Control for pick up. A member of the Border Patrol will be assigned to each of your teams to assist with any overly large or aggressive dogs."

A lead weight grew in my stomach. Overly large dogs—or *wolves* pretending to be dogs?

Before I could think better of it, I interrupted his briefing. "How will they be assisting us, sir?"

Sergeant Millington shot me a look. "They'll be armed."

"I thought the City Guard didn't carry firearms," I shot back. I just couldn't seem to stop myself.

"In certain situations, the Border Patrol is authorized to carry. The decision to shoot will be theirs and theirs alone. I suggest you stay out of their way." He glared at me until he was sure I was done talking. "Patrol leaders, come see me for your assignments."

Hours later, we were well into our normal patrol route. So far we'd tranq'd a couple medium-sized strays and called it in to Animal Control for pickup. This was so far out of our norm, it was ridiculous. My gut said the City Council knew Matt and his team were in town and were trying to flush them out. And they were using the City Guard, using *me*, to do it. Worse, I had no way to contact Matt to warn him. Fuck, this wasn't good.

I tried to spin my ID band around my wrist, but it wasn't there anymore. I tugged my sleeve lower to hide my bare skin and kept walking.

I eyed the Border Patrol guard suspiciously. The nametag on his uniform said Riker. He hadn't bothered to tell us his first name. I'd never seen him before, or any of the border guys assigned to the other teams. They were all older, and had that grizzled, tough as nails feel to them, like they'd seen some shit at some point and were prepared for more. Alarm bells went off anytime I got too close to the guy, and I was more than happy to let him take point. I did *not* want him at my back. Especially armed.

We were nearing the end of our patrol when it all went to hell. Hendricks and Sanchez were bringing yet another tranq'd dog out to animal control, leaving the rest of us standing in an alley, trying to ignore the smell rising from one of the dumpsters. I looked around and realized it was the same damn alley from last night. The alley where I first saw Matt in wolf form.

Two dogs—no, *wolves*—came trotting out of a side alley, one gray, one a sandy brown with Matt's green and gold eyes. Fuck. I frantically waved at them to go back, but it was too late.

Riker saw them and instantly raised his rifle. He hadn't looked twice at any of the other animals we'd come across. Judging by the expression on his face, he knew exactly what he was looking at now. So I did something really stupid. I got in his way.

I held my hands up desperately. "Don't shoot them!"

Riker didn't break his focus. His eyes narrowed on the two wolves slowly backing away.

"Hannah!" Jena shouted in alarm. She tried to grab my arm, but I dodged her attempt.

I glared at Riker. "They're friendly, there's no need to shoot them."

"Get the fuck out of my way," he growled as the gray wolf backed around the corner and out of sight.

The big man was faster than he looked. He shoved me out of the way before I could blink, and I hit the ground hard. He took aim at Matt. I raised a hand and screamed, a wordless cry of fear and rage. And the wind answered.

A violent gust of wind came out of nowhere and slammed Riker into the wall. He lost his grip on the rifle and it skittered under a dumpster. Holy shit. The Border Patrol guard slumped to the ground and looked over at me with a mix of fear and hatred on his face.

"You're one of *them*," he slurred.

Crap. I staggered to my feet and looked over at Jena. My best friend and partner of four years just looked at me, eyes wide. I reached for her, but she stepped back with a look of fear.

"What the hell was that?" she gasped, backing further away from me.

I glanced over my shoulder. Riker had risen to his knees, one hand on the wall to steady himself, eyes already searching for his lost weapon. There was no time.

"I'm sorry, Jena." I spun around and dashed around the corner where Matt waited for me alone, the gray wolf nowhere in sight.

I spent the next hour running behind Matt's furry butt as he took a twisting route through what felt like every back alley in the city. Along the way, I stripped away everything that could identify me as City Guard—my vest with my radio and cell phone, my patrol cap, my uniform jacket. I felt like I'd stripped away part of who I was.

By the time the border wall was finally in sight, I was down to black cargo pants and a black t-shirt. Matt held up a paw for me to stay and walked into a recessed doorway. I paced while I waited, trying to keep my muscles from locking up. The sweat from our run turned ice cold as the sun fell below the horizon and the temperature dropped.

After a few minutes of pained grunts and rustling clothes, he walked back out dressed in a similar style. He tossed me his dark jacket when he saw me shivering. I pulled it on gratefully.

He tapped his fingers on his leg. "What are you going to do, Hannah?"

He didn't tell me what to do, he asked. I was grateful for that, too. I sighed. I was pretty sure I would have gone with Matt tonight anyway, but that damn guard had taken away my choice.

In less than twenty-four hours, everything had changed. I felt like something was about to break. I just wish I knew if it was the clockwork path I was on, or me. Maybe it was both.

I looked up into Matt's green and gold eyes. They were full of love and hope, and something inside me settled into place. I stepped closer, drawn to him like always. This time, I pulled *him* into a searing kiss. His arms wrapped around me tight, one around my waist and the other gripping the back of my neck. I felt cherished, like I was the only one in the world who mattered.

His kiss shattered me. But I didn't break. The fear keeping me chained in place did.

I drew back far enough to look into the green and gold eyes I loved.

I smiled. "I'm going with you."

He gave me that wicked grin in reply. "That's my girl."

We made it over the wall that night. I had no idea what my future would be, but I wasn't afraid. The days ahead no longer looked gray, gloomy, or endless. I wasn't alone anymore.

I'd broken free of my clockwork path.

* * * * *

Melissa Olthoff Bio

Melissa Olthoff grew up on Star Trek, Star Wars and pretty much every Arnold Schwarzenegger movie ever made. She was lucky enough to have an amazing dad that supported her out-of-control reading addiction—and her goal of joining the military. In 2005, she commissioned as an US Air Force officer and briefly achieved her dream of becoming a pilot. While she loved flying, her ears did not, so she cross-trained into Airfield Operations where she spent the rest of her military career. Her last assignment was Seymour Johnson AFB, a F-15E Strike Eagle base. She swore she wouldn't date a fighter pilot, but accidentally left a loophole and ended up marrying one. She now works as an accountant (seriously) to pay the bills and her husband flies cargo. They like to joke that they used to be cool and do cool things. Then they had children. They currently live in Tennessee with two kids and two oversized German Shepherds.

# # # # #

Dark Side of the Sun by Monalisa Foster

June 20th, 2025

Eliana pulled her sedan up to the curb, right under the biggest oak she'd ever seen. Its canopy cast welcome shade from the scorching mid-day sun. Ahead, an ambulance was pulled under a mansion's porte cochère. Four black-and-whites were also present, their lights twirling madly: one behind the ambulance, the others scattered along the curb.

A young cop was putting up barricades, while another was stringing crime scene tape between them. Another pair was gently encouraging five curious neighbors to back away. By the look of it, the gawkers were nannies and housewives, each with an obligatory kid or two in tow.

Eliana pulled her too-big jacket on. Simple, lightweight, and cut to hide the full-size Sig Sauer 1911 behind her right hip, it was still another layer of clothing she'd rather not have on in suburban Phoenix's triple-digit heat. She pulled her purse to her shoulder and stepped out. The car door slid shut, and she made her way across the just-watered grass. It left drops on her flats, but even those were sucked dry by the greedy heat of day.

She showed her credentials to the middle-aged cop that barred her way. It wasn't exactly a badge, but the Order of Soteria was well-known and respected. His gaze flickered back and forth as he compared her photograph to the one on the card. When the picture had been taken, her pale, blonde hair had been short and curly. Now that she'd let it grow out, it was straighter, and she wore it in a tight bun at the back of her neck. Bodyguard work didn't exactly pair well with flowing anything.

Besides, there was an appearance code. It could be summed up as "understated." Armed nannies didn't need to stand out. And they didn't need to give wives any reason to worry that their husbands might find them interesting either. That's why the Order went out of its way to emphasize the Bible's version of Soteria as salvation from penalty, power, presence, and most importantly, the pleasures of sin.

Hence the flats. The lack of makeup. The conservative suit cut not just to hide weapons, but de-emphasize a woman's shape. And a vow of chastity. The idea of mortal sin had regained its power when the supernatural had become less "super" and more "natural."

There'd been a reason why the myths and legends of old had seen a rebirth during the last part of the twentieth century. The world was being prepared for the mainstreaming of vampires and shifters and witches. With the death of privacy, with the ubiquitous monitoring of everything, it had been inevitable. Science had tried to explain it all using reason and logic, but the world had been so ready to embrace the supernatural that it hadn't mattered why things were. For most, accepting reality was easier than qualifying and quantifying it.

Some had feared the world would fall back into a dark age of superstition, but that hadn't happened. Science and technology still had their uses. In truth, the supernatural had always co-existed quite nicely alongside science and reason in most men's minds.

The cop used the mic at his shoulder to verify that she was expected and handed back her card.

"Go on in, Sister, they're expecting you."

"Thank you, Officer."

She crossed the cobblestoned driveway. The mansion was not the biggest in the gated neighborhood, but it was in a cul-de-sac, which were usually prime lots. The owner had obviously chosen it for privacy. It didn't back up to any other homes, and it had been placed as far away from the neighboring properties as possible. Every single window had roll-down shutters masterfully made to look like anything but. And there were cameras everywhere, some better hidden than others. The cameras were not that unusual. The shutters were.

The entryway's double doors swung open, and an EMT backed out, dragging a gurney with a bodybag strapped to it.

His partner, a woman, was pushing from the other end. By the look on her face, this might well have been her first day on the job. She looked more than a little green.

"A moment please," Eliana said and showed her ID again. The EMT pulled at the bodybag's zipper. It parted to reveal a woman's face. Her eyes were closed, her face pale, her lips blue. She looked about forty, with gray in her short, wispy hair. Forty was about fifteen years too old for this to be Sister Isadora Conley.

There was one way to be sure.

"Would you mind turning her head so I can look behind her right ear?" Eliana asked. No point in getting gloved up when the EMTs already were.

The rookie EMT complied, gently nudging the corpse's head and folding her ear. A laurel wreath crown was inked into the skin. Eliana fished her UV flashlight from her purse and aimed it at the tattoo. There was enough shade under the porte cochère that a barcode was revealed within the circle of the wreath.

Definitely Sister Conley. Eliana sighed as she put the flashlight away.

The fact that Sister Conley looked forty meant that she hadn't just died because she'd been shot. She'd died because someone had drained her anima. According to her file, she was magic sensitive, but not a magic-user. Not all of the Sisters were witches. But even the sensitives became users in the face of a powerful enough threat. Which meant Sister Conley had been in a desperate fight for her life even before the bullet found her.

Eliana nodded at the EMT, who pulled the zipper shut. They loaded the gurney into the back of the ambulance, grunting as they lifted it.

One of the cops was holding the mansion's left front door open, and Eliana stepped into a foyer. Staircases curved upward on the left and the right and a chandelier hung from a heavy chain above.

Underneath it, three men and a woman with "Forensics" stamped on their jackets were busy taking photographs, measurements, and bagging things handled with tweezers. Blood pooled on the floor, and numerical tent markers littered the marble tiles.

Two sets of couches that could each seat six filled the large room beyond the foyer. Its tall, wide windows were sealed against the sunlight by the rolling shutters. If it hadn't been for the portable lights that the forensics people had set up, the house would be pitch black.

Sweat trickled down Eliana's back. No air conditioning.

"Power's out," a voice from behind her said.

Despite the heat, her skin pebbled. Her heart skipped a beat and then sped up. Thorne's voice descended—as it always had—right past her brain, to her stomach, sending it, and lower things, aflutter.

Even now, even here, with the stench of death still lingering in the air. Even after all these years. Would it ever lose its power? Would she ever be able to purge him from her system?

She swore under her breath. *He* was the last person she wanted to see or deal with in the whole world.

Eliana turned.

"The bloodsuckers' bloodsucker," she said. "I should've known."

Thorne had acquired a few more crows' feet around his eyes— and a few gray hairs—but he was every bit as stunning as when he'd broken her heart six years ago. He looked like he'd just come from the courthouse too, with his tie undone, the top of his collar unbuttoned, and his shirt sleeves rolled up, revealing tanned muscles. The kind you didn't get just by going to the gym or by lying on the beach, but the kind you got by working outdoors.

Thorne was good with his hands. Good at building things. Good with horses. And boats. Good at a lot of things. And he knew it.

"It's good to see you too, Eliana."

"Sister Kammer."

His lips pressed into a line like he was holding something back. A joke or quip no doubt. Probably something designed to make her feel at ease, get her to drop her guard. Something charming she'd fall for and then hate herself for letting it work on her. Instead, the moment passed in silence, like a splash of cold water that quenched the anger burning inside her.

Professionalism. Calm professionalism. That's what was called for. She should apologize for her remark, but she just didn't have it in her. After all these years, the wounds he'd left on her heart and soul were still there, neither healed nor scarred over enough.

"I will ask the Order to send someone else," Eliana said. She didn't need her personal issues getting in the way of her job, and it was obvious she had not cast them aside.

She headed for the door.

Thorne stepped into her path, barring her way with his six-foot-two frame and an extra hundred-or-so pounds of muscle. She tilted her head up slightly to catch his gaze. Thick, dark lashes framed coal-black eyes that betrayed fear. Not of her, but of someone—or given whom he worked for—something.

"Don't," he whispered, his voice low and pleading like she'd never heard it before. "I asked for the most powerful member of the Order. Can we go talk in private?"

She should have said no. Her anima and her anger didn't work well together. Instead, she nodded.

He led her down a hallway lit with red light strips along the floor. Led her right into an office bathed in the low glow of backup lighting falling from high, coffered ceilings. Her eyes adjusted, following Thorne as he walked past a plush chair and a huge desk.

The curtains were drawn and the windows behind them were, no doubt, shuttered as well. And if that oversized fireplace was real, she'd eat her holster.

"A child is missing," he said as he opened a mini-fridge and filled a glass with melting ice. He topped it with sparkling water and held it out to her.

She took it, careful not to let her fingers touch his. If his voice still had power over her, so would his touch. Not something she wanted to test under these circumstances.

Water beaded on the glass and slid down her hand as she raised it to her lips. The air inside the house was stifling. She drank, letting a few of the half-melted ice cubes slide down her throat along with the water.

Thorne gestured for her to take a seat and poured a glass for himself. He watched her over its rim.

"And I know a child is missing," she said as she sank into the overstuffed chair in front of the desk. "That's why the Order sent me."

She worked with the Order's Warranty and Recovery department, making things right when they'd already gone wrong. She'd done protection for a few years and found that she got too attached to the children in her care. She blamed Thorne for that too.

On the night she'd learned he'd been cheating on her, her anger-fueled anima had manifested for the first time. She lost control of it, and it had almost killed her. Days before, she'd accepted his ring. They'd set a date. She'd been blissfully happy. The simple, normal life of marriage and family were all she'd ever wanted.

But once her anima had manifested, she'd had to learn to control it. If the Order of Soteria hadn't taken her in, taught her how to lock her power down, channel it, it would have consumed her and anyone close to her.

She'd been oblivious to the warning signs. Even when she and Thorne had made love and she'd felt her anima stir, she'd dismissed its presence as natural, as just the way things were. She'd never been in love before. That's all she'd thought it was—the power of love.

She'd had no reason to think otherwise. No one in her family had an iota of magical ability.

She'd sought to fill the void their breakup had left behind with the love of children not her own, children who quickly outgrew their need for her.

"As the child's legal guardian, I'd like for this to be handled with discretion."

Something twisted in her gut.

"You're the child's guardian?"

He gave her a rueful smile. "Vampires can't have custody of children, remember?"

"Nor should they."

He took a long-suffering breath. "It's not their fault they were turned."

"Of course not," she said. "No one's ever bought their way in."

"That would be illegal," he said in his courtroom voice.

"Yes. It would." But that didn't mean it wasn't done. And it didn't mean that the Vampire Guild wasn't above trading immortality for money, even if they couldn't guarantee the results. A painful death was far more likely than not. And who was going to file a complaint and piss them off? No one.

Thorne cleared his throat. "In this case, the child in question—whose name is Clara and she's five—is the granddaughter of one of my clients. Clara's parents were killed in a car accident when she was just a few months old. Elizabeth is the only mother she's ever known."

"Any other blood relatives?" Eliana asked.

Thorne's attempt at gaining her sympathy had fallen flat. Well, almost. The photo in the Order's file had shown a doll of a child, with dark brown pigtails and big, dark eyes. Wearing a private school uniform with a plaid skirt and black patent leather Mary-Janes, Clara was the picture of adorable innocence.

"No one qualified," Thorne said.

"Meaning?"

"An uncle by marriage—not blood—who drinks. A great-grandmother in a nursing home, and a cousin of the mother who's a junkie."

Thorne turned a picture on the desk toward her. Within a gold-leaf frame, little Clara sat atop a horse with a familiar blaze down its nose. Sunshine, one of Thorne's sorrel mares if memory served.

Eliana set her water aside and took the picture with both hands, running a wet fingertip across the image. There was something familiar about the child, and she hadn't seen it before when studying the image in the case file because Thorne hadn't been sitting in front of her. Clara was not only the right age, but her eyes, hair, and complexion matched his so well, they screamed his paternity.

Rage and envy threaded together, blooming like a poisonous weed. It fueled her anima, made it course through her veins. And with her anima invoked, a sense of peril, of terror, of helplessness hit her. The frame cracked in her grip, and with it, the glass. It sounded like a thousand mirrors all shattering at once. On the desk, the water glass vibrated. It took all her willpower to shut down her anima. Fatigue pulled at her, deep and strong, as it always did when she had to fight her power.

She raised her gaze to Thorne's. He was sitting with his elbow on his chair's arm, his chin resting lightly on his knuckles, watching her with those dark eyes of his. How much did he really understand of what he was seeing?

"It's not what you think," he said.

"And what am I thinking?"

"That I am the father."

Right on, as always. It was part of his job to read people, and he'd always been good at it. And far too good at figuring her out. A wonderful thing when you're in love. Dreadful when you were not. But it wasn't dread she was feeling.

She set the picture back on the table, flat on its back, not trusting her trembling hands not to betray her. It was just fatigue, that's all. It had to be.

"How long has this Elizabeth been a vampire? Less than five years I'm willing to bet."

He reached into a drawer and pushed a sheet of paper toward her. A birth certificate, stamped and sealed, naming the child's mother and father, a Donata Davins-Smith and a Caleb Smith.

"Donata was Elizabeth's daughter," Thorne said.

"*The* Elizabeth Davins," Eliana said evenly. "Your former law partner."

His face remained as impassive as ever, but darkness crept into his eyes, altering his features ever so slightly.

"Are we going to waste time with the wreckage of our past or are you going to do your job?"

She pushed herself up from the chair, despite the weight that had been settling on her shoulders.

"I will have the Order send someone else."

"And what reason are you going to give them?"

A shiver ran up her spine, despite the sweat that had plastered her shirt to her skin.

"The truth. I cannot work this case."

"You have to."

He pulled a smartphone from his pocket and placed it face up. It showed a picture of Clara with tears streaking down her face. She was holding a sign with hand-scribbled lettering naming a deadline less than two hours away; an address deep within the city; and a fifteen-million-dollar ransom.

Eliana's heart twisted in her chest. Clara's eyes were haunted in a way no five-year-old's should be. Peril. Terror. Helplessness. And it had only been hours.

"Why?" Eliana asked softly. "Why does it have to be me?"

"There's no time to get someone else, and I need help. Powerful help," he said, eyeing her. "And I can't involve the police."

"Why not?" Pointless question really. The Guild might go through the pretense of getting the police's help, but they'd take care of the problem themselves. No one pissed off the Guild and lived to tell the tale. In some ways that made the kidnappers more dangerous. Stupidity was its own hazard.

"Elizabeth won't risk involving the police. And I agree. After we get Clara back, the police can chase the perpetrators down."

The desperation of a father clung to his voice. Going along with it would be folly. The Order would never sanction this. He was too close to it, no matter what that piece of paper said. One quick phone call would end this misadventure before it began.

"Most kidnappings aren't that simple, Thorne. Surely you know that. We need the police in on this. We can't go running around on our own—"

"We don't have a choice. I'm not going to fail Clara because of technicalities."

Nor face yourself, either. She understood the loss of a great love all too well. She couldn't do that to him. Fates save her, but she couldn't. What had she done to earn such ire from the Fates? To make them pursue her in this way?

"Where is Elizabeth?" she asked.

"On a private jet, flying back. She's been overseas on Guild business. She'll land after sunset, but as you can see, we are running out of time."

He was right. They'd barely have enough time to get to the address.

"And today is the summer solstice," he said. "The longest day of the year, the day on which vampires are at their weakest. The sun does not set until 8:35PM. Whoever chose this day to take a vampire's grandchild must have counted on the power of the solstice working against the Guild."

It was also the day when witches were at their strongest. Witches who didn't have to use their will to fight their magic. Sighing, she pushed the phone back at him.

"They're not going to like it when you show up with a witch at your side."

A slow smile touched his lips. "No. No, they're not."

Thorne set an empty briefcase atop the desk, stood up, and opened the safe behind him. Stacks of bearer bonds joined the briefcase.

"They'll probably ditch the case," he said. "Can you make the bonds themselves traceable?"

"Yes."

"Do it," he said. "Please."

She stood up and slipped into the hallway. The forensics team was still in the foyer, moving about.

Eliana shut the door and locked it. She slipped the too-hot jacket off. Her shirt clung to her as if she'd been soaked down with a hose.

Sweat ran down Thorne's cheek and throat, glistening in the low light.

Was she really going to do this? Was she really going to undo what had taken years of discipline to attain? She had no choice. She'd shut her anima down. It would take time for her to recover her strength.

She slid around to his side of the table, set her palm down on the stack of bearer bonds, and took hold of his hand.

Power hummed at the touch, making the hairs on her arm rise. Thorne flinched away, but she grabbed his arm again.

"You have to trust me," she said. "This won't work without trust."

A half-truth. It would work better. So much better. But it would be wrong. *I'm not a dark witch. I'm not.*

He swallowed, making the sweat clinging to his throat run down to his chest. The scent of him, of her, mixed together in the room's sticky air pulled at her memories of making love on a distant beach, on the top deck of his boat, in the shade of Lake Powell's canyon walls…

This is really going to suck.

She grabbed his neck and brought his face to hers. "Kiss me."

He did. Without hesitation. Without reservation. His tongue parted her lips. His hand went to the small of her back. Magic flowed, tingling along her arm, her fingertips, right into the paper.

She deepened the kiss, curled her fingers in his hair. He tugged her closer. She had to be careful. Not let her anima take over or get out of control. Just enough to enchant the paper. Just the paper. Nothing else. Nothing for herself. Nothing to break her vows. Nothing sinful.

No penalty. Heat pooled in low, dark places, making her squeeze her thighs together as if that would alleviate the ache.

No power. His tongue explored with a rising hunger that fed her own.

No presence. Magic and musk filled the room.

No sin.

Liar.

* * *

Memories rushed at Thorne, springing forth unbidden. The tingle of magic in the room. The feel of a woman atop him, moving back and forth as he slid in and out of her. He'd thought himself caught in a dream. At first, it had been pleasant. The woman was Eliana, powerful and brilliant like the sun, glowing with life and love. The hand caressing his chest bore the engagement ring she'd just accepted. He'd grabbed her hips, dug his fingers into her flesh, and thrust up into her, lost in a flood of sensation.

Such a pleasant dream, he'd told himself as she'd quickened her pace and they climaxed together.

But then the dream had chilled, as if storm clouds had rolled in to quench the sun. The light that he'd thought to be Eliana faded.

Thorne had tried to touch her, pull her back toward him, save her from the encroaching darkness, but his limbs wouldn't obey. It was then that he'd panicked.

Laughter had lifted the veil of magic from his eyes.

The woman atop him wasn't Eliana—but Donata.

Her laughter was joined by a deeper rumble. Caleb, her husband, was in the room. A hulking man—covered in tattoos, piercings, and leather—he fit the stereotypical image of a bad-boy biker. A barely legal Donata had been drawn to him like a moth to a flame. At first, to get back at her straight-laced mother. Later, because she'd embraced his world, one that had started with petty crimes and malicious mischief and moved on to violent crime sprees. It had broken Elizabeth's heart, just as Donata had intended.

Caleb moved from the shadows along the wall, gliding forward, wrapped in a cloak of dark fog.

His gloved hand had wrapped around Donata's throat and his lips brushed hers. "Well done, my dear."

"Shall we do it again, just to be sure?" she'd asked with a sly smile.

"If you wish," Caleb had said. Light sparked in the dark pits of his eyes as he gave Thorne a malicious look. The fog surrounding Caleb crawled toward Thorne.

Trapped and bound by Caleb's magic, Thorne hadn't been able to move. He hadn't been able to speak, or scream, or beg.

And when they'd finished with him, Donata had bent to whisper a message in his ear. "Mama will have to let me—let us—back into her life now. Nothing like a grandchild to make a dying woman forgive all."

Magic had flowed around him again as Caleb chanted. The pits of his eyes darkened, deepened, and the dark light within them burned and crackled like coals, spitting out sparks. It had been the first time Thorne had seen dark magic.

Back then he hadn't known that magic often made users infertile. That knowledge had come later.

Thorne severed the kiss with Eliana and stumbled backward on unsteady legs, catching his breath.

"I'm sorry," Eliana said. "I don't know how much of my own anima I will need, if we're…"

"If we're going to save Clara," he finished for her. That last word came out strangled. He brushed his hand through his hair.

With hands steadier than he'd expected, he arranged the bearer bonds in the briefcase and snapped it shut.

"You can take all you need," he whispered, unable to meet her gaze.

He hadn't thought he'd ever be able to let another magic-user ever touch him again, much less enjoy it. Guilt and shame crawled over his skin. He wanted to scrub his skin raw the way he had once Donata and Caleb had been done with him. It had been months until he'd felt clean again. He still didn't feel whole. Not even their deaths had erased what they'd done to him. If anything, their deaths had denied him closure. They'd always be the ghosts that haunted him.

Eliana picked up her jacket and slipped it on. "Clara means very much to you."

Of course she did. She *was* his daughter, no matter how ill-begotten. He would never hear the words "daddy" from Clara's lips, but if "uncle" was all he could have, he would gladly take it. As long as she was alive and safe again, it didn't matter what she called him.

"Let's go," he said. "We don't have a lot of time."

He grabbed the briefcase and moved toward the fireplace. With a casual gesture, he nudged the vase perched on one end, and a latch clicked. The entire wall swung inward, leading into a dark tunnel.

"Light-tight escape route," he explained. "My car is on the other side."

The sound of her footsteps followed as he hurried into the dark. The red light of the guide strips moved with them. The air within wasn't moving at all though. Whoever had taken out the power had done quite a job. It shouldn't be taking so long to bring it back up.

"What's the plan?" Eliana asked.

"We go to the address. Wait for them to show up. Exchange the money for Clara. Your job is to get Clara out safely, protect her, take her back to the Guild."

"What about you?" she asked.

"What about me?" He kept moving, eager to get out of the tunnel.

"You sound like a man who doesn't plan on making it out alive."

He kept walking.

"Or one bent on revenge," she added, her voice fading. "I think you're too close to this."

He stopped and turned around. She was just standing there, expectantly.

"Perhaps I am. But, I'm not the contracted protectee. Clara is. Sister Kammer."

She frowned as if considering his invocation of her title. He was right, technically and legally, and she must know that. She moved toward him. He picked up the pace and checked his watch.

"Can we expect help from your … friends?" she asked.

"The vampires, I trust. But they won't be able to help us until dark. The humans who work for the Guild, not so much."

"You think it was an inside job."

"Had to be," he said. "Someone was in the house. Sister Conley walked into a trap. They knew she'd be alone with Clara."

"Who has access?"

"Elizabeth, myself, Sister Conley, the cleaning staff, the security company."

"I don't think we're up against janitors or rent-a-cops. Does Elizabeth have any enemies?"

"We all have enemies," he said. "It's part of the job."

"How was she turned?"

"She was dying. Cancer. She'd worked for the Guild a long time. They decided it was worth the risk. She didn't ask for it, or pay for it, if that's what you're thinking."

"But she agreed."

"How could she not, Eliana? She'd just lost her daughter. She had a granddaughter to raise. She didn't want to leave Clara twice-orphaned."

"I almost believe you," she whispered.

They'd reached the end of the tunnel. He punched a code into the keypad, and they emerged from a utility shed at the edge of the neighborhood park. Heat rose off the swings, slides, and merry-go-round, even with the shaded canopy above.

He shoved the briefcase into the back of a black SUV and got in. Eliana slid into the passenger seat. He put the air conditioning on full blast and typed their destination into the navigation system.

"Why do you hate vampires so much?" he asked. "I could never figure that one out. You didn't used to care much for magic-users either, even though you were one yourself. When were you going to tell me I was about to marry a witch?"

"I didn't know I was one. Not until you broke me." Her voice had lost its previous spite. The distance in it hurt far worse than the spite had. Later. There would be time to sort it all out later.

He drove in silence, overriding the car's warnings about exceeding the speed limit. It wasn't until he got a second warning that the controls were going to be overridden that he slowed down. By then they'd made up for the time lost.

They entered an uncontrolled lane that led to an abandoned road. Deep within the seediest part of the city, it was made up more of potholes than asphalt. It looked like it hadn't seen an actual vehicle in years. No cameras, no cell towers, not even electricity, just abandoned warehouses with their broken windows and caved-in roofs.

They'd entered a no-man's land. He checked his watch. Ten minutes to spare. Three hours to sunset.

He shut the car off and pulled the briefcase from the back. Eliana's gaze swept their surroundings with an expert eye.

Clouds rolled in, making the pools of sunshine leaking through the buildings fade.

"Your vampire friends?" Eliana asked.

"No, I don't think so."

He'd worked with the vampires for over a decade now. Most of them were too young to daywalk. They really were at their weakest during the day, and while Elizabeth might well risk herself in the sunlight, the more powerful members of the Guild would see to it that she did not. She was one of them. Clara was not.

"After you," Eliana said.

* * *

Eliana had never felt anything as dead as this place Thorne had brought them to. There was not a breath of wind. No insects scurried. No birds. No stray cats or dogs. Nothing but shadows and the tingling feeling of wrongness.

If it had been night she'd have thought that every vampire in town was here.

I should've brought more ammo. Or a shotgun. Or three.

She followed Thorne up the steps fronting a loading dock. The giant rolling doors were pulled down tight. Weeds sprouted from the asphalt. Old tires piled high in a corner leaned toward a half dozen storage drums that had seen better days.

Hinges creaked as Thorne pushed a steel side-door inward and stepped inside cautiously. Their steps echoed over the concrete flooring, crunching dirt and broken glass. A crumbling, metal staircase led up to what must once have been an office, its window frames still holding onto bits of glass. Another walkway that looked like it would come crashing down at any moment crawled up the far wall. Empty rafters cast shadows across the rusting walls.

Thorne came to a stop in the center and set the briefcase down. He backed away from it, brushing Eliana's hand.

Her anima stirred at his touch—spark to kindling…

Dark magic hit them in waves.

Maniacal laughter spun around them, bouncing off the high steel girders and concrete floor.

She drew on her anima and used its power to cocoon them both in a shield. Her Sig was a reassuring weight behind her right hip. No matter how strong dark magic was, it didn't work against sanctified bullets. And there was enough silver in her ammo to give even a vampire pause.

"I've got your money," Thorne said. "Where's Clara?"

"Clara, Clara, Clara," echoed around them in a high-pitched whine. "Always about precious little Clara."

Eliana pushed the cocoon of her anima outward, nudging it to expand a bit at a time, hoping it would reveal the source of the voice. The problem with her shield was that it worked both ways. It kept the dark magic out but also limited the magic she could sense outside of it. Dared she risk dropping it? They'd be defenseless without it. She didn't know whom she was up against. A master's dark magic was faster than her draw, and she needed a target.

From behind one of the rusting pillars, a woman stepped forward. She made up for her lack of height with two-inch thick platform boots. Buckles rode the boots all the way up to her knees. The rest of her was clad in layers of black leather, spikes, and buckles. Her neck was inked; her hair, a rat's nest of black; lips to match.

She'd made herself up like a calavera. White paint. Stitching drawn in to extend from the edge of her lips to her ears. Dark circles under her eyes rimmed with red dots. Hard to tell if it was part of a spell or a way to thwart facial recognition.

A sneer distorted the illusion of a skull as the woman stalked closer.

"This one?" All hiss and spit. "Why did you have to bring *her*?"

"Thorne?" Eliana asked in a low voice. The woman was not a magic-user. That much she could tell even without extending her anima. But she was protected by dark magic. She reeked of it.

The woman made an exaggerated pout. "Oh dear. Don't recognize me? How droll."

"One of those enemies you couldn't tell me about?" Eliana asked as she put her back against Thorne's, keeping him close.

The woman squatted down by the briefcase, running a gloved finger along the edges. She pushed it over and clicked the latches open.

"I have no idea who she is," Thorne said.

The woman looked up and snapped the lid of the briefcase shut. "I'm so hurt. We shared such a wonderful night."

She moved forward, finger pointed at Eliana. "Didn't he tell you?"

"Tell me what?" Eliana asked, lowering her shield so she could send out threads of magic to explore the shadows. There was someone else here. She was certain.

"How he called your name. How he thought I was you."

"Donata?" Thorne said, his voice thick with shock.

Eliana twisted around. "I thought she was dead."

"I did too."

She believed him. The Fates having their fun again.

"Caleb," Eliana whispered. "If she's alive, he is too. He's the dark magic user. He's here."

Thunder split the air between them, throwing Eliana one way and Thorne the other. She landed with a thud that knocked the air out of her lungs. Rolling, she drew her gun. She had the sights aligned on Donata and was about to pull the trigger, when her vision went dark. She blinked, drawing on her anima to chase away the magic blinding her.

Her vision flickered like an old film with missing frames. She pushed herself up, catching snatches of clarity as her own magic fought with the blindness. But they didn't last long enough for her to pull the trigger with any confidence.

Donata had something in her hand.

Swirling fog clouded Eliana's vision. She used her anima to burn it away.

The tip of the stick in Donata's hand sparked. A shifter-zapper. Designed to bring shifters under control, it was more powerful than a bull-zapper and could be used by non-magic users.

A veil dropped between them like a bolt of unfurling cloth.

Eliana's anima brought forth flame to scorch the veil.

Ozone filled the air, swirling around her.

The dust and debris pulled itself off the concrete to twist around her. Bits of dust flew at her, stinging her eyes, filling her nose and mouth with a metallic taste.

Spinning away from the crackling sound of the zapper, Eliana exhaled, clearing her nose and mouth.

Lightning caught her at the small of her back.

Her body spasmed. She lost her grip on the gun.

Pain reached through the shield of her failing anima, pierced it, tore it apart.

As she lay on the dirt-covered concrete, she caught a glimpse of Thorne being knocked back by Caleb. A big man, he too was decked out with a calavera and the regalia of a biker. He seemed unaffected by the heat of the day, even covered in leather. A duster billowed around him like wings.

Another touch from the zapper jolted the remaining sensation out of Eliana's right arm. Donata was having fun.

Eliana's anima howled deep within.

Another zap. She gasped for air as a million needles were driven into every nerve. Her muscles tightened so hard, they felt like they were tearing themselves apart. Her limbs twitched. Fire scorched its way up her spine and into her skull.

Drain it. Drain it, bitch. And then I'll show you.

Eliana raised her head despite the pain. A few yards away, Caleb pummeled Thorne's face with spiked gloves. The sickening sound of crushed bone, of rasping breath, of a heart struggling to beat, came together in a terrible chorus.

Her gun. It had spun away and landed just a few feet away. She still had feeling in her left arm. She used it to pull herself toward the Sig.

Pain jolted her left side, rendering her arm useless.

Donata's gloating smile came into view. Triumph danced in her eyes.

Eliana ignored her. The stun was wearing off, but she had to lay still, pretend it wasn't. Just until enough sensation returned so she could use her anima. She'd kept reign on her anima. Through the pain. Through the fear. That's all that mattered.

A shadow came to stand over them both. Caleb. Hands on his hips, the dark wizard looked down at her.

"How's that vow of chastity working out for you, Sister?" he asked as he squatted down in front of her.

Eliana glared into his soulless face.

He leered at her. "Oh, I'm going to wait for the stun to wear off, don't you worry about that."

* * *

It was the pain, Thorne decided.

Caleb fed off pain.

And it's what was going to keep them both alive. Caleb and Donata couldn't have their malicious fun with them dead.

He opened one eye. As they'd fought, one of the spikes on Caleb's glove had caught his left eye and pierced it. Caleb's black lips had thinned as they pulled back over his teeth. A moue of disappointment had played over his features when Thorne's pain had dulled to a throbbing ache. Caleb had broken his left arm and pinned his right leg to the concrete floor with a rebar shaft. Pinned it right through the thigh.

Thorne watched helplessly as Caleb hoisted Eliana over his shoulder.

Donata trailed in his wake, hugging the briefcase to her chest, humming "The Itsy-Bitsy Spider."

Caleb dumped Eliana on the ground beside Thorne and gave her abdomen a kick. Blood welled and spilled out of Eliana's mouth. Her blue eyes glowed for an instant. He'd seen that glow before, thought he'd imagined it when they'd made love. But it hadn't been his imagination then, and it wasn't now. It was her magic, held, restrained, lurking underneath the surface.

A chanting Caleb left them and paced the interior perimeter, a trail of fog swirling in his wake. His threat to Eliana wasn't an idle one. The bastard was going to use her, abuse her.

He'd thought nothing would ever make him feel as helpless as he'd been that night. He'd been wrong. This would be worse. He needed to find a way to grab Caleb's attention, distract him, make himself the target once again.

But how?

Donata. She was the key. Caleb had some need for her, or he wouldn't have kept her around.

She sat on the ground, cross-legged, transferring the bearer bonds from the briefcase to a backpack, stopping several times to bring a bundle of the paper to her nose and inhale deeply. Then she'd let out a cackle and resume her song. A madwoman high on something... but on what?

"Can you move yet?" he asked Eliana.

"Not well," she whispered. "I need my gun."

Donata dropped the bundle of bearer bonds she'd been stuffing into the backpack and pushed up from the ground. She walked over to the Sig and picked it up.

Eliana's eyes widened in surprise and shook her head ever so slightly. Her lips moved, but no words came out. A prayer perhaps, or a spell.

"What are you doing?" Thorne asked.

"She's susceptible to suggestion," Eliana said.

"Good," Thorne said, wincing. They were running out of time.

"Compulsion is not white magic."

"Screw white magic," he said.

She shot him a glare. "Easy for you to say."

Eliana took a deep breath. Her face hardened, brows drawing together, mouth compressing to a grim line.

"Bring me my gun," Eliana whispered.

Gun in hand, Donata moved toward them.

A dark blur streaked across the open space between them. Caleb slapped Eliana hard across the face. She coughed up blood and spit it on the ground between them.

Caleb's hand palmed Eliana's head and pulled her limp form up by her hair.

"Witch!" His other hand went around her throat and squeezed.

Thorne dug in his heel and pushed. The leg Caleb had impaled with the rebar made a cracking sound as metal scraped bone and a scream escaped from Thorne's throat.

Caleb dropped Eliana. She coughed and gulped air greedily.

"Figured it out, have you?" Caleb said as he lowered himself over Thorne. The pits of his eyes darkened, and his pupils turned to glowing coals again. "Do you like being a hero?"

Thorne's nostrils flared. He'd never felt such hatred for anyone before. For the first time in his life, he envied the magic users their power.

"Do you, hero?" Caleb twisted the rebar in Thorne's leg.

Dutifully, Thorne screamed.

Caleb threw his head back, mouth open in a silent rictus of pleasure.

Donata came up behind him, holding the gun loosely. She spider-walked her fingers from the base of Caleb's skull up and over his tattooed scalp.

"You were going to break her for me, remember," she said as she leaned over and licked along the curve of Caleb's ear. Her eyes shone with malice as she cast her glance in Thorne's direction.

Caleb let out an inhuman groan. Energy pulsed out of him like a wave, flowing over the ground, stirring up puffs of dust.

"He's still in love with her," Donata said. "Her pain will hurt him. Think of it. Two. For. One."

Caleb grabbed Eliana again and pulled her up. She staggered and fell. Using her clothes, he hauled her up again and shoved her up against one of the rusting steel pillars. A chain dangled from an anchor point above. Caleb wrapped it around Eliana's wrists and mumbled a spell. The chain tightened around Eliana's wrists and yanked her up, pulling her up on her toes.

"Thorne!"

Oh God, please no.

A small figure rushed at Thorne.

Clara had been crying. She was shaking, but she seemed to be okay. She wrapped her little arms tight around his neck. He put his good arm around her, pulling her face into his chest.

Hard to believe a mother would do this to her own child. There had always been something off with Donata. Elizabeth had spent a fortune on therapists and doctors, always believing that she could "fix" whatever was wrong with her daughter. Some had simply called Donata "wild." Hooking up with a dark magic user hadn't improved her. It had done the opposite: drawn out everything evil. He just hoped none of it ever manifested in Clara. Evil wasn't genetic.

Caleb and Eliana faced each other. He pulled out a knife with a serrated edge and sliced her shirt and bra open.

"Clara," Thorne whispered. "Honey, don't look. No matter what you hear, promise me you won't look."

She curled up tighter into him, burying her head into his shoulder.

"Promise," he prompted.

"Promise." Barely a whisper.

He wished he'd been armed. He wished he'd brought backup. He knew enough cops who might have been convinced to help. He should've listened to Eliana.

Caleb unzipped his pants.

Donata was standing back, arms crossed, practically salivating, gun casually dangling from her hand.

"Oh look, darling," she said. "Thorne is being a good boy and watching."

Clara put her hands over her ears.

Caleb's hands grabbed Eliana's hips. He ran his hands up to her bare breasts, cupping them as he leaned closer.

"Stun hasn't worn off yet," he grumbled.

Thorne pushed up so he could hold Clara tighter. The pain in his leg spiked again.

A growl rumbled in Caleb's throat as his head snapped to look at Thorne.

"Trying to distract me, pretty boy? Don't worry, you'll get your turn."

He bit into the space between Eliana's shoulder and neck.

Eliana screamed.

Donata cackled.

* * *

*N*o *penalty.* Not this time. I took the pain around me—Eliana's pain, Thorne's pain, Clara's pain— and drew it into myself. Like ribbons unrolling from a spool, gossamer-thin, it floated around me.

No power. Wrong. It was all around me, left by Caleb's magic, by Donata's madness, by the ghosts that haunted this place. They had left their pain and sorrow—decades of it—in the metal around us as sweat that had been spilled over hot forges, blood that had been spilled by accident and on purpose. There were fifty years of power imbued into every mote of dust, every molecule of rust. And now it was mine, all mine.

No presence. Wrong again. I was not just present, I was uncontainable. I shook the rafters, sending debris down, making the ground shake.

No sin. Caleb was full of it. Murder. Rape. Torture. A sadist through and through, a deep well of darkness and mad pleasure derived from the pain of others. People who denied the existence of evil had obviously never had Caleb's hands on their bodies, nor his teeth in their flesh.

Caleb's teeth tugged, trying to pull free.

I laughed.

Oh no, it's not going to be that easy.

Donata's cackle rang out again as she skipped around us. "Tear into her! Tear her apart."

Stupid bitch.

Couldn't see what was going on in front of her own eyes.

Caleb's fingers tightened, spikes digging into Eliana's hips. Blood welled, ran down her legs as she struggled against him. He liked that, oh yes, sadist that he was.

I made her let out a whimper. She was fighting me, but I was stronger.

Caleb bit down harder. I knew he was not going to be satisfied with a nibble. No, he was going to take Eliana's flesh and swallow it, drink her blood for its magic, drain her dry.

I made her push into him like she wanted him inside her body.

Oops. Wrong move.

He tried to pull away, his heart beating in a frenzied panic against Eliana's bare breasts. Too late, Caleb.

I flowed out, spilling over his skin, lighting it up from the inside.

He roared, deep inside his throat, caught in my power.

Soulless bastard. How does it feel to burn? Just wait and see. This. Here and now. This is nothing.

I took him, bit by bit, from the inside out, digging my talons into his heart, his brain. I became a forest of flaming thorns, alive under his skin. He would get his fill of pain. I would make sure.

He struggled, fought me, calling on his own dark magic. Arrogant ass. One cannot throw up shields against one's own defining power. Hadn't anyone taught him that?

Probably not. Just as well.

My light had Caleb in its insatiable grip. I saw myself reflected in Thorne's dark eye. Caleb was going to pay for that too.

An eye for an eye. I had always liked that.

No, Eliana insisted.

The liquid of Caleb's eye hit her neck with a hot, wet plop, and slithered down over her breastbone, accompanied by black blood.

Caleb freed his teeth from her shoulder and screamed. His right hand lifted off her hip before I could stop it, but I kept his left one on her.

Oh no, I'm not letting you go. Not until I'm done with you.

Donata stopped prancing, her eyes going wide, her mouth opening.

"Stop!" she screeched.

I reached out and took hold of Donata's pain, drew it into myself.

Careful, Eliana reminded me.

Too late for careful. Much too late.

The oath. Eliana again.

Yes, I might lose my soul, my life, but so be it. What good was an oath one was not willing to carry through because one wanted to live?

Caleb's heart was still beating. I felt it, loud and clear, its rhythm a frenzy. Plenty of life left in him, in that foul, black blood of his.

The power of it tingled in his veins, coursed through his blood, pulsed in his bones. I could gorge myself on it.

Greed is a sin. Eliana, always the good girl, doing the right thing, saying the right thing, being so very careful to hold me in check, to use me sparingly, or not at all.

Denying me. Starving me. How dare she speak to me of greed?

Stop fighting me. Or do you want to die? Do you want Thorne to die? Are you out to punish him for the way he hurt you? How about Clara? Would you punish her for the sin of being born?

No.

Of course she had to say it. I was right. And with Donata holding the Sig and pointing it at her—at us—what choice did she have?

I made Eliana grin, letting it turn into the same kind of leer I'd seen on Caleb.

Donata's face twisted. Her agony was delicious. Exquisite.

Skip, skip, skip, one little hop at a time, the ink-black ribbon of Donata's pain spilled out of her and slithered up Eliana's leg.

I was done with Caleb. He was a pillar of ash. The weight of studded leather pulled at what was left of him and landed in a heap at Eliana's feet. The chains with which he'd bound her snapped open and fell to the floor, the sound echoing in the silence.

I turned Eliana to face Donata, made her flick the gore of Caleb's eye off her shoulder with a careless gesture.

What a sight I must be. Their calaveras seemed comical now. A farce.

"You wanted to play with death, did you not?" I said, using Eliana's voice.

The black ribbon spilling out of Donata thickened, became a sheet floating on an updraft.

I pulled it toward me, fed it to what was left of Caleb inside me and then … let him out.

Fog rose around me, dark as the night. It twined with the ribbons and veils I'd been gathering to me. Rising higher and higher, they swirled above me like gathering thunder clouds, blocking out the failing sun.

Time slowed, flowing like syrup. I'd have to let Eliana have her body back soon.

I, her anima, had reached my peak and holding on too long would destroy me, rob me of my sapience, pull me back into the ether of magic that had always permeated the universe.

Donata pivoted, aiming the gun at Clara.

Thorne rolled. The pain of shredding his leg hit Eliana like a fist to the gut. She doubled over, landed on her knees, battered by Clara's screams.

Again, I wrestled Eliana for control. My work wasn't yet done. There was a new monster to kill.

Donata raised the Sig and pulled the trigger. Click.

"Oops, try it again."

She put both hands around the grip. Tugged at the trigger.

Idiot.

"One more chance."

But I didn't really give her one. I grabbed Donata's wrist with one hand, took the gun with the other. Clicked the safety off as she struggled.

The muzzle touched her temple.

Click-boom, a moment too quick for my taste.

Bile rose in Eliana's throat.

Poor Eliana. She didn't understand that Donata's pain was too short-lived.

Too quick.

Too clean.

Pity.

* * *

Eliana pushed herself up from the hot concrete, favoring her torn shoulder. The scent of gunpowder hung in the hot air. Sweat had pooled at the small of her back, her knees. It ran down between her breasts. Her hair was plastered to her scalp. Some of it had fallen loose and was dangling in front of her eyes, wet like she'd been swimming.

The warehouse was darker than it should have been. Storm clouds. Heavy ones. Phoenix's famous summer monsoon hadn't been in the day's forecast.

She wiped at her eyes. It only made them sting. She blinked them clear.

Someone was crying.

Half-naked, she was covered in soot and gore, her wrists circled with her own blood. She grabbed her shirttails and tied them together, covering her chest. She took a step forward and fell. Crawled to Thorne's side.

He'd rolled onto his back, holding onto Clara's hand, his laboring breath accompanied by blood. His leg was torn open, squirting blood with each heartbeat.

Clara looked at Eliana with pleading eyes full of tears. They were rolling down her blood-stained cheeks. One of her pigtails had come loose. The other was dripping blood. Stains covered her white shirt. Her knees were scraped and bloodied below the hem of her plaid skirt.

"Clara, are you hurt?" Eliana asked as she pushed herself to her knees. The zapper's stun was wearing off, letting the pain of her injuries burn and throb and stab. Letting her know she was alive.

"No. Thorne is."

Another squelch of blood from his leg. Eliana applied pressure with her bare hands. Her arms shook with the effort.

"Thorne," Clara said, leaning down to place her head on his chest. "You can't die. Please don't die."

"I'm trying, sweetie. I am," Thorne said. The wet, gurgling sound of it said he wasn't going to make it.

Clara lifted her head, looking at Eliana with eyes that would never be innocent again.

Fates, make her forget. Let her forget.

"Save him," Clara said, grabbing Eliana's hand and dragging her palm atop Thorne's struggling chest.

"I can't," Eliana said.

It would be some time before she could use her anima again, if at all. If she ever dared use it again. Let it use *her* again. And healing had never been part of her magic. She'd tried to heal a sparrow with a broken wing once. She'd never forget the screeching, the foul stench of burnt feathers and scorched flesh.

If she got him to the SUV. If she got them to a hospital. She needed a tourniquet. She pushed herself up, cursing the zapper and her weakness.

Vampires rained down.

A dozen of them.

They floated down through the open roof, some landing near, others far. Respirator masks covered their faces, to filter out the scent of blood, no doubt. Others came in through the door, armed with rifles—even a vampire's answer to dark magic came in the form of a gun and lots and lots of bullets.

A pair of them—a man and a woman—landed by Thorne's head. The man looked like a bodyguard or a mob enforcer dressed up in a business suit.

The woman wore a courthouse business suit—tailored pantsuit, silk shirt, heels. Her hair was done up in a tasteful chignon that looked so much the better for being a bit rumpled by flying. Elizabeth no doubt.

Clara launched herself at the woman. "Grandma. Thorne is hurt. Fix him." She tugged at Elizabeth's hand, pulling her down toward Thorne.

Kneeling, Elizabeth removed her respirator and lifted Thorne's head into her lap.

Eliana tensed. Blood and vampires didn't mix well. She shifted her weight, ready to spring into action, no matter how meager.

But if the blood bothered Elizabeth she let no signs of it show.

Clara stood over Elizabeth expectantly. "Grandma." Her soft voice trembled with a rising sob.

Eliana looked away. What had this child seen? What was she about to see?

Whispers. Elizabeth asking Thorne if he wanted to live. Him saying no.

Clara bursting into tears.

Eliana turned back just in time to see another vampire pick Clara up and speed off with her kicking and screaming over his shoulder. If she'd had the strength, she'd have gone after him. Or would she?

She was weak and drained. The vampire wasn't going to hurt Clara. And Eliana couldn't leave Thorne now. Not now. Fates help her, she wanted to be here for him, even if she couldn't do anything.

Elizabeth was stroking Thorne's hair with long, gentle fingers. She touched his brow above the eye he'd lost.

"She always liked it when you played pirate for her," Elizabeth said.

It made him laugh. He coughed up blood.

"I can save you, but you'll lose the sun," Elizabeth said and cast a sideways glance at Eliana. "I know how much you like the sun. The open skies. The horses."

He mumbled something Eliana did not catch.

"You'll have to watch her grow and then grow old and die," Elizabeth said and bent to kiss his forehead.

Something tore inside Eliana. Tore and slashed, and she fell back to her knees.

"You'll never be able to have another child." Elizabeth again.

If she'd had the strength, Eliana would have taken hold of Elizabeth, shaken her. He was suffering. Dying. Couldn't she see that? Why was she drawing this out? Why hadn't they called for an ambulance? If they'd brought guns why hadn't they brought the cops?

"Have something to say, Sister?" Elizabeth asked in a tone that chilled the air.

Eliana had just sucked the life force out of Caleb. Shot this woman's daughter in the head. Broken her vows. Violated everything her Order stood for. Who was she to judge?

She closed her eyes with a rattling sigh, unable to speak, weighed down by six years of suffering, of jealousy. Misplaced jealousy. The love in Elizabeth's eyes was not that of a lover, but of a sister. She could see it now. Could have seen it at any time in the past if she'd only given Thorne a chance to explain, if she'd confronted Elizabeth, if she'd taken the time to entertain anything but her own hurt feelings.

She could continue blaming her magic, the odd nature of her anima that fed on sex, on intimacy. She'd rationalized it in so many ways. Feared it. Craved it. Wrestled with controlling it, even when all she wanted was to surrender to it.

It was her love for Thorne that had allowed her anima to the surface once again, that had given it sapience. It was her love for him that had sustained it. That's how the Order would explain it too.

She'd been warned. Love was the most powerful force in the universe. She wasn't the first to kill for it. Or die for it.

"I love him," Eliana blurted out.

Elizabeth raised an elegant brow. "Will you still love him when he's a bloodsucker?"

Eliana let out a gasp. The Fates weren't just pursuing her. They were hounding her soul.

"Yes," Eliana said, tears filling her eyes once again.

Elizabeth held out her hand, and the man standing over her shoulder handed her a blade. She sliced her wrist and placed it over Thorne's mouth.

Weakly, he turned his head in Eliana's direction. Elizabeth's blood hit his cheek and ran down toward his ear.

"Drink, damn you." Eliana surged forward, took hold of his hand. It was as cold as ice.

"Drink while you have the strength," Elizabeth said. "My blood isn't strong enough to reanimate a corpse."

"Drink," Eliana pleaded, raising his hand to her wet cheek. He was cold. So cold. She couldn't bear it. To never see him again, never feel his breath whisper across her neck, never hear his laughter.

He turned his head and opened his mouth.

Elizabeth shoved her bleeding wrist between his lips. She hissed as if in pain, her fangs descending.

Yes, drink. Drink and live.

It was life. It had to be. They moved, they spoke, and from the look on Elizabeth's face, they felt. Sorrow, fear, love. It was all there, in Elizabeth's actions. The dead cared for nothing and no one. They were free of the burdens of the living. Of caring for a child. Of caring for a friend. Of fear from destruction.

Behind those cold façades, the vampires suffered. She hadn't seen it before because she'd not wanted to. It could not be otherwise, for if it was, she'd just condemned Thorne to a fate worse than death.

He went deathly still.

Eliana pressed her trembling fingers against his wrist. No pulse.

"What now?" she asked, voice shaking.

"We wait," Elizabeth said.

"How long?"

"Three days."

* * *

Thorne was caught in a fog. Sometimes it cleared, giving him glimpses of clarity. Then he'd lose his grip on it and it would slip away.

I'm dying. I'm dead. I'm in Hell.

But he could still breathe. That surprised him. It shouldn't have. He'd been around enough vampires to know that they drew breath. They spoke, after all. It was a fleeting thought that fell prey to a red fog chased by a strange voice saying, "Sleep. It's morning."

When he came back out of the red sleep, it was in a dark room. Within a sconce on the wall above him, a small light burned, but he could barely look at it. It was blinding, leaving after-images as if he'd been staring at the sun.

His vision returned slowly as he fought his way back out of the red sleep once again. Despite the bed, the nightstand, the room felt like a tomb.

The red sleep retreated in the face of a more powerful force made up of hunger and thirst. More potent than anything he'd felt before, its power threatened to consume him, rob him of what was left of his mind. He'd risen from the bed, rattled the locked door, screamed until he had no voice and darkness took him into its embrace once again.

Elizabeth had come to him. At first, he'd thought her an apparition, something brought forth in Hell to torment him.

She sat at his bedside, offered him her wrist. It dripped blood. He didn't remember grabbing it, or drinking, but he must have. His sight and strength returned.

Every time the red fog let him go, she was there, ready to feed him from her wrist.

"I feel like a child," he complained.

She gave him a smile. "Aren't you? Newly born. In need of sustenance. Think of it as mother's milk."

He groaned. And drank. Sometimes petulantly, waiting until he could bear it no more.

Every time, she met his petulance with patience. "I understand. Believe me, I understand."

"How long do I have to keep doing this?" he asked.

"Until you're healed."

"And then what?"

She smiled as he drifted back to oblivion. "Hush now. We'll worry about that later."

The later came in the form of donated blood, freshly drawn and brought to him in a shot glass. Despite being ravenously hungry, he wasn't able to hold it down.

More "mother's milk."

"Will I have to drink directly from the source?" he asked after he'd failed to hold the drawn blood for the twentieth time.

"Perhaps," Elizabeth said.

"I can't keep drinking from you." He didn't want to. His guilt would drive him to starve himself. Then, weak with hunger, he'd eventually give in. She never forced it on him. Merely offered, then turned away when he refused.

His fangs came in with a vengeance, pushing through one day, waking him from an exhausted stupor. He'd only thought he'd known hunger until then. And that's when he realized that he could never be around Clara. Or any other human.

It was then that he'd kept the shot of human blood down. He'd been determined. Single-minded. He needed enough strength to end it. Walk into the sunlight. Let it cleanse and scorch him. He wanted to burn. To be flame. To be ash.

He wasn't the first one to try. The vampires caring for him had been ready. He hadn't gotten very far. They'd dragged him back to his bed, tied him down. Forced human blood down via a feeding tube.

"Where's Elizabeth?" he'd demanded once they removed the tube.

"You can see her when you're strong enough to break free," Samuel, the stone-faced vampire assigned to care for him, had declared. A good head taller than Thorne, he must have been a wrestler or something in his human life.

Thorne suffered through the indignity of being treated like an invalid. He drank the blood. Kept more of it down each day. Hated himself. Hated her.

Dreamt of the sun. Of Eliana.

Woke from a nightmare where he bit her and drank her dry.

Broke his bonds that night.

"I want animal blood."

Samuel had crossed his arms and looked down on him as Thorne struggled to stand, still reeling from the nightmare. "You can't live on diet blood. You'll merely starve slower."

Thorne had thrown a clumsy punch. It had landed and bounced off Samuel, who'd merely grunted and given him a scolding look.

Elizabeth came back, all prim and proper. She hugged him. Kissed his cheek. Didn't feed him. He hadn't asked. She hadn't offered. Showed him pictures of Clara. Left them behind as motivation. Explained how resilient Clara was. How she kept asking for him.

That's when he found out he could cry. That he could hurt. That he still had a soul and a conscience.

"When are you going to let me out of here?"

"When you can feed yourself," Samuel said.

They brought him a man. A fire-fighter, strong and fit, with too much iron in his blood.

"Look, buddy. I'm not into you either," Andrew said. "But it's either this, or I have to donate to the Red Cross."

"Why don't you? Save some lives."

"Guild saved my life. I'm paying it forward."

It was awkward for both of them. Thorne had taken no pleasure from it. Wondered if he ever would. Knew he'd hate himself either way. His gaze fixed on the picture of Clara on the side table, he thought only of seeing her again, of being able to hold her.

"Damn clumsy, Thorne," Andrew said, wiping the mess off his neck. "But don't worry, you'll get better at it."

A friendly pat on the shoulder as he left.

By the fifth time, there were two neat holes that sealed up quickly. Guilt still gnawed at him. Every time. And every time, he'd hold on to Clara's picture. And dream of Eliana.

The first time they brought Clara to him, he wept. He held her close to his chest, with her head cradled against his neck, and he was just a father, holding his daughter, grateful that she was alive.

Elizabeth looked on, smiling. "I think he's ready to check out, Samuel. Don't you?"

Samuel grunted, as eloquent as ever, but there was a smile in his eyes.

Thorne mouthed a thank you as he held Clara against his shoulder.

* * *

Soteria soared above Eliana in the Order's atrium.

The stone statue had always reminded Eliana of the Statue of Liberty. Unlike Lady Liberty though, she thrust a sword into the sky, wore a laurel wreath around her head, and held a toddler on her hip. Her gaze swept out in front of her as she held the child in a protective embrace.

Sunlight filled the atrium, shining down through a glass roof.

After services for Sister Conley, an inquiry had been held. She had told the priestess everything. That her anima had taken on a life of its own. That she'd lost control of it. That she'd sinned, in her heart and soul, if not in flesh.

And awaited judgement.

Today, she had been summoned back.

Her body had healed. She had a black scar on her shoulder, one that had defied all attempts to fix it. A permanent black mark in the shape of a ragged circle—a dark sun. She didn't mind.

A young witch, maybe thirteen if she was a day, crossed the atrium. Dressed in a blue pencil skirt, flats, and a long-sleeved white shirt, she looked very solemn.

"The Arch Priestess will see you now."

Eliana followed her down a corridor. The young witch opened a door and gestured for her to go in.

Tall, thin windows cut into beige walls covered with photographs of the Arch Priestess's predecessors. Books were stacked high on her wide cherrywood desk. No computer. No phone. A cabinet lined the wall behind her.

The Arch Priestess lifted her head of gray hair from the book she was reading and gestured for Eliana to sit down across from her. Dark eyes full of power blinked at her, their edges aglow behind thick lenses with heavy frames. She wore the same style of starched white shirt that the young witch had. And no doubt, the same type of blue skirt. A pendant with the Order's logo hung around her neck. It was the only sign of rank.

Eliana sank into the straight-backed chair. Her heart raced. The carefully prepared words she'd been working on for the last few days were gone.

"There are still many things that we don't want the world to know," the Arch Priestess said. "Besides, it would be really hard to prove, given that the Guild has taken care of things on their end."

Eliana closed her mouth with a snap.

"Oh don't worry, dear, you're not dreaming," the Arch Priestess said, humor in her aging voice. She pushed her glasses back up her nose only to have them slide back down again.

"What do I do now?" Eliana asked.

"I've taken the liberty of having your resignation typed up for you." She reached into a folder and pulled out a piece of paper with the Order's logo on it. "You'll sign it, of course."

Eliana signed with trembling hands. There was no point in reading it, even if her addled mind could focus enough to do so.

The Arch Priestess took the paper, stamped it, and set it back into her folder. She stood up and opened the cabinet behind her.

"Now that you've resigned, we're just friends, chatting. You may call me Maria." She pushed some books aside and set two crystal glasses down.

Maria lifted a decanter with an amber liquid from its shelf in the cabinet, pulled the stopper, and splashed some scotch into each glass. Then she settled back into her seat and regarded Eliana as her finger circled the rim of the glass.

"The Order lost a very powerful witch today," she said without judgement and took a sip.

Eliana took the glass and did the same. A second sip gave her the courage to speak. "That's it. Just my resignation?"

Maria smiled. "Well, I suppose we could do something more drastic, but I figured it would be a bad idea. That anima of yours is a nasty thing. Vicious. Powerful."

"Dark," Eliana amended.

Maria shrugged. "Dark or white magic is more about what you do with it than what you label it."

"You're afraid of me."

Maria swirled the liquid around in the glass, making rainbows scatter across the room as it reflected the sunlight.

"Several of us, working together, could destroy you. I suggest you keep that in mind."

"But you're not going to." She set the glass down.

Maria poured more scotch into both their glasses.

"You did your job. You saved the protectee and our reputation. And despite all that darkness inside you, you've never done anything evil."

"I drew the life force out of a man. Turned his body to ash. Used my magic to block out the sun. Made a woman shoot herself in the head."

"And now we're back to all the things we don't want the world to know." Another sip. Another knowing look.

Eliana rubbed her forehead.

"I would like to give you a piece of advice, if you'll take it," Maria said.

Did she have a choice? Well, she was no longer a Sister. Technically, the road ahead of her was full of choices. None of which she was prepared for.

"Find some way to drain that anima of yours on a regular basis or next time you *have* to use it," Maria said, taking her silence for assent, "it will overpower you again."

Eliana blinked. Her throat went dry. She sipped at the scotch. It burned its way down her throat, providing no relief.

"Drain it how?" she asked and swiped at her lips. Her stomach was on fire now too.

"Why do you think we ask for a vow of chastity, my dear?"

"So the wives don't see us as competition."

A chuckle. "Yes, that's the official reason. But your anima rises when you fuck, does it not?"

Eliana choked.

"Of course for most of us, our anima is not the problem it is for you. You need someone for whom your anima will rise, but who can drain it when it does." A slow smile stretched Maria's lips. "It can't be a human of course. Too fragile."

"Someone like a vampire?" Eliana asked.

"Oh yes, a vampire would do nicely."

* * *

Thorne had been staring at the same page for what seemed like eternity. A small pool of light from an antique lamp fell over his shoulder as he sat in the winged chair, book in his lap. He'd been living in Elizabeth's guest-room for almost a month now. Since she was technically responsible for him, she'd insisted. And he hadn't argued. It gave him time with Clara.

He and Elizabeth had had a very long discussion about Clara. It would be too confusing to reveal himself as her father right now. Maybe in a few years.

He'd tucked her into bed a few hours ago and watched her fall asleep, curled around a teddy bear.

You'll have to watch her grow and then grow old and die. Elizabeth's voice echoed in his memory, night after night. Yet, she had chosen to do the same. His "choice" had been less clear, but that's just how things happened in life. And death. Or whatever this altered existence, this "differently alive" really was.

As a vampire, he'd be able to protect Clara, at least when the sun wasn't up. Moving north was another option they'd discussed. But a place with longer nights also had more vampires, usually older ones, and bringing a child into that world was not without problems. Just like humans, some were good and some were not. As much as the Guild tried to police its own, it could only do so much.

The Guild had successfully kept things in-house. Sister Conley's murder had been ruled just that. The official story was that Clara hadn't been with her, but had been on a playdate at a friend's house. The Order of Soteria had been accommodating as well, backing up the story. There had been no mention of a kidnapping. Clara had no memory of it. For which he was grateful even if it had involved "glamour."

And now that Donata and Caleb were well and truly dead, there had been no point in telling the police about them either.

That they'd faked their deaths shouldn't have come as a surprise. Elizabeth hadn't played into their original extortion scheme. They'd wanted her money, but hadn't counted on her being turned. And once Clara had been born, they'd wanted nothing to do with their own child—not if she wasn't going to get them what they really wanted. He was glad they were dead. Wished he'd played a greater part in it.

He snapped the book shut, annoyed with his line of thinking. He'd never been the vengeful sort. Was this part of being a vampire? Or was it the result of seeing the three people he loved most in the world, threatened, tortured, and terrified? Was it guilt from not being able to do more? Not being able to protect his own?

The only loose thread was Eliana. He worried about her. For her.

Officially, she'd resigned, but he knew that the Guild had had a hand in that as well. Witches and vampires working together. Strange bedfellows and all that.

Elizabeth was away on Guild business again. It was just him, Clara, and two vampire bodyguards. The guards were there not just for Clara, but for him. He'd successfully transitioned, but until he could prove that he could be out and about on his own—without harming humans—he would never be alone. He had a year to prove he wasn't a liability. The Guild "took care" of their own in more ways than one.

A soft knock on the door.

"Mr. Carmichael. You have a visitor."

Liam, the older of the guards. Very formal. Would've made a good butler to some Brit. Probably had been one. He certainly had all the mannerisms.

Thorne glanced at his watch. Midnight. Still seemed strange to have visitors so late. Perhaps he'd been more immersed in that book than he'd thought. He hadn't heard anyone come up to the house.

"Come in." He set the book aside and stood up, reaching to adjust a tie that wasn't there. Habit. He was casually dressed in jeans and a T-shirt, his feet bare. He hadn't planned on visitors.

The door swung inward.

Eliana.

Breath left his body in a whoosh.

She was—as always—a vision. Long, blonde hair fell freely across her shoulders. A tank top and shorts showed off her curves. Sandals gave her a carefree look. One he hadn't seen in almost seven years.

It made his heart skip a beat.

Liam withdrew, closing the door behind him.

Thorne cursed and turned away, leaning on the desk with both hands. Bastard. Leaving him alone with a human. One he wanted now more than ever. One who'd haunted his nightmares, made him curse his Maker, one for whom he'd walk into the sun. Become flame. Become ash.

"Nice to see you too, Thorne," she said smoothly. No malice. No fear. No judgement.

He closed his eyes, tried not to breathe. She smelled of sunshine and fresh bread, of honey and fruit, all the things he would never be able to experience for himself again. And he wanted to take her in his arms, breathe her in, never let her go.

His fangs ached. And if she stayed, other things would too.

Leave. He wanted to shout it. Couldn't.

"You're alone with a newly made vampire," he said. When had his voice become so grating?

"I know. I told them I wanted to see you alone."

"Why?" He made his hands into fists, leaned into the surface of the desk carefully. Sometimes his strength got away from him. At least with Clara there seemed to be some mechanism at work that made it much easier to be around her. Probably because she was his own blood.

The sound of Eliana's steps approaching were like thunder. He shook his head.

Block her out. Pretend she isn't here.

The light-tight tunnel was just steps away. He could flee. She'd never catch him.

Coward.

She placed her hand on his shoulder, ran it down his arm.

He spun, backed her into the bookcase, pinned her to it. Looked down into her eyes.

There was a glow in those baby-blues, like the sun was shining beneath them. And a smile. A smile in her eyes. On her lips.

"I've missed you too," she said.

He wet his lips. His mouth was watering. The ache from his fangs throbbed, sending pulses all the way down his body.

Eliana's heartbeat flared at her throat. Called to him. It was the only sound for what seemed like an eternity. He bargained with each one. *Just one more. I can take one more. And another.*

"I need you, Thorne." She closed in and placed a kiss on his jaw. Trailed it down to his throat.

Thump. Thump. Thump.

One more. Just one.

"And I think that you need me as well, do you not?" she added as she retraced the path of kisses. They were like sparks traveling across his skin. Vicious. Enticing.

He could lose himself in this. Lose himself forever.

He'd changed. He'd never know if it was from being turned, or because he'd almost lost them, or because it had been in him all along but never been needed. He liked the aggression. He liked being strong. He never wanted to feel helpless again.

"It won't be like before," he said in warning.

More kisses, each one harder than the last. Her teeth grazed against his skin. Her tongue swept his pulse point.

"I'm counting on it," she said.

* * * * *

Monalisa Foster Bio

Monalisa won life's lottery when she escaped communism and became an unhyphenated American citizen. Her works tend to explore themes of freedom, liberty, and personal responsibility. Despite her degree in physics, she's worked in several fields including engineering and medicine. She and her husband (who is a writer-once-removed via their marriage) are living their happily ever after in Texas. Her epic space opera, Ravages of Honor, is out now.

Link for author page: https://www.amazon.com/Monalisa-Foster/e/B075Z7SDJ1

# # # # #

Ever the Dreamer by Donea Lee Weaver

My skin was warm and sticky the moment we strolled out of our hotel room. New Orleans never had cold, dry weather, or so the guy at the reception desk had told us. Trumpet notes and savory smells of Cajun BBQ wafted to us from nearby Frenchmen's Street—our destination for the night. I smoothed down my barely-there yellow sundress and smacked the lip-gloss on my lips. The attractive male tourists wouldn't mind a little warm and sticky, I was pretty sure of that.

As we descended the stairs from our third-floor room, my platform heels protested. Another thing the reception guy had told us—no elevators were allowed in "historic" hotels. The enclosed courtyard was empty, and the windows from the surrounding rooms gloomed dark. We seemed to be the only visitors staying at the Jean Lafitte house who were out for a good time.

Once we exited the property onto Esplanade, that changed. The street was abuzz with life and chatter and more music. Spanish moss wafted in a slight and welcome breeze, hanging from enchanting trees with twisty branches, up and down the lane. The beauty of them, sadly, didn't match our experience at ground level—the air was thick and smelled like hot garbage.

Kylie tucked her index finger under her nose. "Ugh." She grimaced. "I could never live here. No way I'd ever get used to that smell."

"Well, lucky we don't live here, then," I said.

"Chloe, the eternal smart ass." My other friend, Jen, looped her arm through mine after leaping over a crack in the sidewalk.

"I do what I can." Kylie glared at us before relenting and looping her arm through my free one.

We picked our way through the craggy sidewalks and streets for a few blocks—our excitement growing as the crowds got bigger and the music got louder. Frenchmen Street was an equally cool, but less touristy "Bourbon Street," and one a lot of the locals frequented. Local or tourist, however, we girls were on a mission. We'd joked on every trip we'd gone on together that we'd kiss some random stranger. Hadn't happened yet—but NOLA seemed the perfect place to get a little...somethin'.

Gorgeous baskets full of brightly colored pansies, snapdragons, sweet alyssum, and lush greens hung from second-floor balconies on equally colorful buildings. It was as if the designers of this street had decided to use every hue of paint in their collections. We snapped pictures of iconic architecture on places like Dat Dog and Adolfo's and other buildings and businesses you wouldn't find in our boring little hamlet back home.

A troupe of players blew their horns on the street corner—jazzy sounds that almost transported you back into a different era. Oh, it was brilliant.

"Where to first?" Kylie asked.

"There's an open artist's market halfway down that way, I think."

We turned left and danced through the crowds of people to get to our first stop. The Frenchmen Art Market, small but charming, sat in the middle of a row of buildings, with food and booze on either side of it. Rows and rows of bright yellow string lights were strewn overhead, some of them even wrapping around tree trunks and branches. Murals dotted the inside walls, and vendors threw in their own special flavor to the place with their various wares.

I loved the artwork of New Orleans, in particular—the steamboats, the jazz clubs, the iconic buildings, churches, and its colors—it was a town unlike any other. Enchanting.

Stopping at one booth in particular, I gazed at the stunning painted landscapes that seemed transportive. I could almost see myself floating along a river in the moonlight or dancing on a private terrace at some lovely country villa.

"Do you like them?" The smoothest voice I'd ever heard sounded behind me, deep and made sexier by the slightest French accent.

Goosebumps raised along my forearms, despite the muggy atmosphere. "I do."

I heard him shift beside me and turned to see the most stunning man. His skin was black as midnight, but his eyes were the blue of a sunny day. He leaned closer to me.

"I can see you in this place," he said, his breath hot on my cheek. "It's warm, but not like here. Comfortable. The stars are dotting the night sky, and fireflies float around the trunks of nearby trees. The rising moon glints off the river running by. You're in your lover's arms, swirling in a dance so light, it's as if gravity doesn't exist."

As he described the scene, I closed my eyes and could see it all, so vividly, like a waking dream. The only incomprehensible thing was the face of the man who held me. In a fanciful wish, I placed the handsome stranger in the role. "Mmm, I see it. It's wonderful."

A sudden throat-clearing sounded behind me and I was pushed forward—lightly, but I still stumbled. I whipped around, circles and circles, but the strange, intoxicating man had vanished. The scent of him and the feel of dancing in his arms lingered for a few moments, and then I had a hard time even remembering what he'd looked like.

"Chloe?"

I scanned the square, but my eyes took in nothing.

"Chloe? Hey, are you okay?"

A light hand touched my shoulder, and I jerked it away.

"Whoa. Chloe. What the heck. It's just Jen."

"Jen?" My words sounded far away. I rubbed my temples and tried to focus on the face in front of me. Jen. Oh, yes—my best friend. "Where have you been?"

She tossed a curly strand of dark hair behind her shoulder and squinted at me. "Where have I been? I came back for you and found you looking like you'd just taken a super-sonic acid trip." She touched me again, and I only flinched a little this time. "Are you okay?"

I gazed at the booth in front of me, my eyes lingering on a vibrantly-colored picture of two people dancing near a river. "I was talking to the artist...I think."

"Umm," an older man with silver hair and a goatee approached us from the left, "I'm the artist. Is there something I can help you ladies find?"

I stared at him blankly before shaking my head and grinning at him. "I love your work. That one in particular. Do you have a print of it?"

"As a matter of fact, I do."

* * *

The rest of the night was a blur. We ate beignets and Cajun shrimp pasta at the Marigny Brasserie, grooved to good music, and then got a little tipsy at the Spotted Cat. Every single one of us whined when we got back to the hotel, gazing up at the three flights of stairs we had to go up. Somehow, I made it out of my clothes and into a bed to get a few hours of sleep. My dreams were fitful, though. There was a man in them, a man I wanted, but every time I reached for him, he seemed to slip from my grasp.

"Wakey, wakey," Kylie sang her wake-up call to me, bouncing on the end of my bed for a minute. "Get up, sleepyhead. We've got a big day ahead of us."

"I love you, and I hate you right now," I muttered, pulling a pillow over my head.

"I know." She chuckled as she shuffled away from me, and moments later I smelled coffee brewing. One thing my friend and I definitely didn't have in common—she was a morning person.

When we were dressed and ready, we walked to the end of Esplanade to catch a streetcar to the Dumaine St. station. We were up early enough that the crowds at Café Du Monde probably wouldn't be too bad, but it was nearly eighty degrees outside already. We'd suited up in light-colored clothing, sun hats, and generous amounts of sunscreen.

After twenty minutes in line, we were seated at a small round table in the middle of the café and ordered the recommended plate of three beignets and their famous café au lait. Dusting powdered sugar off my fingers, I gazed around the room, hoping I might see my mystery man from last night. It was a ridiculous thought, really. New Orleans had tens of thousands of people milling around. That we'd be in the same spot at the exact same time, twice, seemed incredible.

"Oh my gosh, I could eat about twenty of these," Kylie said, her lips white and pasty.

Jen and I giggled at Kylie's overindulgence and at the beautiful day ahead of us. Perhaps last night had been a bizarre daydream. At any rate, the guy hadn't wanted to stick around, so why was I wasting valuable vacation thoughts on him?

"Where to next?" Jen asked. "We have a few hours before our bayou tour leaves."

"Jackson Square?" I suggested. "There's a few shops around there, more artwork, and the St. Louis Cathedral at the back."

"Sounds like a plan," Kylie said between finger-licks.

More vendors lined the outside walls of the square, and though I tried to resist the artwork, I secretly hoped I'd see the artist from last night. He wasn't the man of my dreams, but Mr. French-accent from last night and I did seem to have the same taste in artists.

As we rounded the corner and headed toward the entrance to the Cathedral, a group of sketchy-looking guys catcalled to us. One whistled low and approached Jen. "Hey, pretty lady. Wanna see me blow my horn?"

"Ignore them," I whispered, and we picked up the pace, practically sprinting to the church. Collectively sighing once we were inside, we gazed up at the murals on the ceiling, happy to replace outside's ugliness with something so beautiful.

I wrapped an arm around my friend's shoulders. "You okay?"

"Yeah." She shrugged it off with a forced grin. "I just hate it when that happens, you know?"

"Don't we all."

I sat in a pew at the back of the cathedral, away from the tourists, away from the worshippers, and even away from my friends, who strolled the outside aisles taking pictures of the lovely stained-glass windows. There was a certain reverence and sense of peace in every cathedral I'd ever visited—didn't seem to matter what city or country you were in. I loved to just sit and let it wash over me. It seemed to reset some of my life's stresses, or at least kept them at bay for a while.

I could sense someone scooting through the pew behind me and was a little irked as the wood squeaked when they sat down. Of all the other available places to sit...

"There's nothing quite like the tranquility of an old church to soothe one's soul, is there?" The voice behind me was warm and familiar. I hesitated to turn around and see him there. Like he'd disappear again the moment I did.

"No," I said. "Nothing quite like it."

"May I sit with you?" His voice was hot on my skin again, but it still made me shiver.

"I guess."

The wood creaked again, and seconds later the man of my dreams shuffled into my pew and sat next to me. I stiffened as he sat too close and looped an arm onto the backrest behind me.

"You're a Dream Walker, aren't you." It wasn't a question.

"A what?" It took me a moment to process his words. "No. No, I'm not."

He gripped my hand firmly, but not too hard, and turned to face me, narrowing his eyes and staring. Straight into my soul, it seemed. "I'm not wrong about that," he said, reaching out to touch my left temple. "Ah! You're just new."

I slapped his hand away, the sound echoing, and shrank down in the pew. "Hey, now. Don't touch me like you know me. We just met, buddy."

He threw his hands up. "My apologies." But then he cocked his head to the side and appraised me. "Surely, though, you must detect that we're the same. We're both Dream Walkers."

"What are you talking about?" I hissed low. "Dream whatever? That's ridiculous."

"You don't believe me? Try it," he challenged, "on your friends tonight. While they sleep, it's simple. Much harder when they're awake."

"No." Not that I believed anyone could walk in someone else's dreams, anyhow. It was...a violation. And not possibly real. How could something like this be real? "Even if I believed you, they'd think I'm a total creeper. Oh, and by the way, I don't believe you."

He narrowed his eyes at me before he leaned back. "Sheltered upbringing, I see. Where are you from? Midwest?"

"None of your business." I *psh*ed.

"Utah." The pew in front of us groaned as Jen sat down and looked between the two of us. "Who's your friend, Chloe?"

"Tyson Laveau." He stiffened at Jen's presence and didn't take her hand when she offered it.

"Oh-kay," she said, frowning. "Laveau? Like the Voodoo Queen?"

He straightened, his frame impressively tall even seated, and looked down at Jen. "The surname is more common in this city than you might think."

I nudged him. "Knock it off," I whispered. "You're being rude."

He raised his dark, perfectly shaped brows at me and sighed. "Here." He pressed a strange coin into my palm. "If you'd like to know more, you can find me at the Maison tonight." He nodded curtly at Jen before sashaying away from us and out the front doors.

Jen huffed when Tyson was completely out of view. "What was that all about? Is that the same guy from last night?"

I studied the coin in my hand. There was a crescent moon engulfing a sun on one side, and an open hand on the other, shaped kind of like the hands you saw on trendy, boho reflexology posters or something. I shoved it into my pocket. "Yes, same guy. And...honestly, I have no idea what he was talking about."

Not yet, anyhow. Crazy as pretty much everything he said to me was...I had to admit, I was curious.

* * *

While my friends clambered half over the sides of the pontoon boat that guided us around the bayou looking for alligators to snap pictures of, I texted my mom.

Our family doesn't have any freaky dream powers, do we?

Subtle.

Yet she replied within seconds.

OMG, you're drunk. R U drinking? I know I shld hv had dad come with you girls...

Oh, geez. I was twenty-three years old, with a BS degree in psychology, currently working on my masters…yet she still treated me like I was nine, sometimes. Sheltered. Tyson's word came back to me like a flick in the nose, and to be honest…maybe he was right. If not exactly "sheltered," definitely "over-protected."

I'd traveled a decent amount on my own after graduating high school, but I had to admit, there was still a bit of a naivety to me when it came to the darker, grittier workings of the world. And I'd certainly never experienced anything that would make me believe the supernatural actually existed. I hadn't even seen a ghost!

My brain strained. Or had I? One thing I could claim—I remembered my dreams. A lot of people don't. I could pinpoint details in my dreams even hours or days after I'd had them. I also experienced a seemingly abnormal amount of déjà vu. But, dream walking? Huh.

No, mom. Not drinking or drunk. Just random. Never mind. Luv u!

"Holy cow, look at that one. It's huge!"

Kylie's squeaky excitement caught my attention, and I switched my phone over from text to camera. The day was sunny, and the light reflecting off the water made me happy I'd picked a pontoon boat tour, quiet and covered, instead of one of those noisy fan-boat tours that left your skin at the mercy of the elements.

The boat waded through watery lanes flanked by tons of green brush and drippy moss and trees. Oh, and alligators. Our guide baited them with fluffy marshmallows, and every time one of them jumped out of the water to snatch one, someone on the boat applauded. Smiling, I snapped a picture of a small alligator sunning itself on a fallen tree trunk near the riverbank. They were kind of…cute, really.

Kylie plopped down on the bench seat next to me and took a long swig of water. "So, who was that guy at the cathedral?"

"His name is Tyson Laveau."

"Huh." She shoved her water bottle back into a slot on the side of her backpack. "So, does he have friends?"

My eyes rolled before I could stop them. "I really don't even know this guy. I doubt I'll even see him again."

"Jen said we were meeting him at the Maison tonight? Is that not the case?"

Oh, Jen. If I'd waffled about meeting with Tyson again and listening to more of his insane Dream Walker talk, well...the decision had just been made for me.

"I guess we're going."

She flashed me a smug grin and wiped the face of her phone on her shorts to clean it. "Awesome. Now, if you'll excuse me, I've got more alligators to bait."

Awesome, indeed.

* * *

The Maison took us back to Frenchmen Street. We'd avoided the club the other night because it was packed. Standing room only—or maybe not even that. Even with three levels of venue space, it was hard to find a place to squeeze into, let alone breathe. A standing marquee outside the entrance announced a band called "Dysfunktional Bone" was playing, and the distinctive notes from a trombone, tuba, and trumpet drifted out to us.

"Wow." Jen grimaced at the crowd just inside the doors. "Even if I dropped ten pounds right this instant, I still don't think I could squeeze into that place."

My forehead creased. I had to agree with her. I even hated eating at noisy restaurants, but then this was all part of the New Orleans experience, right? "I think we have to try."

"Really?" She looked genuinely surprised by my response.

Rubbing the coin Tyson had given me, still in my pocket, I nodded. "Really."

"We'll be fine," Kylie said, stepping ahead of us and pressing herself into the fray.

If it was hot outside, cramming into a sweaty crowd in a poorly ventilated building made it even hotter. Holding hands, we finagled our way toward the bar, ordering water before any drinks. As I guzzled the lukewarm liquid, I scanned the crowd. Picking Tyson out of this mess of people would be a challenge, for sure. But as if he knew I was there looking for him, a voice in my head told me to look up. There he was, on the second-floor balcony looking down at me, his crystal blue eyes even more brilliant in the red-lit dimness of the room.

I pointed at him, nudging Jen's shoulder. "I'm headed up there," I shouted.

She cupped a hand behind her ear. "Huh?"

I pointed again, and we both looked up to see Tyson grinning seductively down at us. It clicked for Jen then, and she nodded. I think she said, "Be safe," but it was honestly hard to hear my own thoughts. I swiped a hand across the back of my neck, trying to slick away some of the sweat. The musty smell of warm bodies assaulted my nose, and I chastised myself for not grabbing more water before I tried to slosh my way to the second floor.

Yet the moment I reached the top step, Tyson was there to greet me. He grabbed my hand, and the crowds seemed to part far enough away from each other that we could get through the sea of people nearly untouched. We headed around another corner and up another flight of stairs, until we were in the highest and furthest back corner of the building. He touched the wall, and another door appeared. Really, it was just hard to see…not like it magically came into being or anything.

He cracked it open, and the outside air, cooler than the inside, was refreshingly welcome. The world, once he'd closed the door behind us, was also much quieter. As we scaled another few steps to a roof top, I sucked in a deep breath and sighed.

You could still hear the music, but the din was bearable up here. Tyson pulled me close into a dance hold, and we swayed together under a black sky. A few stars beat out the city lights and abundant neon, but the moon must've been a new one.

"I'm glad you came," he said.

"I am, too," I said, and I meant it.

"Where should we be dancing?" he asked.

I really knew nothing about this man, but I eased my head against his shoulder like it was the most natural thing. "I don't know. Right here seems pretty good to me."

He chuckled softly. "Yes. But if you could be anywhere else, where would it be?"

It wasn't the most obvious venue for dancing, but the courtyard outside the Louvre popped into my mind. "Okay. I've got a place."

"And I can put us there." He pulled me closer, and before I could drop my jaw in awe, there we were, dancing between the pyramid and the Seine.

I laughed out loud, delighted, staring around at a city I'd only visited once, but whose details were so ingrained in my memory. The fountain, all the lamp posts, the statues of long-gone aristocrats gazing down at us from their second-story stoops.

"That's amazing." My voice seemed disembodied. "How...why...I...I just never imagined something like this was possible." I gazed up at Tyson, who took a long blink, and then we were back on a roof top in NOLA.

"We're rare," he said, stroking my cheek. "The stories say our kind are always searching for each other. That we have a second half, a soulmate, and if we can find each other, our powers will increase tenfold."

My skin buzzed as I considered that it was hard enough to find a soulmate when you were just a regular old human. "Have there ever been any? Any who've found each other."

He let out a low sigh. "A few."

"Like?"

He pulled away from me, shrugging. Tyson paced to the edge of the roof and gazed down at the crowds still drinking and dancing along Frenchmen. "Adolf and Eva come to mind. Napoleon and Josephine, too."

I laced my fingers together and frowned. "Oh, great. So we're evil?"

Tyson laughed, shaking his head. "There's also Pierre and Marie Curie, and Franklin and Eleanor Roosevelt. When these Dream Couples come together, they can decide how to use their power, to what extent they'll influence, and for how long. Unless, of course, they're someone like Hitler, or that tiny Frenchman who would be emperor. Then the rest of us come together to stop them."

"Hitler did atrocious things for years."

"I didn't say stopping them was *easy*." In a whirl of fancy footwork, Tyson was in front of me again, pulling me into a dance hold. "Do you want to know if you're my soulmate?"

A lightness overcame me, like someone was pumping air into my body, like a balloon, and at any second I might float far, far away. "How can you know? For certain?"

"We can start with a kiss."

As he pulled my body closer to his, all warm and moist and willing, my head tilted back easily. I didn't close my eyes right away, and neither did he. We stared into each other until our faces were so close that our vision naturally blurred, and then his full lips were pressed against mine.

Fire ignited in my gut, and I tugged him tighter against me. His hands dug into my back as our tongues spoke a tangled language only lovers knew. Damn. It got harder to breathe, but I didn't want to stop. Ever.

A loud *POP* rang out in the night, and we fell away from each other, though reluctantly. I sucked in a deep breath, desperate for the oxygen, and wanted to ask him, "So? Do you know?" I couldn't get the words out, so I did some kind of questioning, floppy-handed shrug motion.

He half-smiled, touching his lips and nodding. "It's promising."

* * *

I'd rejoined my friends to tell them, yes. I kissed my random "vacation stranger." However, if we ended up being DW soulmates after this, would it count? Hmm.

"How was it?" Jen asked.

My grin meant more than she'd know. "Magical."

We toasted this victorious goal with Cosmos from the bar and danced and drank more until the wee hours of the morning. When we'd dragged ourselves back to our room, Jen and Kylie fell asleep almost immediately. Jen hadn't even taken the time to undress or wash off her makeup.

Worn out as my body was, my mind still buzzed with thoughts and questions about this new potential reality of mine. Dream Walkers. Dream. Walkers. The most I knew about them were from movies like Nightmare on Elm Street. If I entered my friends' dreams, would my coffin-shaped acrylics become long, deadly razors?

Still, as I watched Jen sleeping in the twin bed next to mine...gawd! The temptation to enter her dreams was...damned hard to resist. Maybe just a peek...

Tyson had affected my daydreams with such ease—he'd just had to be near me. But I knew it wouldn't be that easy for me. I stood at the side of Jen's bed, gazing down at her like a total creeper. Should I sit? Should I continue standing? Should I crouch down to the floor and just reach my hand up? Or maybe I needed to lay down beside her?

Ugh. No. None of those options sounded right. I glanced over at the table by the kitchen. Chairs. That would work. I walked over to grab one and carried it back to the bedside as stealthily as I could. Placing it next to my sleeping friend, I sat down and reached out a hand. Just a peek, I reminded myself. Harmless.

I touched the side of her head softly and closed my eyes. All the stuff in my brain quieted down, and it was filled instead with fuzzy images that weren't my own. I just knew, somehow. Not knowing how to get the images in focus, I clenched my eyes tighter, tilted my head, bit the inside of my cheek, and strained my brain harder than I thought possible. None of it worked.

Leaning into the chair, I let out a long sigh. "I give up," I whispered. I drew my hand away slowly, but just as the tips of my fingers started to come away from Jen's dark, curly hair, an image tightened into sharp focus.

We were back in the Maison, but the background noise and faces were muted. Tyson was there, whispering things into my ear and stroking my arm while I flirt-laughed and twirled my hair like some ditz. Awesome. Suddenly, the band started to riff some rhythmic Latin music, and Jen stamped the floor in a sexy Tango pose that got Tyson's attention right away.

He abandoned me, sliding across the floor to take her into his arms. The faceless crowds parted, giving them the space. And, oh boy, did they work a fast, spicy tango around the room. Ditz-me dropped her jaw in protest, then stomped out of the room like a bratty child.

"I don't know what I ever saw in her," Tyson admitted to Jen.

"Well, you have me now." Jen batted her longer-than-normal eyelashes at him, then he dipped her, and they kissed. They *really* kissed.

I felt…embarrassed for her. For me, too. This was such a violation…not to mention it kind of pissed me off. Jen hadn't said a thing to me about being interested in Tyson, so it was hard to see her cast me in such a light when she hadn't even given me an opportunity to…what? Defend myself? Defend him? Tell her I'd let her take her shot with him? But then, knowing Jen, she'd never say a word about any of the things she was truly feeling.

It made me question our friendship, and that certainly wasn't fair. How many times had I had private thoughts about either her or Kylie, thoughts I was ashamed of and was so happy later to know they were only in my head?

So what was the point of being here?

An idea popped into my head, and before I knew it, Tyson had stopped kissing Jen and actually dropped her to the floor.

"Hey!" Jen scrambled upright and rubbed the side of her hip. "What did you do that for?"

Tyson stroked his chin and looked her up and down. "You're not the girl for me. Sorry. You should find yourself a nice man."

Jen blinked a few times and shook her head like she was trying to rearrange her thoughts. "Aren't you a nice man?"

He sauntered up to her, placing his index finger under her chin so she'd gaze up at him. "Not really."

The way he said it gave me chills…but this was just Jen's dream version of Tyson, right?

He kissed her on the forehead, and then it was as if everything zapped back into its proper place—people thick against each other, faces in focus, music blaring so you could barely hear yourself think. Strangers pushed and prodded me, and before I knew it, I'd been thrown against a wall, smacking the back of my head on a particularly sharp edge of exposed brick. "Out!"

The moment I shouted the word, I was back in the chair beside Jen's bed, and all she did was snore and turn to her other side. I rubbed my head, which still smarted a little here in the real world.

That couldn't be good. Tyson definitely had more things to tell me about how all of this worked.

* * *

I spent my morning in quiet reflection while my friends buzzed around me, excited for our plans for the day. The dream-walking last night had shaken me to the core—a feeling that had been reinforced when I mentioned Tyson to Jen earlier this morning.

She'd blinked in weird, random succession, like her brain was robotic, and she'd attempted a reboot. And then she'd said, "Tyson? Hmm. Why are you interested in him, anyhow? Me, I'd rather find myself a nice man."

Nice man. Those were my words, not hers. I'd influenced her against her will. Nothing about that felt right, and I had to wonder--what was the real value or function of a dream walker? I would have been okay, I thought, if this ability had never been awakened in me. What would I possibly do with it? And *should* I even do anything?

Someone touched my shoulder, and I jerked, spilling coffee on the table.

"Whoa," Kylie said. "Sorry I startled you."

I grabbed a napkin to wipe up the liquid. "It's okay."

She sat down across from me and put her hand over mine. "You sure? You're kind of a million miles away this morning."

I glanced over at Jen. She sat on the edge of her bed, putting her sneakers on, smiling, humming a familiar tune, and completely oblivious that her dreams had been messed with last night.

I tried to shrug off my guilt. "I'll be fine. Bad dream last night is all."

"Okay, then." Kylie didn't look convinced, but she patted my hand and smiled. "Excited for the Aquarium today?"

"Yeah." I actually was excited. The Aquarium, followed by the Butterfly Museum, a little shopping, and then we'd top the night off with a steamboat cruise on the Mississippi. "Should be a fun day."

She moved to stand up but plopped back down in the chair. "Ooh, do you think we'll see that cute guy from the club again?"

Oh my gosh, not her, too…

Tyson Laveau.

Google didn't have much on the guy. I'd looked last night. Repeatedly. No Facebook profile, no blurbs in the local news, not even a graduation announcement. He possibly had an Instagram account, but it was private to only his friends. And since I didn't want to look like a creepy stalker, I didn't send a follow request. We weren't friends, not really. Not yet. I wasn't really sure what we were. Could I really see this guy as my soulmate?

"Well, he hasn't texted or anything." I slid a finger over my phone, lying, because I knew there was at least one message there. "Besides, I've had my little vacay fling. It's time to focus on you two. Maybe there'll be some cute guys on the cruise?"

Kylie grinned wide and rubbed her hands together. "I hope so!"

"Yeah," Jen chimed in. "Hopefully some nice guys."

Sigh.

* * *

We boarded the steamboat *Natchez* just before seven p.m. It would be nice to sit, eat, and listen to jazz music as we floated along the Mississippi river. My feet felt like we'd walked twenty miles. I eased onto a bench on the upper deck and kicked my sandals off. Heaven.

Jen and Kylie were at the bar, getting us mango daiquiris, and I relished a moment alone. I closed my eyes and tried to block out the din of enthusiastic tourists. I pictured myself back in that lovely balcony canvas where I'd first met Tyson—moonlight and dancing, and just the two of us. He was a complete mystery to me, and I didn't fully trust him. But I'd be lying to myself if I said I wasn't fire-in-my-gut drawn to him.

As before, the man dancing with me was indeterminate until I actively put Tyson in his place. When his face came into focus, he looked down at me, surprised.

"Well," he said, "hello there."

I sprang away from him, embarrassed. "Oh, my gosh, it's really you, isn't it?"

He waltzed forward, pulling me into his arms again. "Who were you expecting?"

My cheeks flushed hot, and I bit my lip. "I don't know. Dream you, I guess."

He chuckled low before pulling me closer, grabbing one hand and spinning me out and back in. "As a dream walker, you can pull me in anywhere. If…" he held up one finger, "I want to be pulled in. I could have declined."

"How?"

A shooting star spanned the sky overhead, making his eyes twinkle. "You can feel the pull, like someone's looped a string around your wrist and wants to guide you somewhere. You can snip that string with a thought."

He spun me again, and when I returned against him, I laid my head on his chest. "Is there a handbook for all this? Seriously. I have so many questions."

"Don't worry," he said softly against my ear. "It's more intuitive than you think." He looked off into the distance then, squinting at the moonlight. "Your friends are returning with drinks. You never answered my text from earlier."

He'd asked me to meet him at Harrah's Casino just prior to midnight—told me to bring the strange coin he'd given me. "That's awfully late for a young girl like me to be out all by myself in the French Quarter."

"Bring your friends and call a car to take you home. As long as you stay away from the alleys, you should be fine." He lifted my chin with his index finger and kissed me. "Perhaps that will persuade you?"

"Mmm." I nodded. I did enjoy kissing him. "We'll see."

"Until tonight, then." He pulled away, bowing to kiss my hand before vanishing.

And then I was back on the paddleboat. A couple in front of me were dancing until the man pulled out of it and bowed down to kiss the woman's hand. They both look startled immediately after, the woman blushing, and the man looking bewildered.

"My apologies, ma'am. I…" He shrugged and backed away slowly.

"It's okay?"

My mouth dropped open just as Kylie held a drink in front of my face.

"Wow," she said. "What was that?"

I grabbed the drink from her, gulping it down until it gave me brain freeze. No less than I deserved. Somehow I knew I had influenced those people—two random strangers—into doing something they wouldn't have done otherwise. Sure, it seemed innocent enough. This time. Surely, if there was a way to ignore a dream walker's invite, there was a way to keep all your dreams private and to yourself. I rubbed the ache away from my temple and shook my head.

"No idea," I lied.

* * *

We dragged ourselves into our hotel room around eleven p.m., exhausted and wishing we all had boyfriends waiting in bed for us, begging to give us foot massages. With no carpet or even a fluffy rug in our temporary living space, the only refuge for achy feet was to lie in bed.

"Oh, I could sleep for a year," Jen mumbled, as she fell face first onto the mattress. "What are we doing tomorrow? Just sleeping in? That sounds good, right?"

We had tickets for a plantation tour in the morning, but I didn't want to ruin her impending good night's sleep.

"Yep. Sounds good."

"Erm...kay." Yeah, she was out.

Kylie called down from the top of a spiral staircase that led to the only bathroom in the place, and her room upstairs. "Think I'm gonna take a shower before I call it a night. Do you need to get in here first?"

I let out a long breath. Did I? The smart thing would be to head up there, wash my makeup off, and change into my PJs. I'd mentioned going to Harrah's to my friends after we'd gorged ourselves on crawdads and hush puppies on the *Natchez*. They weren't interested. Not remotely. I'd be a fool to go by myself. Even Tyson had said so. And yet…

"I've got a makeup wipe down here. Think I'll use that and call it a night. I'll shower in the morning."

"Okay, then. Night!"

"Night."

The moment I heard the water run and double-checked that Jen was indeed out for the count, I snuck out of the room.

Holding my hotel key like a mini-dagger, I blended with the crowds still heading to Frenchmen Street, until I reached the streetcar stop at the bottom of Esplanade. There was another stop that would take me straight to Harrah's.

"By your lonesome, miss?" the conductor asked me.

"I'm meeting someone." I tried to keep the doubt from my voice and tightened my grip on my key.

"Careful, careful," he said, waggling a finger at me. "Stay clear o' them alleys."

"I will." The closer to the casino we got, the stupider I felt. My friends should be with me. Or I should have just waited. What was I thinking? "Thanks."

The neon blue sphere with "Harrah's" wide across it was a welcome sight as I jumped off the streetcar and walked to the entrance of the casino. I stared up at the Greek figures sculpted at the top of the building and wondered—could they have been real, too?

"Hey!" A man with multi-colored Mardi Gras beads and a large plastic boot filled with booze nudged me out of the way. "Look in front of you, not up." He spewed a few choice expletives before stumbling down the steps and into the street.

His rudeness only added to my unease. My hands fisted at my sides as I warred with my decision—go in? Go home? But then a warm breeze brushed up behind me, and a man's low voice hummed in my ear.

"I wasn't sure you'd come," Tyson said.

My whole body sighed as I turned and fell against him. "Oh, thank goodness." I grabbed his hand, and he held mine tight. "I wasn't sure, either. What are we doing here?"

"You'll see." He winked and pulled me along with him into the casino, and a cacophony of bright lights, jingling, gamblers, and cigarette smoke.

We weaved through so many slot machines, poker tables, and party-goers, I lost myself. Everything started to look the same the deeper we got into the casino. Every which way I looked was a reflection of itself. You really could lose time and yourself in a place like this.

The commotion dimmed as we closed in on a large silver slot machine in a curiously quiet corner. A picture of an imposing and ancient man, flanked on either side by a sun and a moon, stared down at us as we approached. He was frighteningly familiar, but I didn't know why.

"Who is that?" My voice came out in a whisper.

Tyson stopped to gaze up at the man in almost reverence. "Morpheus," he said. "God of Dreams."

Gulping, my mouth dried as I wondered why this mythical person looked familiar to me. I'd studied Greek mythology in college, watched plenty of mythology-inspired movies and TV shows, and read novels aplenty. Still…there was something about that depiction of the god that rang truer to me than anything before. Maybe I'd seen him in a dream?

Tearing my eyes away from his image, I clutched at the coin in my pocket. "What do we need to do?"

Tyson stared at me, curious, but didn't ask the question I thought might be in his head. He pointed to two coin slots on either side of the machine. "We put our coins into the machine at the same time, pull the handles in unison, and it will tell us if we're meant to be."

I snorted. "You're kidding. I thought all the making out we were doing was supposed to tell us that."

"That was just for fun," he said, grinning. "There are tests like this all over the world. In New Orleans, it just happens to be a slot machine in a casino."

I chuckled at the weird ridiculousness of it. A slot machine was going to confirm my soulmate for me? No way. Still...I was curious to see what fortune it would give us, if any.

"Are you ready?" he asked, positioning his coin near the slot opening.

I did the same. "Ready as I'll ever be, I guess."

"Count of three?"

"Sure."

"One...two..."

We dropped our coins on three, grabbed the handles on our respective sides, and pulled. Images spun and spun until the first one clicked into place.

Soulmate.

More clicking, incessant clicking.

Soulmate.

"Oh, c'mon!" I hissed at it.

Just kidding.

Our coins fell back out into the silver collection plate at the bottom. Tyson and I both stood with our arms folded, glaring down at the shiny-faced moon/sun side of them. My neck craned back, and I actually guffawed.

"Well." Tyson side-stepped next to me and patted me on the shoulder. "That sucks."

* * *

"**D**o you want me to follow you back to your hotel?" he asked, hands in his pockets and shuffling from one foot to the other on a sidewalk beside Canal Street.

I cringed at the jangling *boop-boop-boop*s of cash machines that echoed every time someone walked out of Harrah's. I didn't know how to feel about what had just happened. Tyson and me...we didn't really make sense. I barely knew the guy. Still...the idea of finding a magical soulmate in New Orleans? It was interesting. Much more so than my regular life.

"No."

His eyebrows crinkled. "You're sure? I really think..."

"Yes, I'm sure. I'll be fine. Really."

He chewed the inside of his lip and shook his head. "I don't know."

Touching his arm, I noticed the zing I'd felt shoot through me when I touched him before wasn't really there anymore. "What would be the point?"

He frowned.

"Sorry. I didn't mean it that way. I just…" I leaned in to give him a side hug. "You can walk me to the streetcar station, okay?"

"Okay."

He looked sad as I waved goodbye to him, and the streetcar *tut-ted* away toward its next stop. The short trip to my stop on Esplanade went by in a blur, and my feet and shoulders felt heavy as I descended its stairs and made my way back to the hotel.

A few people still milled around on Esplanade, but not enough to blend in with. And the ones there weren't exactly people I'd want to blend with anyhow. A number of homeless people were camped on the sidewalk near the station and the Jazz Museum, so I crossed to the other side of the road. Better safe than sorry.

I watched them from the corner of my eye until I'd gotten past them. My body tensed with nerves, and the sweat above my brows seemed to bead from more than just the heat. Why had this trip turned me into a moron? I never took chances like this, not in a strange place. I should've taken Tyson's offer…

"Well, hello there, pretty lady."

The scratchy male voice prickled in my ears, and my body froze as a man emerged from the shadows of a building along my way. My key was still gripped at my side, but I couldn't seem to move my arm.

"I said 'hello.'" His already deep voice lowered as he stumbled closer to me. "What? No manners in you young things?"

I took a step back and stumbled in a missing chunk of sidewalk. "Excuse me," I said. "Please." I found my footing and tried to side-step around him, but he was too close to me in an instant.

"Mmm. You are pretty." His breath smelled like the sewer-like air of the streets. He sniffed hard. "You smell good, too."

"Please, leave me alone." I fought the urge to close my eyes.

He bumped my shoulder. "Why you being so mean, lady? I gave you a compliment. Don't you young girls like compliments anymore?"

"Please, just let me pass. I don't want any trouble." My throat was tight, dry, and my heartbeat ran races in my chest. I started feeling dizzy. "You don't want to do this."

"Do what?!" He shouted the words straight into my face, his spit landing against my cheeks. He gripped my arm tight, twisting the skin, and I think I screamed.

The next thing I knew, we were floating in space. In literal *space*. The Earth glowed green and blue below us. I hovered above it, safe in an astronaut's protective suit. I could feel the oxygen flowing into the mask.

The creepy jerk who'd tried to assault me floated in space, too. But he had no mask. His hands were cuffed at this throat, and he gasped for air.

"Good!" I shouted into the void. "You deserve what you get!"

But the realization of what was actually happening hit me like gravity. As I watched his face turn blue and his eyes start to bulge, I remembered the hit to the back side of my head, the spot that still ached in the waking world after a dream.

I was killing this man.

"No. No, no, no, no, no." My arms flailed as I tried to swim toward him, but the closer I got, the further he floated away. "Out!" I shouted. It had worked with Jen.

Nothing.

I couldn't breathe. My helmet…still in place…but my lungs…

"Please, no!" The man was nearly purple now, and I knew in moments he'd be gone.

In a quick flash of light, Tyson was there. And then he wasn't. Landing with a painful thud, the three of us were suddenly back on Esplanade. The man gasped for air, wheezing and wide-eyed.

"Are you all right?" Tyson checked me over first, and when I nodded, he advanced on the man.

"Stay away from me, you freaks!" The creeper bolted, crashing into garbage cans, then he scrambled up and fled into the darkness.

"How...?" I leaned against a wall and tried to collect my nerves.

"I followed you on the next streetcar. I thought maybe..." Tyson shrugged. "I'm just glad I made it in time."

I couldn't reply. As I looked into his eyes, my eyes watered, and his face blurred into the background. And then I sobbed. He held me against his chest, our bodies rocking gently, and he whispered something in French into my ear. I had no idea what he said, but I knew the words were meant to be comforting.

He helped me to my hotel, and I managed to punch the code in to get through the door. We stopped in the silent courtyard and dropped onto a bench near the stairs that would take me to my room.

I leaned into him and dabbed at my eyes. Breathe in. Breathe out. "Thank you," I finally managed to say.

"Of course."

I pulled my lips into a tight line and shook my head. "I...gosh. I don't even know what to say. I'd meant to ask you if I could be harmed in dreams."

"Are you hurt?" He whipped sideways to check me over.

Rubbing the back of my head, I waved a hand. "Not tonight. It happened the other night. It doesn't matter, really. I just hit my head. But...I never imagined I could also hurt other people."

He stared into my eyes for a moment before answering. "I'm surprised, actually. Most Dream Walkers aren't capable of something like that right away. Especially if they've never had a mentor."

"There are mentors?" I needed one. "Do you have one? How do you find one?"

Tyson chuckled. "Slow down. There's time for those questions later. But yes, I had one. He passed away last year, sadly. And you don't usually find one. They find you."

I sighed and tried to relax against the back of the bench. A mentor would've been nice to have. It would've been nice to know, long ago, what I might be capable of. Instead I'd been born with an ability no one had cared to tell me about or even how to use it. Or explain to me why I even existed.

"We'll stay in touch," Tyson assured me as if my internal questions were plain on my face. "Don't worry about that."

"Promise?"

"Of course."

He watched me until I made it to my room and waved goodbye to him. I opened the door with a soft click and tip-toed into the dark room. Nothing stirred—well, I could hear my friend's heavy breathing. The room upstairs was silent, too. Clearly, neither of my friends knew I had left. And maybe it was better if they never found out.

And as I finally crawled into bed and closed my eyes, I hoped tonight I wouldn't dream at all.

* * *

I did my best to enjoy the rest of our trip, and for the most part, I did. But relief washed over me like a warm shower when we made it to the airport Thursday afternoon. I didn't know what being home would be like for me, not now that I had this new truth. I'm sure I'd figure it out. I could message Tyson any time I wanted.

Someone tapped my shoulder, and as I turned, Tyson winked at me, smiling that bright smile of his. "I thought I'd see you off," he said.

I dropped my backpack on the floor and grabbed him around the middle. "I appreciate that. And you."

He flashed some kissing lips at me next and asked, "One for the road?"

My gut fluttered. "Yeah. Sure. Why not."

This kiss wasn't like the blazing make-out sessions we'd had a few times before—it was soft, lingering, light tongue mixed with a little sadness and regret.

As he pulled away, he pressed his forehead to mine and sighed. "Don't stop looking for your other half. I'm sorry it couldn't be the two of us."

I pulled back, cupping his cheek and losing myself one last time in his sea-colored eyes. "I'm sorry, too."

"We may not be soulmates, but we can certainly be mates. I'm here for you, Dream Walker."

I pulled the coin from my pocket and offered it to him. "I imagine you might need this back?"

He closed my hand back over it and shook his head. "Keep it. Perhaps the planets will align differently someday, and we'll use it again?"

"Maybe."

"Safe travels, chérie."

"Thanks. And happy hunting."

He nodded, playfully snarling like a stalking tiger. And then he was gone.

Somewhere deep down, I think I knew Tyson wasn't really the one for me. The idea of us had been fun to play with, at least for a while.

Rare.

He'd told me from the start finding my Dream Walker soulmate might never happen. But I knew beyond a doubt I'd never stop looking.

* * * * *

Donea Lee Weaver Bio

Donea Lee Weaver is a perpetual daydreamer who has been creating and telling stories since her elementary school days. When she's not writing about the things she loves (all things romance, fantasy, sci-fi, and yes, even a little horror) you can probably find her planning her next vacation, playing games with the girls, reading, taking the scenic route or cuddling on the couch, with her daughter and her dog, binge-watching a favorite show. She was born and raised in Utah and earned a BA in English from Weber State University. She's also a member of The League of UT Writers and attends a variety of writing conferences every year.

You can find additional stories by Donea Lee on Amazon. Feel free to contact her at donealee@gmail.com or find her on Twitter and Instagram: @donealee.

# # # # #

At the Still Point by Marisa Wolf

An aquarium's worth of water sloshed in Emery's stomach, and the aftertaste of chlorine tablets and fish pellets lodged in the back of her throat.

"And I said, I don't give a shit about your theory, Detective. Stomach, throat, and liver all had damage consistent with one-time, guaranteed-to-deliver poisoning. Patterns would have been different for long-term—did this asshole just hang up on me?"

Keri slammed the phone back on its receiver, then lifted and slammed it down again for good measure. Emery did her best to blend in with the metal wall of cold drawers. Her almost best, really, given she made no effort to shift the coloring of her skin. Keri's loud anger tended to be safer than her ferocious silences.

"If they would just read the gods-damned reports I damn well send them, they would—Emery Middle Name Mimnesko, are you trying to hide from me?" Keri switched her tone mid-sentence, tugging impatiently at her long white coat and glaring.

Emery straightened, hoping she didn't look as guilty as she felt, and crossed her arms defensively. Keri had thrown 'Middle Name' in there, which meant the other woman's anger had blown out as fast as it had come in, but Keri in a foul mood could loosen Emery's grip on herself on even a medium day. Today, from spilled coffee to broken shoelaces to overbearing detectives, had left medium behind and barreled right into crappy territory.

"That's the third time Detective Abraham's called today, and you hate him to begin with." Emery rocked onto her toes. "And it's been a day."

"It's always a day." Keri blew out her breath, ran her hands through her hair, realized belatedly she'd ruined her bun, and glowered again. She bent forward to secure her hair, craning her neck to keep her eyes on Emery. "You're ok though. Right?"

"Tasting aquarium." Emery shrugged, a chill wrapping around the back of her neck.

Both of them paused, glancing to the far end of the morgue. Against the bare concrete wall a seventy-five-gallon tank stood on a metal frame, empty save for a handful of small rocks scattered against the glass.

Keri finished fixing her hair and straightened, her ID fluttering off her lapel. It landed face up between them, a smaller version of Keri's unsmiling face staring at them next to the official lettering of 'Doctor Keres Nikotonos, Medical Examiner, Bard City Morgue.' Keri groaned, crouched to pick her ID up, and tossed it onto the nearest stainless steel table.

"Nothing bad is happening, Em. Just a normal dick with his nuts in a twist." Keri shrugged, took the handful of steps to cross the narrow part of the morgue, and put her hands on Emery's shoulders. "Nothing's scheduled to come in today, so we can finish up our reports and have a nice, quiet—"

The double doors slammed open so quickly they crashed against the concrete walls and bounced back. Each of the people on either side of the stretcher reflexively caught the doors on the swing and held them open until the two of them got clear with the stretcher.

Emery felt her form shiver, but took a deep breath, and held on-to herself.

"Sorry, sorry, it's been a hell of a day." The man on the left flipped his hand up in an apologetic wave. Blood was splashed on his shirt, dried, but not yet flaking. "You're our last delivery before cleanup."

Keri swiped her badge and clipped it back to her lapel, gesturing at one of the six empty tables. "Nobody called," she said, raising an eyebrow.

Emery shook herself, swallowing the chemical taste back and steadying her thoughts. The morgue was usually peaceful, but she'd felt unbalanced before the series of interruptions from police detectives and bloody EMTs. She straightened and pushed away from the cold drawer, reaching out her hand for the papers the man on the right held.

"It's been a mess," the first man said, shrugging. "Seven dead, thirteen well and truly fucked upstairs in the ER. Professional opinion."

"Seven?" Emery asked, looking down at the paperwork. "This is just for one."

"Others went to the holy men. Couldn't confirm they were down for the count." The second man, paler, twitched his nose. Emery figured him for some breed of the occasionally furry variety, despite the smoothness of his skin. On a better day, she'd feel a measure of fondness for their slight relation. "This one's all the way dead."

"You could have brought them all here," Keri said, tone cool as she watched the men angle the stretcher to the table she'd directed them to. "I'm not the ME for nothing."

"Nothing against you, Dr. Nikotonos. Explosion was particularly suspect; you know what I mean." The first man appeared fully human. Every hair on his arms stood straight up, likely still reacting to the magic he'd been exposed to at the scene.

"My point stands. Mimnesko, what are the orders?" Keri kept her eyes fixed on the EMT, which seemed to keep the man from moving the body.

"Standard autopsy. Cops aren't asking for anything extra, no riders from any of the detectives." Emery flipped the paper over to make sure there were no addendums, then strode toward her desk to grab a clipboard and a tag. As always, it was easier to hold professionalism with a clear task at hand. "No identification on him, so I'll get the fingerprint kit and DNA sampler."

"Any other information we need?" Keri asked the EMTs, tone clipped and bored.

"No, ma'am. Holies will be in touch if they find anything."

"Yes, that sounds like them." Keri rolled her eyes, took the clipboard from Emery, and signed her name at the bottom of the form while the EMTs lifted the body from stretcher to table. She tore it off and handed it to the were-breed EMT, turning the clipboard toward him for his signature on the paper underneath. While he signed, she flipped the sheet from the body's face to ensure it matched the brief description on the paper, and Emery moved over to the second EMT.

"Confirm receipt of male, potentially human, magically inert body." Emery took the clipboard from the EMT and started to fill out a toe tag. "Good luck with the rest of your shift."

Sometimes EMTs needed encouragement to leave, sometimes they vibrated with eagerness to get out of the morgue. These two were somewhere in between, so it didn't hurt to nudge.

"Yeah, we're on for the rest of the nightshift. Hope we don't have to swing by here again," the human said cheerfully, and Emery offered a faint smile of agreement. Keres flipped her hand in something like a wave, turning back to the body.

"Well." The doctor pulled a fresh pair of gloves from her jacket pocket and snapped them on. "Let's see who we have here."

Emery finished the toe tag with a flourish, glancing up as the double doors swung closed behind the EMTs. Keri pulled the covering sheet fully off the body, and Emery reached toward his feet with the tag.

And froze.

"Em?"

Her stomach roiled, but she couldn't find a single word to distract herself or answer Keri. Shudders jumped from the muscles in her back, down her sides, and her outstretched hand began to shake.

"Em!" Keri took two long steps and shoved herself between Emery and the body. "Where are you?" Silence pooled between them, and Keri firmed her voice. "How many kidneys do you have?"

It could have been the question or the tone of Keri's voice that reached her. Emery's eyes snapped from their unseeing distance to meet Keri's darker ones. She dropped her hand and blinked, doing an automatic count of her internal organs. Everything was there; her form had held inside and out, despite the shock.

"I...Keri, he's...he's familiar."

"He's WHAT?" The controlled doctor slipped, her eyes flashing black throughout the sclera. "How? Who is he?"

"No, I...I don't..." Emery's eyes flickered from brown to blue to green to gray to almost the same shade of black as Keri's, wide to narrow to round, as her gaze snapped from her friend to the body and finally, inevitably, to the aquarium.

Four years she'd spent in that glass container, though she remembered it mostly as a series of sensations. Keres had taken painstaking time showing her—reminding her?—how bodies worked, over-explaining every autopsy, every system, every variation of creature that came through the morgue.

Eventually Emery had managed to put herself together and climb out of the aquarium. She'd pulled enough detail from all the bodies that had passed through over the years to build something functional, unrecognizable as any one previously living body. Because she'd, finally, successfully, built such a mishmash, no one personality or set of memories flooded into her. She'd built her mind into usefulness through countless conversations with Keres over the last six years, in small excursions out into the world that eventually became longer as she learned, or relearned, function and living.

As for the time before the aquarium, nothing.

Keri had found her, disintegrated into no more than a thick puddle in an alley. Keri—the half-battle nymph—had been called by an air of cruel brutality, but the crooked space between decrepit apartment buildings only held old garbage and Emery's formless self. The doctor, knowing *what* the puddle was, if not who, had gathered her up and poured her into an old aquarium...and the time before that remained empty and unanswerable.

Until this burning moment, ten years later. Until recognition, faint and nauseating, climbed up her throat alongside the chemical fish taste.

She knew him. Somehow.

And he was dead. A laugh snared against the words she attempted to speak, only gibberish emerging for a long moment. Keri opened her mouth, and Emery shook her head sharply and stepped back.

"Two. I have two kidneys. Two lungs. One liver. A heart. Maybe one of the organs knew him." This was not true; the lie coated her tongue. But how could either of them know? "I don't know anything about him, except he's familiar."

"Ok." Keri blew out her breath and nodded once. "Ok. Luckily, we're very good at our jobs, eh, Diener?"

"Right." Emery took a deep breath and summoned up a solid approximation of a smile. "Was his death unusually brutal, magic-wise?" The body looked intact, but there was no accounting for the invisible ravages of spellcasters.

"What?" Keri rolled her head on her neck and shook out her shoulders. "Not especially. We usually make that note at the end so it doesn't bias our examination." There was the slightest of questions in her tone.

"You've called me 'Diener' twice in the last twenty minutes. You usually go all formal when you're feeling a little more death goddess-y."

"Apologies, Technician Mimnesko." Keri's lips quirked in an al-most-smile. "Would you prefer assistant? Morgue support? Shapeshifting autopsy expert?"

"Extra hands?" Emery added, wiggling her fingers and resisting adding a few digits to sell the feeble joke. She smiled slightly, then went for a clean pair of gloves.

"Let's figure it out."

* * *

Nothing remarkable surfaced about the body. For someone murdered by magical backlash, he'd died relatively peacefully. Not so much as a tremble in Keri's perception, unusual when the method of death had been hinky enough to get the holy men involved.

Emery washed her hands once more, shrugging off her protective coat and tossing it into the biohazard laundry bag.

"Should we change for good measure?" Like any proper morgue attendant, Emery kept a few changes of clothes in her locker in case of a particularly messy or magic-clinging case. Today had neither, overtly, but with any afterwash of unrestrained magic, it always paid to be sure. The loose power couldn't hurt her, but non-shapeshifters weren't as lucky or immune.

Keri closed her eyes, breathing deeply through her mouth, tipping her head back and dropping her jaw for a more thorough assessment.

"Nothing obvious, magic-wise. You could shower to be safe, but we aren't carrying anything out to the unprotected masses. Hungry?"

Before Emery could answer, the phone shrilled. They exchanged looks, and Emery shrugged, crossed over to the bright crystalline display, and acknowledged the request with her palmprint.

"Bard City Morgue," she said cheerfully. Rolling letters, a warm white against the blue face, indicated an internal call.

"Front desk here, Morgue. We've got someone here who's sure their loved one's with you. You have identification?"

"Not yet and more bodies to come. Did the police send the visitor?"

"Said it's a familiar bond, that he felt it happen and tracked the last twinges here. What would you like to do?"

Emery shook her head, muted the display, and tilted her head back toward Keri. "Police said it was an open case, right?" Jurisdiction didn't matter to her, but Keri had to walk the tangled lines of laws and ego, so she tried to be supportive.

"Have them take his identification and send him down. Maybe one less call for us after dinner."

"Is it dinner?" Emery asked, unsure what time it was outside their basement. And it didn't matter, given now that they had more work to do before a break. She shifted her body chemistry, dulling the hunger, and unmuted the phone. "Yes, Desk, we'll take him. Does he need an escort, or you good with him?"

"We'll take ID and send him along." The contact disconnected, and Emery turned to catch the fresh coat Keri tossed to her. "You want to get some food, and I'll walk him through?"

"I'm not leaving you to potential emotional overload on a day you were already tasting aquarium remnants, Em. I'll channel my death goddess ancestors and remind myself something with grease and cheese is just a little bit away."

* * *

He walked in, and Emery's knees locked into place. Heat swept over her shoulders and climbed her neck, and her hold on her form shivered in the space between heartbeats.

Shit. She grabbed hold of herself, firming her body into place inside and out, and forced her legs to work. Keri was speaking to him, and his eyes focused on her, the medical examiner part-death-goddess, not the assistant in the far corner.

Emery steadied herself against the corner of the desk, unable to follow the conversation. His jaw, sharper than it had any business being, tugged at a corner of her. Defined cheekbones, dark eyes, darker hair tousled over his forehead. He looked vaguely like the body. That must be the deep bell-ring of familiarity. She'd spent time studying their new arrival, and…

"Diener, yes. She'll have some forms for you. Mimnesko, if you will?" Keri gestured, and Emery took a deep breath before crossing the room to where they stood over the body.

"I'm sorry for your loss," she said, keeping her eyes fixed on the clipboard. "We just need you to review and sign here. Do you know where you'll be sending your…" she trailed off, trying to remember what Keri had said while she'd been getting a literal hold on herself. "Cousin?"

"I told him not to get involved with the Keepers," the man muttered, and Emery's eyes snapped up to focus on his face.

Mistake.

Her skin shivered, and chlorine crowded in her throat.

"Unfortunately," Keri interjected, stepping neatly between them while grabbing the clipboard from Emery's unresisting hands, "we aren't here to police the Keepers, only to ensure the actual police have what they need. Have you given them a statement?"

Her brisk tone knocked Emery's sense back into her, and she clamped down on her form with a ragged gasp.

Unfortunately not fast enough for him not to notice.

"Shapeshifter, nice." He smiled at her, and the expression warmed his face and the entirety of her body, nearly sending her control spinning again.

"You're familiar with the signs?" Keri's voice cooled. "There aren't many in Bard City."

"I'm not from Bard City," he said, his eyes not leaving Emery's, though his smile faded. Smiles didn't last long in the morgue, nor did warmth. It was meant to be a place of clinical, chemical calm. Everything this man was belonged somewhere definitively elsewhere.

"I can't imagine they're common wherever you're from," Keri continued, still holding the clipboard, "given how long they've been hunted. If you'll sign, Mr. Reynolds."

"Reinhold."

"My mistake." Keri had shifted to aggressively neutral. Emery knew her own lack of control was making Keri worse, so gave herself one more steadying breath before straightening and stepping up next to the ME.

"Mr. Reinhold, I apologize. It's been a long day. As I'm sure it has been for you. Again, we're so sorry for your loss. If you'll sign here confirming the identity of your cousin, we can put you in touch immediately with the detective leading the case. We hope that can bring you some closure."

His eyes returned to hers, and his lips moved as though he would smile again.

She very much hoped he would and was perversely relieved when he didn't. The morgue had space for very limited emotions, which was part of why she felt so at home here. This Reinhold and whatever he'd brought with him rampaged so far from that it was no won-der she couldn't settle.

This was the story she could tell herself.

"Perhaps you'd rather talk in Doctor Nikotonos' office? It can't be easy, standing next to your cousin like this." Emery hoped Keri would take the hint, and of course her oldest and only friend did.

"Yes, our apologies, Mr. Reinhold. Please, come with me." She gestured with the clipboard, and the man looked from Emery to her and back before nodding.

As they stepped through the side door, Emery sagged against the table and only managed to keep from collapsing because the table was already occupied.

* * *

"*W*hat in the ever-loving, nineteen circles of inter-locking hells was that?*" Keri's voice slammed into the room a bare second ahead of the door hitting the wall.

Emery had stowed the body and cleaned every surface again, washing away the living man's scent. It didn't work, because the smell of him hadn't seeped into the bare metal tables, it had seeped into her.

She'd taken refuge in cleaning the aquarium, and then finally slumped to the floor to lean against the metal frame of its base.

Seeing her, Keri moderated her tone, but not by much. "Emery! Stand up. Are you melting? No? Then tell me what has you falling—almost literally, let me add—to pieces today?"

"I know him, Keres." Emery didn't stand up, but pulled her knees in and dropped her head on top of them. "It's like the body, but worse. I know him, and I absolutely don't, and who *is* he?"

"Connor Reinhold. Best I can tell, he's a mage from Seaside and was tethered to his cousin because their mothers requested it, not because he had any fondness or use for his cousin, who apparently has been chasing after Keeper attention since he knew they existed."

Emery didn't bother to repress her shudder. Joining Keeper ranks required killing whatever one loved most in the world, meaning they were often surrounded by hangers-on who loved nothing at all and could never move beyond the outer circle. Or perhaps their hangers-on were normal people slowly corrupted by Keeper influence. Emery had never gotten close enough to find out.

"He's been in Bard City for a little over a year, trying—half-heartedly, I'd say—one last-ditch effort to keep his cousin out of the Keepers' crypts."

"You could say he succeeded…" Emery tried for lightness and was rewarded by Keri's hand on top of her hair. "Though I don't suppose Connor Reinhold has power enough to blow up the Keepers."

"I don't think the Keepers were blown up, little fish. It takes a hell of a lot more power than any one mage has to get them. You want to get some dinner? I'll be nicer to you over food."

She lifted her head at that. "You tell that lie every time." She attempted a smile, and accepted Keri's help getting to her feet.

"Yes, but I get meaner without food, and therefore it's never, entirely, a lie." Keri squeezed her hands once before letting go, and Emery knew they'd return to the topic of how she could possibly know this stranger from out of town. Maybe food would help them both, because Emery had no idea what the answer could be.

They walked through the hospital without incident—no one who'd worked there for long stood between the ME and her post-shift meal—and confirmed with the front desk that Connor Reinhold had checked out in a timely fashion after leaving the morgue.

Emery also made sure to get a look at his address and had a feeling Keri had used the same opportunity—if for different reasons.

By silent accord, they walked around the corner to their favorite diner. By longstanding mutual agreement, exhausted hospital visitors and exhausted hospital staff politely ignored each other under the hiss of the grill and the always unidentifiable murmur of music almost familiar enough to soothe and never grate. A neat spell, and everyone too polite—and exhausted—to learn its origin. The food tasted better the more tired and out of sorts one was, but Emery suspected that was no spell at all.

"Dumplings on the way over, loves." Dizzy, a purple and gold sprite, waved from the grill. "Saw you coming." It was her polite way of saying she'd *felt* them coming, as the empath had a touch for her regulars, and they'd clearly been broadcasting their emotions.

"You're why I never murder anyone, Dizz," Keri replied, sliding into one of the few empty booths and pushing into the corner.

"A record I'll hope lasts a few years more, yet." Dizzy twirled away to another customer, her hair leaving a shimmer in the air for a breath behind her.

Emery smiled after the sprite and pushed into her side of the booth until she could rest her head on the chill window.

"It's going to rain tonight," she said, staring out at the flickering streetlights glowing through the increasing gloom.

"It always rains," Keri answered, eyes never leaving the grill so she wouldn't miss the first sight of the promised dumplings. "That's why I live here."

"I miss the moon."

"I miss the smell of intestines drying on the battlefield, but we can't all have what we want." Keri snorted, her mood lightening as Dizzy delivered the dumplings with a flourish.

Emery tore her eyes from the dark sky and tucked away her longing for the friendly flash of the moon in the sky. It was all superstition anyway, the moon as a patron of shapeshifters, but...

The smell of the dumplings registered, and the events of the day, moon and all, were tucked away for a bit longer.

* * *

Keri let her climb the stairs alone, but Emery didn't hear her friend's door close, meaning Keri had waited in the shadow of her doorway until Emery had safely reached her upstairs apartment. She would have rolled her eyes or called down something teasing, but it had been more than enough day for the both of them.

"Long one, eh?" The low voice issued from the darkness, and Emery snapped on the light with a laugh in her throat.

"You're back!"

"My scrumptious little tenant, how could I stay away? I felt you shaking out of your form from three demesnes north."

The smile faded from her face, and Emery crossed the airy front room to busy herself opening the shades. Little light came through, the moon well and truly hidden by clouds, and the streetlights dimmed by the rain, but the vast spread of the outside world always reminded her she wasn't in the aquarium anymore.

"You didn't have to come back. I'm perfectly—"

"Lie to me, and I'll throw you right back downstairs with your death-eating godling, my moonlet." Zafi threw herself backward into the nearest overstuffed chair and regarded Emery through narrowed blue-black eyes. "Now. Have it out."

Emery told her the story in as much detail as she knew her brownie would require. Zafi had owned the land their sprawling house had been built on for nearly a thousand years and had designed each of the seven apartments that made up the house. She was equally exacting of each tenant, who paid her in money, of course, and trinkets, but also something indefinably their own. Zafi never fully specified what that one thing was to each tenant, but they all had an idea. At any measure, it wouldn't do to disobey a direct request—the protection offered from being a brownie's ward was nothing to take for granted.

When Emery finished, Zafi sat in silence, stroking the vibrant orange and yellow scarf around her neck.

"My sweetened nightbeam, it was only a matter of time. Whatever left you in that alley is circling back around to you at last."

"Connor wasn't in Bard City—"

"What use to you would I be if I couldn't feel the shadow of fate tightening its grip? He's only a part, not the play. I'll keep you as safe as I can, my milkmaid, but I don't know the shape of this well enough yet." Zafi pulled the scarf tight, then loosened and twisted it into a series of improbable patterns. "Will you seek him out?"

Beyond securing his address, she hadn't allowed herself to think any further of it until Zafi had asked.

"Yes." The answer surprised her, but not her brownie.

"Good. I'll stay close these next days. The wind has a color to it I can't..." Zafi frowned into the middle distance, then cleared her expression with a sparkle that almost felt real. "I'll stay close. And so will your guardian battle angel." She gestured in the direction of Keri's apartment.

Emery wanted to protest that she could take care of herself, but after today...after today, it was better to graciously accept the help provided until the world righted around her.

* * *

The neighborhoods of Bard City had long outgrown their origins as havens for different species who'd crossed into this world. Each still radiated out from an anchoring point—a cluster of ancient houses in Keystone, where Emery and Keri lived; the hospital in Setteree, where they worked; and in Fir Alley, where Connor lived, a coffee shop. The uneven stone and moss of the building indicated it had begun its life as something more like a bunyip's keep, but the interior had a welcoming golden light, and the knobby twisted wood of the walls projected a cozy warmth instead of a swamp's threatening shadows.

The counter and various coffee-making magics were new and modern, and the girl behind the counter appeared thoroughly human. Emery's shoulders relaxed as she took in the mixed early-morning crowd scattered across the mismatched tables and chairs. The promising smell of caffeine and the quiet, easy interactions of the shop's denizens ensured her morning wouldn't be completely wasted to her half-considered scheme. At the very least, there would be coffee.

The three-person line moved quickly, everyone sure of their order and ready with their payment. Emery kept the streak going and
moved to a table against the uneven wall to wait for her latte. She slid
into the seat facing the door and dropped her chin into her hands.

Neither Connor nor Keri walked in, and Emery chuckled at herself once she realized she'd expected at least one of them to walk in
right after her. Keri had walked with her through the several neighborhoods between their home and this coffee shop, then peeled off
to run errands—which almost certainly meant she lingered somewhere nearby, but also had things to get done on one of their few
days off from work.

As for Connor…he lived in the area, but that didn't mean he
drank coffee. Or purchased it rather than made it in his house. Or
would come into the shop at the exact bit of time Emery spent there.
She'd told herself she didn't expect to see him here, but only to get a
feel of his neighborhood, but of course that hadn't been entirely true.
Zafi had spoken of fate, and so some part of her believed fate would
deliver Connor into her hands.

"Latte for Emery!"

She stood and collected the cup of precious caffeination with a
smile, and when she turned back toward her table, a familiar face
smiled brilliantly down at her.

"All the coffee shops in all the towns in all the world, and she
walks into mine," he said, a laugh threading his voice.

"Mr. Reinhold," she replied, aiming for professional even as the
brightness of her expression belied it.

"Diener Mimnesko." His formality was as false as hers, given
how his eyes locked on her. "May I join you after I order, or would I
be interrupting?"

"No," she said, then blinked, smiled, and tried again. "No, you wouldn't be interrupting, and yes, I'd love it if you joined me. I'm just relaxing on a day off."

"The best of answers." He touched her elbow and stepped past her to the counter, and she took a sharp breath through her nose.

If morgues were no place for the sort of sensual warmth this mage carried, then also elbows had no business connecting directly to her gut, suffusing the entirety of her lower body with a sudden influx of heat. She breathed out as sharply, reminded herself she'd met men before, and made her way back to her seat without anything else unsettling happening.

Then, of course, Connor joined her.

"Do you live on this side of town?" he asked, leaning toward her in a manner that made the small table seem both invisible and also an impossible hindrance.

The air thickened, and to keep from gasping, Emery took a sip of her coffee instead. It was delicious and near-scalding, which gave her an excuse to breathe.

"No, I've been in Keyhold as long as I've been in Bard City."

"Not from here, then?" He tilted his head, and her gaze went wandering along his jawline.

If she kept floundering like this, she'd never keep the conversation going long enough to figure out how she knew him. Get it together and keep it together, Em.

"I had an...accident a few years ago. I may be from somewhere else, but Bard City's all I know. What about you—I know you mentioned you've only been here a year or two, have you been in Fir Alley the whole time?"

"I have; I like all the old stone buildings. Are you up for talking about the accident, or should we just follow the change in subject?"

"There's not much to tell." She shrugged, her hair sliding over one shoulder before she twisted it back.

Connor froze, and he locked in on her so firmly she felt the shiver of his magic between them.

"Is something wrong?" she asked. In her peripheral vision, nearby patrons rubbed their arms as goosebumps prickled in response to the energy shift from him.

"When did you have your accident?"

"Six years ago—"

The sound he made could have been incantation or curse. The sizzle of magic intensified for a blistering moment, then disappeared so abruptly she sat back in her chair. She released her hair, and he watched it fall before speaking again.

"What happened?"

In a normal situation, she'd likely excuse herself from a conversation like this. His intense interest in her, and in her accident, would grate, sending the taste of chlorine flooding into the back of her throat. But here, now, with him—if she knew him, it had to be from before the alley, before the aquarium. Shapeshifters were immune to magic, so she had no worry the mage could take bits of information and weave a new story she would believe. She could...she could tell him. She would have to, to figure out who he might have been to her.

In the six years she'd been herself, she'd never shared the story. Keri, who knew it even better than Emery herself, had been the one to tell it to the few people who needed to know. And now...

"Do you want to go for a walk?" she offered, tearing her gaze from his and glancing around them. Despite the occasional background noise from behind the counter, the shop remained too peaceful for her to risk talking here. Bard City had been safe for her since the accident, but she'd been careful and well-protected. Shapeshifters were hunted for many reasons, and Bard City had certainly not been safe for her before her accident.

"Yes," he said immediately, standing and offering her his hand.

Emery considered deadening the nerves in her hand to keep some measure of self-control, but dismissed the reaction as overkill. Then his hand closed on hers, her knees threatened to give out under her as she stood, and she silently threatened herself with shutting down her entire nervous system to block out her painful awareness of him.

Blessedly, he let go of her to retrieve his coffee from the counter, and she cupped both her hands around her drink to keep from tempting either of them toward any renewed skin-to-skin contact.

Connor chatted briefly with the barista, and Emery smiled at the girl before walking back outside. She took a quick moment to text Keri they were on the move, then slipped her phone back in her pocket and wrapped her hand around her cup once more.

"There's a park around the block that's kept up by a briggan, if you want to head that way." Connor stood close enough to her she could feel the heat of him. The slightest lean would put her arm against his, and she came within a breath of giving in to the urge.

"Sounds great," she said instead, falling into step beside him.

"I think it's pretty obvious I want to hear your story." He rubbed the back of his neck with one hand, looking ahead rather than at her. "But if you don't want to…" The offer for her to change her mind hung between them for a few more steps, but she already knew her answer.

"Six years ago, I was formless in an alley. You recognized me as a shapeshifter, so you know what that means?"

"You'd changed too much, too fast, or someone had attacked you until you lost control of your form and reverted into...uh, formlessness." He said it quietly, as though aware of what a terrifying thing that would be for a being who survived through control.

"Into goo, yes." A flicker of motion quirked her lips, and she drank more of her coffee. "Keri had decided to cut through the alley on her way to work—something she never did, but she likely sensed something without knowing it. She's from a line of battle-death goddesses."

"Good work for a medical examiner."

"It comes in handy."

They smiled at each other—small smiles, softer, and perhaps a little rueful. The magnetic pull of his first smile upon seeing her still pooled through her, and she had to blink a few times before remembering what came next in her story.

"Thankfully she recognized me for what I was and gathered up as much of my substance as she could."

"That must have taken awhile."

"It wasn't a particularly clean alley, and whatever had happened had been long enough before that I'd spread out. Keri's very detail-oriented, so she did a thorough job, but it kept her from noticing much of anything else about the alley. By the time she had a chance to go back, there wasn't anything to find." Emery chewed her bottom lip until it twinged, then smoothed over it with her tongue.

Connor's eyes locked on her mouth and she covered her reaction to that with another drink.

"There aren't a lot of great ways to store a released shapeshifter, but she found an old aquarium from when the morgue had leeches and got me squared away."

He barked a laugh, and her lips curved in answer. Granted, she'd been more of a rectangle, fitting into the general shape of the aquarium, but the urge to make a stupid joke distracted her from the chemical tang bubbling out of her stomach.

"When I didn't come back right away, she brought me into the morgue proper, so I could watch autopsies."

"How the bodies came apart and went back together." He nodded thoughtfully, then stepped behind her to make way for an enormous blob-shaped nuppeppo on the sidewalk, then moved back to her side and continued, "I can only imagine how helpful that would be if you'd really lost yourself. How long did it—"

"Four years."

He sucked in his breath, then brushed her elbow—that godsdamned, suddenly sensitive elbow—and angled a hairsbreadth closer as they walked in the shade of the tree-lined street.

"Four years? I didn't know…I didn't know a shifter could come back from that."

"Keri said it's soon or never, but like most things about shapeshifters, that's more rumor and story than facts from anyone who's ever known one. Keri's lived in Bard City for almost two hundred years, and I'm only the third she's ever met. Or that she's known that she met." Emery lifted her shoulders, allowed herself to drift closer to him in turn, her shoulder against his upper arm. "We haven't contacted any since I've been back, either."

"So four years went by, and then you...just came back?"

"Pretty much. One day goo, next day...me. A new me, since I don't remember anything from before the aquarium, but..." She shrugged and noticed their surroundings for the first time. The buildings to their right were a mix of connected and freestanding old stone-worked fronts, a mix of stores, offices, and homes. To the left, an assortment of thin-trunked trees with long, trailing branches and mossy leaves. The sidewalk was mossy stone, which they had to themselves.

She knew they hadn't been walking long, and were still in Fir Alley, but beyond the nuppeppo some steps back, she couldn't remember passing anyone else at all. Had she been that caught up in getting the words of her story right? Or was it Connor?

She bit her lip harder this time—she knew better than to ask herself rhetorical questions—and blinked back to the moment at hand. She wasn't the only one in a loop of self-reflection, as Connor's steps had slowed along with her own, he had his cup raised to his mouth as though about to take a sip, and he held it there for another minute longer without drinking.

"Six years," he said finally, so softly she would have missed it if she weren't waiting so hard to hear what he had to say. They turned a corner, and moss and stone and trailing trees opened into vibrant clover and tunnels made of arching trees and woven flowering vines in a cacophony of colors.

By unspoken agreement, they made for a curving tunnel dominated by purple and blue petals, the smell of wisteria and late summer afternoons twining through the air around them.

As they walked deeper into the park, the light shifted, dappling through branches, vines, and flowers, heavy with shade and scent.

Their pace lessened, again and again, until they stopped altogether, looking by turns at each other and their empty cups.

Emery breathed, intended to move away, and hesitated. Connor brushed her cheek, and warmth spilled through her, winding up her spine.

"Six years," he said again. "And four. Are you...could you be?" His voice, soft and wondering, chased shivers after the climbing warmth in her body.

She knew what he was asking. A shapeshifter he'd known, and lost somehow—could she be the same? What she didn't—couldn't—know was the answer to his question. She couldn't even begin to explain how something in his face pulled at a memory that no longer existed for her. A snag from a hole that didn't exist. He opened his mouth to say more, and finally she moved, overwhelmed by all the things she couldn't remember, couldn't know. Emery closed the small distance between them, touching his lips with hers.

His hand slid past her cheek, tangled in her hair. Warmth flashed into fire, and she released the mysteries, trusted this body to do what her mind couldn't. Give her an answer.

The world beyond their embrace vanished, only the strength of his arms holding her together.

Heat and want and need, the wild rush from the base of her skull to the tips of her fingers. The feel of his hair against her palm, the pulse of his body against hers...she let herself drown in it, letting the core of her relax. Her form had too much wanting in it to slip out of focus, but something...something changed.

He left her mouth for her neck, the sensitive spot under her ear, and she heard and felt the change in his breath.

"You smell like her," he whispered, pulling back enough to meet her eyes. His brown eyes sharpened with focused desire. "You're her. It's you."

Her body knew his. She'd kept busy since emerging from the aquarium, relearning how the world worked, building a life, learning a trade. For her body to operate properly, she had to allow it to do its natural things—feel tired, get hungry, stir with interest at someone attractive. The latter had happened perhaps a handful of times, but nothing…nothing like this.

He'd known a shapeshifter. Something in the deep essence of her knew him. Could that be enough?

She dropped her hands, pushing against his chest to put distance between them, to catch either her breath or sense of self or any sense at all. He let her move away, but didn't fully release her, leaning forward until their foreheads touched, their breath mingling in the small space between them.

Emery, reeling, couldn't process what had changed in her body. Everything felt…the same. She'd put every piece of this form together, cell by cell, and system by system. She attempted to match her breathing with his to center herself back in the moment, back in control of her body.

He shifted his head slightly, enough for his eyes to lock on hers, and everything stilled. Even her mind, ever-working to hold her chosen form in place, quieted.

The world around them held its breath, and nothing moved.

Until heat began to climb from her stomach up her spine, riding through her veins. A flush shifted through her, and every feature, every organ…slid into something else.

His eyes widened, his jaw clenched. His hands lifted toward her.

Did she move, or did he?

She didn't know, didn't care.

"It's you," he whispered, close enough that his breath touched the curve of her neck. She angled her head to keep her eyes on his, the intensity of his gaze holding the air in her lungs.

"It's you," he repeated, and then his eyes moved everywhere, taking in every new—or old—curve of her face, sweep of brow. His hand rose further, and the barest edges of his fingers grazed her cheek.

Emery's breath rushed out of her, heat and stillness and long moments without breathing leaving her dizzy. The smell of him leaving her dizzy. The unfamiliar weight of this new body she'd slipped into leaving her dizzy.

She could tell him she still didn't know who she was. She could tell him she had no memory of this shape, that she couldn't even quite feel the contours of it, that it was slipping away from her already, as he drank it—her—in.

Silencing everything but the most pressing of urges, she did none of that and kissed him again instead.

It took a gunshot to pull them apart.

Emery shifted into defensive mode, fingers elongated into claws, jaw distended to make room for larger, pointier teeth.

Connor flattened them both to the ground, the hum of magic springing up around them before collapsing.

"Shapeshifters," he muttered, rolling off her and trying again. She dug her new claws into the rich earth beneath her and called.

A hatch opened to her side, vines and flowers melting away, and a square of light outlined her brownie's face as she took their place.

"Lucky you're in a park with a nice briggan, letting me toddle through. Curtain's up, is it? The play's off and running. What's the man doing? Protecting you? That's nice, my little butterbean. Come along, come through. Bring your boy." Zafi disappeared again, the square between worlds open and waiting behind her.

"Connor," Emery hissed, shifting back to her normal mouth's configuration for ease of speech. Another gunshot from what seemed an entirely different direction.

Connor, crouched ahead of her on the path, turned back and noticed the hatch. Smart enough not to waste time with questions, he launched back toward her, pushing her ahead until they both fell through the brownie's dimensional shunt.

They'd landed back in her bedroom, by which Emery knew her landlord had been paying perhaps even closer attention than necessary.

"I…don't know what to ask first." Connor's voice, ragged from adrenaline, made her leap to her feet.

"Who was shooting? Was it at us?" She paced across her room, yanking her phone out of her pocket to text Keri. Belatedly, she realized she still, somehow, had her empty coffee cup in her hand, and the ridiculousness of it shocked a laugh out of her.

"Those are good questions." Connor climbed upright as well, gestured at her with the crushed cup in his own hand. She pointed at a small trash bucket in the corner and reassured herself that they hadn't littered in a briggan's park and had one less thing to add to their list of worries.

"Is there a lot of gunfire in Fir Alley?" she asked, knowing the answer.

"No, but it's been a hell of a couple days." Connor rubbed the back of his neck and cocked his head at her.

"My landlord is a brownie," she offered, figuring that for one of his questions. "She can open small portals through sympathetic spaces, and she's very protective of her tenants."

Something much larger than a bird thumped on the roof above them, and Emery managed not to wince. Connor immediately spun, hands clenching and magic buzzing, and she hastily crossed the room and pressed her hands on his shoulders. His magic stuttered, then he released it and turned toward her.

"They couldn't have followed us that quickly, even if we were the ones being attacked."

He opened his mouth, tensing under her touch, and she had exactly enough time to wonder if that stormy expression meant he was going to argue with her or return to the kissing, when Zafi appeared on top of the bench under the window.

"Fate and darkness are on the move, my little ducks. Not on my roof, shame on you, mage." The brownie flicked her brilliant scarf at Connor and shook her head. "I can't leave the house, birdling, not at a time like this. Stay close and stay safe."

Zafi disappeared as quickly as she'd arrived, and Connor took two steps toward where she'd been before catching himself.

"Fate and darkness?" He held out his arms, and without thinking, Emery went into them. In the safety of her room, she could relax, could tell him—

Her door flew open behind them, slamming against the wall.

Again the flare of his magic, and she turned, remembering the thump above them.

Keri stood framed in the doorway, her night-black wings visible in dark relief for a heartbeat before she shook them back into the ether. Her glare remained perfectly visible, and Emery stepped back, her back connecting with Connor's chest. He curved an arm around her waist, and a flush climbed upward from her chest.

"The Keepers are moving."

The warmth fled from Emery's body in answer to Keri's flat tone. The Keepers had lived on the outskirts of Bard City for decades, attracting hangers-on, but causing little harm themselves. Then yesterday, the explosion. And now...?

"Detective Abraham called. The Keepers wiped out the holy men that had the other bodies; the entire temple is glassed." Keri frowned, stepped into the room, and turned the full force of her flint stare on Connor. "They sent their stooges out to clean up the EMTs an hour ago. He thinks they're going for the hospital and the morgue next, if they haven't already." Her hands curved into fists, and she snarled, "What do you know about them? Are you working with the Keepers?"

"What do I—"

"You said your cousin was with them, and you were here to try and get him out. But you didn't try very hard. So therefore you must know something about them—or were you here for that at all?" She stalked closer, looking pointedly at his arm around Emery's waist with a vicious curl to her lip.

"If they're hitting the morgue, we can lay a trap—"

"You don't trap after the fact, mage." Keri stopped short and held out her hand, her black fingernails dagger sharp. "Tell us what you know."

"There are only four of them." Connor stiffened against Emery, and she held herself motionless between her friend and her...Connor. "They're ancient—not the most powerful, but they've been hoarding strength for at least as long as they've been here. I..." He sagged, some vital pressure going out of him.

Emery detangled herself from him and half turned, keeping both him and Keri in her sights.

"I've chased Keepers before. It never goes well. First I lost my parents to them, when I was younger. Then my...the woman I loved. A little over ten years ago." His eyes bored into Emery, and her heart hammered in her chest. "My cousin and I fought together at first, but I lost him, too."

"And you thought we could just go to the morgue and lay a trap for them?" Keri scoffed, crossing her arms. "Easy as that?"

"The further they are from their power center, the easier it is to confuse them. And we have the one weapon they can't account for, the one they can't see coming."

Emery felt his next words before he said them, the dread climbing up from her stomach like an aquarium's worth of chemical tang.

"A shapeshifter."

Keri opened her mouth, snapped it closed, and lifted her eyebrows. Emery nodded, a fraction of movement, enough for Keri to register.

"I'll call Abraham." Keri turned on her heel and left the bedroom.

"Emery..."

The softness of Connor's voice hooked somewhere behind her belly button, and she turned fully to him.

"Keepers can't sense shapeshifters until you hurt them. They can't feel you coming or corrupt your thoughts. Can't whisper their filth into your head. You know where they're vulnerable?"

She nodded, silence crowding her throat.

"You went after a pit of them ten years ago. They vanished, and so did you. I thought...I knew you were dead. I felt it. I looked, anyway, for...for years."

"I'm not her." The words belonged to someone else, barely moving her mouth as they emerged.

"Are you about to leave the safety of a brownie's demesne to try and fight Keepers rampaging through your city?"

She nodded, unable to take her eyes from his.

"You are. In every way that matters." Connor leaned closer, and her chin lifted toward him by reflex. He brushed his thumb over her bottom lip. "I—"

Emery quieted him the only way she could, pressing her lips to his and letting the heat of him wash away the taste of chemicals and loss in the back of her throat.

* * *

The Keepers had already taken over the hospital by the time they got there. The folding glass doors hung crooked and shattered from the main entrance, and all the lights left whole shone with a sickly yellow-green glow that shadowed more than they showed.

Sirens echoed, Abraham and his backup on the way, but if the Bard City Police had ever been a match for Keepers, Keepers wouldn't have lived on the outskirts of town for so long.

Keri unfurled her wings, the endless darkness of them dimming the diseased light from the hospital further.

Emery shook her head and held out a hand.

"I'll go first. Don't follow me unless your sisters come."

Keres was formidable on her own, but Keepers could worm into nearly anyone. Only with a flock of her battle-goddess descendants would Keri be safe against the Keepers' whispers.

But Emery was immune to magic; Emery was able to push her form into anything that would help, anything that would kill…Emery the shapeshifter could be their perfect weapon. As long as she didn't shift too far, too fast.

"If I fall apart—" she began, meaning to break some of the tension.

"I'll bring you back together again."

"I won't lose you again."

Keri, then Connor, equally determined. Equally afraid for her, equally willing to go into the building with her. Emery summoned a smile for them, opened her mouth as though she had something else to say, and then turned and ran inside before they changed their minds and tried to stop her.

Bodies—of people she knew, people she'd worked with—lined the halls, rested empty-eyed in doorways. The Keepers had feasted here, turned patient against doctor and nurse against visitor and orderly against…she blinked her eyes clear and forged deeper into the hospital.

The Keepers hadn't set everything to explode, so they wanted something. Nothing stirred in the hospital, so that left the morgue. The emergency staircase dripped in unnatural cold, ice slicking the steps. Emery slipped off her sneakers and shifted her feet, layers of fur and roughened skin giving her the grip of a polar bear.

She moved down the stairs to the basement, to the morgue. To her morgue, where Keri had helped her piece herself back together. Where she had found a purpose. Where the first tinge of her old life had come back to her.

The door was frozen shut, magic and bone-aching cold holding the metal tight. She returned her feet to normal, put her shoes back on, and reinforced the muscles and tendons and bones of her arms and shoulders and midsection, shoving down on the handle and breaking the seal of the door with a combination of ruthless strength and her own natural immunity.

The thunk resonated against her bones, but she ignored that along with the cold and slipped into the hall outside Keri's office. No light leavened the deep pools of darkness around her, and she carefully returned her upper body to its previous state before reconfiguring her eyes and ears to better process what input there was. The doors to the morgue deadened sound; those were easy to locate. Four bodies inside, cold as the air around them, but filling the space with a solidity that grated against her newly built senses.

Chlorine bubbled up her esophagus, and she swallowed it back. No time. She held her breath and took a moment to picture the nuppeppo she'd seen earlier that day in perfect detail. The feel of the creature solid and whole in her mind, she shifted into a large blob and added teeth and sharp edges everywhere.

There were only four Keepers. Usually they grouped in larger numbers, each with their own particular brand of corruption, but for Bard City, for her morgue, only four. Perhaps whomever she'd been, years ago, had wiped out most of their flock and chased the last here.

Perhaps she'd shifted too far too fast and lost herself against them. Perhaps that had never been her, or something else entirely had happened to bring her to that alley.

Regardless of the before, they were here now, and so was she.

She burst into her morgue in a snarl of motion and violence, ripping one solid form to pieces before any of them reacted. Then the voices came.

Shapeshifter, one hissed, the voice roiling through her thoughts, leaving an aftertaste in her mind she couldn't shift away from.

Leave us this body. Leave us the weapon. The second voice wrapped around the twisted spine that supported her misshapen body.

They sent you here to die. They don't care. You can't stop us. Shifters always try. Shifters never win. The third boiled the liquid of her body, warping it.

You'll never win.

You'll never—

She shifted again, removing bones, replacing fluid, shifting teeth for claws and claws for teeth and sharpening everything until she had no concept of the whole of her form.

She knew only that she hated, and what she hated, and that she could destroy what she hated.

So she did.

They fought her, and screamed, and she changed and changed again and flowed around them, into them, through them, choking them and drowning them and rending them and finally, finally, ending them.

The cold, clean floor of the morgue ran with fluids of every kind, and she couldn't separate what was hers from what had been her enemies. Slowly she ebbed toward the drain in the far end of the long room. Slowly she forgot that she moved at all.

Before she reached the drain, something flashed, reflected off glass. An aquarium in a far corner, catching light from some motion.

"EMERY!"

A voice she knew, strained by an unfamiliar panic. The beat of wings, so many wings.

A ripple of sharp chlorine and salt.

"Emery." Another voice, low. Male. Worried and cracking and on the very edge of breaking.

A tug followed by another. Something in the voices, pulling her back.

Reminding her she was a *who*, not a *what*.

She swirled away from the drain, closer to the aquarium. A voice she didn't know, shouting, and then all around her, hands.

In moments or hours, she put herself back together again, finding the form that was Emery—that was hers.

Keri glared at her and kissed her on the forehead, waving her sisters away. Connor grinned and caught her in his arms.

She flattened her body against his, feeling the surety of her form molding into him without changing. She still didn't know who she had been, but here, in his arms, in her stillness and his warmth…

She knew who she wanted to be.

* * * * *

Marisa Wolf Bio

Marisa Wolf was born in New England, and raised on Boston sports teams, Star Wars, Star Trek, and the longest books in the library (usually fantasy). Over the years she majored in English in part to get credits for reading (this...only partly worked), taught middle school, was headbutted by an alligator, built a career in education, earned a black belt in Tae Kwon Do, and finally decided to finish all those half-started stories in her head.

She currently lives in Texas with three absurd rescue dogs, one deeply understanding husband, and more books than seems sensible. Learn more at http://www.marisawolf.net.

# # # # #

Promised by
Dawn Witzke

"You can't make me marry him!"

The cold water hit my naked back as two of my mother's goons dropped me through the steel hatch into the massive isolation tank at Boru City Aquarium's non-public area, where I sank fourteen feet to the bottom. The tank filled the space between the 1st and 2nd floor of the Aquatics Building. By the time I reached the bottom, my legs had given way to a tail, and my lungs were processing the oxygen from the saltwater. Where my breasts once were was flattened and covered with scales.

On the first floor of the building, my uncle, Lucas Arnott, stood next to my mother in the viewing room; they watched me descend to the bottom of the tank. Lucas was my father's brother, as well as the primary shareholder and general manager of the Aquarium. We had both inherited the clan's signature tall, stately figure and black hair, while my mother, Serina, was shorter, with the blond hair of the Richards' clan.

I screamed at the two through our telepathic link. When I got free of the tank and away from my family, I was going to cut my hair short and dye it blue so I couldn't be mistaken for one of the Arnott clan. I might even move as far away from the ocean as I could get where no one would know I was an Astakide mermaid.

It has already been decided, Ayame, she replied, speaking to me as if I were a child. *In two weeks, you'll be Mrs. Luini Calabrese, whether you like it or not. This marriage will solidify the treaty between our two clans.*

In that moment, I hated her. I hated my father. I hated our culture's draconian ways. I hated everything about being an Astakide.

I rammed my shoulder into the glass front. The brightly colored fish contained in the tank huddled in the back corner, far out of my way. *You can't keep me in here.*

My uncle eyed me from the other side of the glass. *Dear, it's for your own safety. This marriage is going to make waves.*

Then end it, I pleaded.

Stop with the dramatics. You had no objections at the betrothal party.

I was nine!

There had been a private ceremony between our clan and theirs, which had required—though I don't recall it—Luini and I to consent. There was absolutely no way I understood the gravity of the situation, nor did I understand what I was consenting to. After a dozen years, it was little more than a faint memory of a party where I stood next to an eleven-year-old boy who wouldn't even talk to me. And now they were holding me to a nine-year-old's declaration. I hated them.

And now, you're almost twenty-one. More than old enough to understand that an heir to a throne must sometimes sacrifice their happiness for the good of their people. My mother was quite condescending in her declaration.

I swam up to the glass and slapped my hands against it. The sound inside the tank was deafening, but I kept hitting it over and over until my mother and my uncle disappeared out the door. Damn them.

The tank, it seemed, would be my prison until I was wed. I swam its perimeter looking for any way out. It was the size of an Olympic swimming pool and filled with coral and several schools of fish from the Atlantic. The fish avoided me, as they should. A predator had just been dumped into their home. At least I knew the fish wanted me out of there.

I settled into a corner where I could think. As I watched the fish swim frantically to keep away from me, I realized there was another option. If my family wouldn't let me out of the marriage, maybe I could convince Luini that he didn't want me as his wife. While the law bound me to the betrothal, the groom was free to end it if he found being married to his future bride disagreeable. If he didn't want me, the family couldn't force the marriage. I smiled to myself. If my parents wanted to stick with the old ways, I'd use it against them.

* * *

The next morning, I awoke to the scent of blood in the water and a feeling of terror. I looked around for the source. Something was in the tank with me. From behind a particularly large section of coral reef swam a tiger shark, about ten feet long. It swam toward me, having already killed almost half of the fish in the tank. I screamed telepathically, hoping someone would hear me. I'd have to get to the surface to get help from the humans, but that would make me easy prey for the shark.

Like a stampede, the remaining fish fled before it, desperate to get out of its way. They slammed into me in their fear, obscuring my view of the attacking shark. I sank to the bottom of the tank, laying as close to the floor as I could get, with the coral protruding through the sandy bottom. It just missed my arm when it passed overhead. My heart raced. I was going to die.

Astakide lore is filled with tales of the tiger shark—devil of the sea who thought nothing of killing entire clans and anything else that ventured into its territory. None of the stories, however, mentioned how to survive an encounter with one. If I could stay out of its reach, maybe it would tire out before I did. But I had grown up on land in a house with a pool. It had spent its whole life chasing prey through the water. *I am so screwed.*

I moved before it could come back. At ten feet long, it needed room to turn around, which meant swimming to the open waters above the reef. This gave me enough time to duck into a thicket of Elkhorn coral growing along the south side of the tank. The coral had thick hard branches, but I still wasn't sure it would be strong enough to keep the shark out.

It sped through the water, ramming its body against the stone-like structure protecting me. Branches above me broke. The impact spooked a parrotfish, who darted out of its hiding place to its death in the shark's jaws. The distraction was enough to make it forget it was trying to kill me. I pulled myself farther under the thicker flat plates near the base growing between two sections of rock, hopefully providing more protection from the creature.

Ayame? The voice in my head was deep and melodic. Someone had heard me.

Help! Help! was all the words I could form as the tiger shark again rammed the coral, breaking through a section near my tail. There was no room for me to pull it up near my body. I screamed when the shark grabbed hold of my fin with his teeth and pulled. The coral ripped through the skin of my hands as the beast pulled me from my hiding spot. With all the strength I could muster, I pummeled it with my fists until it to let go of me. Pain shot through me as the shark ripped a chunk of fin from my tail.

Swim to the hatch, the voice said.

It'll get me.

The hatch above opened, and a mass of bloody fish parts were dumped into the water. Fish parts rained down around us, sending the shark into a frenzy. It snapped at me but didn't get a hold. I didn't wait for the shark to stop its feeding. I took off toward the hatch with it close on my tail. This would be my only chance.

An arm reached into the water. I latched onto it and was pulled out of the tank, but the shark lunged up through the hatch after me. I screamed as it snapped onto my fin, taking another section with him as he splashed back down into the tank.

The man who had rescued me slammed the hatch closed before coming to my side. His forearm had formed scales where he'd gotten wet. They quickly disappeared as he wiped his arm on his shirt.

An Astakide.

"What were you doing in a tank with a shark? Are you crazy?"

I glared at him. For someone who looked like he could be a Greek statue, he didn't seem all that bright.

He knelt next to me; his eyes roamed over my naked body, which had started changing to its human form. I sucked in my breath when he touched by ankle. Half expecting to see one of my feet gone, I saw only shallow red scrapes along my leg. Transformation from Astakide to human was a great mystery. If I transformed back into my mermaid form, my tail would still be missing a chunk. I was taught that the human form is nothing more than glamour that hides our true nature, but I never believed it. I think legs and tails are separate parts of our being. Damage to one doesn't mean damage to the other. Maybe science will be able to figure out the mystery someday. But at that moment, I was just relieved to know I still had all my body parts.

"There don't appear to be any injuries." His hands moved over my legs.

The higher he went, the more chills ran up my spine. I wondered if he was going to examine all of me. Had I gone from one kind of shark to another?

He looked up at me. "Why were you in there?"

I pushed myself into a sitting position; his hands dropped away.

"My mother put me in there. To keep me safe." My voice dripped with disdain. "I don't know how the shark got in there. It wasn't there yesterday."

"Well, you're safe now."

"Thank you." I felt guilty for not saying that right away. He'd gone out of his way to help me, and I was being a bitch.

I looked down to notice the front of his khakis stretched tight. It was completely by accident that I was looking where I was, because I don't make a habit of looking at men's crotches. His eyes were, however, fixed on my returning breasts. They were always the last part of me to change. In human terms, I wasn't well endowed, but it appeared to be enough to interest him. His attraction to breasts was strange for an Astakide male. They tended to be more into legs.

He pulled off the green polo that had Boru City Aquarium stitched into the pocket and handed it to me. "You can wear this until I find you some clothes."

It was my turn for unwanted physical reaction. His face and arms weren't the only parts of him that looked like they'd been carved from marble. His chest and abs were defined in a way that would make David jealous.

His shirt hung almost to my knees, but I was somewhat warm again, and covered. That didn't stop him from staring at me. I'm sure I looked a mess.

"You know my name, what's yours?" I asked.

"Lou."

"Thank you, Lou, for rescuing me."

"My plan was to rescue you from hunger, not from a shark. Your mother didn't tell me you were in the tank. I thought you were being protected in one of the unused rooms."

Until that moment I hadn't noticed the paper bag on the floor.

He stood, holding his hand out to me. "Shall we find somewhere more comfortable so you can eat?"

Comfortable. Naughty thoughts ran through my head as he pulled me to my feet.

I followed him through a series of doorways to a lounge, where we took a seat at one of several tables. The room was large, with vending machines and tables in one half, and clusters of comfortable looking chairs and a sectional couch facing a large screen television in the other half.

He took the containers from the bag and set them before me.

"Eat."

The containers were filled with sushi rolls, cucumber salad, and edamame in the shell. One after another, I devoured the sushi rolls while Lou stared.

"You must be really hungry. When was the last time that you ate?"

"Yesterday morning, before my mother locked me in the tank."

"What did you do to deserve such a punishment? Run over her dog?"

I shoved another sushi roll in my mouth before answering.

"I refused the marriage she arranged for me."

"Do you not like him?"

"I haven't seen him in a dozen years. But my mother doesn't care. She only cares about the alliance this marriage will secure."

"Maybe you'll like him."

"Or maybe I won't. Either way, I have a plan to get out of it." I had no idea why I was telling him this. He would likely run back to Mother and tell her everything. But he seemed like he might actually care about someone other than himself, unlike my mother.

"Maybe you should try getting to know him first. You never know, you might like him."

You, I like. A spoiled Astakide, not so much. "I'm not going to marry a stranger."

"He wouldn't be a stranger if you got to know him."

"Thank you for the advice, Lou, but I'm going to stick with my plan."

I finished eating in silence. Lou gathered the empty containers and tossed them in the trash.

"I'll be back in a few hours. You should probably stay in here until I figure out what I'm supposed to do with you."

"Sure. It'll be a dryer prison cell than the tank, with no sharks."

He smiled at my sarcastic remark.

"I'll bring you clothes when I come back." He dropped some cash on the table. "In case you need something from the machines."

He paused before leaving the room. "By the way, do you like chess?"

"I do."

I might have escaped, but the promise of Lou's return kept me in the lounge. If I was expected to make the lounge my prison for the remainder of the time, I'd have to ask for some books or something to do while I waited. At least in the tank, I had the fish to watch. I flipped mindlessly through the 119 channels on the television filled with human entertainment.

By the time Lou returned, I wanted to poke my eyes out rather than watch another minute of human entertainment. He came in the room with a couple of tote bags.

"Serina sent these along for you." He handed me one of the bags.

I took the bag and looked through it. There were several changes of clothes, along with my hairbrush and makeup. Obviously my mother had packed the bag. Only she would care if she had makeup while she was being held captive.

"Oh. So you're staying?" I shouldn't feel so excited about spending time with one of Mother's lackeys, but it was better than being alone. Plus what little I knew about Lou, I liked.

"Yes. For your safety. For the next two weeks, you'll have a bodyguard twenty-four, seven. The shark has been returned to his own tank, but that won't prevent another incident. We think someone with magic put him in there with you, and we'd prefer you alive."

'We'd prefer you alive.' Did that mean mister rock hard muscles cared what happened to me? I could definitely like this.

"Great. A fairy wants me dead." I was only half joking.

"There are other creatures who have magic besides fairies."

"That's so much more reassuring." I let the sarcasm drip from my words.

He sat down in a chair across from me at the table. "Okay, then. What would you like to do?"

Unbutton that shirt you're wearing, was what I wanted to say. He was really nice to look at half naked, after all. "I don't know. Didn't you say something about chess earlier?"

"Chess it is." He opened the other bag and pulled out a wooden box.

"I'll warn you," he said as he laid out the pieces, "I'm really good."

"So am I."

After ten games of me losing, I had to admit he was far better at it than I was. But I wasn't planning to give up. At some point, he'd make a mistake, and I'd beat him.

"Time for sleep," he said, yawning. "Your mother will be here in the morning to decide what to do with you."

"Ugh."

Lou left the room for a few minutes, returning with pillows and several blankets. He tossed me a pillow.

"We can move the furniture and sleep on the rug. It should be soft enough."

I was supposed to be getting married soon, and I was thinking more about sleeping with the man keeping me company than how I was going to get out of the marriage. Lou was quickly checking off everything I had ever dreamed of in a husband. He was good looking, heroic, smart, and kind. If he cooked and cleaned, he'd be my ideal.

He laid out the blankets next to each other. I guess he wasn't planning to let anyone get near me. My insides tingled at the thought of him being that close all night.

His eyes went wide when I pulled his shirt over my head.

He looked down at the floor. He was obviously uncomfortable.

"What?" For an Astakide, he sure had weird hangups about nudity. When you're getting in and out of the water frequently, you just get kind of used to seeing everyone's different appearances. Maybe he'd spent too much time around humans.

He crawled under the blanket and turned his back to me.

"Goodnight." I said before crawling under my own blanket.

"Goodnight."

* * *

Lou was gone when I woke the next morning. Instead, my mother sat in one of the plush chairs watching me. I would've rather been back in the tank with the shark. At least I knew the shark wanted to eat me. With my mother, I could never tell. She was dressed in a crepe off-white dress suit. Probably taking a few minutes to torture me before heading into the office.

My father owned the largest chain of antique bookstores on the eastern seaboard. The last I'd heard he was somewhere in Europe, where he was looking to buy a private collection of seventeenth century tomes. Mother ran the business end of things.

"Have you come to your senses?" she asked in that condescending tone of hers.

"Did you put that shark in the tank? To get me to change my mind?" I asked.

The look on her face was one of pure annoyance.

"Don't be absurd. You're worth far more alive than dead."

I swallowed the flippant reply on my lips. "I want to meet him."

"You'll have a lifetime to get to know one another after you're married."

"I want to get to know him before we're married."

She looked at me as if trying to decide if it was worth fighting me over.

"Fine," she said after a long silence. "I'll make the arrangements."

I was going to have to make the one meeting count. There wouldn't be another chance. "Can I at least stay somewhere other than this room? It is dreadfully dull."

"Considering the shark attack, you're no longer safer here than anywhere else. You can return home, but since I don't trust you not to break the treaty, nor do I trust whoever is trying to kill you, you'll be under guard. I'd rather you not end up dead."

"I'm glad to know you care."

"Whether you believe it or not, this treaty will bring prosperity to both of our clans. When you're the leader of your own clan, you'll understand the sacrifices you'll have to make for your people."

"What do you know of sacrifice? You and Father chose each other. You've never wanted for anything."

My mother stiffened. She glared at me through narrowed eyes.

"You have no idea what I've sacrificed for our people."

* * *

"I brought you something." Lou said when he appeared that evening at the house for his shift as guard. He wore the same green polo and khakis I'd last seen him in.

He stood in the doorway of my bedroom holding a wooden box that looked remarkably like the chess set he'd had with him in the lounge.

"Besides food?" I feigned ignorance. Honestly, I was just as bored at home as I was at the Aquarium. Lou was my only respite from guards who watched everything I did, but never spoke. It was worse than having only fish to watch.

"Yes."

He pulled the chess set from under his arm.

"Oh, good, another chance for me to lose to you," I said, smiling. It was probably a terrible idea to become friendly with the help, but if I ended up having to get married, I wanted my last days to be interesting.

My heart skipped a beat at the smile that appeared on his face. Dear Lord, he was handsome. It wasn't just the good looks. It was everything about him. And those eyes. They were the color of seaweed where the light didn't quite reach. But it was the smile every time he looked at me that was most appealing.

He began setting up the board for us to play. I munched on my dinner of reheated clam chowder and biscuits as I watched him meticulously place the pieces.

My heart skipped a few more beats when he looked at me again. Why couldn't he be my intended instead of some jerk? *Once I'm free of the marriage,* I promised myself, *I'll see where this leads.*

Our hands touched when I went to move a pawn. It sent shivers through me.

"What's with the Aquarium uniform?" I asked trying to distract myself.

"I volunteer as a tour guide when I have spare time."

I had a ton of questions, but I let the subject drop when he didn't elaborate.

We played into the wee hours of the morning. He took his leave when the next guard came on duty, citing having to be back at the Aquarium by noon. I thought of asking him to stay, but if Mother found out, she'd never allow him to be there again.

* * *

"The meeting has been arranged."

I looked up from the book I was reading. My mother stood in the hall outside my room in an evening dress and diamonds. She did love her galas where she could show off her wealth and her "caring."

"When?" I kept the elation I was feeling to myself. I didn't want to give my mother a reason to change her mind. She'd never let me meet him if she knew what I was planning.

"Next Wednesday."

"Seriously? Three days before the wedding? Why not sooner?" I tried to keep the desperation out of my voice, but some slipped through.

"You can wait until the wedding day if you'd prefer."

She knew she held all the power, and I was at her mercy. I'd have to take it.

"Fine. I'll meet him on Wednesday."

"You'll be on your best behavior, or you'll regret it. His parents are coming along, and afterward we're all going out for dinner."

I perked up. Going out would give me a chance to escape.

"Except for you. You'll remain here."

I must have let my mask slip.

"I hate you."

"I know you do, dear." She said it like she didn't believe me—or maybe she just didn't care. "I'll be home late. Don't wait up."

* * *

Lou didn't show up until late the next day without the chess board. I wasn't sure he was going to be back at all.

"I can't stay long. My parents are in town, and I have to entertain them. Someone else will be taking my shift tonight. Sorry."

I sat down on the bench in the hall outside the library.

"Do they visit often?"

He sat down next to me, our legs touching.

"No. They spend most of their time in Italy. They loathe the Americas and only visit when they deem it necessary."

"I wish my parents lived far away, then I could live my own life instead of being a pawn in theirs."

"Don't let them living on the other side of the world fool you. My father still pulls the strings, since it's his business I manage. I just don't have to see them all that often."

"My mother set the meeting up for next week. I only get one shot at getting out of this stupid marriage."

"Or maybe you'll fall madly in love with him? At least give it a chance."

"Doubtful. How am I supposed to fall in love with someone I don't even know?"

"Love at first sight happens."

"Only in fairytales, Lou. Real love takes time to grow."

"If you say so."

His face was inches from mine. How easy it would have been to close that gap and kiss him. His replacement walked in just as I got the courage up to try.

* * *

"Tell me about yourself, Lou."

We sat at the kitchen table, the chess board between us and a plate of reheated fish tacos next to it. I had found them in a bag in the refrigerator, obviously left there by one of the staff for me. My mother wouldn't have thought to make sure I had anything to eat. We didn't have a maid, and rarely kept food in the house, since my parents were out every night of the week.

"I grew up in Italy, came here for college, and never left. I manage my father's fishing business when I'm not at the Aquarium or here. My life is very boring."

"No wife and kids?"

I bit into the taco. It was spicier than I usually liked my food, but it was good.

"Not yet."

"Anyone special in your life?"

I think he could tell I was fishing.

"There's Matilda, but she's a Baleen whale."

I swallowed hard trying not to choke. That wasn't at all what I'd expected from him. Finding out he was single made me giddy inside. I wouldn't have to feel guilty about wanting to spend time with him.

"Sounds like a match made in Heaven."

"Oh, it is. She almost died of loneliness in the tanks. Since I began swimming with her, she's cheered up. I also worked with management to change how they kept the animals. None are housed alone anymore. They're kept in more natural habitats, where they're happier. Except for Matilda. There just isn't the space for a second one her size, so I spend time with her."

"That's sweet."

"You'll have to meet her sometime."

"Yeah." My answer came out flatter than I'd wanted it to. The marriage would change everything. But I was going to get out of it, so I'd get to keep seeing Lou and meet Matilda. A little voice in the back of my mind whispered that Lou and I could never happen.

Then the room spun.

"Ayame?"

I answered by leaning over and vomiting.

Lou rushed to my side. I felt his arms on my shoulders.

"Bad tacos?"

I shook my head no. It wasn't food poisoning. My heart raced and breathing was becoming difficult.

He helped me to the sink, where I rinsed my mouth. After the burning of stomach acid subsided, a bitter taste was left in my mouth. More rinsing didn't remove it.

"I think I've been poisoned." I got the words out through shallow breaths before collapsing.

Lou picked me up in his arms. "Please don't die."

* * *

I sat up in the hospital bed, an IV stuck in my left hand. My uncle stopped in to check on my recovery.

"Your mother sends her regrets that she can't come

herself. The fish tacos were laced with cyanide. You're lucky to be alive."

"I guess whoever is trying to kill me hadn't planned on Lou being there to save me."

A look of annoyance flickered across his face. Annoyance at what, I wasn't sure.

"It seems you're recovering nicely. Your mother and I have been working to root out the culprit. So far, we've turned up nothing. The Ao Sí are also looking into the matter."

"Do you trust the fae?"

"Not at all, but an inquiry might scare off whoever is trying to kill you."

"Maybe. When can I go home?"

"The doctor says you can go home in a day or two. I should go so you can get rest."

Lou entered the room after my uncle was gone. I'd been told by the nurses that Lou hadn't left my side for more than a few moments during the two days I'd been in the hospital.

"Would you like to leave your room for a while?"

"Won't you get in trouble for going against doctor's orders?"

"Not if you don't tell on me," he said.

He took a robe from the bag he was carrying and handed it to me. I slipped it on over the hospital gown.

He turned. His eyes roamed up and down me as if trying to picture what I looked like under the robe. He blushed when his eyes met mine. I rather liked this bit of power I had over him. I wondered how much he'd blush if I wasn't wearing the robe and the hospital gown gaped open? I inwardly laughed at the shocked expression I imagined would be on Lou's face.

He took my arm and led me off the ward and through the halls of the hospital to the North Tower. It had been turned into a library with spiral staircases and replicas of classic art.

"Have you ever been here before?" he asked.

"I haven't. It's beautiful."

"You're beautiful."

I didn't know what to say, so I said nothing.

Lou walked over to a painting of an ocean scene. It was gorgeous, with deep blues and greens of the water against a bright red and yellow sky. The gold plate on the frame read Ivan Aivazovsky, The Ninth Wave. It was mesmerizing.

"Have you ever been in the open ocean before?" Lou asked.

"No. My only exposure to the ocean was on holiday to the Caribbean. We stayed in the shallows, except for a brief jaunt to see colorful reefs."

His eyes lit up like a kid on Christmas morning. "The ocean is a magical place filled with some of the brightest and weirdest fish you've ever seen."

"Have you ever been out there?"

"Yeah. A few times. It was amazing. You should go if you ever get the chance."

I wanted to believe him, but I'd heard the stories others tell of the dangers of the sea. We were lucky to be able to live among the humans and never have to face those dangers again.

"Hey, cheer up. You can have the same experience at the Aquarium, without the dangers of the open sea."

I gave him a smile, though I didn't feel it.

He pulled me into a hug, stroking his hand through my hair. I could hear his heart beat inside his chest. There was something so seductive about being in his arms. Something that made me not want to ever leave. He must have felt it too, because he pulled me closer. I melted into the planes of his hard muscles.

I don't know how long we stayed that way, but I felt a sense of loss when he moved away.

But then, before I could register what was happening, his head came forward, and he was kissing me. A moan escaped my lips at the sheer pleasure of it. Our tongues danced together to a tune that could be felt more than heard. This was the kind of kiss I'd dreamed I would have with my husband. A kiss that made me feel loved.

Without warning, he pulled away.

"I'm sorry." He walked across the room and back. "I shouldn't have done that."

"It's okay. I'm not married yet."

"That's not the point."

"Then what is the point?"

He stared at me. "Never mind. I should return you to your room."

I was speechless and hurt. How could he kiss me so sweetly, then act like I disgusted him?

We returned to my room without seeing the rest of the North Tower and sat in silence until Frank came.

"Not staying?" Frank asked as Lou grabbed his coat from the back of the chair.

"Not tonight."

My heart broke when he walked out the door without even a goodbye.

* * *

It was another two days before I went home. Lou hadn't returned to the hospital, nor did I see him at the house. I kept to my room, trying to think of anyone but him. It didn't work. He was all I could think about. Even my pending nuptials were barely a concern. I wanted to see Lou again.

I waited by the door an hour before he usually showed up in the hopes he'd be there. To my happy surprise, he was. I practically threw myself into his arms.

"Did you miss me?" he asked.

I debated on how to answer that, but finally settled on the truth. "Yes."

"Good. Then my magic is working."

"What magic? Astakides don't have magic."

"Oh, it's magic, but not that kind of magic. I'm talking about the magic of making you madly in love with me."

I rolled my eyes. "I'm getting married at the end of the week."

"I thought you said you were getting out of it?"

"I am, but Plan A could fall apart."

"Do you expect it to?"

"No. But..."

"Then you have nothing to worry about if you do fall in love with me."

He had me backed into a corner, but I wasn't about to admit it to him. "We'll see."

He bent down and kissed me.

"Mmmmm."

"Are you ready to lose again?" he asked, pulling the chess set out.

"No, because I'm not going to."

I followed him to the library, where he laid out the board on the floor in front of the electric fireplace. My interest at the new location was piqued. The library was a massive room filled with books. Some of the shelves were double and triple stacked. There were even piles of books on the floor and most flat surfaces. My father was a book addict, having collected and read more books that the entirety of the

Boru City population combined. It would surprise no one that he owns more than one bookstore in the city—the Trove, an antique book shop, being his favorite. He spent far more time there than he ever did at home with his family.

I reclined on my stomach to play.

"You first," he said to me.

I started strong, but it wasn't long before he'd taken most of my pieces. After losing three games in a row, I decided I was going to win the fourth game, even if I had to cheat. I inched the hem of my skirt up just past the tops of my thigh highs.

"How about we make this game a bit more interesting?" I said.

He looked at me. His eyes were little more than pupils. Good, he'd noticed.

"Is something wrong?" I asked.

"No." His voice cracked. "What did you have in mind?"

"For each piece captured, a piece of clothing gets removed."

"I don't think that's a good idea."

"Afraid you'll lose?"

I unbuttoned the top button of my blouse. I knew I was playing a dangerous game, but I'd be meeting my betrothed tomorrow. This was my last night before reality smacked me in the face.

"Afraid I'll win."

The chess board was all but forgotten as he kissed me. I grabbed his shirt and pulled him to me.

"You have entirely too many clothes on," I said.

I ran my hands up under his shirt, forcing it upward until his chest was exposed. It was a hard plane of muscle. He shifted to pull it the rest of the way off.

I tugged at his pants, but he brushed away my hand. "Not so fast."

He rolled me on my back and settled between my legs. I gasped at the feel of him against me. I'd had no idea how much I wanted him until then. I didn't want to marry some unknown stranger, I wanted Lou. All of him.

My eyes closed to experience the feel of his lips against my neck, soft trails of tingling kisses followed his fingers as he unbuttoned my shirt. The moan that reached my ears had been from me. I ran my fingers into his hair, holding him close. I'm not completely unknown to passion; after all, I've been betrothed since I was nine. There have been stolen kisses from interested boys and some handsy stuff. But this? This was something that felt so amazing. I wanted so much more. There was a hurtful longing when he pulled away to remove his pants.

"Are you okay?" he asked when he moved above me, our bodies not quite touching.

"Uh huh," was all I could say.

I was too lost in his kiss to notice when he closed the gap between us. He was warm against me.

His hand touched my hip, then slid down my skin, setting off a trail of fire. He caught my leg behind the knee, and lifted, opening more space for his hips.

"Ayame." My name was soft on his lips.

I gasped when he entered me. Not so much from the pain, but from the flood of sensations running through me. He was all I wanted at that moment. He was on top of me, inside me. I wrapped my legs around his hips, pulling him deeper. I couldn't get enough of him.

A rumble came from his throat, sending a chill through me. He wanted me, too.

"What the hell are you doing?" My mother's voice rang loud, jarring me out of the ecstasy I was oh, so enjoying.

"Luini!" a male voice shouted.

Luini? Oh shit! The meeting was supposed to be tomorrow. I looked over at my mother and the man standing next to her. He was too old to be Luini. There was no one else with them. Where was Luini?

Lou grabbed his shirt and covered me with it before rolling off. He scrambled into his jeans.

"Father, I can explain."

"Explain how you've dishonored your clan by not waiting to seal the marriage vows?"

"Luini?" Lou was Luini? Something inside me broke. I'd been having sex with the man I was being forced to marry?

He didn't say anything. In fact, he wouldn't even look at me. That confirmed it.

"Ayame, get dressed," my mother said, disgust in her voice.

My uncle came in as mother was leaving.

"I told you she couldn't be trusted. You should have listened." My uncle feigned a whisper, but I could tell he meant for me to overhear.

The jumble of emotions quickly turned to anger. I straightened my clothes and followed them into the sitting room. I stood near the door with my arms crossed.

"Now there's no question about whether you two will be married on Saturday," Lou's father stated. "You've already consummated the marriage, and by tradition, you're already married. The ceremony is simply a formality for the civil authorities."

"The traditions hold no weight in this matter, Father. When our clan took on human customs, we took on their traditions, as well. Marriage must be consented to by both of us. If she wishes to decline, I'll free her."

"Then you'll destroy our people."

"Our people will deal with it. The treaty shouldn't hinge on us being married."

"What say you, girl?"

"You won't talk to my daughter like that," Mother interrupted.

"Ayame." Lou turned to me. "It's your choice. I'll marry you if you want."

There was no, "I love you." No, "I want to be married to you." Marriage should be between two people who love one another, not a duty or treaty deal. But what did I expect?

"No." Without risking tears in front of them, I turned and walked away. I prayed to Poseidon he would come after me. Tell me he loved me. Convince me I should marry him. The tears began to flow when he hadn't by the time I reached the door to the garden. Outside, my walk turned into a run.

I ran all the way to the ocean. I could dive into the water and swim away from the heartbreak I was feeling. Lou had lied to me. He'd made me fall in love with him. Well, a version of him. A fake version. I stopped before I reached the water.

Strong arms wrapped around me. At first I thought it might be Lou, but then I felt my feet leaving the ground. The scream that ripped from my throat was muffled by the hand covering my mouth. I twisted from the arms holding me only to be wrapped in magical bindings. I turned to see the fairy working the magic. He was young, probably working for hire, considering the worn state of his clothing.

"My dear. You cannot get free, so please stop before you hurt yourself." My uncle's voice came from behind me.

In my confusion, I went still. What was going on? "Why are you doing this?"

"Because my daughter, not you, is going to marry into the wealthiest Astakide family on earth. She will stand in your place once you're out of the way. And since this idiot can't get the job done, I'll have to kill you myself."

He smacked the fae on the back of the head.

"Take her to the boat."

Before the fae could pick me up, I heard Lou yelling. I used the moment to get free. The bindings were loose around my calves, allowing me just enough movement to get a few yards away. I didn't look back when I heard Lou and my uncle arguing. The fairy, unfortunately, wasn't part of the argument, because I felt myself hitting the sand face first as he pulled on the bindings from where he stood.

"Let me go!" I screamed, trying to free myself from the magic. It was a pointless effort, but I was too angry to care. I was nothing more than a political pawn, to be used or discarded at others' whims. I grabbed the line of magic between myself and the fairy and pulled with all my might. It came free from his hands and dissipated. In the sand next to me was a piece of driftwood that must have washed ashore. I picked it up and carried the makeshift club toward the fairy.

When I reached him, I hit him and hit him until he was bruised and bloody. How *dare* he put a shark in my tank? And how *dare* he try to poison me? And how *dare* he try to kidnap me? He tried to crawl away. With a whispered word, he disappeared before I could hit him again.

My uncle was lying in the sand, Lou standing over him.

"If you ever go near her again, I'll kill you. Do you hear me? I'll kill you!" The anger in Lou's voice was raw.

It tugged at my heart a bit, but my anger at him overrode any feelings I had for him.

He approached me. "I'm sorry. I tried to tell you more than once, but I guess I was scared."

"Scared of what? That I'd learn you were a liar? That you didn't really care for me at all?"

"Scared you'd hate me. When I was told we'd be married, I wanted to know what you were like without the trappings of our positions. I wanted you to marry me be because of who I am, not because you were forced to."

He took a deep breath before continuing. He followed me as I walked.

"And you ended up hating me anyway. I've made it clear to our parents that I wouldn't marry you without your consent. My father's threatening to disown me, if that's any consolation." He stopped. "Anyway, I'm sorry. I love you, and it's killing me to know that I've ruined it."

I didn't say anything. I just kept walking as a fresh round of tears flowed down my cheeks. I didn't know what to do. My heart was breaking. He'd hurt me, and I didn't know if I could forgive that.

* * *

I spent the next couple days alone in my room. Neither my mother nor Lou's father would release me simply because Lou refused to marry me. I would still be wed on Saturday to one of their clan.

Saturday morning, my mother came to get me. She carried a pile of clothes for me to dress in. I said nothing as I entered the Meeting House of the Clans. Members of both Clans were there, along with the magistrate who would bind our clans together.

My mother ushered me into a room with my wedding dress. "Get changed. The ceremony is in an hour."

"Who am I to marry?"

She walked away without saying.

The gown was beautiful. It made me look beautiful, which made it all the more tragic. It should have been one of the happiest days of my life, and I was numb. I just wanted it over with. As a wife, I could request my own room so I only had to be with my husband for the purpose of making children. There would be no intimacy, no love.

I let the guard outside my door know I was ready for the attendants to do my hair and makeup.

I sat in the chair and waited. The door opened and closed behind me.

"Ayame."

My heart skipped a beat at Lou's voice.

"I only have a couple of minutes." He pulled up a chair next to me and took my hand. "I came to tell you that you'll be marrying me."

"What? You said I could make that choice."

"That's why I'm here. If you truly don't want to marry me, I will bow out. But I don't want to see you end up in a bad marriage. With me, you'll have your freedom until such time as you want to be husband and wife. I'll make no requests of you without your consent. I'll make that sacrifice for you."

"Why would you do that? You're free. You can marry anyone you want to. You don't have to be stuck with me."

"Because I love you. I won't be *stuck* with you at all. I'll be the richest man alive if I have you. I know I screwed up, but I want a chance to fix it. Please, marry me."

I heard myself say yes. I don't know why I agreed, except that I believed him.

"Never lie to me again."

A grin spread across his face. "I won't."

He went in for a kiss, then stopped. "May I kiss you?"

It was hard not to smile when he looked so happy. "After we're married."

"Deal." He left as the attendants walked in.

The remainder of the hour didn't seem like time on death row.

* * * * *

Dawn Witzke Bio

Dawn Witzke writes eclectic speculative fiction tales of vice and virtue. She is the author of the Underground Series and a bunch of short stories. She hails from flyover country where she lives with her husband, evil minions, and their flock of birds.

#####

Pictures for Pleasure by Terry Maggert

"Bertie, you out there?" Stella picked her way across the damp grass, feet bare. It was late October, and things were cooling down at night. Finally.

"Yeah," came the answer, the voice oddly muffled.

"What is it?" Stella asked, moving closer to the fence. She could smell cigarette smoke in the still air. It was just past ten on a Saturday night, and if her sister Bertie was already smoking menthols, it must've been an interesting night next door.

"Take a look at my face, and you tell me," Bertie said, blowing a plume of smoke skyward. She silently held the pack out to Stella, who took one without thinking. At the fence on a Saturday was the only time she ever smoked, at least since high school.

"What is—oh. What. The. Hell?" Stella asked, fighting a laugh.

Bertie leaned into the oval of light from the flood over the shed. It lit up a small zone at the fence, where they could both stand in or out of it as the mood dictated. Right now Bertie was in, but then she leaned back out, letting the shadows drink her back in.

Stella lit up with the proffered lighter, dragging hard. Jimmy had been—vigorous. She could still taste him in her mouth, and the smoke covered the taste of the fried appetizers they'd eaten at dinner two hours earlier. Fried things and wine, then home with Jimmy. He was a good man, but lord if he didn't get wound up on Saturdays. Just like Bertie's man, Clete.

"You, ah, wanna tell me about that makeup?" Stella asked, fighting a smirk.

Bertie sighed, then lifted her shoulders in a shrug. She was still a small gal, even thirty years out of school, and pretty. She hadn't thickened like Stella, though both of them were still lookers compared to everyone else in their class. Or neighborhood, for that matter.

Her red lipstick looked like a crime scene, and she had a fake eyelash hanging at a rakish angle. She laughed then, and so did Stella. "The sumbitch got a bottle of pills and asked me to put on heels and makeup before we went to the steakhouse," Bertie said. She flicked her ashes, looking back at the house. It was dark, except for the light over the stove. The day it went out, the world was going to end, as far as she was concerned.

"Same for me. He thinks I don't know. He snuck a pill, flushed redder than a buck in the rut, and then came at me twice in an hour. I'm lucky to be alive. You know what he's got goin' on down there," Stella said, her voice low. In high school, the joke had been that Jimmy needed to wear a manhole cover in his football pants just to give his dick a little protection. Clete was no shrinking violet either, according to Bertie.

And now both their husbands had found the wonders of modern chemistry, and Saturdays—which had been a one and done kind of affair—were a lot more complicated.

A lot more demanding.

"Did the boy at least ring your bell?" Bertie asked.

"Helllll no. He came close the second time, but—"

"Second time?" Bertie asked, spitting the words like they were poison.

Stella dragged on her smoke again, nodding and holding up three fingers.

"Three...what? Oh, hell no. Hell. No. We got to do something about this, sis. What happens after football? They be on us like ducks on a June bug, and I—well—" Bertie spluttered.

"I kinda like it, too," Stella said. "But damn if they ain't selfish about it. I mean, come on. We been married all these years, and they're winning. We'll never catch up. And now with Clete watching internet videos about rekindling your fire and all that shit—I mean, look at this makeup. He gets overheated just watching me put it on. He ain't gonna stop going for round three until his heart blows up," Bertie said, getting rid of her cigarette with a rebellious wrist flick. "Damn those little pills."

"Damn the internet," Stella said.

"Damn them finishing before we do," Bertie said.

Stella's face lit as she came back into the oval of light. Her lip was curled in conspiracy. "What if the internet was our friend?"

"What about it?"

"I mean, I got plenty of time to screw around at the office. I can do a little...searching. See if there's something to help us out. Not them," Stella said.

"A pill?"

"Maybe. Maybe something even better. Who knows? Little Rock is only thirty miles away. This is a modern world, sis. We can't be the only two women in the world with husbands who turned into jackhammers after they started taking pills. Let me see if I can find us a little help of our own," Stella said. She'd always been a bit wilder than Bertie, even when they were kids.

Bertie hesitated, then the back door of her house opened, and Jimmy called out into the night.

"Babe? You coming back to bed? Caught my second wind," Jimmy said.

"Oh, Christ a'mighty. I can practically hear the heartbeat in his dick from here," Stella said, and they both snorted with laughter.

"Stella! Come on back in, darlin. I got something to show you," Clete bellowed from the other house.

"We're fucked," Bertie said. "Really."

Stella turned back to her house, lips set in a grim line. "First thing Monday morning, I'm doing research. We're gonna get what's coming to us for a change."

"At least we'll come," Bertie said, patting her sister's hand.

In answer, Stella held up three fingers over her head as she vanished inside. Optimist.

* * *

Life got in the way of research, or so Stella thought, as she hadn't seen hide nor hair of her sister all week, but then Saturday rolled around, and it was time for dinner and romance.

And Clete had been ready. More than ready, as it turned out.

Bertie was waiting for her at the fence, her hair a moving disaster of cowlicks and whorls, like a salt block left in the pasture for a month.

"What the hell happened to you?" Stella asked, eyes round with shock.

Bertie took a moment to answer. There was a patina of sweat on her forehead, and her lipstick was worn to a pink ring around her mouth, like a clown who'd slept in her makeup.

"Could ask you the same thing, sis. Wow," Bertie said, lifting a brow. "What's that on your cheek?"

"Gawd damned glitter, that's what. He had me covered in body spray like some teenager in a backseat, and the sumbitch—well, uh, did you notice anything different about Clete?" Bertie asked.

Stella said nothing, but her brow furrowed slightly in the glow of the light. The air was cooler than the week before, and she had a sweater on over her robe. She fished a pack of menthols from her robe, lit one up, and handed it to Bertie, who took a drag and waited for her sister to speak.

When Bertie looked at Stella, her face was laced with suspicion. "Maybe. Why?"

"You know why. Don't be sassy. Tell me."

Bertie smiled grudgingly. She could never deny her sister. They shared a brain in some ways, being kin and all. "Christ. Alright. Two things, if they're even possible. I swear his dick's getting bigger, and he can last three times as long. I used to—well, I used to be able to fit at least some of that thing in my mouth—"

"On the couch when y'all tried to stay quiet for the kids, right?"

"Oh. My. God. You skank. How dare you—" Bertie said, but she was smiling. "How did you know that was what it was?"

"I can see the TV. He would put on a documentary. Clete does the same thing. Neither of those boys ever gave a damn about no French documentary unless they were puttin' their dicks in our mouths. They're twins that way," Stella said.

"He tried to convince me he was interested in penguins. The nerve of that man," Bertie said, laughing.

"That's what you get for your reputation, woman. If you hadn't—"

"Don't you say it—"

"Well, it's true. You coulda suck started a leaf blower in high school. You can't blame Jimmy, can you?" Stella asked.

Bertie held up her hands in surrender. "Can't fight it. I'm an artist. But that doesn't mean something isn't going on with those pills. I don't think he got 'em from a doctor. I mean, you're good with numbers, and I can manage people, but we both know bullshit when we see it. There ain't a pill to make a man's pecker actually grow, no matter what every smut page on the internet says."

"Not so sure about that," Stella said, holding up a business card. "Found it in his wallet, where he hides his emergency beer money. Take a look."

Bertie held the plain card up to the light, reading as her lips went into a circle.

Naram-sin

Beloved of the Moon God Sumerian King, Warlock, and Love Doctor Also Plumbing and Minor Electrical Work 259 West Pine Blvd. Closed Tuesdays

"Fuckin' weirdo," Bertie said.

"I know. Who closes on Tuesdays?"

"I—right, but—hey. Closed Tuesdays? Like the paint place, you know?" Bertie said.

Stella's eyes lit up. "Right. The wine and paint or whatever. Just opened. Where the old bowling alley was?"

"Yep," Bertie said. She finished her smoke and pointed downtown. "We're taking Tuesday off work, sis."

Stella nodded, grim but determined. "He's so full of shit."

"I took history in college. Ain't no Sumerian warlocks anywhere, let alone Arkansas. We'll see this guy in person and ask him what the hell he's giving the boys. I'm gonna have to buy new sheets if Jimmy don't stop taking these pills, and I know that's what's doing it," Bertie said.

"Tuesday."

"Tuesday," Bertie agreed.

The sisters walked back to their homes delicately. It was a Saturday night, after all.

* * *

Bertie sat in her Altima, smoking furiously with the window cracked as she waited for Stella.

"Come on," she hissed.

Stella opened the door with a sedate gesture, sliding into the seat and then proceeding to waste thirty seconds adjusting herself like a hitter in the batter's box. When she was done, she clicked her seat belt and then turned a gimlet eye to Bertie.

"What?" Stella said, tossing the butt and looking nervous.

"I can't move that fast today. He cornered me last night. Three times. This shit's out of hand," Bertie said, grimacing.

"Three—wait, how? It was a Monday night," Stella said, elegant with her facts.

"The sumbitch lured me like he was noodlin' catfish. I couldn't find him—it was just before bed, 'bout nine—and then I hear music in the bedroom."

"Music? What kind? Like a band?" Bertie asked.

"I wish. It was the music from—"

"Don't you say it—" Bertie warned. "You didn't."

"—I did. He had the DVD in and a bottle of wine on the nightstand. It was even cold. Before I knew it, the opening credits were on and, well, he had a hand down my sweatpants and a hardon like he was fixin' to split wood." Stella looked down at the floorboard, her lips pursed in a moue. "I didn't even get to see the movie."

"You seen the English Patient a hundred times," Bertie protested, then switched to a softer voice. "He lured you like a buck over a corn lot. And to think he did it with Ralph Fiennes. He knows that's your weakness, the miserable dog."

"That's not all," Stella said. "He had a whole stack of Sam Elliot movies in reserve. I'm lucky to be alive."

"Jesus God Almighty. You might still be gettin' thrown around."

"I know," Stella said, her voice turning hard. "But I made it out—a bit sore, and the boy *did* manage to get me there a couple times—"

"He did?"

"Twice. Well, two and a half if you count the fourth time for him."

"Fourth time? What in the hell?" Bertie's voice had risen to a shriek, and she gunned the car away from the curb, pointed toward Pine Boulevard and the origin of their problems. "We'll see if you're a warlock, you bastard."

"Yeah. We'll see."

* * *

"That's it?" Bertie asked.

"Guess so. Don't look like much," Stella agreed, opening the car door and stepping out. They were parked in front of the alleged warlock's place of business. The street was active but not crowded, the sun peeking fretfully through an overcast sky.

"No sign of him," Bertie muttered, peering into the wide front glass. Someone with a damned steady hand had painted 'Pictures for Pleasure: BYOB Painting Studio' across the door. The script was somehow vintage and seductive at once, and Bertie caught herself running a finger over the lettering, her lips pulled thoughtfully to one side.

"His sign don't look like a drug dealer works here," Bertie said.

"Hmph." Stella cocked a hip, frowning. "What he's givin' the boys ain't drugs. It's something else. I aim to find out." She lifted her hand and pounded on the door, making the heavy glass warble. The sisters waited a gravid moment, shrugged in unison, and turned to go around the building. If no one answered the door, they'd be only too happy to let themselves in. There was more than one way to skin a cat.

"We really gonna break in?" Stella asked as they skirted a dumpster filled to bursting with bags of reeking food.

"We are," Bertie said, serene as could be.

"And if we get caught?" Stella lifted a brow in challenge.

"Then I'll simper and shake my tits at Doyle. He's wanted me since high school, and I ain't above using the girls as a get out of jail free card," Bertie said, squeezing her breasts together.

"Just 'cause the sheriff didn't shag you at Prom—"

"He came close," Bertie said.

"He did? I thought you said—car coming," Stella said. The sisters ducked behind the stinking dumpster with a comical attempt at stealth.

It was a red corvette, one of the new ones that looked like a rolling erection and got shitty gas mileage. And Doyle Burton was driving it, wearing aviator shades and whistling tunelessly, his sheriff's uniform straining at his generous neck.

When the car passed, Stella hissed, "Did you see his hair?"

"Yeah. As in, it's all there. And looks damned good, too. That ain't no rug."

"Do you think—maybe—"

416 | KENNEDY & WANDREY

"He's taking the pills, too? I'd bet my best skillet on it. The sum-bitch is one of, well—them. Like our boys," Bertie said, her voice sour. "I wonder if every man over forty in this town has got his lady hidin' in the shed thanks to those pills."

Stella took out a credit card, sidling up to the back door. "I don't know, but we're about to find out. I saw this on, um, all the cop shows. Gonna try it." To her utter amazement, when she slid the credit card down in the door gap by the lock, it clicked—

—And opened.

And there stood Naram-sin, the supposed Warlock of Arkansas.

He was tall and broad shouldered, with thick black hair, and a beard that curled at the edges over a square jaw. Black eyes glittered with mischief, and there were crow's feet hinting at a tendency to-ward laughter. His smile was a brilliant panel of white, even in the shadow of the doorway. He wore jeans and a shirt with more paint colors than a makeup test counter, and when he moved toward the door, the sisters had to crane their necks to look up at him. Bertie took a sniff, thinking that for a warlock, he smelled pretty damned good. It was somewhere between old books and cedar. Maybe both, and for a mute second, both women were rapt, waiting for him to speak.

"How're y'all? I'm—"

"The sumbitch who's making my hooha into a clown car!" Bertie said, regaining her righteous anger with ease.

"Clown car?" he asked. Stella put a hand on her hip, and the oth-er on Bertie's shoulder. They presented a united front, with faces like matching thunderclouds.

Bertie jabbed a finger at him. "You heard me, boy. Since you gave them pills to my husband, he's practically set up shop down there, if you know—"

"—what she means," Stella finished. "Same for me. We know you're the one who gave the stuff to our husbands, and we want to know why."

The man rocked back on his heels, then opened the door and waved the women inside. "I'm only too happy to show you, but you gotta come inside."

"Fine, we will," Bertie and Stella said in unison, stomping past the warlock.

The studio was an open space with worn pine floors and the scent of paint hanging in the air, cut with—

"What's that smell?" Bertie demanded. "Kinda fancy."

"It's my other job. The one you ladies seem to think of as drugs, which ain't nothing of the sort. What you're smelling is herbs and flowers, and the things I need to help. I don't hurt people. Not anymore, anyways," the man said, a touch defensively.

Stella gave a derisive snort. "Got a name?"

"Apologies. Call me Gus."

"Gus?" Bertie asked, dubious. "That ain't the name on your fancy card."

"I go by Gus, and I more or less know why you're here. And y'all are?" Gus asked.

"Stella. That's my sister, Bertie. You mighta heard of us. We're two of the wives getting' pounded like flank steak every time the wind blows and gets our husbands—"

"Ah. Right. Clete and Jimmy, of course," Gus said.

"Hmph." Stella cocked her head like a bird again, but this time she was pure predator. "So you know our boys. Mind tellin' us how they found you, and more importantly, what in hell did you give them?"

Gus sat on a tall stool and waved the ladies to sit—there were chairs lined up in a rough circle, the wide-open studio dotted with easels at regular intervals. Stella and Bertie sat, swiveling their gaze up to Gus as the silence stretched between them.

"I don't make much from the painting thing, so I moonlight a little." He held up a hand to forestall any questions, and the sisters relaxed, but just barely. "I got a lot of experience with herbs and remedies. You might say it's in my blood, and I go way back with, ah—problems between husbands and wives. But what I gave those boys won't hurt them, unless you two decide to put a whippin' on them for getting too friendly, too often."

"I'm about there," Stella said.

"Same," Bertie added.

Gus shrugged. "Then the fault is mine. I thought I had the mix just right to help a little. Not—what did you say was happening, anyway?"

Stella flushed red as a stoplight, then glanced at Bertie, who gave an imperceptible nod. "Um, well—you see, I'm a good Christian woman, so—"

"Your secrets are safe here, ma'am. After all, this is my fault," Gus interjected smoothly.

"Well, not to be crude, but both—right sis?—both of our husbands can go like lumberjacks in bed, and I swear that his, uh." Stella waved helplessly.

"His manhood is getting bigger?" Gus asked.

"Yes. And I know that's bullshit, if you pardon my language, because if it was true, you'd be a bajillionaire, and not livin' in a small town in Arkansas."

"Maybe I like Arkansas," Gus said.

"Good for you. But that doesn't change the fact that his pecker oughta have its own zip code now, and it was pretty damned big to start with," Stella said.

Gus exhaled, letting his hands fall to the rough fabric of his painter's pants. "That wasn't in the formula."

"The hell it ain't," Bertie said.

Gus held up his hands, placating. "Okay. You're right, and I'm wrong. I—well, I can't take the gift away from them—"

"Gift? You call that a gift?" Stella whooped.

"In my culture, yes. It's a sacred thing, to help people in love. Your husbands love you, and they were brought to me by one of their friends—"

"Please don't say Doyle," Stella muttered.

"It was the constable, Doyle. Sorry about that. He came to me for a different problem, though my gift can help with a lot of things that, uh—that get men into feelin' bad about themselves. At least in this place," Gus said.

"Whaddaya mean, this place?" Bertie asked him, eyes narrowed with suspicion. She didn't miss a trick.

"Well, Arkansas is…" Gus said, hesitating for a moment. When he spoke again, there was no trace of a southern accent. His voice was deep, clear, and free of the folksy patois he'd had only seconds earlier. "Your home is a recent addition in my travels. A pleasant diversion, one might say, brought about by years of boredom." He leaned forward, smiling, and the sisters felt themselves drawn to him in that instant. "I've seen many places. Many people. Always the same problems, and always the same solutions. If lovers come together, things are—better. More peaceable. I rather enjoy the peace."

"I, uh—we do too?" Bertie asked, unsure what was happening.

"We do," Stella said, but with only the thinnest whisper of confidence. Gus was a different man from when the door had opened, and she sensed it in the depths of her animal instincts.

He stood, clapping his hands together and grinning. "Then let us approach your problem with a good heart. Ladies, you wish to know the pleasure your husbands have acquired from my...gift?"

"We...do?" Stella said, but it was a question. Bertie touched her arm, and they both swallowed, nerves wound tight in the moment.

"Excellent. Then I beg of you this—go home. Come back tomorrow night, after the sun is long down, and I'll help you both," Gus said.

"Help us how?" Stella asked.

His grin was kind. "Your husbands shouldn't be the only lovers with gifts, but for the female spirit, we need something far more complicated than a simple pill."

Stella shrugged. "Ain't that the truth?"

* * *

Stella sat at the wheel of her car, exhaling a long plume of smoke, her hair in three directions at once as Bertie slid into the seat, then drew back in alarm.

"Jesus in Heaven, what happened?" Bertie asked.

Stella flicked her cigarette out of the open window, patting at her hair as she looked in the rearview mirror. "No more smoking. I'm too worn out to—starting tomorrow, I think I'm going to be a vegetarian or something."

"What? Are you—did you fall and hit your head? What's wrong?"

Stella looked to Bertie, and there were circles under her eyes—the kind she hadn't seen since they both had infants, a long time ago. "Sort of. If you consider bouncin' off the headboard all night to be hittin' my head."

Bertie's hand went to her mouth in shock. "Lord Jesus. What set him off again? On a Wednesday, no less!"

All Stella could do at first was nod, then she took a swig of her Mountain Dew and found a voice. "Delivery came yesterday. Brown paper box with a woman's handwriting on it—"

"Is he cheating? I'll shoot his ass, that horny old—"

"Not cheatin', no. He…bought me something. Off the internet," Stella said.

"Oh, no."

"Oh, yes."

"Was it—dirty sex stuff? Like handcuffs and leather with feathers?" Bertie asked.

Stella barked a short laugh. "I wish."

Bertie's eyes got even wider, if such a thing was possible. "What was it?"

"The sumbitch spent seven hundred dollars on—on a vintage stewardess outfit. From Pan Am. Nametag read Jenni, with an I."

"Ain't they called flight attendants now?" Bertie asked. "What with gender equity and all?"

"Thank you for the lesson in feminism, but you ain't the one who's cooch got taken over by an invading army all night. Oh, and the army was wearing mirrored sunglasses and wanted me to call him Captain Intruder. For. Six. Hours," Stella said. "He was already stiffer than a Baptist minister tryin' to dance when he came down the hall. Naked, I might add, 'cept for the pilot's hat and the tie around his neck."

"I—honey, I'm sorry. Um, why is your upper lip all red?" Bertie asked.

"He put on a fake mustache. This is from friction," Stella said. "Did you know a man can have eight orgasms in one night?"

"Um…no." Bertie looked stricken. "Did you…"

"Seventeen times. We gotta do something. I'm gonna die. Happy, but still, I can't handle any more nights like that."

Bertie reached over and turned the key, firing up the engine. "Drive. That's enough of that nonsense. I want this so-called warlock to put up or shut up."

Stella put the car in gear and pulled away, grinning for the first time. "Good. Maybe my captain would like a dose of his own medicine."

* * *

Gus was waiting for them, despite a CLOSED sign hanging on the door. He waved them in grandly, a single overhead light casting a buttery circle on the scarred pine floor. In the space stood two easels, paint at the ready, and between them a tall table with a stone crock and two bowls of odd design.

"We ain't here to paint like some soccer mom gettin' tipsy with her crew," Bertie said.

"And you shan't be doing anything of the sort," Gus said with unusual gallantry. "I assure you, what I have planned is exactly what you're asking for, if you'll only take a seat." He spread his hands in a placating gesture, then led Stella by the elbow to one of the stools. Bertie trailed behind, suddenly compliant in the wake of his powerful magnetism. Gus had changed once again. Not only was the accent gone, but he seemed—taller. More masculine, even on the cusp of dangerous.

Settled, the women looked to him, still holding onto their vestigial suspicion.

Bertie pointed at the crock and bowls, resting on a table between their seats. "What the hell is that?"

The bowls were wide, looked like stone, and had an odd straw built into the edge. Gus lifted one, giving it a long, approving look. "A cup."

"A cup." Stella snorted. "Gus, if you think a cup is going to help us against the sex monsters you done created with your—"

"Not just any cup," Gus interrupted smoothly. "This is a cup made by my people, to hold one of the most sacred things ever known."

"You mean beer?" Bertie said, laughing.

"I mean exactly that. How did you know? Are you a student of history?" Gus asked, his brow lifted in surprise.

"Honey, we're southerners. Not fools," Bertie said.

"I stand impressed. This beer might be a bit different from anything you've ever known," Gus said.

"Is it a magic panty-dropper? Because beer already does that, and I'm startin' to think you're full of shi—" Stella said with heat, but Gus put a hand on her arm, calming her with a touch.

"Not just any beer. Mine. Songs have been sung about what you will taste, and stories carved about what will come next. From my cup comes a power like you've never known, and I share with you to atone for my sins," Gus said.

"So it tastes like shit then, right? Otherwise you wouldn't be so damned slow to pour it. Let's git to gittin', if you're really magic, Gus," Bertie said.

"As you will," he said, sweeping up the crock and pouring a thin, golden liquid into the cups, then handing one each to the sisters. "Through the straw, if you please. There's cereal in my brew—it gives it the power of the land, and my own lineage. You're taking part in something bigger than the mind can imagine."

Bertie drank first, her face screwing up like she'd bitten a lemon. "Damn, Gus. Sour."

Stella was more phlegmatic about the entire affair, but it was likely her post-orgasmic state of exhaustion had something to do with that. She drank, lifted her brows, then drank again. "Okay, so do I have a magic hooha yet, or what?"

Gus snorted, then held out two plain black brushes. "Not quite. You have the artistry in you. Now, you must paint for me."

They took their brushes, staring at them as their cheeks began to flush.

"I feel—strange," Bertie said.

"Same. You didn't drug us, did you?" Stella asked, knowing it was a bit late to complain.

"On my honor, no. Are you feeling anything inside, like a flutter? Wings unfolding, perhaps?" he asked them.

It seemed improper to call him Gus, for some reason, so the sisters felt their internal thoughts shifting. He was changing again, even as the golden liquid warmed them from within, delicate kisses of movement all along their throats, their necks…and lower.

"I—I am," Bertie admitted, her voice a sensual purr. "I feel beautiful."

"I do, too. I love…me," Stella said, frank wonder in her voice.

"Yessss," he said, watching them both as their lids drooped, the brushes held inert, waiting for purpose. "I told you I would give you that which you most want. It begins here, on the canvas before you. Paint your true self."

"True…self?" Bertie asked, her tongue thick.

He stood very close to them now, his huge presence filling the space. Touching Bertie's face with a delicacy that surprised her, he leaned close, speaking low into her ear. Something tickled at her senses. It was him, seeing her memory. Her past.

He found what he was looking for. Bertie, standing tall, her breasts proud as she disrobed in front of the boy she thought she loved. When he reached for her, his breath ragged, face a sheen of naked lust, she saw him. He was small—not worth her body, or her mind. Not even worth her time. He spat a curse and got dressed when she said no, and Bertie knew in that moment she was right. Somehow, she knew the man who called himself Gus could see the scene, and he wanted her to paint herself in that moment.

Her true self. More than a thing. More than a tired woman. She was a *goddess*.

The brush began to move of its own accord, and he turned to Stella, his mind probing her with equal ease. Her secret was far closer to the surface—her wedding day, a memory that was neither bitter nor sad. There was joy, muted by the whirlwind of the day. She saw herself in the cheap dress, yellow flowers stolen from the park in her hair, a smile as wide as all the world. Her lips were red, her hair up, the scent of barbecue in the air from the church kitchen downstairs. An expectant hum filled the church as the organist Miss Winnie warmed up for the fifth time, missing more notes than she hit. Then Stella stepped into the outer room, and the sun came through to light her up like she was cast in pure gold.

"That's it—that's your true self. Paint, Stella. Paint with all your will, and I promise you shall have what you want," he said.

They painted. The brushes flew, paint spattering wild, yet leaving the canvas untouched where it wasn't welcome, and in moments, shapes began to emerge, though neither sister could have drawn a stick figure an hour earlier.

Bertie's painting took shape first, a floating angel with dark wings and a spear made of silver so bright it looked alive on the canvas. The being—it was Bertie, there could be no doubt—hovered over a field strewn with broken flowers and mud churned from war horses too numerous to count. Arrows lay everywhere, and overhead, even the crows looked away, so fearful of meeting her terrible beauty that they might not survive the slightest glance. Her breasts were encased in armor streaked with the day's brutality, but even in her terrible truth, there was a beauty so perfect it defied the eye.

"Do you see?" he asked.

"I do," Bertie said. "I'm…a fighter?"

"You're a goddess of war. You are victory itself, if only you were given the right canvas," he said.

She continued to paint—a sun, fleeing over hills where fires burned, still bright with the light of her truth. Then, as suddenly as it began, she was done, slumping to the side, only to be caught in Naram-sin's powerful arms. He lowered her to the floor, where the brush fell from her open, stained fingers, her lips parted in a sensual pose like a painter's dream.

Then it was Stella's turn to reach the apex of her purpose. Where Bertie had been a dark goddess, she was light—bright, white, cleansing—a beatific saint walking over gardens of green and gold. She was life itself, her robe open to expose pink flesh and the hue of all that was good in the universe. She was love. She was birth. Her smile was incandescent, a smear of brilliance that threatened to sear the canvas it was painted on, and Stella finally stopped after one final, delicate swipe as she painted crimson lips, then the brush fell with a clatter.

"You are goodness and light," his voice growled, then he caught her, too, and in a moment, they both slipped quietly into a sleep so deep that not even the stars dared disturb them.

* * *

"It need not be hung. It simply will be," Naram-sin told both sisters when they awoke, the sun long since gone to other places.

Stella and Bertie felt an electric chill as they looked at the packages, wrapped in a fine cloth and handed to them both without a word.

"How much do we—" Bertie said, but Naram-sin waved her concerns away.

Stella hesitated, then asked, "What if it don't work?"

He smiled at her, and she felt—not small, but seen.

"It is as you wish. Place the talismans above your bed, and you will have what you asked. I give you my word," he said.

"Not much of a guarantee, but okay," Bertie said, recovering some of her natural sass.

When Naram-sin turned to her, the world shifted, but Stella caught her elbow. He was—different again. Taller. His hair, blacker than midnight, oiled curls gleaming, and a hypnotic power that reached into her essence. For an instant she knew fear, then he smiled, touching her shoulder with two fingers spread wide in an ancient gesture of life and blessing. She could feel the heat of him even through her coat.

"It's more guarantee than you could ever have, lady." He stared at her, his black eyes gleaming with the power of eternity. "What I give you is the word...of a god."

* * *

Clete stared at her, his eyes goggling at the woman who waited on the bed.

"Stell?" His question was everything—his want, his need, and—fear. He felt a touch of fear. She was luminous, her body supine but somehow waiting, like a trap.

"Come to bed, dear," she commanded.

He got on the bed as her legs fell apart, welcoming him inside. Above her, the picture pulsed as they began to move against each other, the bed shrieking in protest as he reached a shattering end less than a minute later.

"Damn—um, sorry, honey. I'll just—" he said, but she only smiled, clamping her legs around him like a velvet vise.

"Where do you think you're going?" she asked. Her voice had a feral note that made his senses come alive.

"I—well, I'm done, so—"

She reached back, touching the picture with a lover's caress, then waved toward his groin. He was erect again—instantly, painfully so—and sweat sprang out on his forehead before running down each cheek to fall on his chest in a fitful patter.

From outside the open window, a howl of panic split the air from next door.

"I guess Jimmy got the news, too," she said, laughing as she moved against him, and his hips began to move in unison, like when they were young. "New rules around here, pardner." Her eyes closed as she began a long, slow grind against him, each second stretching into eternity. "*I'll* tell *you* when we're done."

* * * * *

Terry Maggert Bio

Left-handed. I like dragons, coffee, waffles, running, and giraffes; order unimportant. I write the Halfway Witchy, Messenger, Starcaster, and Shattered Skies series. I'm a long-time advocate for audiobooks, volunteer for animal rescue, and may be found eating, baking, or eating while baking.

I don't sleep, but you probably guessed that already.

Find my books here, and let's be online pals, too. https://amzn.to/2yDrwyf

# # # # #

About the Editors

Sheellah Kennedy was born in Toronto, Ontario, Canada, and raised in a remote area of British Columbia. From the time she was a little girl, she loved to read. It's no surprise that she became a children's librarian for several years. She is pleased to have her first ever short story published in "Flights of Fantasy," and intends to turn it into a full-length book. Her family means everything to her. She would like to thank her three children, Ryan, Adrienne, and Erika for continuing to love her despite her unconventional ways. She would also like to thank her parents, Rodney and Gloria Jewell, for always pushing her to believe in herself, and of course her ever-patient husband, Chris Kennedy, who continues to believe in her, giving her the courage and strength to try new things even when she doubts herself.

Born and raised in central Indiana, Joy Wandrey holds a Master of Library Science degree from IUPUI and has worked in literary fields for much of her adult life. An accomplished fiber artist and reenactor specializing in 18th century America, she also runs her own small creative arts business. Now turning her interest to publishing, she's joined forces with Sheellah Kennedy to form Wyld Stallions Press, an imprint of Chris Kennedy Publishing. Living a full time RV lifestyle with her bestselling author husband, Mark Wandrey, and two chihuahuas, Joy can be found at large somewhere in the United States.

* * * * *

Made in the USA
Coppell, TX
03 January 2021

47392170R00236